Praise for the nov

'Susanna Quinn is a b

'Gripping

'I read *Glass Geishas* in one sitting, with a break for sleep.
This does not usually happen. It's a terrific read.'
Fay Weldon

'A fascinating thriller that delves into the Japanese sex
industry and into the murky world of hostess clubs'
Daily Express

'An involving read' *Financial Times*

'A sinister and seedy tale about the dark side of
Tokyo's night scene. I stayed up late to find out what
happened next.' Natasha Solomons

'A gripping, thrilling insight into the world of Japanese
hostess bars. A seriously skilful page turner . . . don't read it
on the beach unless you want sunburn.' Kate Harrison

'The writing is skilful and vivid and the tension doesn't let
up. Susanna Quinn is one to watch.' Julia Gregson

Also by Susanna Quinn

Glass Geishas

About the author

Susanna Quinn has worked as a journalist, ghost writer, book designer, hostess, club dancer and party masseuse. She lives in Brighton with her partner, baby daughter and many flocks of seagulls. She keeps a website at www.bookgroupbooks.com and can be found on Facebook and twitter.com/susannaquinn.

SUSANNA QUINN

Show, Don't Tell

HODDER

For my soul mate, Demi

First published in Great Britain in 2013 by Hodder & Stoughton
An Hachette UK company

First published in paperback in 2013

1

A CIP catalogue record for this title is available from the British Library

ISBN 978 1 444 73362 4

Printed and bound by CPI Group (UK) Ltd, Croydon, CR0 4YY

Hodder & Stoughton policy is to use papers that are natural, renewable and
recyclable products and made from wood grown in sustainable forests. The
logging and manufacturing processes are expected to conform to the
environmental regulations of the country of origin.

Hodder & Stoughton Ltd
338 Euston Road
London NW1 3BH

www.hodder.co.uk

Act I

Curtain Up!

Life's a Stage by Lili Allure

My thoughts on dealing with a mother's suicide:

Wear a corset. A well-fitted corset hugs you like a stern pair of arms, reminding you the best performers stay in perfect control of their feelings. The show must go on.

LOVE MORGAN b.1831, d.1865.

Love Morgan 1831 – 1865

Vivienne Morgan b.1965

As a striptease performer, Lili believed 'conceal and reveal' came down to perfect timing. Concealing her body with feathered fans, then revealing twirling tassels and a crystal thong, was captivating only if the timing was perfect.

The trick was to reveal at exactly the right moment. Being taken to her mum's flat only days after the body was found was a reveal too soon.

'I haven't cried yet,' Lili told PC Maureen Fletcher, as they reached the boarded-up door to Viv Morgan's flat. 'Who doesn't cry when their mum dies? I must be a monster.'

'People deal with death in all sorts of ways.' The family liaison officer, a pale, rounded woman with downturned eyes, inserted a crowbar and began levering.

'Who do you think bunged up the lock?' Lili glanced at the police padlock covered in chewing gum.

'Probably just kids. You know, seeing the place again, it might help you understand things a bit better. Your mum was in something of a strange place when she passed.'

Lili lit a cigarette and took shaky puffs. 'She was something of a strange woman.' Smoke floated from her red lips, wreathing three reddish-brown victory rolls set above her forehead.

Beneath the make-up, Lili had a handsome face with a long nose and strong, straight teeth. Her boyish good looks were only feminine with the right cosmetics. Her body was a different story.

'People experience all sorts of feelings when a loved one passes away,' said the police officer. 'All part of the grieving process.'

'I don't think I'm grieving,' said Lili. 'I just feel angry.' Both her hands were shaking. 'And scared. I'm scared to see Mum's flat again. Petrified, actually.'

The police officer stopped working the crowbar. 'You're sure you're ready for all this?'

'I'll never be ready. But I may as well get it over with.' Lili's eyes were tight and hot, but tears just wouldn't come.

'Right.' PC Fletcher began prising wood again. 'Looks like the lock works. As soon as I get their board off, you'll be fully operational.'

Crack!

'If Mum was here right now, do you know what I'd do?'

'What?' PC Fletcher's eyes softened.

'I'd strangle her.'

'Oh.'

'I mean, not literally, but . . . I hate her for doing this. I can't think straight, I can't eat . . . I'm on a diet of coffee and fags . . .'

'This time of year, sad to say, suicide isn't uncommon,' said PC Fletcher. 'The January blues.'

'She was sad all year round.' Lili swallowed and looked away.

'I hope you don't mind me saying this but the way your mum was living . . . it would get anyone down.'

Crack!

'She's always been messy.' Lili watched shadows appear behind net-curtained windows as tower block residents came to stare. It was an unusual view – a tall girl in seamed stockings, long gloves and bright red lipstick breaking into one of the flats. 'I lived with her for years.'

'It's not just the mess.' PC Fletcher worked the crowbar back and forth. 'Did the station give you our bereavement leaflet?'

'No. But it's fine. I don't feel bereaved. Just angry.'

'I'll have them send you one. What's your address?'

'Kate Hamilton's Supper Club.'

'Not work, love. Your *home* address.'

'That *is* my home address.' Smoke zigzagged from the cigarette in Lili's trembling glove. 'It's not permanent, but the manager lets me stay in the main dressing-room.'

Crr..ack!

Wood bounced to the floor, revealing the familiar brown front door Lili had lived behind for too many years.

Every other front door in the tower block had been repainted since the council-issued decoration of the 1970s, but not Viv Morgan's. The brown paint had stayed, just like the aluminium window frames, gas fire and orange-and-lime painted kitchen.

'You're an actress then.' PC Fletcher pushed open the battered front door. 'You look familiar.'

'No, a burlesque dancer,' said Lili, wondering how on earth PC Fletcher hadn't heard of Kate Hamilton's. The police tried to close down the club every other weekend for licence violation. Only a few weeks ago Lili had been practically naked on stage, boobs covered in glitter, shouting at a police officer who was trying, and failing, to arrest her.

This is art, you fucking idiot! Look at the stage – how many strip clubs have you seen with fake snow?

'Ah ha.' The policewoman gave a nod as if to say, 'That explains everything'. 'Yes, now I come to think of it, I've seen posters of you. You were quite the thing a few years back, weren't you?' She patted Lili on the shoulder, her hand meeting fake fur. 'You might want to compose yourself before we go inside. Get yourself calm.'

'Okay. Calm.' Lili's throat tightened. Her eyelids stung under thick eyeliner as PC Fletcher stood aside and let her into the hallway, but she didn't cry.

Together, Lili and PC Fletcher walked into the lounge.

In eighteen years, nothing had changed.

The red-tasselled sofa leaned against the far wall, facing a Blu-tacked magazine page of a young Viv in a 1970s advertisement. Viv was proud of her modelling days. Her girl-next-door looks meant, as a young woman, she'd always been cast as the perfect, pretty housewife.

Drayton's fully-fitted carpet makes any *house a home.*

Viv's flat, however, was far from picture-perfect.

There were cereal bowls and mugs filled to the brim with lipstick-stained cigarette butts, and a row of empty wine bottles lined up on the TV. And, of course, the boxes. Boxes, boxes everywhere, piles of them slumping over themselves in great, brown stacks.

'She was a hoarder,' said Lili, feeling blood stinging her white-powdered cheeks. 'There weren't so many boxes when I lived here. But it's all the same, really. The mess, the fag ends, the wine bottles. And all the things she couldn't bear to throw away. Just the same.'

The guilt was still there too, woven into the stained carpet, lounging on the sagging sofa.

The day Lili left home, she'd put Viv's lifestyle away in a dark corner of her mind, like the empty Ibuprofen packets Viv hid under the sofa cushions. But Lili's guilt had never gone away.

No matter how thick a curtain Lili pulled around thoughts of her mother, she was still the heartless daughter. The one who'd left. Who should have stayed to help Viv pull herself together.

'She was such a mess,' said Lili. 'Such a complete fucking mess. I'd die if I ended up like her.' She dropped her cigarette into an overflowing ashtray.

PC Fletcher gave an uncomfortable cough. 'You know, grief—'

'She couldn't throw anything away,' Lili interrupted, looking into one of the boxes and seeing crumpled clothing. Another was full of old handbags.

Someone, probably a police officer, had been thoughtful enough to open a window, but no amount of fresh air could remove years the smell of tobacco and damp that clung to the boxes.

'I never understood it,' said Lili. 'She kept such rubbish. Things she was never going to use.' She lit another cigarette. 'I hadn't seen her in years, she was never really a mum to me, but . . . I should be crying, shouldn't I?' She looked at her cigarette.

'I think I should stay with you while you look around.' PC Fletcher's palm pressed on Lili's shoulder. 'There's more to see. In the bedroom. I must warn you, it's . . . you might feel a bit emotional. People in a state of depression sometimes exhibit manic behaviour. It can be upsetting for relatives.'

Lili took another puff of cigarette to steady her voice. She pulled white fur around her shoulders. 'No, I've already taken up too much of your time. It's so nice of you to come up here with me, but you're busy. You get back to the station.'

Officer Fletcher looked uncomfortable. 'Is there anyone else who could come up, keep you company? Your family? And feel free to call me Maureen, by the way.'

'I don't really talk to my family.'

'Right. What about your mum's boyfriend?'

'Ben? I wouldn't feel right about it – not yet.' Lili ran gloved fingers over a frayed sofa arm. 'How's he taking it all?'

'Not so well. He's seeing one of our bereavement counsellors.'

'I wouldn't feel comfortable talking to him anyway. I don't really know him. Me and Mum . . . I hadn't seen her for a long time. I wasn't involved with her life.'

'It would be best to have someone here when you look in the bedroom—'

'No, really.' Lili shook her head, curls wobbling in their hair-pins. 'I want to deal with this by myself. I'm not freaking out. I'm fine.'

'Right. They've kept your mum's door key for investigation, but you said on the phone—'

'It's all right.' Lili reached into her bag and pulled out a key. 'I've still got mine. After all these years.'

Maureen inspected the front-door lock. 'Someone's made a pig's ear of fixing this. Still – looks like it works, that's the main thing.' The Yale lock was on the latch, so Maureen snapped it free, checking it still secured the door. 'Safe and sound. I'll send someone to take the board away. Well, good luck. Call us if you need anything.'

'All right, thanks.' Lili took a long drag of her cigarette, feeling the filter burn her gloved fingers. She heard the letter-box rattle as PC Fletcher closed the door behind her.

She looked around the living room. The sofa was, she noticed, leaking green stuffing now and sagging like an old lady.

She waited long enough for PC Fletcher to walk down the stairs, then said: 'How could you do this, Mum? How could you do this?'

She grabbed handfuls of sofa stuffing and punched dusty cushions.

'You selfish woman. You stupid, selfish woman.' She buried her head in the sofa and felt embroidered cushion on her nose and cheeks, but still no tears.

Getting to her feet, Lili took deep breaths and walked into the kitchen. Dirty, chocolate-brown mugs and plates floated in a sink of cold water.

Lili picked up a wet plate. She hurled it at the wall and broken china fell on to the draining board. She aimed a mug at the wall too, but then emptiness overwhelmed her. She let the mug slide back into the washing-up bowl, where it bobbed and sank. What was the point? Her mum would never see the broken pieces.

She went into her mum's bedroom, feeling metal struts dig into her ribs as she moved.

Most performers couldn't bear to wear a corset off stage, but Lili liked to be laced in at all times. Her childhood and teenage years had been chaos. Then she'd found burlesque and taken control of her life through her body. Happiness was a pulled-in waist. All these years of wearing a corset and she'd never got a single scar.

Lili chewed her lip when she saw her mum's double bed. Its brass headboard was like something from a 1940s film.

The familiar crumpled duvet, covered in bobbly four-leaf clovers, sat in a heap on a wrinkled blue sheet. She and Darren used to balance on the headboard, eating sliced-white toast with Milky Way bars melted on top.

She knew she should be crying, but she couldn't.

It took a minute before she noticed her mum's bedroom wall but, when she did, she understood why PC Fletcher had thought she might get emotional. Lili put a hand to her mouth.

'Oh holy Christ,' she said. 'Mum, what were you thinking?'

Life's a Stage by Lili Allure

My Darling Kate Hamilton

Kate Hamilton's Supper Club is the envy of burlesque performers all over the world. What the Crazy Horse is to Paris, Kate's is to London. Decadent costumes, flawless choreography and brilliant dancers.

When I first saw Kate's stage-of-a-thousand-lights, I knew she had to be mine. But if you'd have told me in two years' time I'd still be performing here, I wouldn't have believed you. Yet here I still am.

Kate's is named after a famous Covent Garden supper room and 'night house' of the 1800s where gentlemen could pay young ladies for sexual encounters. This Victorian house of sin was run by a lady called, of course, Kate Hamilton.

History says Kate weighed twenty stone, wore low-cut bodices, drank champagne all night long and shook like a jelly when she laughed.

Lili rested her Parker pen on the open pink notebook and stared out of the taxi window.

'Here we are,' said the driver, as the cab pulled up outside Kate Hamilton's Supper Club, with its icing-sugar-coloured plaster and polished wood doors.

Lili's fountain pen skidded across the page and she felt oddly disconcerted by the spiky scribble. She snapped the book closed.

'What are you writing?' asked the cabby. 'A diary or something?'

'Something like that,' said Lili. 'I thought maybe I'd write a book some day – a sort of coffee table thing. So I make little notes for it sometimes. Just things I know about burlesque and London and doing the shows.'

'I've always wanted to see your show,' said the driver, turning to look at her through the plastic screen.

'Oh.' Lili stared out of the taxi window, but didn't really see the beautiful, closed-up theatre. 'Right. Thanks.' Since leaving the flat, she hadn't noticed much of anything. She couldn't remember walking to Liverpool Street to hail a cab, or telling the driver where to take her.

'Are you okay?' the driver asked, as Lili emptied the contents of her handbag on to the taxi floor.

'Fine.' Lili watched perfume miniatures and an Estée Lauder lipstick rolling over the rubber floor. Absent-mindedly, she handed him her passport.

'Have you got a tenner hidden in here or something?' said the cab driver, flicking through pages stamped with all the countries Lili had performed in and shaking the pages. He reached her photo. It was a publicity shot, bare shoulders, smouldering eyes and perfectly set, victory rolled hair. 'There's no money in here, love.'

'Sorry. I don't know what I'm doing. Sorry. What was I looking for?'

'I'd hazard a guess you were looking to pay me.'

'Oh. Right. Sorry.' Lili opened a vintage Chanel purse and gave him a fifty pound note. 'Keep the change.'

'Famous, beautiful and generous too,' remarked the driver, as Lili gathered up her things and stepped out. 'I'll come see your show sometime. But knowing me, by the time I get around to it you'll be halfway round the world again.'

'I don't think that's very likely,' said Lili.

'You used to do shows all over, didn't you? New York, Las Vegas . . .'

'Used to.' Lili closed the cab door. She saw the cabby pick up his mobile phone and guessed there'd be a tabloid headline tomorrow: 'Lili Allure Tipsy Before Show'.

Lili looked up at the three-storey Victorian theatre, curved around the corner of two streets. It had shiny, dark-wood doors with brass handles and two tiers of white plaster climbing up into the sky, finishing in domes and flourishes like a wedding cake.

Its beauty usually took Lili's breath away, but today she barely noticed it.

'Home at last,' she whispered, checking her watch. 'Oh shit.'

Lili went around to the stage entrance and hurried down the dark, stone tunnel to the huge basement dressing room under the theatre. Her heels echoed on the concrete. She could hear the dancers getting ready and the fizz of pre-show chatter.

'I'm late,' Lili shouted, as she hurried into the dressing room. For the past two years the underground space had been more than a changing area for Lili. It was her makeshift apartment, and she slept on its scuffed, leather settee beside theatre props and glitter tubes. She washed her clothes and herself in a sink permanently marked with greasepaint.

'You? Late?' Pete, the theatre manager, sat on a counter top holding a mug of tea laced with vodka. 'The world's gone topsy turvy.'

'Sorry, sorry. It's been a weird day.'

'It must have been.'

Lili's backing dancer, Bryony, was struggling into a G-string and gluing on sparkling, sea-blue pasties. She turned to look at Lili with relief and surprise.

'Is something wrong, Lils?' Pete looked like a thirty-five year old trying to be thirteen, with his punked-up blond hair, bicycle chain accessories and pinstriped jacket. He loved fashion, but fashion would have preferred someone a bit younger.

Lili and Pete sometimes slept together when they were drunk, which meant they tried to act indifferent to each other while sober.

'Sort of. But it doesn't matter right now.'

Music boomed through the floorboards, and the girls hurried to get ready for the opening number.

Pete caught his reflection in the mirror and finger-spiked his hair. Beautiful G-stringed buttocks lifted and fell around him, but Pete paid no attention. He'd long ago been desensitised to female nudity, and the girls treated him as their slightly dotty sister. 'You look like you've seen a ghost.'

'I need to get ready.' Lili went to her clothes rail. She took off her shoes and stockings, and thumbed through her costumes. Her first number was 'Starlight', for which she wore an all-glitter gown that dazzled like a firecracker.

She'd glued extra silver glitter to the thousands of sequins on that gown, just to give it the wow she wanted, and then hand sewn each one in place. It had taken months. For a whole summer, her fingers had been bumpy with glue and her hair and skin had sparkled with stray glitter.

'Lils.' Pete picked at an eyelash. 'Didn't you go to your mum's place today?'

At the word 'mum', Lili felt her insides wobble. She kept searching through her costumes. Some would call it paranoid, but Lili always did a quick check to make sure everything was ready before the show. She didn't want to find something was missing while the audience waited for her to change between acts.

'Pete, what am I doing?'

'You're checking your costumes.'

'No, I mean here. Living in this dressing room. Working at this club. I still haven't sorted myself out a place to live.' Lili's fingers ran over her costumes. She found the tightly tailored, floor-length coat embroidered with bright blue snowflakes that she used for her Snow Queen number. 'It's like I'm scared to change things.'

'What happened at your mum's place?'

'I'll tell you later.'

'I would have gone with you. You do know that, don't you? Or Bryony or Carol-Ann.'

'No.' Lili patted on pearly foundation. 'I'm glad you didn't. There were things there . . . It's given me plenty to think about, put it that way. I hadn't seen Mum for years. I'd forgotten a lot of things. What she was like.'

'What do you mean?'

'I thought me and Mum were so different, but maybe we're not. I've been angry at her for years, just like she was angry at her family. Don't worry about me. The show will be fine.'

'I'm not worried,' said Pete. 'I've seen you perform with a broken rib. You're not a quitter.'

'I did quit.' Lili avoided her own eyes in the mirror.

'What?'

'After that Janey thing. I stopped touring when I came here. And I've been stuck ever since.'

'Carol-Ann offered you a good job here. You took a new opportunity—'

'No, I came here to hide away.' Lili picked up a lipstick.

'What's going on, Lils?'

'Honestly? I'm not sure. But maybe there's nothing wrong with hiding. Hiding keeps you safe.'

4

Life's a Stage by Lili Allure

Lili's songs – *Starlight* by Muse

Burlesque is about more than seeing lovely naked ladies. Believe it or not, those of us who are any good put a lot of thought into our performances, and that includes song choice. The song has to do more than just sound good. It has to tell a story.

Some burlesque girls like the classics (how many times have I heard Big Spender?) but I'm what they call a neo-burlesque dancer, so I like bringing alternative tracks to the stage. I edit the songs to go with my performance, often rearranging the lyrics. The song and the dance work together to tell the story. I always tell two stories. One for the audience, and one secret story just for me.

Lili had a secret she'd never told anyone. She got stage fright. Before every performance, as Bryony took hold of her corset strings, put a bare foot on her back and pulled, pulled, pulled, Lili silently prayed that she wouldn't fall apart on stage.

Now, waiting alone in the wings, she saw the dark shadows of the audience and felt sick with terror. More sick than she'd felt in a long time.

With a shaking hand, she felt inside her gown to the long metal clasp at the front of her corset. *Where is it?* Her teeth began to chatter. *It's okay, it's okay, it's okay.* She found the cold head of a sewing needle hidden within the fabric, and pinched it free with her nails.

Lili put the needle inside her mouth, and pushed its sharp

point slowly through her cheek. Her eyes watered in pain, but all the bad feelings, the fear and the rage and the sadness, were washed away – just for a moment.

I haven't needed to do this in a long time, she thought. Her hands shook as she threaded the needle out of her cheek, then pushed it back into her corset. She felt lighter, but she knew the lightness wouldn't last long.

Da, da, da, da, da, da . . . The thrum of guitar started on the *Starlight* track. Lili marched on stage in time with the music, a gleaming smile on her face, her eyes looking over the audience.

The stage dazzled with hundreds of tiny white lights, and a giant, curved blue moon set with squares of glass lit up Lili's face and shimmering gown. Six glowing stars hung at different heights around the stage.

Those who looked very closely might just notice the faint outline of black under the stars, and realise they were attached to a hidden staircase.

Lili turned to see Bryony appear in the wings. Bryony had bouncy, brown curly hair that she'd forced straight and set into a gleaming French pleat. Everything about her was soft and curvy, even her cheekbones, elbows and knees. She was looking at Lili with concern.

The stage became so bright the audience shielded their eyes. Bryony danced on stage in a silver corset and stockings, miming being blinded by a dazzling Lili Allure.

Starlight by Muse began to play.

Lili's heart beat faster as the words wove their way through her thoughts. She felt stiff, and her flowing hips became a lumpy shuffle. She knew she wasn't smiling.

I've been chasing the starlight, she thought. *And I haven't stopped chasing it since I left home.*

Bryony touched her arm. 'You should be on the stars, Lils,' she whispered.

Lili climbed on to the first star, and clumsily pulled at a glove that should have been off already. She heard someone in the audience say, '*She looks drunk.*' Lili glanced into the crowd and nearly missed her footing on the next star.

No, no, what's wrong with me?

Stage fright or not, Lili's performances were always flawless. Always.

In private Lili could let it all out, be messy, be frightened. But on stage, in public, absolutely not. No fans were ever allowed backstage. The real Lili wasn't on show. No one could ever know that the glamorous, immaculate Lili Allure had wonky red stitching holding together the undersides of her corsets.

Lili took another step upwards and stumbled again, but this time she managed to catch up with the music. Moments later she was dancing among the stars, just as always, albeit a little stiffly. Then she jumped on to the moon and began swinging over the stage, removing her corset as the moon rose higher.

The applause was half-hearted as Lili was lowered to the floor. She darted to the wings, where Bryony waited with her discarded gloves, stockings, hat and corset.

Carol-Ann, the house manager, stood there too, her pretty, pointy face dotted with eczema like smears of jam. Her hair was gelled back into a bun and she wore a fitted black trouser suit.

'Lili, my love.' Carol-Ann took Lili's arm. 'Come on. Let's go have a cup of tea.'

Lili slumped on to the burgundy bar stool, resting her elbows on the brass bar. She caught her reflection in the shiny yellow metal and sat up straight.

'The door's locked, isn't it?'

'It's all right,' said Carol-Ann, going behind the bar and filling a white travel kettle. 'This bar's closed tonight. What's going on?'

'Was I that bad?'

'Honestly?'

'Perhaps not completely honestly. Just give me a rough idea.'

'You looked lost up there.'

'Right.'

'Pete said you went to your mum's flat today.' Carol-Ann

dropped two sugars in a mug and made Lili a milky tea. 'There you go. A Carol-Ann special. So. How was it?'

'Ugh.' Lili rested her head next to the mug. 'It was horrible. There was a family liaison officer there, and I was trying to hold it all together. All the things I want to say to Mum were just going round and round in my head. It's like I've been cut off in the middle of a row, and now I'm just walking around furious.'

'I can understand that.' Carol-Ann put an arm round Lili's back. 'When I lost my dad it took a long time to get my head straight. But everything passes in time.'

'No.' Lili sat up. 'I don't think this will pass. Not unless I do something about it.'

'Lili – your mum's flat, was everything okay there? It's just, you seem so shook up—'

'No, it wasn't okay. It was . . . Oh, I don't know. It was Mum. There was some stuff in the bedroom.'

'What stuff?'

'It's hard to explain. I need to go back and get my head around it. It's time to stop hiding.'

'Hiding?' Carol-Ann squeezed her shoulder. 'You're one of the bravest people I know. You and me – the runaway sisters. We've had it tough. We don't hide from things.'

'I have been hiding, Caz.'

'From what?'

'From me.' Lili took a sip of tea.

'So what's new?' said Carol-Ann. 'You've been hiding from you for years. Most performers take their corsets off when they leave the stage. You keep yours on all day, every day. And all that make-up you wear from the moment you get up. You keep the real you hidden from everyone except us.'

'I know. You all know what I'm like, what a mess I can be, but I'd die if the public found out.' Lili sighed. 'But I think the real me, the mess, is coming out. It won't stay hidden now. Even on stage.'

'What exactly was in your mum's bedroom?'

'Seriously, Caz, if Mum was here I'd kill her. Not literally, but you know what I mean. I can't believe she's done this to me. I can't take feeling this way for much longer.'

'So what are you going to do?'

'First thing tomorrow I'm going back to the flat. It's time to face things I should have dealt with years ago. Or I'm going to turn out just like my mum.'

LOVE MORGAN b.1831, d.1865.

Love Morgan 1831 – 1865

Vivienne Morgan b.1965

5

Life's a Stage by Lili Allure

Ah . . . the corset

Stage corsets are rather different from those designed for daily wear. Although they can still be tightly laced at the back for an eye-wateringly small waist (mine goes to 19 inches), they have long, metal grips at the front that come apart for easy removal.

I must tell you, not every burlesque performer wears a corset for every act. It's a cliché to think so. But corsets do sum up the glamour, sexiness and vintage allure of burlesque in one beautiful, laced-up curve maker.

The gorgeous Dita Von Teese loves Parisian corsetière, Mr Pearl, but if you can't afford a trip to Paris, let alone Mr Pearl's prices, you can find good corsets nearer to home. Or you can make your own. Scour vintage shops for bargains and make the necessary adjustments with a needle, thread and lots of glue.

Lili's hand shook as she threaded her key into Viv's front door. She remembered the little jog the key needed to make it turn, and she held her breath as the front door snapped open.

She'd spent all last night curled up on the dressing-room sofa in the dark, trying to make sense of what she'd seen yesterday. Her thoughts felt sour and electric, and she hadn't fallen asleep until daylight.

She'd been tempted to turn up on Pete's doorstep and spend the night with him to dull the pain, but recently he'd started talking about relationships and the future.

The flat was silent. Cobwebs waved along the ceiling in the gentle stairwell breeze.

There's no point messing around, Lili decided. She marched straight to her mother's bedroom and stood on the threshold.

The bedroom was just as it had been when she'd lived there. Bed unmade, boxes slumped around. It was the walls that were different. In all her years in theatre, Lili had never seen anything so dramatic.

Her mother's woodchip wallpaper was covered, *covered*, in angry felt tip, as if a two-year old had scribbled out an all-day tantrum.

She felt her knees go and sat heavily on the floor. Her long, white fingers came up to her face. 'You were always so angry, Mum,' she told the carpet. 'But this isn't just anger. This is madness.'

By the skirting board was a pile of used Berol pens, the sort Lili remembered from junior school, their nibs blunted, puffy, ink leached out of them. But what was written between scribbled lines and circles was anything but childish. Sad, manic, angry sentences. Some parts were capitalised and underlined in red.

Lili stared at the words. She stood up, reached out and touched the felt tip marks.

Mine, mine, mine, I'll FIND THEM or die trying.

Love Morgan murdered by family for the letters. LOVE'S YELLOW LETTERS show why.
  I've looked BEHIND ME and they're telling lies.

I know the family secret.
       I am nothing. I will die today.

'What family secret?' Lili asked the wall.

Being back in Viv's flat after all these years, seeing the madness on the wall, the fact Viv was dead . . . it was like a dream washing over her in a great wave. Nothing was real.

Lili felt like a bad actress struggling to play a part. She knew there were certain emotions she was supposed to feel. Sadness. Shock. But she didn't feel them. Only a low, simmering rage at what her mother had let herself become.

Lili took a step forward and let the ugly writing swarm all around her, words and phrases leaping out.

Then she saw a word that made her step back again.

Her own name, *LILIAN*. It seemed to glow on the wall.

LILIAN – Find Love's yellow letters
Find LOVE'S YELLOW letters
Find Love's yellow LETTERS
Find Love's yellow letters
Find LOVE'S YELLOW letters
Find Love's yellow LETTERS
Find Love's yellow letters
Find LOVE'S YELLOW letters
Find Love's yellow LETTERS

'What letters?' Lili asked. 'Mum, what letters do you want me to find?'

There was a final sentence set apart, written in bright green.

GRETCHEN, don't go in the lounge. Tell your mum to come up, she'll know what to do.

Don't go in the lounge.

Lili felt sick. The police said a young girl had found the body, but they hadn't mentioned a name.

Beside the repetitive sentences, Viv had drawn some sort of diagram composed of hard, scraggly scribbles.

Lili looked closer.

The chipboard wallpaper was a mess of angry black lines, stabbing at what appeared to be names and dates.

Family names, Lili realised, seeing several 'Morgans' near the skirting board, their birth dates circled beside them.

There were lots of blank spaces above, with lines pointing upwards.

Around the names, lines and spaces, Viv had drawn branches with spiky leaves and menacing black birds.

'What is it – a half-finished family tree?' Lili asked the wall, and felt a lump in her throat.

At the top of the wall, above the blank spaces, was written:

Love Morgan, b1831, d1865.

The words were underlined many times, as if this were a name that made Viv particularly angry.

To the police, the felt-tip marks were probably the scrawlings of a mad woman. A clear-cut case of someone losing her mind and ending her own life.

But Lili knew her mother, a drama queen infusing everything she did with anger, passion and chaos. To Lili, the wall proved there was more to her mother's death than depression or madness. She'd been thinking of the family and Lili when she died.

'It's a family tree,' said a voice.

'Oh!' Lili spun around and saw a girl, maybe fifteen or sixteen years old, hovering in the doorway. 'Who are you?'

The girl's face was a perfect, tan-coloured oval, and her long, brown hair was blow-dried to Hollywood thickness around skinny shoulders. Her eyes were big and brown.

She wore a cable-knit jumper flecked like wholemeal bread, jeans a good inch too short and dusty plimsolls. The jeans had been pulled down as low as possible, and the jumper stretched and pulled over one shoulder, but still the outfit was decidedly dowdy for a teenager.

'You're Lili, aren't you?' said the girl. 'Viv told me about you.'

Lili breathed out slowly, staring at her. 'Yes . . . And you are?'

'Gretchen,' said the girl. 'I live in the flat below.' Gretchen looked at the chipped, purple polish on her fingernails. 'It was me who called the police.'

'Oh.' Lili glanced at the wall. *Gretchen*. 'Yes. The police said a girl found Mum. In the lounge. After the overdose.'

Gretchen shrugged. 'It was like a film, really. Not real. I'll probably have some trauma about it when I'm older.'

'Not real,' said Lili. 'I know what you mean. Mum wrote your name on the wall. Did the two of you get on well?'

Gretchen nodded. 'Sort of. I came up and saw her sometimes, after school. We used to watch TV and stuff. My mum didn't like me coming up here.'

'It's horrible you had to find her. I'm so sorry.'

'I think she wanted me to find her,' said Gretchen. 'She knew I'd go in the lounge before I looked in the bedroom. She wanted it to be someone she knew. It's weird to think I'll never see her again. Sad and weird.'

Lili watched Gretchen's emotionless face, and saw something she didn't expect. Herself, years ago, as a tough teenager pretending everything was fine when it wasn't. She wanted to put her arm around Gretchen and tell her it was okay. But she wasn't sure that was true.

'How do you know this is a family tree?' Lili asked.

Gretchen twisted a leather bracelet on her wrist. 'I was helping her with it.'

6

Lili stared at Gretchen. 'What?'

'For my history coursework. I was supposed to be finding out about your family. The ones who've died.' Gretchen peered over the bed at a box in the corner. 'I love all that stuff, you know. Family research. It's like being a detective.'

'Why was Mum doing her family tree?'

'She wanted to find some letters. Belonging to her.' Gretchen pointed at the wall. 'Love Morgan. We were helping each other. I needed to do a family tree for my coursework, so Viv was my project.'

'Letters?' said Lili, looking to where Viv had scrawled: *Love's yellow letters* over and over again. 'What are these letters? Look – Mum's written here. *Lilian find the letters*.'

'Oh yeah.' Gretchen squinted. 'I didn't notice that before. She must have wrote it just before . . . you know.'

'And who's Love Morgan?'

'One of your relatives,' said Gretchen. 'She lived years ago, in the eighteen hundreds. Viv wanted to track back so we could work out what happened to her yellow letters.'

'And did you find anything?'

'We'd only just got started,' said Gretchen. She thought for a moment. 'How come Mrs Morgan never told you she was doing her family tree?'

'I haven't spoken to my mum in years.' Lili looked at the wall again. 'She was always so angry about our family, but she never said anything about any yellow letters. I don't get it, I really don't.' She looked at the cigarette burns on the carpet. 'Are you sure Mum wasn't just making up stories?'

'Maybe.' Gretchen shrugged.

'Did Mum's boyfriend know about all this? That she drew all this stuff over the walls? Why didn't he do something? Call a doctor or take her to hospital?'

'Ben wasn't with her over Christmas. Viv told him she wanted time away from him. It's a shame. She was much more normal when he was around. He kept her calm. But she was always breaking up with him.'

There was a pause.

'Did Mum ever talk about me?' Lili felt the self-consciousness of the words.

'All the time.'

'Really?'

'Yes. About how you were in the theatre and everything. A stripper at somewhere called Katie's.'

'She talked about me all the time?' Lili's hands began to tremble. 'Then why didn't she . . . she could have found me before . . . why didn't she come looking for me?'

'I'd love to do what you do,' Gretchen said, her voice whizzing along. 'But I'm too fat. I'd love to be in the theatre. All the costumes and make-up. It's so glamorous.'

Lili sighed, and glanced at Gretchen. 'You're not fat.'

'I did drama at school and dancing,' Gretchen continued. 'I'm trying so hard to get thinner. I don't go to lessons any more, but I'd get really good marks if I went.'

'You know something, Gretchen? You remind me of me when I was your age.'

'I do?' Gretchen's face lit up.

'Yes. All the bravado, but I see you. You're as scared as I was, deep down.' Lili felt herself smile. 'Excuse me – as I *am*. Maybe I'll grow out of it one day.'

'All the what?'

'Oh, it doesn't matter.' Lili looked at the wall. 'So this course-work you were doing?'

'I hadn't really got started on the investigative side of things,' said Gretchen. 'I was helping Viv with the basics, mainly. Just how to draw a family tree. There are lots of names missing, still. And dates. But it was such fun. History is my favourite subject. I always get As. My coursework was shaping up to be brilliant. No one else would have done a family tree.'

'It's nice to have a talent,' said Lili, reading the wall. From Love Morgan's name, lines spread downwards like a chemistry diagram, but no lines met with names until they reached the bottom. 'When did Mum start on this?'

'Just before she died,' said Gretchen. 'But it was all to find the letters. She was *mad* about finding those letters. The letters, the letters, the letters. That's all she talked about. "Gretchen, you've got to help me. I have to find them. Please help me."'

'Do you think she found them? If they even existed.'

'No,' said Gretchen. 'We'd got nowhere near finding them. We hadn't even worked out if they survived. They could have been destroyed. Or maybe they never existed, like you say. I don't mean this in a bad way, but Viv's stories were always changing. And she was a bit, you know, nuts that last week.'

'Right.' Lili's chest burned. *God, why can't I cry about all this? What's wrong with me?* She reread part of the wall: *Now I know the family secret. I am nothing, I will die today.*

'What she's written here,' said Lili. 'Do you know what it means?'

'No idea,' said Gretchen.

'Did you find out anything about our family?'

'Only stuff about Love Morgan,' said Gretchen. 'She was from the Vic-tor-rian age. Most of it your mum told me from family stories passed down.'

'What sort of stories?'

'Like, Love was a big, fat woman who had sex with men for money. She couldn't care less what anyone thought of her. She was always getting into rows and getting arrested.

'Back in Victorian times, women were supposed to be all nice and polite and not show even their *ankles*. But Love drank a lot and didn't do what people told her, and she hated the workhouse and the factory, so she was a prostitute instead.'

'Go on.'

'She married a man called Tom, who was five years younger than her, and everyone said he was scared of her. Your mum said Tom didn't want to marry Love, but Love went on and on until he said yes.'

'This man here?' said Lili, pointing at the words 'Tom Morgan', linked to Love Morgan with a hair-thin pencil line.

'That's him.' Gretchen took some chewing gum from her pocket and nibbled it like a hamster. 'I love what you're wearing. Where did you get your shoes?'

'Paris.'

Gretchen sighed. 'I'd *love* to go to Paris. Mum never lets me go anywhere. I suppose I'd better get my photocopy and get out of here. I told Mum I'd only be a minute.'

'What photocopy?'

'The article about Love Morgan.' Gretchen went to a cardboard box with *McCoy's Crisps* written on its side and tipped it on to the floor. Papers spilled out.

'About Love Morgan?'

'Yes, the newspaper article,' said Gretchen, as if Lili was stupid for asking. 'I made it for Viv, but I need it for my coursework.' She picked up a single sheet of paper. 'Here it is. It's about Love Morgan's murder.' Gretchen held the paper out to Lili.

It was a photocopy of a Victorian newspaper called *The Star*. The headline said: **Arsenic Death**.

Lili took the photocopied page and began to read.

Arsenic Death!

*During the early hours of yesterday morning, the body of a
woman was found in a downstairs lodging room at 31 Nichol
Street, Whitechapel. Her death was the result of arsenic poisoning.*

*The woman, Mrs Love Morgan, was said to be thirty-four
years of age, with the appearance of one who is in the late stages
of syphilis. Her nose was missing in part, and one of her eye
sockets overtaken with disease.*

*Although Mrs Morgan resided in a common lodging room with
her husband, Thomas Morgan and son James Morgan, she was
not thought to be of the class known as 'unfortunates'. However,
Love Morgan was known to be somewhat addicted to drink and
described by a neighbour as living a 'loose and immoral life'.*

*The night before her death, Love Morgan was seen at The
Mall . . .*

From there, the photocopy had been cut off.

The article was dated 15th February 1865.

'I only had twenty pence for the copier,' Gretchen said, taking
the paper back. Something in her pocket bleeped. 'I have to go.'

'Do you mind if I borrow this?' Lili asked.

'I suppose so . . . How long for?'

'Just a few hours. I'll make another copy at work.'

'Okay.' Gretchen tucked the paper into Lili's handbag. 'I have
to go.' She disappeared into the hall.

'Wait!' Lili hurried after her to the stairwell. 'Do you know . . . are you sure Mum didn't find these letters? Could they be in the flat?'

Gretchen shook her head. 'I doubt it. Anyway, if she found them, why would she write that on the wall? You know, about *Lilian find the letters.*'

'I don't know. Mum liked to play games sometimes.'

'So are you going to look for the letters too?'

'I suppose I . . . Yes, I will.'

'Why?'

'Because Mum asked me to. Which means maybe these letters – they'll help me understand why Mum did this. Why she didn't say goodbye. Okay, actually that's not quite true. I want to find them because maybe, in some way, they'll *be* a goodbye. It's so stupid. I hadn't seen her in years, but she's still my mum. I still want her love. I want her to care enough to say goodbye to me.'

Gretchen's face was blank. 'You think some old letters will tell you that?'

'It's no coincidence she was thinking about family before she died,' said Lili. 'She was always so angry with our family. She used to say there were secrets that made her the way she was. But I never understood. These letters – they're something to do with family, right?'

'Yes, and she thought someone in your family *had* the letters too,' said Gretchen. 'Why don't you ask your relatives about them?'

'What?'

'Your family.'

'Mum thought someone in our family *had* the letters?'

'Yes. But like I say, Viv was always changing her mind about things. Anyway, why don't you talk to your family and find out?'

'I can't do that.'

'Why not?' Gretchen hovered in the hall.

'It's hard to explain.' But curiosity prickled, replacing the duller, sickly feelings of guilt she'd carried since hearing about Viv's death. 'Maybe I'll search the flat.'

'Good luck with that. It'll take a year just to look in all those boxes.'

'Tell me about it.' Lili went to take a cigarette from her bag, but seeing the young girl in front of her, changed her mind.

Gretchen watched the silver cigarette case with interest. 'Can I have one?'

'No,' said Lili. 'It's a filthy habit.' She thought of Viv's cracked, yellow feet in pink slippers, bending to light cigarettes on the gas fire.

'I wasn't the only one your mum talked to about finding the letters,' Gretchen said.

'Gretchen!' A voice shouted up the stairwell.

Gretchen looked over the railing. 'Shit! It's Mum. I've got to go.'

'Who else did she talk to?'

'A man,' Gretchen called over her shoulder as she ran down the stairs. 'Ian someone. She was always on the phone to him. She visited him too.'

'Ian? Do you know his last name? Or how I could contact him?'

Gretchen scrunched up her forehead. 'I've seen him on flyers. There was one in your mum's flat. Dr Ian something.'

'GRETCHEN!'

'I'd better go.'

8

The flyer didn't take long to find. It was resting on Viv's pink toilet cistern next to an empty packet of Mayfairs. The paper was orangey damp and curled at the edges.

Lili nearly laughed when she read it.

Dr Ian Batty – Clairvoyant, medium, tarot reader, mystic, palm expert, psychic detective, spiritual healer and historian.

   Greetings. *I am renowned psychic expert Ian Batty. My famous abilities (as featured on the Health Channel's 'Mediums') can help you look into your past and see your future. Genuine connections with the spirit world and psychic healings. Historical knowledge and family investigation. Where there was dark, let there be light!*

   Blessings, Ian.

   Visit my Psychic Chapel. Drop-ins welcome.

   99 Mile End Road (above the kebab shop).

Oh, Mum. You still believed in all that rubbish.

Walking to 99 Mile End Road in high heels was tougher than finding the flyer. Unlike the West End, where cabs regularly mounted the curb to get Lili's custom, on a winter morning in Whitechapel there wasn't a taxi in sight.

By the time Lili reached Ian's 'psychic chapel', located in a muddy backyard behind Mile End Kebabs, her feet ached.

'Hello?' Lili shouted into the rusty speaker beside a door covered in bird droppings.

Walking from her mum's flat to Mile End Road, whilst

stopping to rub her blisters, she'd seen a glimpse of something dark over her shoulder. As if someone was following her.

But that's Whitechapel. Shadows everywhere. You've just got too posh and forgotten what it's like to walk along a real street.

As she waited for Ian Batty to answer, shoes sinking into mud, she caught another dark blur of something from the street. But then a bus swayed past and the shape was gone.

'Who is it?' a voice crackled through the speaker and Lili jumped.

Calm down, she told herself, pulling her handbag straighter.

'My name's Lili Allure.'

There was a pounding as someone came downstairs. The door squeaked open, just a crack, and a man's face appeared. He had a huge quiff of silver hair and heavy, grey eyebrows that leapt around his forehead.

'What do you want?' the man boomed. He was very tall and thin, and wore a tweed suit with a red-silk rose in the buttonhole.

Lili was a little taken aback by both his volume and his unfriendliness.

'Are you Ian Batty?' Lili asked.

'*Dr* Ian Batty. That I am.'

'I'd like to talk to you about someone.'

'My dear girl,' said Ian, with a cynical smile, 'have I not been perfectly clear? I *refuse* to talk to any more journalists.'

'I'm not a journalist—'

'Go back to your editor, and tell him Ian Batty *will not be made a fool of again.*' With that, the man slammed the door. Lili heard the creaking of stairs.

'Wait!' She hammered on soft paint, wincing at the damage she was doing to her lovely white knuckles in their black glove. 'I'm here about my mum. I'm here about Viv Morgan.'

There was a pause. Then Lili heard Ian creak back down the stairs. The door opened.

'Vivienne Morgan?'

'Yes. I'm her daughter. Lili.'

'Not a journalist?'

'No.'

Ian looked at her, frowning. 'Her *daughter*. Yes, of course you are.' He opened the door a little wider. 'Vivienne is a dear lady. Deeply troubled, of course, but I'm helping her through it. Please understand, I'm being hounded by the gutter press . . . a recent case I was involved with – anyhow. May I help you in some way?'

'When did you last see my mother?'

Ian thought for a moment. 'Perhaps seven days ago. We had a very long and productive session.' His forehead furrowed again. 'May I ask what this is concerning?'

'Did she talk to you about letters? That she was looking for old letters?'

'Indeed she did, but—'

Lili grasped his hand. 'Then I need to talk to you. I'll pay you, of course.'

'My dear!' Ian looked horrified. 'I'm not *paid* for the work I do. What sort of person do you think I am?'

That took Lili by surprise. She'd never heard of a medium who didn't charge. 'But this is your job, isn't it?'

'Not exactly. I'm retired now. This is my hobby. And a very blessed hobby at that. I distribute love from the spirit world to those in the mortal realm, and for that I couldn't possibly charge.'

'Right. Well. Like I said, I need to talk to you about Mum and these letters.'

'May I ask why you can't talk to Vivienne herself about this matter?' asked Ian.

'Well, perhaps, as a medium, you can tell me. She passed away a few days ago.'

Ian turned to her, his wrinkly eyes searching her face. 'Passed on? To the spirit world?'

'I suppose you could put it that way.'

Ian's face fell. 'So *very* sad. Dear, dear. Do come in.' He retreated up the stairs and beckoned her to follow. 'But the spirit world is a happy place. We mustn't feel too sorry for the departed. Would you be kind enough to shut the door *firmly* behind you? The pigeons have a nasty habit of getting in when it isn't closed properly.'

Lili put her hand to the door, not quite committed to closing it.

'Come into my consultation studio,' Ian nodded to the door at the top of the stairs, 'and we'll talk. Your name is . . .' he turned and pointed at her, '*Lilly*. Am I right?'

'Li-*li*.' *I just told you my name.* She had a vision of Viv, excited to be in the company of a 'mystic' like Ian, believing all his nonsense. Not long ago Viv had been standing right here, living, breathing . . . probably complaining.

Lili blinked and black shadows appeared, then disappeared.

'Li-*li*. I do apologise. My psychic blessings are manifold,' said Ian with a smile, opening the door, 'but sometimes I can be a little hard of hearing when it comes to names.'

The little room smelt damp, but an electric heater, its element bright red, took the chill from the air. Crystals were lined up along a black fireplace and artificial roses in a vase.

In one corner, newspaper articles about Ian were tacked to the wall, alongside a Parapsychology Degree certificate from the Centre of Consciousness Studies in Arizona, and an MA in History from the University of Edinburgh.

'So . . . may I ask,' said Lili, reading the certificates, 'what are you exactly? Psychic, historian . . . what?'

'Good question!' Ian sounded delighted. 'I don't believe we have to box ourselves. I have abilities on the spiritual plane, of course, but I also have knowledge of history which I use to help people investigate relatives who have long since passed.'

'These degrees are from America . . . Scotland . . .' said Lili. 'How did you end up here – Mile End Road, London?'

'A snap decision,' said Ian, going to a loose window frame which had begun to whistle in the wind. He took a Guardian newspaper from a little table, tore up pages and stuffed them in the rattling gap. The whistling stopped.

'I've spent my life travelling all over the world,' Ian continued.

'I was in the army – it gave me a love of travel and foreign places. And I've been all over. Europe, America, Africa. But this year I realised – I've never tried London. Can you imagine!'

'You had all of London to choose from and you picked Mile End Road,' said Lili, watching heavy traffic on the grey road outside.

'I had a calling,' said Ian. 'Something about this area . . . its history. And of course, rental prices here are very reasonable.'

'That's because it's a shit hole.'

'People see beauty in different things,' said Ian. 'I love Mile End. To me it says life. Take a seat, my dear. I shall make us some coffee. I have the very best Folgers coffee granules, all the way from America.'

He returned with two cups of coffee on mismatched saucers.

'I'd like to find out if these letters are real,' said Lili. 'Mum thought they belonged to a relative of ours, Love Morgan.'

'Did Vivienne discuss our consultations with you?' Ian raised a heavy eyebrow.

'I hadn't spoken to her in years.'

Ian nodded. 'There's a distance between the two of you. But you live nearby?'

Lili shook her head. 'No.'

Ian pursed his chapped lips. 'Very strange. I really had a feeling – close but distant. Where do you live?'

'I live in the West End,' said Lili. 'As far away from this place as possible.'

'I had a feeling you were *very* near,' said Ian.

'No.' Lili shook her head. 'I haven't lived near her for years.'

'You're a performer, of course.' Ian took a sip of coffee and leaned forward. 'You look like your mother, did you know that? The same eyes.'

'Did she talk about me?' Once again, the words fell from Lili's mouth before she could stop them.

'We didn't discuss living relatives,' said Ian kindly. 'There was something very particular Vivienne needed help with. A detective assignment. She required my psychic abilities to help trace these

letters you've spoken of. Love's yellow letters, she called them.
And you're looking for these letters too?'

'Yes.'

'May I ask why? Are they an inheritance of some kind?'

'No, that's not it,' said Lili, trying not to feel offended. 'Mum
asked me to find them. She wrote "Lilian, find the letters" on
her bedroom wall. Right before she died. These letters . . . Mum
seemed obsessed by them. And . . .' She paused. 'Mum killed
herself.'

9

So far, only the police and Lili's theatre friends knew the nature of Viv's death, and Lili wanted to keep it that way. She felt ashamed. A failure. Good daughters didn't have mums who committed suicide, and she was terrified of the newspapers finding out. But, for some reason, she didn't feel ashamed with Ian.

'They suspect suicide?' Ian closed his eyes, apparently in pain. 'I'm so very sorry. Then there will be an inquest.'

'The police said something about that,' said Lili. 'I wasn't really listening. They said I might want to get a solicitor and put a case together. But the thing is – I don't want to prove anything. I just want to know the truth about *why* she did what she did.'

'You can't rely on the coroner to reach a definite conclusion,' said Ian. 'Most likely he'll give an open verdict, if suicide is suspected. He'll think he's doing your family a favour, sparing you the shame. Anyway. You're looking for the letters because your mother left you a message asking you to do so? Is that right?'

'Yes.' Lili let her eyes wander over the crystals and certificates. 'And I think they might help me. You know. She was always so angry with our family, and perhaps these letters will explain why. And if I can understand why she was how she was, maybe I can forgive her and let go.'

'Let go?'

'I feel so angry with her. Furious. It's like I can't move with it. Every moment of the day, my head comes up with new things I want to shout at her, about what a bad mum she was and how suicide is the most selfish, awful thing you can do. It's driving me mad. As long as I'm angry, I'm just like she was. Stuck. Going nowhere.'

'Yes, indeed.'

'How long had Mum been coming to you?'

'I've known Vivienne for some time, but I was only acting for her in my counselling capacity for, oh goodness me, less than a week. But our sessions were very full – she came to me every day.'

'I really want to understand,' said Lili. 'What was she thinking those last few days? Do you think these letters really exist?'

'Certainly, I believe they exist,' said Ian, his voice slowing as he stirred his coffee. 'And I can help you locate them. Vivienne and I were making a connection with the spirit of dearly departed Love Morgan in order to track them down.'

'Love Morgan?'

Ian nodded. 'I have a gift, you see. For contacting troubled souls. Your usual deaths, I can do nothing with, but troubled passings . . . murders . . .' He paused, dramatically. '*Suicides* too. They're my speciality.'

Lili found her gloved fingers had interlaced. 'Mum wrote that Love was murdered for the letters.'

'Indeed, Vivienne believed she was.' Ian drummed his fingers together. 'But you'll forgive me . . . I'm long past my crossword prime, and my memory for exact details . . . Wait there a moment.'

He left the room and returned with a ring-binder, then took reading glasses from his shirt pocket and began to read.

'My notes on the case,' he explained, reading from the single piece of paper inside. 'Love's yellow letters were written in the eighteen hundreds, and were passed down through the Morgan family, your mother believed.'

'But Mum's stories . . . She was always making things up. Do you really think—'

Ian cleared his throat. 'Vivienne and I have spoken to Love Morgan. She is something of a character. High-spirited. Troublesome. Violent. And a prostitute. But many poor women were back then. She was murdered in East London many, many years before Jack the Ripper began his killing spree.'

Lili thought back to the wall in her mother's flat, and the dates written next to Love's name.

'Did Mum say what she thought was in these letters? Or why she was so desperate to find them?'

'I had a feeling she had an idea, but she didn't say much about that,' said Ian. 'Just that she wanted to find out if they were still in the family. Who they were handed down to, that sort of thing. I'm sorry, my dear. My memory is dreadful, and I haven't been as professional as I should have been in making notes.'

'But she never found the letters?'

'We were getting closer.' Ian looked up from the folder. 'During our consultations, I ventured into the spirit world. It seems most of your family have had trouble-free passings, but then we hit the jackpot. I made contact with Love herself, the owner of the letters. A restless lady, not at peace, poor thing. She told us a great deal. I can help you too, to make contact.'

The spirit world. Lili had never believed in mediums or an afterlife. But perhaps contacting Love's 'spirit' was as good a way as any to refresh Ian's memory about the consultations with her mother.

'Okay,' said Lili. 'Can you contact her now?'

'My dear,' said Ian with a smile. 'It's not that simple. There are things I need. To make a connection. Let's start at the beginning. Tell me something about yourself – a memory. Something that happened in your past.'

'No.' Lili was surprised by the force in her voice. 'I hate talking about the past.'

Ian snapped the folder closed. He was perfectly still, then said: 'You know, I can try . . . if it's agreeable to you, to make a connection with your mother in spirit. Her passing was troubled too. In fact . . . yes. I feel she is trying to talk to us.'

Lili felt a jolt. The idea of Viv talking to her, even in make-believe, was frightening.

'I don't believe in ghosts.'

'Her spirit is here,' Ian insisted. 'She is seeking a connection with us.'

Lili dropped her cup and saucer with a clatter. 'This is stupid.' She leapt to her feet. 'I don't believe in any of this stuff. I have to get going.'

Lili hurried down the stairs and on to the street. The thought of some old charlatan pretending to channel her mother . . . no, she couldn't bear it. Maybe she should forget about these letters, forget about dealing with her feelings about Viv. Maybe it was better to just stay where she was. Sure, she was hiding. Stuck. But at least she couldn't get hurt that way.

I don't believe in spirits or mediums, she thought, walking as fast as she could, skirt fabric pulling around her knees. She'd worked in the theatre long enough to know mediums were nothing more than sleight-of-hand artists, playing easy tricks on the vulnerable.

It was only a few hours until showtime. She should make up for yesterday by being ready in plenty of time.

A white minicab waited at a red light, and Lili couldn't believe her luck.

She raised her hand.

'Kate Hamilton's Supper Club.'

Life's a Stage by Lili Allure

Lili Allure's signature burlesque routines

1. Starlight

Dressed in a gown that shimmers with silver crystals, I appear on stage under tiny spotlights that flash all over my pale skin. Then I dance among the stars, hung on a hidden staircase on stage. Finally, I strip and spin from a moon-shaped hoop hanging from the ceiling.

2. The Snow Queen

On a feather-covered sledge, I strip under falling snow, then perform ice-skating moves on a tiny circle of plastic ice.

Kate Hamilton's welcomed Lili into its cool underground corridors. She tip-tapped towards her makeshift living space but, as she opened the dressing-room door, she saw at once something was wrong.

A thin breeze wheezed through the dark room, brushing her bare neck.

She turned on the light.

The single dressing-room window, which led to a side alley, had a jagged hole smashed into it. Costumes, make-up and props lay scattered around the room.

Lili stood so still she could hear her own pulse beating at her wrists and throat.

Da-dunk, da-dunk, da-dunk.

All around her were smashed props and torn outfits – her own creativity and hard work in pieces by her feet. Although Lili bought day clothes from vintage clothing stores, every stage costume she owned was made by her own, sore, pin-pricked hands.

In a daze, Lili knelt beside her 'Starlight' gown, which had been thrown to the floor and, by the looks of things, trampled on.

The tiny glass jewels she'd spent weeks sewing on the dress were crushed and strewn over the bare floorboards. She put her cheek to the empty claw settings and felt the rough metal.

Above her, a row of ruined sailor costumes hung from a rail. They were scribbled over with heavy red marker, buttons and trim ripped and pulled. The club's famous opening routine, 'Hornpipe', would have to be cancelled tonight.

Her dressing-table make-up remained a messy mountain of brushes, lipstick-blotted tissues and kohl-marked cotton buds. No change there, and she was relieved to see nothing appeared to be missing.

Save for a few lipsticks in her handbag, she kept all her make-up at the club and it was as precious to her as jewels. Without make-up, she wouldn't go out on the street, let alone on stage.

She was about to push a shelving unit in front of the broken window, when she noticed writing on the full-length mirror beside her dressing table.

Lili looked closer. Written in black felt-tip on the oval glass were the words:

'The letters are MINE. Stay away.'

Lili stared at the mirror, her open mouth making a black hole behind the word 'MINE'. Unsure of her own eyes, she wiped at the letters with her fingertips. Sure enough, lines cut through the black ink. The writing was real.

Her teeth chattering, she covered the broken window with a tall shelving unit. Still, she didn't feel safe in the savaged room. Her insides felt like they'd been stirred into a sickly, hot soup.

Someone's been watching me. How else could anyone know I'd decided to look for these old letters?

She glanced at the mirror, and a shiver ran through her body.

A reflection caught her eye – her Snow Queen sledge, or rather, the remains of it. Raw, smashed wood poked up between silver-glitter paint and feathers. Suddenly she couldn't breathe.

Pulling her dress over her head, she yanked at the corset strings that criss-crossed up her spine. When the strings gave way she fell, palms flat against her dressing table, breathing hard.

The writing glowed malevolently in front of her.

Lips pressed into a thin, tight line, Lili rubbed and rubbed at the glass until the writing was gone. Black ink replaced dust on her fabric-covered fingertips. She ripped off her gloves and threw them to the floor.

'Whoever you are, Pete's going to beat the shit out of you,' Lili shouted. 'Why do you want to stop me looking for Love's letters? Who are you?'

Lili picked up her ruined gown and lay it on her knee. It wasn't beyond repair. Another pound of rhinestones, some strong thread . . . She'd always wished she'd sewn on the jewels with fishing wire anyway. She could make the corset even better.

Who could know I wanted to find those letters?

Only psychic Ian and the young girl – Gretchen. She couldn't imagine Gretchen trashing her dressing room, and she'd been with Ian Batty only ten minutes ago.

Gretchen said Mum thought someone in the family had the letters. Did the family know Mum was looking for them? Could someone have guessed Mum would ask me to find them too?

Lili picked off broken rhinestones.

No one threatens me. Ping! A metal claw-setting bounced to the floor. *No one does this to my theatre.* Ping! And another. There were so many to remove, it would take hours. Throwing the gown to the floor, she stared at herself in the mirror.

It was only then she saw her photos – the ones she'd been saving to make a coffee-table book. The collection of her in all sorts of outfits, 1940s, fetish, cheesecake pin-up, had been hurled over the sofa she slept on at night.

She gathered them up. The first picture was of her in a hip-length mac, suspenders and high heels.

You look like your mother, did you know that? The same eyes.

Lili saw her mother's big, bright eyes looking back at her. *I'm nothing like her. I'd never do what she's done to us.* She gripped the slippery picture and ripped and ripped. Soon there was nothing left but tiny, frayed squares. *I hate you. Do you know that? I hate you. If those yellow letters aren't your way of saying goodbye – or apologising – I'll hate you for the rest of my life.*

She picked up another shot of her, this time wearing nothing but a pink tutu and heels, riding on a candy cane. Her eyes looked straight ahead at the camera. Lili scratched at the face, then ripped that photo too.

Then she got to her feet. For once, preparing for tonight's show would have to wait.

It was dark by the time Lili reached Ian Batty's home. He opened the door without a word and showed her upstairs.

'I knew you'd be back,' he said, taking a seat and folding bony fingers in his lap. 'But I must confess, I didn't expect to see you so soon.'

Lili's cheeks were flushed with anger. 'My dressing room was vandalised. Someone's trying to scare me off looking for the letters. Which means now I'm definitely going to find them.'

'My dear.' Ian's eyebrows shot up. 'Someone *vandalised* your dressing room? You should go to the police.'

Lili shook her head.

'Goodness me, why on earth not?'

'Only a few people knew about the letters. You. A teenager called Gretchen. I can't imagine her vandalising anything. And my family. If it was someone in my family, I'm going to find out myself who did it. I don't need to get the police involved.'

'That seems a little foolish.'

'I need your help,' said Lili. 'Even if I have to deal with . . . things I'd rather not. You were probably the last person to talk to my mum. She might have told you something that can help me.'

'You're in a safe place here.' Ian lifted a box of tissues and handed it to Lili. 'Let your feelings come out, whatever they may be.'

'Ian, I'd love to.' Lili looked sadly at the tissue. 'But I haven't cried. It's all stuck inside.' She patted her throat. 'I'm more angry than sad. But maybe if I find these letters . . . if Mum's using them to send me a message somehow . . . I can let go.'

'I'm sure you'll let it out at some stage. Grief often catches you unawares.'

'I know you feel you have this gift,' said Lili. 'But instead of talking about the spirit world, I'd rather you just told me what you and Mum spoke about.'

Ian tapped the wooden arm of the chair. 'I would,' he said, looking tired. 'But regrettably, as I explained before, a good memory is no longer a strength of mine. But! With every gift he takes, the Lord imparts another. And I was blessed with different, less tangible powers. What I don't recall, the spirits help me remember.'

Lili watched Ian, his eyebrows shooting up and down, hands gesturing all over the place. Her mum had talked to this man just days before she'd passed away. He'd witnessed Viv's last thoughts, her state of mind.

'The channels are open right now,' said Ian, taking a deep breath and exhaling slowly. 'But I need something that will draw the spirits to us.'

'What do you mean?'

'To connect I need a bridge. Information from the past. What do you know about this lady? About Love?'

Lili shrugged. 'Less than you do, probably. The only thing I have is half a newspaper article about her death.'

'Do you have it here?'

'A copy of it – yes.' Lili reached into her bag and handed him Gretchen's folded photocopy.

'Marvellous.' Ian read the page, then grasped it firmly, as if it might jump from his hands. 'Then we're ready.'

Lili felt uncomfortable. There was nowhere to look in the tiny room other than at Ian, his forehead rippling with concentration, his chest puffing up and down.

'Goodness!' Ian shouted. 'My. I'd forgotten. She has quite an energy, this lady. She is strong. A survivor. A firecracker, I think you could say. Ever so tall and large. Big and broad.' Ian squared his shoulders. 'She says exactly what she thinks, and *no one* will tell her what to do.'

It was all Lili could do not to sigh out loud. He was repeating exactly what Viv had told Gretchen about Love Morgan. Lili had worked in the theatre too long to believe in parlour tricks, but if this was the only way to jog Ian's memory then so be it.

'Love lived many years ago. In Victorian times. Things were very different back then. Do you know much about London in those days, my dear?'

'Only what I learned at school. It wasn't a very glamorous time.'

'Well, lucky for you one of us is interested in the rich and wonderful history this city has to offer. Love lived only a few roads away from here. Did you know that?' Ian tapped the newspaper article. 'Old Nichol Street. The slum area. In the days when Love was alive, East London was polluted, dirty and dangerous. Life was cheap. As a poor woman, Love was next to worthless.

'The rich lived in big houses in the city – you've seen many of those houses, I'm sure. Bloomsbury. Clerkenwell. They're still there. Those rich people ran the factories and lodging houses in the East End. The poor were their servants, their workforce, their tenants . . . and their sexual entertainment.

'Women like Love lived in lodging rooms, rented by the night or the week. Those rooms were over-priced, dirty and tumbledown. Nicer places weren't given to the people like Love, who certainly drank more than was good for them and may or may not have prostituted themselves.'

'You certainly seem to know your history,' said Lili, thinking, *If nothing else, I can learn something about when Love was alive.*

'Oh my dear, it's a passion of mine – the Victorian period, in particular. Where was I? Ah yes. In those days, there were schools, certainly, and more and more people were learning to read and write. But life was hard for any poor person lucky enough to reach adulthood. A daily struggle to survive starvation, sexually transmitted diseases, rotten housing and sickness. If you didn't have a family to take care of you, you certainly didn't want to reach old age.

'Of course, the Victorians had many things we have today.

Newspapers.' Ian shook the photocopy. 'Cafés, theatres, dance halls of sorts – nightclubs, I suppose you could call them. Many of the buildings you see around you were built in those days, including the very one you are standing in.'

'This is fascinating,' said Lili. 'But can we just stick to the point? I thought you were making a connection with Love.'

'Right you are.' Ian closed his eyes. 'Love? Yes. We are here, my dear. Ah ha! Yes. Goodness she has a strong energy.' He tapped the table. 'She is not at peace. No, not at peace at all. I have a relative of yours here, Love, my dear. She has a newspaper article about your passing. She'd like to know more about you, if she may.'

He turned to Lili. 'She wonders, may she talk about the night she died?'

12

'Okay.' Lili shifted in her chair.

Ian closed his eyes and shivered. 'I am there now, with her. She is taking us back. She tells me the night was very cold.'

Lili glanced at the newspaper page Ian had handed back to her. It was dated February.

'She is alone.' Ian squinted as if someone had turned off the light. 'She is walking on grass but it's hard to see. It's Green Park. Yes. The Mall, she's calling it, but it's Green Park. A notorious area for prostitution in those days. For old women, diseased women, desperate women – prostitutes who couldn't get business anywhere else. There are no lights.

'Love is telling me she hates gas lights – she won't make her money if men can see her face.' Ian passed a hand over his nose. 'There is a hole. Here. Where the disease has taken part of the bone.

Lili's eyes fell to the newspaper again.

'She has lesions too.' Ian held a hand to his forehead. 'Over her left eye, so she can no longer open it.' He waved fingers over his eyes. 'To look at her, you would know the sort of life she led.'

Ian held his hand over his face for a moment, then let it drop. 'And why are you walking the Mall, Love? Ah. I see. You need money for your rent. One more good customer and you can go home.

'Come again? Oh, dear. A man asked you to do something, not moments ago, that made you feel quite sick. If it wasn't for the gin, you don't know how you would have stood it.

'You've seen two men dressed as ladies tonight, and men who meet other men . . . but it's dark in the Mall, and a great many strange things go on away from the street lights. And of course, for women who don't look as good as they did, well, it's the only place they can make a living.

'What? I don't think you'll shock me, my dear. Attitudes are quite different now. You engage in . . . beg your pardon? Things only good for animals.

'Oh. She means oral sex. And anal sex. Yes, yes I understand. Most people of your time find those things quite disgusting. Yes, well I imagine the pay would be good. You can't work any of the fancier districts anyway, and as you say, someone has to offer relief to those poor, sick devils.

'What? Oh. Love doesn't care what people say about her. Quite right. Who are they to judge? Yes, I see. She says she's done the business with princes and paupers and everyone in between.

'Plenty of gentlemen from fancy houses come to the Mall, she says. They are some of the worst, those "fine" men. She's had a gentleman ask to kiss between her legs this week, and another wanting her to break wind on him – both things that would make a Nichol man blush.'

'Who?' Lili asked.

'A man from the Nichol slum. Where Love lives. What's that over your face, my dear? A veil? Of course. Everything kept in shadows. You hide in the dark, offer the business to passing men, and lift the veil where no one can see your face so you can offer . . . well, we would call it oral sex.

'Disease has ruined her face, but she was a ruined woman long before, she is saying. She'd sooner be ruined than work in the factories. She sees poor souls so overworked their hands work the machines in their sleep. At least she has a few spare coins for gin, and she's been jolly enough in her time.

'Who was that, Love, my dear? A man just left her. She sees his shadow at the far side of the park. He asked for . . .' Ian cleared his throat. 'Don't be shy, my dear. Flagellation. He wanted to be beaten. He came with a horse whip and asked her to do the necessary. The man in question was well-dressed and young. Perhaps only sixteen, Love thinks.

'I'm sorry to hear that, my dear. Love is feeling unwell. More than the usual aches and pains. It has been building all day.

'There is tightness in her throat, like she's been swallowing sand, and a prickly feeling. And she has a great thirst. She stumbles on the dark grass and realises she is too sick to work any longer tonight.

'She is walking home now, pulling her veil tight as she reaches the lit streets. A terrible, black headache comes on. She has pains in her stomach too. And her abdomen feels tight as a sail on a windy day.

'She stops and vomits burning water. And then again. And again. She leans against some brickwork and sees red and yellow, and something green. It's nothing new for Love to feel poorly, but there is a fearsomeness to this illness that takes her by surprise.

'In alleyways and passages between the Mall and Whitechapel she sees women with men, many just dollymops, ordinary, married women out to make a few extra pence. She wishes she was somewhere dark and quiet.

'Now she has violent diarrhoea, and she feels water flow from her backside, down her legs. Her petticoat is wet with it, and sticks to her as she walks.

'She is too weary to go on now, and rests on a bench. She is woken by shouting and sees a man astride a woman, pulling up her skirts, the woman screaming, hysterical, beating the man about the head.

'Love is too weak to do anything but walk on. She prays for the woman as she falls over the cobble-stones. The world goes black and blue. Somehow, she reaches the dark streets of Whitechapel. She hears laughter.

'Men and women, being jolly. Drinking.

'Her home is in the Old Nichol, where front doors are burned for the fire and rooms have their own fog, come rain or shine. She does better than most, because she'll take what work she can and doesn't care what people say about it.

'She passes a factory and feels she must go again. The pains are bad now, and she catches sight of blood under gaslight as she lifts her skirts and bogs over a grille. With pain passing for a moment, she walks up Bethnal Green Road towards Old Nichol Street.

'She is so thirsty. Now there are aches and pains in her body like rats gnawing her bones. She is close to home, and knows she is dying. The taste in her mouth is like burning. Her insides are boiling. She stops to bog again, but can't make the alleyway so goes in the street and sees nothing but blood.

'When she reaches her lodgings, sweat is running from her face.

'Tom asks her whatever is the matter. She falls down beside him into blackness. When she awakes she tastes burning again. And then . . .'

Ian fell silent.

'And then what?'

'Tom is asking about letters,' said Ian. 'She is too sick to tell him where they are. She believes she has been poisoned.'

A pause.

'She's not telling me any more,' Ian told Lili. He opened his eyes. 'No. She is silent. I need to have something more of hers – more than this newspaper article.'

Of course, thought Lili. *So you can carry on this parlour trick.* But she wanted to hear more. It was strangely compelling. Whatever he was telling her, he'd probably told Viv before she died. The more he talked, the more she was likely to find out.

She checked her watch. Showtime was creeping forward, but she wanted Ian to keep talking.

'What sort of thing do you need?' Lili heard herself ask.

'Something that builds a link to Love. Papers, objects. Historical documents. Old possessions if you have them. Something that tells me about her life.'

'I'll see what I can find.'

'I'd be much obliged.'

Out on the street, Lili pictured Bryony and Doll arriving at the dressing room, staring at the smashed equipment, worrying over torn costumes and photographs. Pete would be raging and swearing.

She knew she should get back, help mend outfits and props. They needed her. But what would she be going back to? The same old stage and routines, before falling asleep on the same old dressing-room sofa.

This is my chance, she realised. *To break free. Those letters could mean finally letting go of this anger – not just about the suicide and not saying goodbye, but about Mum never coming to find me when I left home.*

Lili headed towards Whitechapel and Viv Morgan's flat.

13

By the time Lili reached the tower block, she had fifteen missed calls on her mobile phone, all from Kate Hamilton's. She felt terrible for letting the club down. Awful. But if she searched Viv's flat quickly for something, anything Ian could use, she could still get to the theatre in time for curtain up.

The mess and chaos inside her old family home were so depressing that for a moment Lili wanted to turn around and walk right out again. Remembering the mirror writing kept her focused, and she moved purposefully, pulling boxes around and rummaging through their contents.

What can I find for Ian? Where would Mum have kept things about Love?

Viv's hoarding had got much worse since Lili left. There were boxes of the most ridiculous things – Happy Meal toys from the 1980s, old magazines, broken kitchen appliances. Lili felt the usual dislike of the place she'd called home for too many years.

In the hallway, she noticed the familiar slide locks on the outside of every door. One drunken Sunday, Viv had found a box of locks in the street. She'd brought them home, inhaled a panda-pop bottle of cannabis smoke, then fitted them all over the house.

Lili had got out of the bath to find herself locked in from the outside.

It was only when the Lambrini and marijuana wore off, Viv realised fitting locks to the outside of internal doors did little to deter burglars. Still, she was happy with the afternoon's project, and declared the house safe and sound.

Lili had written an essay about the afternoon for her English homework. She'd got an F because she was supposed to be writing about real life. The teacher didn't believe she wasn't making it up.

As Lili's hand slid into a box of crumpled clothes, she heard something.

A human sound, like quiet laughter.

She pulled her hand back and listened. But there was only silence and she reasoned it was probably old pipes. Or rats.

She kept searching, not clear what she was looking for, but feeling she'd know it if she found it. Perhaps Viv had kept old family papers, or some heirloom from years ago. Or perhaps she'd find the letters themselves.

Goosebumps kept her company as she searched.

After a fruitless half-hour, Lili went to the kitchen for a glass of water and noticed something that made her heart rate double.

All the kitchen cupboards were open. They'd been closed when she'd visited with PC Fletcher. The lime-green doors hung out limply on old hinges. Lili slammed them shut and leaned against the counter.

She felt hard corset bones at her chest, and noticed Viv's old tin kettle lying on its side on the gas cooker, like a felled tree.

Unnerved, Lili touched it.

It was warm.

She snatched away her hand. A shadow flashed past the kitchen window and she bit back a scream, then rested her hand on her chest. It was just someone walking past outside.

Okay, okay. Calm down. Maybe the police came back and made a cup of tea. The noises are old pipes or something. That seemed rational. More rational than . . . Lili chased the thought away.

I need to keep searching.

Heart thumping, she went into Viv's bedroom. She avoided looking at Viv's angry writing on the bedroom wall.

Then she noticed something.

The *McCoy's Crisps* box wasn't on its side any more, and the bed . . . someone had *made the bed.*

Lili took a step back, skinny fingers clenching and unclenching, trying to keep herself calm.

Maybe I'm just remembering wrong. Maybe the bed was made before. Maybe I picked up the box.

But she knew it hadn't been. The duvet had been in a tired heap on faded, blue sheets. Now the sheets were covered. And she'd left the box as Gretchen had left it.

Maybe the police . . . But why would they make the bed? Or move a box?

Lili felt the angry scrawl on the walls shouting at her, closing in all around her.

There was a reason for how I was, the writing said. *You shouldn't have left me.*

She put her hands over her ears and shut her eyes, backing out of the room.

There was a knocking and Lili screamed. Her eyes sprang open. It took a moment to realise someone was at the front door. Cautiously, she turned the Yale lock, expecting to see PC Fletcher outside.

It was Gretchen, looking curiously at Lili. 'Are you all right?'

Gretchen wore an immaculate school uniform with a pleated navy skirt that fell unflatteringly around her calves. Her thick brown hair was tied in a navy scrunchy, but she'd pulled strands free around her face. Her school tie had been knotted the skinny way round too – another little act of rebellion.

'Fine.' Lili realised she still had her hands over her ears, and let them fall to her sides. 'Yes. I'm fine. Did you make the bed?'

'What bed?'

'Mum's bed.'

Gretchen frowned. 'Are you mental? Why would I do that?'

'Okay,' said Lili. 'Well, did you make a cup of tea up here or something? The kettle is warm.'

'No. What, you think we don't have our own kitchen?'

Lili shook her head. 'Sorry. It's just the bed, and the box in the corner . . . It's like someone's been in here.'

'Well, it wasn't me,' said Gretchen. 'I came up to see you.'

'How did you know I was here?'

'We're right underneath. I heard you,' said Gretchen, tapping the floor with her plimsoll. 'Sound carries all through these flats.'

'Oh.' *That explains that weird noise earlier*, Lili thought. Someone in another flat. But she didn't remember hearing other people's noise when she lived here. The floors were concrete, after all.

Lili smiled at the awkward teenager, who clearly wanted to be invited in but was too proud to show it.

'It's good to see you,' said Lili, and she meant it.

Lili felt a warmth towards Gretchen. She knew instinctively that Gretchen didn't like herself all that much. She was exactly like Lili used to be at that age, and Lili wished she could take her under her wing. *But I've got too many of my own issues to be of any use to anyone else.*

'What did you want to see me about?'

'I wondered whether you'll let me help you find out more about Love.' Gretchen looked at the floor.

'Maybe,' said Lili, impressed that Gretchen was fearless enough to visit Viv's flat after what she must have seen. Impressed and a little unnerved. 'Why do you want to help me?'

'Because I'm *good* at this stuff and I'm not a baby,' said Gretchen.

'I never said you were a baby.'

'I don't know. It's what some people think.'

'So you really want to spend time with me and help me out?'

Gretchen stared at her. 'You're joking, right? You're Lili Allure. I'm lucky to be even in the same *room* as you. Everyone at school talks about your shows. Why wouldn't I want to help you? And of course, there's the little matter of my history coursework, which needs to be in next week.'

'Coursework?'

'I started this family tree project with Viv, because Mum wouldn't let me research my own family tree. But the more I researched it, the more I realised I was learning *tools*, you know? Stuff I could use to find out about my own family when I'm eighteen and leave home.'

'Is finding out about your family important to you?'

'It is. Well, it will be. When I leave home and I'm allowed to look into them.'

'You can't look now?'

'Mum would go mad.'

'Right.' Lili nodded. 'So we'd be helping each other in a way. Good. Listen, I'm after more information about Love, as it happens. Like that newspaper article you gave me. Do you have anything else like that?'

Gretchen shook her head. 'No. Not yet. But I can get it.'

'Okay.' Lili stepped on an empty crisp packet. 'How about I come down to your flat and we'll talk there? It's horrible up here.'

Gretchen looked at Lili's pinched-in waist, seamed stockings and high heels. 'I suppose you can come down.' She seemed uncomfortable. 'But Mum . . . she's a bit funny about some things.'

'Let me speak to her. It'll be fine.'

'Okay,' said Gretchen. 'You can try.'

14

'Mum! I'm back.'

Gretchen pushed open the front door with a crash, revealing a spotless hallway laid with wooden flooring. Lili had noticed potted herbs on the concrete balcony outside.

She smiled. This council block had come a long way since she had left. Gentrified, she believed was the word. Who'd have thought the middle classes would want to live in an ugly old tower block? But they did.

'She's breathing down my neck right now,' Gretchen whispered, showing Lili into a dust-free, dirt-free lounge decorated with tasteful African ornaments and dried flowers. 'She's gone mental since Dad left.'

'Your dad doesn't live with you?' Lili asked, surprised. The flat seemed to belong to the sort of person who'd tough out a miserable marriage rather than risk being frowned upon as a single mum.

'Which one?' said Gretchen. 'I've got two. Neither of them want me. That's why I'm so messed up.'

'Two?'

'Her ex-husband,' said Gretchen, pointing a thumb at the kitchen. 'That's Daniel. My foster dad, who I never see. The one who left. And then my real dad. The biological one. I've never even *met* him.'

'Okay,' said Lili, confused.

'I'm fostered,' said Gretchen, as if that explained everything.

'Oh. So the woman you live with—'

'Isn't my real mum. But I've lived with her all my life. My real mum was a family friend. She gave me up when I was a baby, and Carol and Daniel said they'd look after me.'

'So Carol's your foster mum?'

'Yes.' Gretchen nodded. 'It's called private fostering. When you agree with your friends that you'll look after their kids. Carol used to talk about adopting me, but she doesn't any more. Not since Daniel left. Now she just wants to control everything I do.'

'I get it.' Lili looked hard at Gretchen. 'So that's why all the family tree stuff, right? You want to learn how to trace your real family?'

'Shush!' Gretchen flapped her hands. 'Keep your voice down. But yes. I want to learn all about how to trace relatives.' She looked stonily at the wall. 'They live abroad, they don't want to meet me, but when I find them I know they'll change their minds.'

'Did you learn much from Mum about tracing relatives?'

'More the other way around. That's why I liked hanging out with Viv. She was nice to me – she didn't treat me like a baby. Not always telling me how to do things, asking me a million questions.'

'I'm sure your foster mum loves you,' said Lili.

Gretchen laughed. 'She's miserable and I can't do *anything*. If I step out of line, she stops all my money, takes my computer away, picks me up and drops me *at the school gates* so all the kids think I'm a weirdo. As if it isn't bad enough there already.'

'I know what it feels like when you think your parents don't love you,' said Lili. 'It makes you feel worthless.'

Gretchen blinked, and for a moment the indifference left her face and she looked softer. 'Yes. It does.'

'It sounds like your foster mum is trying her best, though. I mean, my mum couldn't even be bothered to get out of bed in the morning.'

'She tries too hard. I wish my biological parents cared enough to come and get me. But they don't want me to know who they are, and Mum thinks it's all for the best.' Gretchen lowered her voice to a whisper. 'I'm going to run away. Somewhere Mum can't find me.'

Lili felt in her bag for cigarettes, an automatic gesture. 'Don't run away.' She looked at her silver cigarette case, then realised she shouldn't smoke in someone else's home or in front of Gretchen.

'Why not?'

Lili wasn't sure how to answer that one. After all, *she'd* run away. Who was she to tell Gretchen to stay in an unhappy home? Clean and tidy didn't always mean happy, just like messy didn't always mean miserable.

'Because if you run away you're always running,' she heard herself say. 'And you can't hide for ever. One day, whatever you're running from will catch up with you.'

'Gretchen?' A pinched, frantic woman with limp, brown hair and rectangular-framed glasses darted out from the kitchen. She looked Lili up and down. 'Who are you?'

'Hiya, nice to meet you.' Lili stretched out a hand, but the woman didn't take it.

'I'm Gretchen's mother. Carol,' said the woman, credentials on the table.

'Hello.' Lili smiled straight teeth and stretched lipstick. 'I'm Viv Morgan's daughter.'

Carol stared at her for a moment. Then she blinked, and something seemed to click. 'Oh! Viv. You're her daughter? Yes, of course. She had two grown-up children, didn't she? Such a tragedy. Terrible. A terrible thing to happen.'

'Did you know my mum?'

'Oh, barely.' Carol looked at the floor.

'You *did* know her,' said Gretchen.

'Well, I suppose I did.' Carol gave a worried smile. 'It was such a tragedy to have something like that happen in the building.'

'You were always trying to avoid her,' said Gretchen.

'Goodness me, don't be ridiculous.' Carol twisted the checked tea towel in her hands. She turned to Lili. 'What are you doing here?'

'I wondered if it would be okay to talk to Gretchen for a bit. I know she and Mum were friends . . .'

'Not *friends*.' The woman gave Gretchen a disapproving look. 'I never liked Gretchen going up there.'

There was a pause as Lili sensed the word Gretchen's mum hadn't said out loud.

Dirty.

Lili wanted to rub herself clean. It had been years since she'd felt like that. Eighteen years in fact.

'Well. Gretchen probably knew her better than I do right now,' said Lili. 'So, I was wondering if we could talk.'

Carol looked uncertain, holding her arms closer to her body as if fending off something dangerous. 'I don't really want Gretchen exposed . . . I'm not sure it's appropriate . . .'

'Just for a little while, Carol.'

'No. I don't think it's a good idea.'

'She's helping me with my coursework, Mum,' said Gretchen.

'No. It's not a good idea.' Carol shook her head. She disappeared into the kitchen, negotiations apparently over.

'It's no use arguing,' Gretchen whispered. 'Let's talk at the door.' In a louder voice she said, 'I'm just showing Lili to the door, Mum.'

On the draughty stairwell, Lili said, 'Okay, so how's this going to work? Clearly your mum doesn't approve of me.'

'Don't take it personally. It's just because you're Viv's daughter.'

'How about this? You carry on your research, then call me and we'll compare notes.'

'I'm not allowed to make phone calls without asking Mum. But I can sneak out and meet you. Are you going to work? To *Kate's*?' Gretchen said the word breathlessly.

'God, yes. But right now, this seems more important than performing. Wow. I've never said that before.'

'I can *see your theatre!*' Gretchen giggled with excitement.

'How do you know where I work?'

'You told me. And anyway, who doesn't know? You're Lili Allure. You're famous.'

'I think the word is notorious,' said Lili.

'I saw a video of one of your shows,' Gretchen whispered. 'On YouTube. You were a naked bird flying round the stage, you looked so beautiful. It was all artistic. I'd love to come and see—'

'I don't do that act any more,' Lili said. 'I only do two acts now.'

'Can I come see your show—'

'No. Your mum won't let you and I don't think it's a good idea to be sneaking around. It must be getting late.' Lili checked her watch. *Oh my God.* Panic seized her. It was getting *very* late. There were costumes and props to fix. 'I'll come back tomorrow and see if I can win your mum over.'

'Good luck,' said Gretchen. 'I've lived with her all my life and *I've* never been able to win her over.'

'Worth a try, though.' Lili thought of the audience crowding in and dearly hoped Pete and the girls had the wherewithal to arrange some new outfits for the opening number. Then she had her own acts to repair or reinvent. 'I'd better run.'

'Wait,' Gretchen said. 'Can I just tell you one thing? About Mrs Morgan and the letters.'

'Gretchen!' Carol banged on the kitchen window.

'Of course you can.' Lili's eyes widened. 'Please. Tell me whatever you know.'

'I remembered something,' said Gretchen, holding the front door. 'Mrs Morgan said there was a secret in the letters – a family secret. Love was murdered to keep it quiet.'

Lili thought about the bedroom wall, and the words *Murdered for the letters.* 'That's what she said? Can you remember anything else?'

'No, I really can't. Honest. But I can help you find out about Love.'

'GRETCHEN!' Bang, bang, bang.

'I'll see you soon,' Gretchen whispered, hurrying inside.

15

Lili Allure's Favourite Burlesque and Cabaret Houses:

Crazy Horse, Paris
Pussycat Dolls Lounge, Las Vegas
And of course, my very own Kate Hamilton's Supper Club
After touring the world, I've let my wings be clipped and have performed at Kate's and only Kate's for the last two years now. It's unusual for a burlesque girl to stay in one place so long, so I'm grateful to the management at Kate's for letting me.

They treat me well and I treat them well right back. I share my make-up and champagne, make sure every performance is perfect and always, always, perform on time.

'Oh my God, oh my God.' Lili hurried past the ticket office, noticing guests already seated at tables.

True to its name, Kate Hamilton's Supper Club served supper. Guests enjoyed three gourmet courses and champagne while watching the nude delights on stage. Grilled-scallop starters were already being placed on tables.

By the time Lili reached the dark stone corridors underneath the theatre, she was running.

'I'm so sorry.' She burst into the dressing room. Bryony and the other dancers, who were pulling on white socks and Boy Scout uniforms with neckties, looked up, bewildered. The broken props and torn costumes had been cleared up. Pete was on a stepladder taping cardboard to the window.

'Pete—'

'Lili.' Pete jumped down. 'Where were you? Did you know about the dressing room? Your pictures—'

'What are the girls *wearing*?' Lili countered.

'We had to improvise. Lost property from the church hall. Anyway. Lils, the dressing room.'

'I need to get ready.' Lili went to her clothes rail.

'Sod getting ready.'

'The show—'

'Lils, the dressing room . . . Charlie saw you – a few hours ago. Coming in the stage entrance.'

'What?' Lili's stomach lurched. 'You don't think . . . Pete, it wasn't me who ruined the costumes. The window was broken.'

'So you *do* know the dressing room had been trashed?'

Lili stared intently at a row of mascaras. 'I knew.'

'So what's going on?'

'I didn't do anything to the dressing room. Except my pictures – I ripped them up. I was angry. But the rest, it was like that when I came in before.'

'Why didn't you call me?'

'I had things I needed to do.'

'What things?'

'I need to get ready.' But of course, her costumes were ruined. 'I need two new costumes and routines,' said Lili, pushing past Pete and going to an old wardrobe of props and material. She pulled a roll of pink satin from the top shelf. 'Where are the pins?'

'In the dresser.'

Lili arranged the fabric around herself, then placed pins strategically to hold everything in place. 'One pin at a time. The fabric falls to the floor.' She hurried to her dressing table. 'Glue?'

'You're going to glue it to you?'

'I'm making some more pasties. Pink ones.'

Lili opened and closed drawers, pulling out tubes of glue and other fixing agents.

'Lili—'

'Okay, okay.' Lili knew Pete wouldn't give up. 'I think someone

in my family might have vandalised the dressing room.' Lili didn't
meet Pete's eye.

'Your family?' said Pete, making a fist. 'Who in your family?'

'No! Please don't do anything.' Lili grabbed his hand.

'What's going on, Lils?'

'I'm not sure yet. That's what I'm trying to find out.'

The applause was thunderous as Lili left the stage, pink satin
gathered up under her arm.

'I love seeing you ad lib,' said Pete, standing in the wings.

'I've always got a few routines up my sleeve for when it all
goes wrong,' said Lili, with a wink.

'There's a girl come to see you.'

'A girl?' Lili held the satin to her ribs.

'I showed her into the dressing room,' said Pete. 'I thought she
was a bit young to be out on the club floor.'

'It must be Gretchen,' said Lili, hurrying past Pete to the tunnel
leading underground. 'God, what time is it now? Ten o'clock or
something. I told her not to come. Her mum's going to kill her.'

In the dressing room, Gretchen was examining one of Lili's
feathered fans, experimentally waving it around her shoulders.

'Lili!' Gretchen sounded delighted to see her.

Usually, Lili's stomach turned at the thought of a stranger
seeing her dressing area, with its mess of make up and inside-out
clothing showing ugly hand-stitched repairs. But Gretchen didn't
feel like a stranger. Still, her fans were fragile.

'Put that down. You shouldn't be here.' Lili sat at her dressing
table and hurriedly removed pink lipstick. The outfit change
meant all her make up needed changing too. Her fingers grappled among broken make-up cases and pencil shavings. 'I've got
a show to do.' Her eyes fastened on a sheaf of print-outs in
Gretchen's hand. 'What's that? What do you have?'

'On stage in fifteen, Lili,' came a shout from outside.

'Something about Love,' said Gretchen, holding out the papers.
'It took me ages to find, but it's there. I promise. And there aren't
many women called Love around.'

Lili stopped dotting silver lipstick on her lips and eyebrows. Her eyes scanned the document. *The Women in Our Workhouses*, had been written for the Charity Organisation Society by a Mrs Cynthia Barton Lay of St Jude's Vicarage, Whitechapel. It was dated November, 1864.

'It's a workhouse report,' Gretchen explained. 'There's something in it about Love, and a little bit about her husband Tom.'

Lili flicked through the pages, hearing a clash of cymbals from the stage.

'It's written by a charity woman,' said Gretchen, helping her find the right spot. 'She talks about all sorts of different women who came into the workhouse.'

LOVE MORGAN b. 1831, d. 1865.

Love Morgan
(1831 - 1865)

James Morgan
(1864 - 1889)

Vivienne Morgan
(b. 1965)

16

Gretchen turned pages and began to read.

'The walls so blank, that my shadow I thank, for sometimes falling there.'

That's an inmate's description of the Whitechapel Workhouse in the eighteen hundreds. Okay, wait. Here's the bit about Love:

'From September 1859 to September 1864 there have been no less than 59 mothers who have entered the infirmaries.'

'Infirmaries?' Lili asked.

'Means they're pregnant,' Gretchen explained, 'and going into the workhouse to give birth. Okay. This is the bit about Love:

'Love Morgan, a married woman of thirty-three years, came into the workhouse to seek shelter as she was soon to become a mother. A rough, low-class sort of woman, Love has a great fondness for drink and is known for her temper and foul language.

'Love's husband, Tom Morgan, is not in work, although Love says she and Tom were both servants for William Peavy, some years previously. However, they were dismissed and now they can't find work elsewhere.'

'William Peavy?' Lili interrupted. 'The famous author? Really?'

'Yes,' said Gretchen. 'You know who he is?'

'Of course I do.'

Even girls like Lili, who'd left school at fifteen, had heard of the Victorian novelist, William Peavy. His books had enjoyed worldwide fame and been turned into countless films and dramas. Lili had even read one of his novels: *The Emerald Peril*. It was a book about . . . Lili thought for a moment.

Arsenic poisoning.

She leaned over the page and read where Gretchen had left off.

Love says her husband is out late most nights and she has little idea where he goes.

'It is our opinion that Love has been living a loose, immoral life because she has syphilis sores. She is known to walk the streets late at night, and we can only pray that now she is a mother those dissolute ways are behind her. It is God's miracle that she can carry a child, so we hope she takes this blessing as a sign to mend her ways.

Love has been to the infirmary on no less than three occasions in the last three years. On two occasions her sons were stillborn, and the third child, a daughter, died before reaching her first year.

Our hopes for her new son, named James, surviving life outside the workhouse are not great. Indeed, it is a miracle her child was born alive.

After three weeks in the infirmary, Love decided not to join the able-bodied in the main workhouse, but to go out, as so many women do, and "make the best of it", with her three-week "pretty lamb" at her breast. Love says she has seen children starve to death in the workhouse, and that if her son will die, it is better he breathe his last away from "those blank walls".

On leaving the infirmary, her only possessions were the clothing on her body and a piece of looking glass, the latter she told us "is worth a great deal and must not be lost". The poor often attach great sentiment to the few items in their possession. For many their greatest fear is a precious trinket being lost in the workhouse storeroom.

On making the "best of it", many young women like Love

often make the worst, and succumb to the sin of infanticide.
However, she left the workhouse in fine spirits, and at the very
least to a married situation, which is more than many women of
Whitechapel can say when they find themselves with child.

'Where did you get this?' asked Lili, make-up now forgotten.

'One of my virtual boyfriends,' said Gretchen. 'He got it from an academic library in London. You need a student card.'

The cymbal clashes grew louder – Lili's cue to wait in the wings.

'What do you mean, virtual boyfriend?' Lili watched dancers flow into the dressing room. Soon she'd be expected to appear, wrapped in white fur and silvery blue chiffon, as the Snow Queen – minus her smashed sledge, of course. Some improvisation would be necessary.

'On Facebook.'

'Gretchen, it's pretty weird for a student to be chatting up a fifteen-year old online.'

'He doesn't know I'm fifteen. My profile says eighteen.'

'I don't think you should be – wait.' Lili put a hand to her forehead. 'That's your mum's business, not mine. So you've found . . . what is it? A report from the eighteen hundreds.'

Gretchen nodded. 'There were lots of charities back then, London charities for London poor people. Funny, isn't it? Now it's all starving children in Africa, but back then it was starving children a few roads away. Anyway. Interesting, isn't it? To hear about the life Love had?'

'But we need more definite information,' said Lili. 'We still don't have any proof that these yellow letters exist.'

Gretchen thought for a moment. 'It does tell us something definite. Love had a son. Called James.'

'But did he survive?'

'Well, one of her children must have done,' said Gretchen. 'Or none of your family would be here. Amazing, when you think about it. The chances of a baby being born alive when its mother had syphilis . . . not great. So to think one of Love's children actually survived and had children themselves, especially since Love and Tom lived in the slum . . . Amazing.'

'Yes, yes. Amazing. The more we can find out about Love the better.'

Above them, the Four Seasons, *Winter*, began to play and Lili knew she had seconds to be on stage. She thought of the writing on the mirror and pulled white fur tighter around her shoulders.

'Lili.' Pete's head poked around the dressing-room door. 'What's happening?'

'Sorry.' Lili hurried up to the stage, calling out: 'Gretchen, would you leave those papers on my dressing table? There's someone I think might like to see them. You should go home now. I'll talk to you tomorrow.'

The audience was waiting.

When Lili arrived on Ian's doorstep the next morning, pigeons pecked at a pile of blond breadcrumbs. The sun hurt her eyes. She'd forgotten it could be so bright this early. Usually, champagne (or more often these days, cheap gin or port with lemonade) kept her unconscious until at least 11am.

Lili hadn't slept much, not least because cold sprays of air leaked through the broken window in the dressing room, but mostly because thoughts of Love had churned round and round.

The dressing-room couch had never been particularly comfortable, but now she had something on her mind it was close to unbearable.

Of course, the couch was only temporary. But 'only temporary' had been two years now, and the longer Lili lived in her dressing room, the more difficult it was to change. She was stuck. Frozen. A real-life Snow Queen.

'Ian?' She knocked on the door, extinguishing her cigarette against the slimy brickwork. For a moment she was afraid Ian had gone out, but then there was a clatter. Ian appeared at the front door, tall, dapper and intrigued.

'My dear. How can I help you this morning?' He glanced

at the sheaf of paper poking from her handbag. 'You have something for me. Well. Do come in. I have some exciting refreshments for us.'

Lili was soon settled onto one of Ian's high-backed chairs, and Ian carried through a plate of syrupy cakes and two glasses of orange liquid.

'My American order came through this morning,' he said. 'Kool Aid and Twinkies. Can you think of anything more wonderful? I've found a special website where I can pick up treats from the States. They're very good. So. What do you have there?'

Lili took the pages from her bag. 'It's a report from a charity in the eighteen sixties.'

'Indeed? Goodness me, how wonderful. May I?' Ian took the document and held it close to his face, flicking pages at speed. 'Fascinating. To think, people living on these streets had to make such terrible choices. Infanticide. Ever so common. How lucky we are. Do try a Twinkie.'

'Thanks, but it's a bit early for me and food.'

'Shame. I hope you won't take offence, my dear, but it looks like you could do with the nourishment.' Ian stood and looked out of the tiny, condensation-covered window on to Mile End Road. 'So you know nothing about the history of this area?'

'Not unless you count the eighties as history. I grew up round here, remember.'

'Fancy. To grow up in the area and know nothing of its history. Take a look at the buildings. The trees. Some of these trees have been here longer than we have. And you know, these streets, my dear, these tarmac streets – underneath many of them are the cobble stones that horses and carts used to rush along years ago.'

'I've brought you this document,' Lili said. 'Can you . . . you know. Talk to Love again, or whatever you call it.'

'Patience,' said Ian, taking a bite of syrupy cake. 'This sort of thing can't be hurried.'

'But—'

'We're dealing with the emotional realm. Sometimes the spirits are waiting, sometimes they need to be coaxed. I'd like to learn a little more about you, if I may. The more personal a connection we have, the easier this will be.'

'What do you want to know?'

'Let's start with you and your mother,' said Ian, straightening one of his framed certificates. 'How did you and Vivienne get along?'

17

'You want to know about me and Mum?' Lili placed her cigarette case on her lap. 'Mind if I smoke?'

'I'd rather you didn't. The spirits don't like it. Yes – I'd like to hear how the two of you got along.'

'Right.' Lili turned the cigarette case around and around. 'You say you're psychic. Shouldn't you be telling me things, rather than vice versa?'

'Seriously my dear, you want information and I need a view of your emotional life. So let's help each other.'

'How do *you* think me and Mum got along?' Lili asked.

'You weren't close,' said Ian. 'I thought before you lived near to her – perhaps even in the same building. But I was mistaken. A crossed connection. I was thinking of you in younger years. You lived with your mother as a child. And as a teenager. Then you left home.'

'Yes. Good guess.'

'Why did you leave?'

'Oh. Lots of reasons.' Lili took out a cigarette and fiddled with it.

'Don't be nervous, my dear. I'm just familiarising myself with you.'

'It was years ago. I don't remember much about it. Look, can't we just—'

'Not true.' Ian leaned forward, his eyes sparkling with accusation. 'You remember a great deal about it. A great deal you'd like to forget.'

'Well, who doesn't have things they want to forget?'

'There's not a moment of my life I'd forget,' said Ian. 'It's all precious. So tell me – why did you leave home? You were very young. Too young. Independent, yes, but afraid. I see you with bags full of clothes. Your hair is pale. Much paler than it is now.'

Lili touched her hair. It had been mousy blonde when she was a teenager. She dyed it reddish-brown twice a month and had almost forgotten its natural shade. And it was true – she had been frightened when she left home, and she'd carried everything, all her clothes and belongings, in two carrier bags. But who didn't carry bundles of clothes when they left home?

'Mum must have . . . Did she tell you that?'

'I see you quite clearly,' Ian continued. 'You were very angry that day. Why?'

'Okay, fine.' Lili sighed and tapped the cigarette against her lips. 'I was angry that day because I wanted Mum to pull herself together.'

'In what sense?'

Lili stared out of the window. 'I wanted her to get a hold of her life. For me. So I could stay. And I wanted her to come and find me. And maybe I wanted to be the kind of daughter who would stay and look after her. But I didn't.'

There used to be tears, she remembered, when she spoke about leaving home. Exhausting emotions. Where had they gone? It was like her feelings had been plastic-wrapped. Now there was only a numb sort of irritation that turned to anger when she thought about the suicide.

Ian nodded. 'Things didn't go as planned when you ran away, of course.'

'No.' Lili noticed one of the white half-moons at the base of her red fingernails was smudged. She covered it with her palm. 'My boyfriend's family threw me out after a week, so I lived with some friends in a boarded-up block of flats. Not far from here actually – lots of runaways stay there. It's called the Tower.'

'An abandoned building?'

Lili nodded. 'An old office building. It was horrible. We all used one of the rooms as a toilet. I thought nowhere was as bad as my mum's, but I was wrong. I spent months living off packet noodles and then winter came and some nights I was so cold I thought I might die.

'Mum never came looking for me. I thought, running away, I'd be leaving bad feelings behind, but I took them all with me. I've spent years hating her. Blaming her for everything that went wrong in my life. Telling people what a shit mum she was. But I always sort of thought, one day, she'd come and find me.

'When I found out about the suicide, it was like being dropped into an icy pond. After everything she did, the drinking, all her boyfriends, to go and leave us without saying sorry or goodbye – it was the worst thing she could have done.

'She must hate me and my brother to do that. That's what it feels like. Unless these letters are her way of saying goodbye. So until I find them, I hate her more than ever, but I'm too tired to keep being angry. It's ruining my life. Unless I can understand *why* she did this, why she never came to find me, I think maybe I'll be stuck feeling angry for ever. Just like she was.'

Ian nodded. 'And you think the contents of these letters might help you understand why she took her own life?'

'Yes. She didn't leave a note. But she asked me to find the letters. She liked to play detective games, so . . . I don't know. I'd have to find out what's in them, but they might be her weird way of saying goodbye.

'And there's something else too. She was always so angry with our family. She always said they made her sad. But she never told me why. These letters might.

'And after what happened to my dressing room . . . it seems someone doesn't want me finding these letters. Which makes me even more sure there's something important in them. Something that made Mum . . . I don't know.'

'May I ask,' said Ian, 'how did you survive financially when you ran away?'

'I looked for work,' said Lili. 'But I was fifteen. Too young. I ended up getting a job as a topless dancer in my Uncle Jeff's pub. The customers never guessed my age. Things got better after that. I looked after myself.'

'I see.'

'And I never spoke to Mum again. She never sorted herself out, and I didn't want to know. Darren – my brother – he stayed with her and told me how she was getting along.

'She got a boyfriend, Ben, who sounded all right. And she had a few operations. But I haven't seen or spoken to her since I left. So that's how we got along. Not well.'

Ian looked startled. 'I *am* sensing the spirits moving closer.' He closed his eyes and laughed triumphantly. 'It's her! Love. Welcome, my dear. Welcome.'

Lili thought of the strange, breathy laugh in the flat and felt herself shudder.

'She's asking me for a drop of something. Certainly, madam! A drain of pale. Brandy. Neat? Why of course.' He left the room and returned with a tumbler of golden-brown liquid, which he placed on an oak table beside him.

He's nuts, Lili thought. *But he was one of the last people to speak to Mum.*

'When she is sad, she drinks,' Ian continued. 'And this is a sad night. We're going back now. Before her son James was born. Before this document.' He smacked the page. 'When she still had her bonny baby daughter. She wants to tell me about the day her daughter died. In those days, Love was still a handsome lady. Well built. The syphilis hadn't completely taken hold.'

Lili nodded and, in spite of herself, leaned forward.

'She is . . . Oh, *that's* where you are, my dear. Of course. The Haymarket.'

Lili flinched. He wasn't telling her a fact she'd given him. He was sharing something new.

18

Somehow, even through closed eyes, Ian felt Lili flinch. His eyes sprung open. 'Are you familiar with that area, my dear?'

'Yes. I work near there.'

'Of course. It's something of a theatre district, isn't it? It was in Love's day, too. But it was also something quite different. Sin street, if history remembers correctly. A place where prostitutes offered their services, both inside and outside the shops.

'Women like Love walked the streets and offered themselves for pennies. Other younger prettier girls worked behind shop counters and did a little extra business in back rooms. The shops were just a front, of course. Everything on sale being poorly made and over-priced. Badly stitched bonnets, stale bread, bad meat, that sort of thing.'

'Really.'

Ian closed his eyes again. 'Oh. That's funny. Love is laughing at the men outside the shop doorways. They're plucking up the courage to ask the lady behind the counter what else she has on offer.

'One man – Love can't stop laughing now – has just left a shop with a very ugly bonnet which cost him ten shillings. He is lingering by the window, looking at the lovely lady inside whom he could have bought for much less if he'd had the courage to ask.

'Love doesn't work in the shops. She won't be kept, not by a landlord or a bawdy house keeper. Bawdy house – that means brothel. She walks the streets with no one to answer to.

'Want the business? she is asking the men. Want the business? Yes, I understand you. Skirts up, bend over – sexual relations.

And where . . . Oh, some alleyway or other. She doesn't have a lodging house near here.

'Her baby daughter is at home, wrapped up in swaddling cloth and a bonnet, blue and sickly. Her husband Tom will be out being jolly, but of course neither of them have anything to be truly jolly about. The child is very ill. She screams and screams.

'Love has been walking the Haymarket for hours, hoping to pick someone up, but she is unlucky. The area is busy with all sorts of gay women – other prostitutes, their look and dress finer than hers.

'Some young girls wear lovely dresses so as to entice the men. They look like ladies, but they're prisoners, she tells me. The dresses aren't their own, but the property of some bawdy house. The owners watch the girls night and day and take the profits from their work. The clothes they wear are more valuable than the women underneath.

'Love wanders the street and then from one café to the next. As the night goes on, she becomes more desperate. Some women are allowed into the night houses and supper rooms, where wine is served at twelve shillings a bottle and men are considerably richer and more genteel than on the street. She tries to push her way in, but usually she is thrown out again. Love is not a lady who is normally allowed into such places.

'She goes home penniless.

'At her Whitechapel lodging room, her little baby girl lies perfectly still. Tom is beside her, wasting a candle, waiting for Love to return.

'She died not long ago, Tom tells her. For want of the doctor we could not give her. Love is saddened to madness.'

Ian became silent. 'No. There is nothing more to say.' He cleared his throat and opened his eyes. 'She has nothing more to tell me for now.'

Lili's mind was churning. Ian was weaving elaborate stories around the facts she'd given him, but that didn't mean he wasn't adding things that Viv had told him. Things Lili didn't know.

'Did Mum tell you Love worked at the Haymarket?' Lili asked.

'She may have done.' Ian rubbed his forehead. 'Yes, it is certainly possible. I find it so hard to feel my way between the things clients tell me, and what the spirits divulge.'

Lili's mobile phone rang and she jumped.

It was Gretchen.

'Gretchen? How did you get my number?'

'Your manager.' Gretchen's high voice floated from the receiver. 'I've got to be quick. Mum's in the loo. She doesn't know I'm calling you. I copied the other half of that newspaper article for you. You just wait until you see it. It's bri-lliant.'

Lili turned to Ian. 'There's nothing more you can tell me?'

'Not for now.' Ian's face looked like a deflated balloon. 'Perhaps – a session at another time. If you could bring me something else . . .'

Lili got to her feet. She wasn't sure whether to thank Ian or not.

'I'll come again,' she said, then told Gretchen: 'I'll come to your flat.'

'My mum . . . No, you'd better not.'

'Well, where can we meet?'

'What about your theatre again?' said Gretchen. 'You're sort of living there, aren't you? You can get inside during the day.'

'Yes,' said Lili.

The line went dead, but then the phone immediately rang again.

'Gretchen?'

'No, love.' It was a man's voice, warm cockney with the hint of some more exotic accent.

'Who's this?'

'It's Ben, your mum's boyfriend.'

'Oh.' Lili gripped the phone. 'Look, sorry I didn't call you before. I got your messages but . . . I don't know. I just felt weird about getting in touch.'

'Don't be sorry, love. It's okay.' Ben sighed. 'What a mess, huh?'

'I know. Look Ben, I can't talk right now.'

'Please, love. Just for a minute or two. It's about the funeral. We need to get it sorted—'

'Sorry, Ben, I just can't. The way I feel right now, she doesn't even deserve a funeral.'

Lili disconnected his call, feeling guilt pound at her fingertips. He was a good man, Ben. Even Darren said so. It wasn't fair to take her anger out on him.

19

Life's a Stage by Lili Allure

Pasties. A girl's breast friend.

What's a pastie? No, it's not a wheat-flour snack or the colour of skin in winter. Pasties are decorative nipple covers, sometimes tasselled, always fabulous. A properly positioned pastie makes every breast look divine. Downward-pointing breasts turn into delightfully perky bosoms with the right positioning, and those that fall out to the sides (like mine) can appear to be perfectly centred with a pastie in place.

In the old days of burlesque, the breast-covering pastie stood between a saucy performance and gross indecency. Back then ladies were arrested for showing too much, so a pastie could absolutely not fall off. Glue was so liberally applied it sometimes left ripped skin when the pasties were removed.

You can make your own pasties very easily and most burlesque girls do. I use buckram as a backing, and then glue on whatever I fancy. A word about nipple glue. Some can leave gooey marks or even be painful, so be careful. I use latex glue to attach my pasties, and find as long as my breasts are free from oil and make-up, it works just fine. I've never lost one – yet!

When Lili returned to Covent Garden, tourists surrounded Kate Hamilton's Supper Club, snapping away at the famous old theatre. Kneeling on tarmac, squinting into the sky, jostling with passing shoppers, they took shot after shot of the Victorian building – a highlight of any trip to London.

Lili was immaculately turned out in a floor-length, camel-coloured coat, black stilettos, beige gloves and a clutch bag. The skin on her neck and face, treated daily to the best cosmetics, powders and moisturisers, was porcelain smooth.

Through the crowd of tourists, Lili saw a poster of herself beside the theatre doors. On glossy paper behind lit glass, she wore a Jean Paul Gaultier corset which, she recalled, had been especially painful to pose in.

A nineteen-inch waist looked fabulous in photographs, but in terms of moving and breathing it wasn't ideal. Still, there were no signs of discomfort on her beautiful face, skin white as the moon, red lips giving the hint of a smile.

When it came to performing, Lili was an expert at hiding pain.

She spied Gretchen behind the crowds, waiting by the closed-up theatre door, and pushed through the tourists to reach her. 'Gretchen. Over here.'

'You just wait until you see this article!' Gretchen had done her best to conceal her school uniform by removing the tie and rolling up the skirt, but it was still obvious she was playing truant. A dowdy grey coat hung over her arm, even though she was shivering with cold. A rucksack sat at her feet, and she delved inside for papers.

'Let's go inside. You're freezing.' Lili took off her own coat and wrapped it around Gretchen's trembling shoulders. She remembered what it was like to have the wrong clothes and spend the day hiding them in lockers or under desks.

Tourists with phone cameras snapped Lili as she led Gretchen through the stage door.

It was warm in the underground tunnels. Pete was sitting outside the dressing room, drinking tea from a Starbucks mug with no handle.

'What are you doing here?' Lili asked.

Pete usually arrived at the theatre as late as possible, and even then he usually hung around the stage area, checking lighting, making sure props were in the right places.

'What? Can't I get to the club early?'

'No.'

Pete got to his feet. 'I was doing a last sweep for broken glass. There's a lot of bare feet in that room. Happy?'

'No vodka this morning?'

Pete glanced at Gretchen. 'It's just tea. Do you want one?'

'I don't like tea,' said Gretchen.

'I'm all right,' said Lili. 'Pete, aren't you coming in?'

'I'm happy out here.'

'Suit yourself.' Lili hoped Pete wasn't brooding about the vandalism. It was her problem.

'It's big in here, isn't it?' said Gretchen, spreading out her arms as they entered the dressing room. 'Who would have guessed it? When that guy showed me down yesterday, I was like whoah. A palace.'

It was true. Kate Hamilton's dressing room was a cut above most below-stage areas.

On the far wall were three open cubicles where the dancers kept their make-up, wigs and costumes. Gretchen went to the middle cubicle and stroked a blonde, bobbed wig. 'I suppose you need space for all these things.'

'It's nice to see the glass all cleaned up,' said Lili, placing her clutch bag on a shelf and taking off her high heels. She sat on the sofa, which doubled as her bed at night, and felt the coolness of the floorboards through her stockings. 'So. Let's see this article.'

'Do you smoke weed?' asked Gretchen, picking up a pair of tasselled pasties from a metal shelf stacked with fabrics, glitter pots, glues and tools.

'None of your business,' said Lili. 'Those aren't yours. Put them back.'

'That means yes.' Gretchen put the tassels to her chest. 'Viv did.' Then, seeing Lili's expression, she hurriedly dropped them on the shelf. 'I'll get the article for you. Have *you* found out anything else about the letters?'

Lili went to a stack of dog-eared novels on the tea-chest coffee table and rearranged them into alphabetical order. 'I saw Ian Batty this morning. And twice yesterday. He told me things about

Love . . . I'm thinking – maybe Mum talked to him a lot. How much did she know about Love?'

'Quite a bit,' said Gretchen.

Lili's mobile phone rang and she slid it from her handbag, checking the number to make sure it wasn't Ben.

'Hello?'

'How *old* is that phone?' Gretchen stared at Lili's bulky, baby-pink Nokia, circa 1998. 'It's like an antique.'

'That's why I like it,' said Lili. 'And it works fine, if all you want to do is make calls. I like vintage stuff. Hello?'

It was the family liaison officer, Maureen Fletcher, letting Lili know that the coroner had completed the post-mortem and issued an interim death certificate.

'Your mum's partner is handling the funeral right now,' said Maureen, 'since the family haven't stepped forward. I gave him your number, but he tells me you haven't returned his calls.'

'I spoke to him about an hour ago, actually,' said Lili. 'But there wasn't time to talk. I didn't realise he was actually *doing* the funeral. I'm glad he is. To tell you the truth, I'm not sure I'm up to it.'

'I must say,' said Maureen, 'I've never seen it this way round before. Usually, the family fight with the partner to have it all their way.'

'It's good Ben's taken charge,' said Lili. 'I would have felt a fraud playing the loving daughter.'

'Mr Javadi was quite anxious to get hold of you,' Maureen told Lili. 'He asked me to get in touch on his behalf. He wants a family member to at least give the okay, even if you don't make any of the decisions.'

'I'm happy for him to make all the decisions.'

'Well. So far, he's arranged for your mum to be taken to a local funeral director's near Mile End tube station. He thought you might like to go there, say your farewell to her, and tell them your wishes. He's quite adamant that you or Viv's siblings have a say in things, but I told him you had something of a difficult relationship, so . . .'

'Has he . . . did Ben manage to get in touch with any other family members? My mum's brother and sister. Or my gran?'

'I don't know, love, but they'll know at Mile End, most likely. Funeral directors are always ever so nice. Very understanding. Just pop along and confirm you'd like Mr Javadi to sort everything out.' Maureen gave Lili the address and hung up.

Lili appreciated the call – a kindness from an officer who must have known that, in Lili's current state of mind, she needed guidance in dealing with the official side of things.

'Gretchen, I've got to go tick a few boxes for Mum's funeral.'

'I'll come with you.'

'Shouldn't you be at school?'

'Not today,' said Gretchen, looking at the chipped polish on her fingernails. 'It's a holiday.'

'In January?'

'Every school does things differently.'

It was an obvious lie, but . . . 'Fine,' Lili decided. 'Come with me then. And we'll look at the article when we're done.' She didn't like the idea of Gretchen wandering the streets on her own. Not that she cared, but . . .

'You don't want to look at the article now?' asked Gretchen.

'I can't focus on anything knowing I've got this to do. First things first. Let's get the funeral arrangements out the way. Then I can think clearly.'

20

Life's a Stage by Lili Allure

Lili's London: The East End

There are thousands of funeral directors in London, and the East End has its fair share. Most people don't pay any attention to them until the day they need their services. After that, they notice them everywhere.

Together, Lili and Gretchen entered T & P Bird and Son, a glass-fronted funeral director's off Mile End Road.

It was warm inside, but Gretchen kept Lili's coat on.

A huge vase of fresh flowers stood in the corner, and a grey-suited man sat at a desk with a computer on it.

'I'm Lili Morgan, here to give the okay for my mother's funeral arrangements,' Lili told the man, wondering why 'mum' had suddenly changed to 'mother'. She supposed it was a way of keeping a familiar word like 'mum' away from a word like 'death'.

'Ah, yes.' The man gave Lili a sad smile and directed her to a beige sofa. 'Your mother's partner has given the preliminary instructions, but he's stressed everything can be changed, depending on what you'd like.'

'There's nothing I'd like. What do you need me to do so I can get out of here?'

'It's not so much a question of need. Mr Javadi is happy to arrange things, if the family aren't . . . willing. You can arrange everything or nothing – it's up to you. He was very insistent that your wishes be accommodated, whatever they may be.'

'I'd like him to organise everything.'

'Well. Let's go through it, anyway. Just in case. Did your mother have any last wishes she shared with you?' The man's voice was soothing, as though he were reading a bedtime story.

'A certain type of ceremony, perhaps? Mr Javadi thought she'd like a Christian ceremony. Do you feel a Christian ceremony is suitable?'

'What? Oh. Yeah, I suppose so.' Lili tapped fingers on the desk.

The man nodded. 'Mr Javadi has requested two cars – enough to accommodate Mr Javadi, you, your brother and your mother's mother, brother and sister. Will that be sufficient?'

'I don't know.' Lili felt her lips sticking together. 'Did Mr Javadi get hold of my gran?' She felt a pang of something. Fear . . . guilt . . . she wasn't sure what, but it wasn't a good feeling. 'She's not always easy to track down.'

'He intends to invite all the immediate family.'

'Gran lives in a caravan,' said Lili. 'She travels around. She doesn't have a phone. He'd have to either visit her or send something by post, and I don't know how he would get her address.'

'Well. You'll have to ask him—'

'And I don't know about my brother,' said Lili. 'He's in prison. They might not give him leave. And me – I won't be travelling with the family. I'll make my own way there. If I make it at all.'

The man looked uncomfortable. 'Well. Mr Javadi suggested the funeral be held at St Botolph's Church. Near where your mother lived. So – easy enough to get to if you feel you would like to attend.'

Lili had thought the anger might soften the closer she got to the funeral, but if anything she felt even more furious. It was like an out-of-body experience, hearing the effort being made to throw a last party for Viv, a woman who couldn't even be bothered to attend her own life.

'How about the coffin?' The man looked up, hands poised over his computer keyboard. 'Mr Javadi has requested something quite colourful – daffodils painted on the side and a blue lid.'

'Whatever he wants to do.'

'The funeral has been provisionally booked for this Saturday at eleven o'clock. But if that's too soon, Mr Javadi gave us specific instructions only to pencil in that date until we had your approval about everything. Time, venue, everything.'

'Yes, it's all fine,' said Lili, staring out of the window.

'Here.' The man took a card and scribbled the date on it. 'Sometimes it's hard to remember dates when your head's all in a whirl.'

'Thanks.' Lili folded the card and placed it into her handbag.

'You might like to phone family and friends yourself, just to make sure everyone your mother would have wanted there knows the time and date.'

'No.' Lili pulled her lips tightly together. 'If a get-together is so important for Mum, she should have stayed alive to sort it herself.'

Gretchen whispered, '*You should phone your family and ask about the letters.*'

'I need to find out where they are, first. I haven't seen them in years.'

The man coughed. 'Would you like to see your mother now? She's resting in our chapel. Mr Javadi has already been.'

'No.'

'Are you sure?' the man asked. 'Most people do want to see their relatives.' He patted Lili's hand. 'You don't want to make a decision you might regret later.'

'I can't see her.' Lili slid her hand away. 'She doesn't deserve anyone going to see her. Don't you get it? She left us. She doesn't even deserve a funeral.'

21

Life's a Stage, by Lili Allure

Another song that might go well with a burlesque routine . . .
Mile End, by Pulp

'Wait! Slow down.' Gretchen called. 'I thought you wanted to see the newspaper article.'

Lili stopped, traffic roaring past, and waited for Gretchen to catch up.

'Sorry,' Lili said. 'It was too warm in there.' She welcomed the cold air that numbed her cheeks and fingertips beneath the thin fabric of her gloves. The funeral parlour, with its sympathetic staff, had been uncomfortable.

'Let's take a look.'

'Okay.' Gretchen pulled a piece of paper through a frayed section of her rucksack, nylon string stroking the pages. 'But not here.'

'Why not?'

'We're in *Mile End*. If we hang around on the street here, we'll get stabbed.'

Lili laughed. 'Is that what your mum told you?'

'Yes.'

'Well, that's silly. I grew up around here. It's fine. Sort of.'

'All the same . . .' Gretchen looked over her shoulder.

'All right. We'll walk back to Whitechapel and read it on the way.'

They passed under railway tracks and walked beside a canal

– the same canal Lili used to sit beside with a bunch of friends from school, smoking and drinking.

Lili took the paper from Gretchen. 'Mum never saw the whole article?'

'No.'

The full photocopy of the *Star* front page was dated 15th February 1865, and contained three sensational headlines: **Arsenic Death!**, **Child Stolen by Foreigner** and **Death from Swallowing a Rat**.

'Newspapers haven't changed much, then,' said Lili. 'Is this newspaper based on today's *Daily Star* by any chance?'

'No relation,' said Gretchen. 'Did you know that newspapers used to be printed on cotton-rag fibre?'

Lili shook her head, smiling at Gretchen's arcane historical knowledge. She scanned the small, dense text below the **Arsenic Death!** headline.

'Okay, so she had syphilis, but was poisoned by arsenic.' Lili reread the first paragraphs. 'Married to Tom, addicted to drink, living a loose, immoral sort of life.' She found text she hadn't yet read:

The night before the body was found, Love Morgan was seen at the Mall, and also the home of her former employer, William Peavy, in Holborn.

William Peavy again. 'It says that Love visited William Peavy's house the night before she died.'

'Don't you think it's amazing that your family used to work for him?'

'I suppose so. But the workhouse report said they both lost their jobs. Why would Love be going to his house?'

'Well,' said Gretchen. 'It wouldn't have been a social call. There was a massive class divide back then. Poor people didn't mix with rich men like William Peavy.'

Lili carried on reading.

22

On Wednesday morning at 7 o'clock Police Constable James 967 was summoned to the home of Mrs Love Morgan, who was found dead in the early hours by her husband, Mr Thomas Morgan.

The Police Constable sent for assistance, and Dr Beasley, of Bethnal Green Road, was called upon to attend the scene, where he found Mrs Morgan's body to be cold and estimated her death had occurred some four hours before. Love Morgan's husband, Thomas Morgan, informed Dr Beasley that Mrs Morgan had been in discomfort since the previous night.

After the body was removed to the mortuary, Mrs Morgan's possessions were catalogued, including clothing of a common description, yellow letters wrapped in red cotton rags and one petticoat bearing the stencil stamp of the Whitechapel Workhouse.

Poisoning by arsenic was confirmed by the coroner, but how Love Morgan came to imbibe the poison is at present unknown.

The rest of the article went into detail about the post-mortem examination and chemical testing used to determine arsenic poisoning.

'Yellow letters.' Lili ran her gloved finger over the words. 'Love's yellow letters, they really do exist. So what happened to them?'

Gretchen shrugged. 'I suppose all her possessions would go to the family. Her husband.'

'Tom.' Lili thought of Viv's wall. 'Mum thought Love was murdered for the letters . . .'

'She could have died by accident,' Gretchen pointed out. 'Arsenic came in paper bags, back then. It looked just like flour. People were always making puddings with it by mistake.

'I think she was murdered,' said Lili. 'If not for the letters themselves, than maybe for what was in them. That's what Mum thought and for once I believe her. There's something going on with these letters, Gretchen. They're more than just some old antique. Mum was obsessed with them, she told me to find them and my dressing room—'

'Wait!' Gretchen grabbed Lili's arm. 'We can't carry on walking this way – we'll go past my school.'

'I thought you were on holiday.'

'No – please. Please, Lili, let's go this way.' Gretchen pulled Lili's arm and led her down a pretty street of terraced houses. 'You won't tell Mum, will you?'

Lili shook her head. 'At least your mum cares. When I skived off school, my mum didn't even notice.'

'Is that why you never visited her?' asked Gretchen, as they passed tiny terraced homes that were now worth millions.

'She never came to see me either.' Lili took off a glove and let her hand drag along the privet hedges so the branches scatched her pale skin. 'It used to really bother me, but I sort of got numb to it over time. Then they told me she'd killed herself, and now . . . oh my God. It's like my whole world's gone red. I'm more angry now than when I left home, and I was pretty angry then.'

'You can't taste arsenic,' said Gretchen, seeming not to hear. 'There was a group of women who all poisoned their husbands with it. They bought bags of it for catching rats, then added it to their husbands' meals.'

'What a way to die,' said Lili. 'I hope Mum . . . Well, I hope she didn't suffer. I hope it was quick. Stupid, isn't it? I'd slap her so hard if she was here, but the thought of her actually being in pain . . .'

'Did you know mothers used to poison their children back when Love was alive?' said Gretchen. 'They had these things called burial clubs. Like an insurance policy for poor people. You paid a monthly premium, and if your child died you got a payout.

'Mothers would choose one of their children to poison – they had big families back then. The unlucky one got arsenic added to their food and died so the parents got a payout and could buy food for the others.

'Imagine being the kid that got poisoned. When all your brothers and sisters got to live. They must have known, some of those kids, what was happening. I suppose if it's a choice between all of you going or one of you, you make the sacrifice.'

Lili thought of her brother, Darren. He'd stayed after she'd left.

Her chest ached so badly, for a moment she couldn't bear it.

'I need to start tracking down my family,' said Lili. 'So I can find out what they know about the letters. And who knew Mum was looking for them.' She walked faster, cheered by an abandoned child's tricycle messing up the lines of the neat, smooth pavement.

'You do still want me to help, don't you?' Gretchen ran in front of Lili, walking backwards.

Lili looked at the tall teenager, who, clothing aside, was so similar to herself when she was fifteen. She thought of the vandalised dressing room and the writing on the mirror.

'Actually Gretchen, no. You can't help me with this any more.'

'What?'

'This is something I should do on my own.' Lili looked away.

'But . . . why?' Gretchen's lips began to tremble.

Lili sighed. 'Okay, calm down. It's okay.' She held Gretchen's shoulder. 'I should have told you this before, but my dressing room was vandalised. Something was written on the mirror. About the letters. So I think it might be . . . it's not a good idea for you to look into things until I work out what's going on.'

'Who do you think would do something like that?'

'There aren't many people who'd know,' said Lili. 'Outside of family, only you and Ian. So it must be one of my relatives. Or you or Ian.'

'It's not me!' Gretchen looked outraged.

Lili thought for a moment. 'I should talk to Ben again. Mum might have told him about family stuff.'

'He's really nice,' said Gretchen. 'He was always doing nice things for Viv. Flowers and stuff. Really romantic.'

'He might have family contacts too,' said Lili. 'If he's been arranging the funeral.'

Gretchen blinked. 'I wish I had a family. I've got real parents who don't want me, a foster dad who's left me, a foster mum who hates me—'

'She doesn't hate you.'

'Whatever.'

Lili realised she'd stopped walking. 'I never felt like I had a family either. We never saw them much, growing up. Mum was always so angry with them, but she never said why.

'If I hadn't left home when I did, maybe Mum would have told me more about them, and why she was so messed up about it. And then maybe I wouldn't feel so angry with her, and my life wouldn't be turning out . . . Never mind.' She started walking again. 'The first time I'll see my family in nearly twenty years will be at Mum's funeral, probably.'

'So you're going to go, then?'

'It's as good a way as any to start asking the family about these letters.'

'When is it again?'

'This Saturday. But maybe that's not soon enough. There's one person at least I can see before then. If he's still in the same place.' She began to walk faster.

'Are we going back to your club?' asked Gretchen, doing a side-step beside Lili as they turned on to Whitechapel High Street. 'Can I try on some of your clothes?'

They passed corner shops and cafés and fabric dealers.

'No. We're going somewhere I used to work years ago.' Lili came to a stop outside a gloomy pub. Above the door, a sign said: The Bricklayers Arms. The windows were boarded up, but soft light glowed from inside through the cracks.

In gold letters at the top of a black board were the words: Licensee: Jeff Morgan.

'He still owns it,' said Lili, staring at the building. 'I don't believe it. After all these years.'

'What is this place?' asked Gretchen, trying to peer around the boards. 'I can't see in.'

'That's the idea,' said Lili.

'Is it a pub?' Gretchen asked.

'Not exactly,' said Lili. 'I used to work here as . . . a sort of waitress.'

'It doesn't look like the kind of place to have waitresses,' said Gretchen.

'No.' Lili gave a little laugh. 'I suppose it's not.'

'So what's the big deal? Why are you standing here staring at it?'

'Because, well . . . my Uncle Jeff runs this place.'

23

It's just the same, thought Lili, looking up at a faded Carlsberg sign poking out like a plastic ear from the brickwork. A handwritten note on the door said: 'Five pound door fee, cash only. Customers *must* buy drinks from the bar, ten pound minimum spend.'

The black boards at the window had chalk writing on them, detailing opening times and the fact champagne was on sale.

'Is it closed?' asked Gretchen. 'Why are all these boards outside it?'

'No, it's open.' The loose-hinged door squeaked open and an Asian man hurried out onto the street. Lili pulled Gretchen away from the windows.

There was a beeping sound.

'Oh shit, that's Mum,' said Gretchen. She pulled out her mobile phone. 'Shit, shit, shit.' Her face went pale. 'How did she know? You didn't tell her I was with you, did you?'

To Lili's amazement, Gretchen began to cry. 'I'm in so much trouble. She knows I'm not at school.'

'Tell her it was my fault,' said Lili. 'Say I needed to talk to you.'

Gretchen screwed up her eyes in anguish. 'She's looking for any excuse to ground me and keep me under her thumb.' She snuck a glance over her shoulder. 'I've got to go.'

Gretchen ran towards a red double-decker bus pulling up opposite the tube station.

'Wait,' Lili shouted after her. 'I'll make sure you get home safe.'

'No.' Gretchen jumped onto the bus. 'Just let me know what you find out from your uncle.'

'I'll call you later.'

'No, Mum'll be a nightmare now. She'll probably take my phone away. I'll get out and meet you. Later.'

'Gretchen, we need to—'

The bus pulled out and Gretchen was gone.

Lili watched the double-decker judder down the street, the sign '205 to Paddington' above its rear window getting fainter and fainter.

She turned back to the Bricklayers Arms. It had been so many years since she'd worked behind those unfriendly black boards. Almost as many years as it had been since she'd seen Uncle Jeff.

When she'd worked as a stripper at the Bricklayers, Lili had been a careless teenager who'd left a careless home. Thoughts of her mum had been sharp and painful.

Time had softened and blunted her feelings, and she had no desire to feel those sharp points again. But Viv's death meant lifting the rock of her past and taking a good look at what was squirming underneath.

If she was ever going to move on, she had to confront things she'd long since run away from.

Lili pushed open the door.

The catwalk-style stage still dominated the small pub. A Chinese girl with bleached-orange hair crawled along the narrow platform. She wore nothing but a G-string and high heels, and periodically stopped to lean back and stroke her neck and bare breasts.

Lili felt like an elastic rope had been slung around her middle, wrenching her back eighteen years to the frightened, loud-mouthed, graceless teenager she'd been.

She looked at the silver pole on stage and watched it wobble as the girl began spinning around it. Lili smiled.

They still haven't got that fixed, she thought.

Lili had been on stage doing a handstand against the pole when the screw had dropped out. It had fallen on her with a sprinkle of decades-old plaster, and she'd screamed obscenities at the assistant manager.

The girl was putting on a good performance, Lili thought, except her eyes were scared and self-conscious. The first month Lili worked at the Bricklayers she'd been scared too, not meeting anyone's eye and taking off all her clothes far too soon.

It had taken a long time to realise her eyes held all the power.

The Bricklayers really hadn't changed at all, Lili decided, except for the drinks on sale. When Lili worked there the bar had been stocked with Cinzano, Martini, Bell's whisky and the 'new', fashionable beer of the time, Stella Artois, served by the pump.

Now, only bottled beer and champagne were on sale. A stack of orange Veuve Clicquot buckets looked decidedly out of place behind the glass-tiled bar.

Lili looked around. The same wooden tables, permanently shiny with spilt drink, were dotted around the stage over a carpet of lager stains and ground-in peanuts.

The pub had a few customers, and a familiar man sat at the bar, his back to the room, thinning grey hair combed against his scalp. Lili felt her heart begin to pound. Who'd have thought? *He still drinks all day in his own pub.*

It was Uncle Jeff.

24

Life's a Stage by Lili Allure

Easy? I don't think so!

When I first began in the striptease business, I worked in a spit and sawdust strip club. It was the best training any burlesque girl could get and taught me everything I know.

Mesmerising an audience has more to do with hard work than beauty. I'm the first to admit my physical imperfections: lumps on my upper thighs, a long nose and boyish face. But I've seen beautiful girls bore the audience while girls who are plain or overweight captivate the crowd.

In my first job I learned that, just like anything in life, what looks effortless takes a lot of hard work. The more I practised on that pole, pushed myself into harder and more dangerous moves and pricked my fingers sewing together interesting outfits, the more money I made.

Now I'm a burlesque superstar, but I haven't forgotten the lessons I learned in that strip club. I spend hours perfecting my make-up before a show, and months designing set pieces and practising my routines. You might think burlesque looks easy, but every bump, grind and drop is perfectly timed to the music.

Uncle Jeff's hair had thinned and faded, and his middle was thicker, but other than that he was unchanged. He wore a denim shirt and jeans, just like always, and sat on his usual stool in his usual hunched-over position.

It was like not a day had gone past.

'Are you looking for a job?'

Lili turned to see a fat, shaven-headed man by the door. He had a margarine tub of five-pound notes in his hands.

'No – my uncle.' Lili took five pounds from her purse and dropped the note into the tub. She went to the bar.

'Mine's a bottle of Special K.' Lili took a stool next to Jeff and waited for him to turn around.

'Oh my word.' Jeff looked from Lili's immaculate, shiny hair to her soft coat, stockings and colour-coordinated shoes. 'Look at you. Long time, no see.'

'Likewise. I need to talk to you about Mum.'

Jeff had a pointy face, a big quiff of salt-and-pepper hair, three gold teeth and twenty-five yellow ones of his own. In the wrong light he looked dangerous, but really he was a gentle soul. He was sweating Old Spice. Uncle Jeff always had been a little too liberal with the aftershave.

The last time Jeff had seen Lili, she'd had bleached blonde streaks at the front of her hair, a dolphin navel piercing and a uniform of belly tops and loose jeans.

'You're not looking to work here again, then?'

Lili shook her head. 'Very funny. Like I said. I'm here about Mum.'

Jeff had avoided drinking at the bar while Lili had worked there. Being a borderline alcoholic, this had hurt him deeply, but he didn't want to see his niece with no clothes on.

'I thought you might come back for the funeral,' Jeff said, 'but I didn't have a number for you and . . . well, you know how it's been. I wasn't sure if you wanted to be got in touch with. Thought you might want to distance yourself.'

'I can't say I'm over the moon to be back in East London,' said Lili. 'But I need to ask you something. When was the last time you saw Mum?'

'A few days before she died,' said Jeff. 'She wasn't in a good way.'

'Was she . . . *looking* for something? Stuff about the family or something like that?'

'She was going on about these old letters.'

Lili's body tensed. 'Uncle Jeff, I need to know everything she told you.'

'Oh, there wasn't much. Just asked me if I knew where they were. I told her I didn't. These letters – they belonged to a relative of ours, long since dead.'

'Love Morgan,' said Lili.

Jeff looked at her strangely. 'That's right.'

The girl from the stage, her performance finished, fastened herself back into her underwear and began walking around the pub with an empty pint glass. She knew better than to approach Jeff, but Lili waved her over and stuck a ten-pound note in the glass.

'Please Uncle Jeff – I need to know. What exactly did Mum say? Why did she want to find these letters? Did she know what was in them? Do you?'

Jeff shook his head. 'I've never had a clue, but Viv was doing the family history. She might have found out more than me. Seriously, I don't know, love.'

Lili fiddled with a damp bar mat. 'What did Mum want to know about the letters?'

'Oh – just where they'd ended up. She wanted to look at something I was given when Grandad died. A will.'

'Whose will?' asked Lili

'Love Morgan's husband,' said Jeff. 'A man called Tom.'

'Tom Morgan?' Lili stared at him. 'You've got his will?'

'Dad gave it me when he died. It's been in the family for donkeys' years.'

'Can I see it? I *need* to see it, Uncle Jeff.'

'All right. It's back at the house.'

'Let's go.'

'Right now?'

Lili looked around the room where she'd spent much of her teenage years. It was as dark and lonely as it always had been, not an inch of daylight poked through even at four in the afternoon.

She remembered pacing the pub for notes and coins, begging

for dances and drinks. It was brutal selling herself every night, made harder because she was naked and vulnerable and had to fend off men who acted like she was their girlfriend.

Lili called over the Chinese girl and stuck another ten-pound note in the glass.

'Yes,' she told Jeff. 'Right now.'

25

'Who told you about Mum?' Lili asked, as they headed west towards the skyscrapers of Liverpool Street.

'Ben,' said Jeff. 'He saw the police break into her flat, and he's been sorting everything out since then. The funeral and everything.'

'I know.' Lili felt the guilt again at being an absent daughter.

'The funeral's on Saturday. Did you know?'

Lili nodded.

'I take it you're going?'

'I was hoping to see some of the family there. And to find out more about these letters and what was going through Mum's head those last days.'

'Have you seen any of them since it happened?' Jeff asked.

'You're the first. Do you still have the place near the Ten Bells?'

'No. You know how Shoreditch is now. All citified and clean cut. Don't get me wrong, they can drink in my pub. But I like to live in a place where I don't have to wear a suit to buy my Sunday paper.'

Before Lili could stop him, Jeff disappeared into a corner shop. He returned with two cans of Olde Oake cider. 'It's yuppy paradise now, Shoreditch. Haven't you seen? All over-priced cocktails and falafel. I'm near Bethnal Green. Still enough foreigners round there to keep the City boys away.'

'Can we walk a bit faster?' Lili asked.

They turned up Brick Lane, a little slice of India in the middle of London. The market stalls and electronic shops of Whitechapel Road gave way to Balti houses, Indian sweet shops and sari fabric dealers.

'It's changing round here too,' Jeff told Lili. He pointed to a coffee shop offering decaf and chamomile – one of the many that were fast catching up with the curry restaurants. 'Even Brick Lane's getting posher. You come back here much?'

'No, never,' said Lili, thinking there were fewer women in saris then when she had lived here. The street signs were still in both English and Bengali, but white, middle-class Londoners were fast encroaching on the area, just like they had on Shoreditch. 'So Mum wasn't in a good way when you saw her?'

Jeff nodded, clicking open a can and glugging. He offered the other can to Lili, and for old times' sake she struck it open and took a dainty sip. 'But then she hadn't been for years. You've changed,' he observed. 'Years ago, you'd have downed that in one.'

'Can we hurry up a bit?'

'Calm down,' said Jeff, pulling a key from his pocket. 'We're nearly there.'

The Indian colour of Brick Lane had petered out now they neared Bethnal Green Road, and leather jacket shops and bagel bakeries replaced Indian restaurants.

'You must know something about those letters,' said Lili. 'I mean, there must be family stories about them.'

'They're something to do with an old family secret,' said Jeff. 'That's all I've ever known.'

'Do the whole family know about them?' said Lili.

'There's been talk of them for years, but who knows what or where they are?' said Jeff. 'Or if they even exist any more.'

'Mum thought they still existed.'

They reached a narrow, terraced house, squeezed between a clothes shop and a bakery. It was tiny – Lili guessed one bedroom, one bathroom. There were wooden shutters over the windows, screwed into brown bricks.

In any town in the land, the house would have been a cheap starter home. On Brick Lane, it was prime retail space. Lili knew it was probably worth half a million. The house was classic Jeff. Scruffy looking, but worth a fair bit.

'So tell me about Tom's will,' said Lili, as Jeff turned a key in a duck-egg blue door.

'Dad left it to me, like it was some great treasure,' said Jeff, standing back to let Lili into the dark house. 'It talks about these old yellow letters – that's why Viv wanted to look at it. But it's all very cryptic.'

Lili saw a narrow room, striped with daylight from the shutters. A chandelier bulged against the ceiling, too bulky and ornate for the tiny space. Jeff clicked the light switch and twenty candle bulbs blazed.

The ground floor was open plan: living room, kitchen and a staircase running up the side.

There was a cool, white fireplace with beer mats lined along it, a rickety pine bookcase and a battered leather couch with brass studs. On the bookcase were magazines, paperbacks and empty cider bottles. Pub meets living room.

The house was spotless, as Lili knew it would be. She was willing to bet Jeff spent a good hour a day scrubbing it clean. Unlike Viv, Jeff couldn't abide dirt. Lili knew he wouldn't pay for a cleaner either – not for a job he could do himself. He was probably still the meanest millionaire she knew.

'Why do you think Mum suddenly got interested in the letters?' asked Lili.

'I suppose they're worth a bit,' said Jeff. 'I didn't know she was hurting for money, but then again, I suppose you can always use more money.'

Lili noticed the handle of a knife poking out from under the sofa. She sat down and pulled it free. 'I see you haven't changed,' she said, examining the blade. 'Weapons hidden everywhere. Still paranoid.'

'You've got to be careful round here. But you've changed. For the better.' Jeff coughed mightily into his hand. 'Sad news about Viv, isn't it? I'm still trying to get my head around it.'

Lili nodded. 'I'm trying to figure out how she could do this. Leave us, without a note or a goodbye or anything.'

'Do you want a tea?' He reached in his pocket and pulled out a handful of long-life milk cartons, almost certainly liberated from the local church. Jeff never bought anything he didn't have to.

'I'm all right. And Mum seemed . . . upset? Unhappy when you saw her?'

'Like I said, not all that happy,' said Jeff. 'She and her fella had been rowing. They were taking a break from each other. Everything was getting on top of her – you know how it did sometimes. And she was going on and on about those letters.'

'Can I see the will?'

''Course.' Jeff opened and closed ill-fitting drawers in the bookcase. 'Here it is.' He passed Lili a brown A4 envelope with 'To Jeff', written in faded red ink on the front. 'I should look after it better, I know. It's an antique. At least make a photocopy. But I've never quite got round to it.'

Lili looked inside the envelope. It was empty.

LOVE MORGAN b. 1831,
             d. 1865.

Love Morgan
1831 – 1865

James Morgan
1864 – 1889

Fred Morgan
1899 – 1972

Vivienne Morgan
b.1965

Jeff Morgan b.1958

26

'There's nothing in here, Uncle Jeff.'

'You're joking.' Jeff took the envelope from her and looked inside. Optimistically, he shook it. 'I don't know what to tell you, Lil. It was here before.' He turned a complete, bewildered circle and began hunting amoung magazines. 'Where's it gone?'

'When did you last have it?' Lili asked, uneasy.

'When Viv came round,' said Jeff. 'We looked at it. I put it back. She left. I haven't looked at it since. But I know I put it back in the envelope.' He shook the brown packet accusingly. 'I put it back myself, and then she left.'

He moved to the bookcase.

'Well, well well.' He pulled out a sheet of faded paper. 'What's it doing there?' He shook his head. 'My memory.'

'Someone moved it?' asked Lili, taking the paper.

'I must have,' said Jeff. 'I don't remember though.'

Lili shivered, although the house was warm enough. She began reading.

This is the last Will and Testament of Tom Morgan of 31 Old Nichol Street, Whitechapel, in the county of Middlesex. I give and bequeath unto my son, James Morgan, the trustee and executor of this my Will, three letters on yellow paper written between February 1863 and January 1865, bearing the name of Morgan, which must not be in any way released from his care after my death and during his lifetime.

I do hereby declare that in case the said James Morgan shall desire to be discharged from or refuse or decline or become incapable to act in the duties of this my Will before his duties shall be fully executed and performed, then in such case the letters will be entrusted to Lyde & Jones Solicitors, who will undertake to destroy them.

In taking charge of the letters, James Morgan must ensure they remain in the care of the Morgan family until his death, and further ensure that they are passed to surviving family members and entrusted to their care.

Upon the death of James Morgan, the letters shall belong to all the Morgan family and the descendants thereof.

If James Morgan shall depart this life without leaving any child or children him her or them surviving him, the letters must be entrusted to Lyde & Jones Solicitors, who will undertake to destroy them.

The will was dated 1870.

Lili clasped the paper to her chest. 'They really could still exist then. I mean, I thought they might, but it's right there in black and white. James instructed the yellow letters to be passed down through the family.'

She felt her waist sag with relief against the bones of her corset. It had been an unspoken possibility this whole time: *the letters were destroyed years ago.* And with it, another possibility – of being stiff and angry for ever, trapped in feelings that were getting her nowhere.

She looked at the will again. 'James Morgan. I read about his birth. In the workhouse. He must have survived into adulthood. At least to teenage-hood. Was he Love and Tom's only surviving child?'

'I suppose he must have been,' said Jeff.

'This was written just a few years after Love died. I see what you mean about it being cryptic.'

'Hard to make sense of, isn't it?' said Jeff. He rubbed his fore-head and took another sip of cider. 'Funny old writing. You know how they spoke years ago, all flouncy. More words than you need.'

'So what does it all mean?'

Jeff shrugged. 'I've never been sure.'

'Why was Mum so keen to find the letters *now*?' asked Lili.

'Why not years ago? You've had this will for a long time. She knew you had it, right?'

'God, yes,' said Jeff. 'She knew all right. There was a big row about it.'

'How come?'

'Oh, just a bit of jealousy really. Viv didn't inherit nothing when Dad died. I did, Karen did, but Viv didn't. She was upset about it.'

'How come Grandad didn't give Mum anything?'

'She was the black sheep, wasn't she? Me and Karen both made something of our lives, and Viv flushed hers down the bog, may she rest in peace.'

'What did Aunt Karen get?'

'A load of old clothes from when Mum and Dad were in America. Designer stuff. Dresses and furs and that. Worth a bit.'

Lili read the will again.

'I thought Tom and Love were poor,' she said, thinking of the workhouse report. 'A poor person wouldn't be able to write a will like that, would they?'

'Probably someone wrote it for him,' said Jeff. 'A solicitor. He must have had a bit of cash to pay for it, but who knows where from. He was out of work for most of his life, so I was told.'

'Do you know anything about Love Morgan?'

'Hardly anything,' said Jeff. 'Actually, there is one thing. Before she married Tom, her name was Avery. Love Avery. Grandad always loved birds. He said we came from a family of Averys on Love's side.'

'Spelled like bird aviary – A-V-I-A-R-Y?'

'Don't know how it was spelled. No two people spelled things the same way in them days, anyway.'

'What a strange will. I don't get it.' Lili read the document again. 'Tom Morgan left the letters to his son, James. Do you know anything about him? James Morgan?'

'Plenty. Our grand-uncle Fred used to tell us stories about him all the time.'

'Who?'

'Grand-uncle Fred. He was Grandma Dolly's brother. Him and Dolly were best of friends – they went out to America together.'

'Your grand-uncle knew James Morgan?'

''Course he did. James Morgan – he was Grand-uncle Fred and our Grandma Dolly's grandad. They all grew up round here, Whitechapel area, they all knew each other. Families were close back then.'

'This will was written after Love was poisoned,' said Lili, examining the date at the top. 'Tell me about James Morgan. Tom and Love's son.'

Jeff took out a pouch of herbal tobacco and began rolling a Rizla cigarette. 'You're not interested in all that old stuff, are you? Family stories?'

'Very interested.'

'Well, Grand-uncle Fred told me a few things about James. He liked talking about the past, did Grand-uncle. Didn't like the present all that much. I was sad when he went, I think I was one of his favourites.'

'I bet Mum wasn't one of his favourites,' said Lili. 'She wasn't anyone's favourite. Gran. Grandad. Aunt Karen. None of them liked her.' She chewed her lip. 'I suppose I'll see Gran at some point. And Aunt Karen . . .'

'Aunt Karen has mellowed a bit these last few years,' said Jeff. 'She and Viv had a cup of tea now and then. She was the last to see Viv before she died.'

'Really?' Lili heard the odd tone in her own voice. 'So Aunt Karen saw Mum before she died too?'

'Maybe Viv was saying her goodbyes, in her own way,' said Jeff. 'Seeing us all before she went.'

Lili felt a creeping despair at the thought of Viv saying goodbyes to everyone but her. The daughter who let her down. Hurt must have showed on her face, because Jeff said:

'She was ever so unhappy, Lilian.'

Lili clutched her can of cider so hard it crumpled. The anger swirled around, sour and stuck. She felt sick with it.

'So what did your grand-uncle tell you about James?'

'Plenty.' Jeff took thoughtful puffs of his cinnamon-scented cigarette. 'Get yourself comfortable. I'll tell you all about him.'

27

'We used to see Grand-uncle Fred in the summertime,' Jeff began, watching his cigarette smoke float around the beads of the chandelier. 'When we lived in America with Mum and Dad. They were fun times, travelling around, living out of trunks and boxes.

'Mum and Dad would leave us with him and his wife, Betsy, for the summer, and take off doing their shows and circuses. Grand-uncle would take us to watch the men play baseball in the park. He'd have a beer, we'd have an ice cream – to share, mind. One each would be spoiling us.

'We'd watch the baseball and he'd tell us how he and Grandma Dolly had grown up in England, how hard life had been. He had a story for every day of the year.

'You wouldn't believe what we had to go through, he used to say. Stealing, fighting . . . it was survival back then. We were on the street, robbing market stalls for food, begging for change. Young kids like you were taught to pickpocket, soon as they could walk.'

Jeff rolled his cigarette between yellow fingertips. 'James Morgan and his wife had it especially hard. They spent their lives in and out of workhouses living off church handouts, diseased, miserable, poor.

'James was sick most of his life – had been since he was a young boy. They think he was born with syphilis, and that gives you all sorts of problems. He was always getting sores, and his bones grew funny. He didn't walk right or hear right.

'Somehow, he survived into adulthood and had kids of his own, but Lord knows how. Must have had a guardian angel. He couldn't work most of the time, so he was fed by charity or the workhouse.

'Grand-uncle always said to us, never be too proud to take handouts. For James, handouts meant the difference between living and dying. Eating or starving to death.'

'Where did James live?' asked Lili.

'Whitechapel,' said Jeff. 'Just like all the rest of the family. Funny we're all still here, isn't it? Travelled to the other side of the world, and guess where most of us end up? Back in East London.

'If Grand-uncle Fred could see how this place has changed, he'd have a big old smile about it, I bet. All the coffee shops and restaurants. In his day, people had to choose between a doctor or being fed for a week.'

Jeff went to the sparkling-clean, stainless-steel sink in the kitchen area and began wiping it with a sponge.

'I get it, but tell me about James.'

'Right. Well, James must have been born around eighteen-sixty time. Something like that. Back then, this area was rough as you like. A slum. The Nichol slum, they used to call it. There was crime and prostitution all over – fights, drinking, opium dens, you name it.'

Jeff rinsed the sponge under the tap.

'James was married to a woman called Catherine. Cooky, they called her. No – wait. They weren't married. No. They were common-in-law man and wife. In those days, people didn't bother so much with the wedding side of things. If a man and woman lived together, that was good enough.'

'Cooky?' asked Lili.

'That's right. She was known for cooking up all sorts of things – rats, birds, foxes – when food was low. They were in and out of workhouses, the pair of them, always split up when they went in. Imagine that. Being kept apart from your partner for years on end.

'The stories Grand-uncle told me about the workhouse would turn your hair grey. People were so hungry they stole vegetable peelings, and then they were beaten for it. James was beaten for stealing an onion.' Jeff shook his head. 'Poor sod. Imagine being so hungry you'd eat a raw onion.'

Lili winced. She could taste onion in her mouth, and her eyes watered.

'Grand-uncle said James and Cooky used to pull vegetable peelings out of the workhouse gutter,' said Jeff. 'The kitchen waste went under a grate, and they'd push their hands through and grab what they could, anything that floated past. They were that hungry.

'Couldn't have done their health much good, but then again, neither of them were particularly healthy in the first place. James was born with syphilis and Cooky had a leg missing. Factory accident. It was a miracle they ever had kids.'

'How many kids did they have?'

'Only one survived. Michael. They had six in total, but the rest of them died in the workhouse.'

'That's horrible.'

'Michael was my Grand-uncle Fred's and Grandma Dolly's dad. He did okay in life. A slum businessman. Amazing when you think the start he had. But he had a violent side. A real hard man.'

'Did Mum ask you about all this stuff?' asked Lili.

'She knew it all,' said Jeff. 'Grand-uncle used to tell all three of us the stories. *Oh, you're so lucky. Oh, you don't know you were born.* No, Viv came over to look at the will again. She always liked playing detective.'

Lili's cheeks prickled. 'She played detective games with us when we were little,' she said. 'Me and Darren. Secret notes with invisible ink and treasure trails. She loved all that sort of thing.'

'That she did,' Jeff wheezed.

'She could be fun sometimes,' Lili remembered. 'When she got the Lambrini ratio right. Not too drunk, not too sober. I'd forgotten. Usually, all I remember about Mum is bad stuff.'

'It sounds like James and Cooky had a hell of a life,' Jeff lamented. 'Whenever they were free of the workhouse, they didn't have two pennies to rub together. They moved lodgings every other week to dodge the rent.

'Landlords back then were all toffs, charging the poor four times what they should for some falling-apart room in a falling-down house. And then to cap it all, they'd throw families out on the street for crowding too many into a room. The rich got richer, the poor got poorer.'

Jeff stubbed his rolly into a Fosters ashtray. 'We don't know we're born, do we? I mean, I'm no Richard Branson, but I've got my little place, my pub, my friends. All very comfortable. Lucky as anything, really.' He slapped the wall. 'When you think how people lived, right where we're standing now. Terrible.'

'So what about the son – Michael? James and Cooky's son.'

28

'Grand-uncle Fred's dad?' said Jeff. 'Fred was terrified of him. Barely spoke about him.'

'Why?'

'Personality clash.' Jeff took the sponge from the sink and began wiping the back window. 'Michael was a gangster, and Fred . . . well. He ended up being on the stage, didn't he? You couldn't get much more different. Hardly a man's job, according to Michael.'

'Do you know if the letters were passed to Michael? The will said James had to pass them on to his children.'

'I don't see why he wouldn't have,' said Jeff, glancing at the will. 'I mean, reading that, it's pretty cut and dried. If Michael didn't inherit them, it says there the letters had to be destroyed.'

'Do you think they might have been?' Lili asked.

'No. I think they're somewhere in the family, always have been. That's what Viv thought too.'

'But you don't know where? Or why Mum got a sudden urge to look for them?'

'I really don't, Lilian.'

'Do you have any numbers for the rest of the family? Or addresses? What about Gran? I mean, I can't honestly say I'm dying to talk to her, but I guess she's a good place to start.'

'Mum still moves all over the place. She was in Crystal Palace, last I heard from her, on a caravan site there. That was months ago, but she told me she was fighting with the site owner and wanted to move. She said she'd be in touch, but I haven't heard anything.'

Lili patted her eyes, which felt swollen. 'It scares me, the thought of seeing Gran. I don't know how I'll handle it.'

'She's not the easiest person to get hold of anyway,' said Jeff. 'I haven't seen her since the Christmas before last. You know how she is. Always moving sites. No phone. Only ever gets in touch by letters. You have to wait for her to find you.'

'Does she know about Mum?'

'I'd like to think she found out about it somehow. I don't want to be the one to tell her.'

'So who else are you in touch with?'

'I've got Karen's address from a while back – I helped her out with financing her new house – but I don't know if she's still there. I don't have her number, she was just moving in when I saw her.' Jeff took a tiny address book from the shelf and flicked through. 'Karen . . . Karen . . . there she is. Worth a try.'

He wrote on a Rizla paper. 'She might know something about Michael Morgan. You never know.'

'Okay.' Lili looked at the thin paper. 'Loughton. That's near the end of the central line, isn't it? Where everyone from the East End goes when they've made a bit of money.'

Jeff laughed. 'Muck with brass.'

Lili tucked the paper into her bag. 'I can't say I'm looking forward to seeing her either.'

'She might not even be there any more, Lilian.'

Lili looked at her perfect nails and remembered a time when they were chewed to the finger. 'She always hated me and Darren. She used to make us wash our hands before we touched her furniture.'

'You weren't the best behaved of kids,' Jeff pointed out.

'True.'

Once, when Lili and Darren were junior school age, they'd eaten an entire bowl of whipped cream from Aunt Karen's fridge. They'd been starving. Viv had given them 30p to buy chips for lunch, and they'd put it in the chip shop fruit machine.

Karen had found Lili and Darren on the kitchen floor, scooping out white froth with their palms. The flavour had been heavenly, and Lili had decided when she grew up she'd have a bowl of cream for lunch every day.

Lili shuddered with embarrassment. The past, her own past. No need to go back there. Nothing but horrible memories of a horrible girl.

'So who else could I talk to?'

'Had you thought about your grand-uncle Ron? Dad's brother? Him and Rose are still in Whitechapel somewhere, but I have no idea where. Still, shouldn't be too hard to track down. Ron Morgan – look him up in the phone book.

'And the rest of them are scattered to the four winds. Karen's girls are in West London, and Ron's kids are in Australia.'

'Uncle Jeff, can I borrow the will?'

'I don't know about that, Lilian.' Jeff folded his arms defensively. 'Dad give it me, and it's an old family heirloom. I wouldn't want anything happening—'

'Well, I'm family,' said Lili, putting the will in her bag. 'And I need it. I'll look after it.'

Uncle Jeff winced as if she was scratching keys over his car.

'Think of it as payback for all the money I've made your club,' said Lili.

29

International flags hung outside the reception block at Crystal Palace Caravan Site, and little pots of evergreen shrubs sat by its red brick walls.

'It looks sort of homely,' Lili remarked, as she and Carol-Ann, the Kate Hamilton club manager, approached the block. 'Even in winter.' Lili shivered in her tan coat. There were posters in the reception window for summer fairs that had long since been and gone.

'It's all closed up, though,' said Carol-Ann, putting her face to glass and venetian blind slats. She wore stained ski gloves and an over-sized puffa jacket with a large tear on the shoulder. Carol-Ann resented what she called the 'funeral suits' she had to wear for work, and dressed as casually as possible in her spare time.

'I guess there's no receptionist out of season,' said Lili.

'How does your nan stand this weather?' Carol-Ann wondered. 'I couldn't live in a caravan all through winter, and I'm thirty-one. How old is your nan? Eighty odd?'

'She's always travelled around the place,' said Lili. 'When we were kids, she used to say you don't miss what you never had. So I guess she's used to it. Anyway. Look, it's all locked up, let's go.'

'I think I see someone in there.' Carol-Ann banged on the glass. 'Hello!'

'Look, it's fine.' Lili grabbed her arm. 'It's closed. Let's go.'

'We've come all this way.'

'I know but . . . maybe it's a sign, you know? I didn't really want to talk to Gran just yet anyway.'

'Then why come out here?'

'Because I *should* talk to her.'

There was a creaking sound, and the reception door opened.

'Can I help you?' A sun-tanned blonde lady in wellington boots appeared. She sounded irritated, and deep frown lines cut into her forehead.

'Oh hello,' said Carol-Ann, putting on her best nice-young-lady smile. '*Do* excuse us. We're looking for her gran.' She pointed a thumb at Lili.

'What?'

'My gran,' said Lili. 'I heard she was staying here, but . . . it's fine. We're sorry to have bothered you.'

'Who's your gran?' the woman asked.

'Ginny Morgan.'

'Oh! Ginny. Yes, lovely old dear. Completely off her rocker of course, but that's how we like them.'

'Is she here?' Lili felt herself squeezing Carol-Ann's arm.

'No. I'm afraid she left us. She had a falling out with my husband, in . . . ooh, I suppose that must have been summer time.'

'Do you know where she went?'

'Haven't the foggiest.'

'Perhaps some of the other residents here know her,' said Carol-Ann.

'*Residents*? This is a caravan park, not a retirement home. Holidaymakers. Ginny was the only one who stayed for more than a few weeks. I'm ever so sorry, I just don't know. Have you tried the other London sites?'

'No worries,' said Lili. 'Come on, Caz. Let's go.' They turned and walked up the spotless concrete road.

'I feel better now.' Lili took out her Nokia. 'It's too soon to see Nan. I should track down Aunt Karen first. Work my way into the family gradually.' She dialled directory enquiries. 'Yes, hello. Do you have a number for Karen Baker in Loughton? No? Okay, how about a Ron Tanning. Whitechapel area. Bethnal Green? Or Stepney? Could he be ex-directory? Oh, you can't say. Okay, fine.' Lili hung up.

'No luck?'

'None of them are registered.'

'What about the electoral roll?' Carol-Ann pulled out her iPhone and tapped the screen. 'I've got access to it on one of my marketing apps. Let me have a look. Karen . . . what was it, Baker?'

'Yes. And Ron and Rose Tanning.'

'You know we're all here for you, don't you, Lils?' said Carol-Ann, pressing her finger over the screen. 'Me, Pete, Bry. We've always looked after you.'

'You feel like you've been looking after me?'

'No, I didn't mean . . . well, sort of. You know, since that thing with Janey. Well, you needed looking after, didn't you? And now this has happened with your mum . . . We're still here, that's what I'm trying to say. We know the real you – the one the public doesn't see. The one who drinks port and lemonade and swears and worries that no one fancies her, or that her show is no good. And we love you.'

'I know I've been a mess,' said Lili. 'I've been stuck for a long time, but since this thing with Mum happened – I can't explain to you how angry I feel. It's beyond words. I want to hurt someone, and the only person I can get to is myself.'

'What about Pete? You've been hurting him since you came to Kate's.'

'Not on purpose. And he can look after himself. Jesus Christ.' Lili smacked her hands together. 'Right now, I feel like I'll never forgive Mum for what she did. Like I'll hate her for ever. That's not right, is it?'

'You're too hard on yourself. Your mum killed herself; you're bound to feel all sorts of things.' Carol-Ann looked back at her phone. 'No Ron and Rose Tanning. Look, Lils, maybe it's not just your mum you're angry with. Maybe it's yourself you need to forgive.'

'What for?'

'You tell me. Wait . . . I've got a Karen Baker. Loughton.'

Lili looked at Carol-Ann's phone. 'That's the same address Uncle Jeff gave me. Well, that's something. I can go visit her home.'

'Do you want me to come with you?'

'No, it's fine. There's someone else I'm meeting first, anyway. This guy my mum knew. Look, I really will sort myself out, Caz. I don't want to lean on you guys any more. I'm trying to turn a corner. Just give me time.'

LOVE MORGAN b. 1831, d. 1865.

Nee Avary

Love Morgan
1831 - 1865

James Morgan
1864 - 1889

Fred Morgan
1899 - 1972

Vivienne Morgan
b.1965

Jeff Morgan b.1958

Life's a Stage by Lili Allure

Lili's London: Altab Ali Park in Whitechapel

The shade of my tree is offered to those who come and go fleetingly.

Sign at Altab Ali Park, from a poem by Rabindranath Tagore

Near Aldgate tube station lies Altab Ali Park, a green haven from the covered market stalls, pubs, supermarkets and cars of Whitechapel Road. Grass and trees are woven around the foundations of an old chapel and graveyard destroyed in World War II. The limestone lines of chapel walls poke up through yellowing, patchy grass, and parts of tombs and graves are dotted all around.

'Thanks for meeting me,' called Lili. She shaded her eyes from lunchtime sun as Ian strolled towards her. He carried a gold-tipped walking stick which he threw out far in front with every step, smacking it onto the gravel with decided clicks.

'Not at all.' Ian sat beside Lili on a bench of wooden circles, which sprouted from the ground like mushrooms. It was one of Altab Ali Park's many modern decorations. The new, industrial sculptures of white metal mingled with old, beautiful trees and the remains of St Mary Matfelon's Chapel.

'Do excuse me.' Ian swung a leather satchel from his shoulder and opened it. 'You've caught me in the middle of lunch.' He took out a paper bag of hot samosas and a slim, silver flask of green tea. 'Would you care for a bite to eat?'

'No. I'm fine. I just want to get in touch with Love. As quickly as possible.'

'The samosas are quite excellent,' said Ian, holding one to the light. 'A jolly good friend of mine makes them. Has done for the last twenty years. So he knows what he's doing.'

Ian looked different outside his flat. His face was paler and older than it had appeared indoors, but his manner was altogether more flamboyant and lively. Being in public brought out the performer in him.

'Can we hurry things along a bit?' Lili asked, her gaze resting on a white tombstone smudged with green mould. A half-full McDonald's cup lay beside it, indifferent to the dead body inside. 'This place is giving me the creeps.'

'But it shouldn't do.' Ian took a bite of samosa. 'It's very good for our purposes. I know what you're thinking. Tombs, old graves, dead people . . . good for meeting the spirits. But that's not why I chose this spot.

'In my experience, the dead like to be around the living. After all, if you'd passed on, would you want to linger around the remains of departed ancestors? I think not. Graveyards are death. Endings. When I contact the spirits, I'm looking for re-awakenings.'

'So why meet here, then?'

'Look around you,' said Ian, waving his hand, a piece of potato flying from his samosa. The spiced vegetable was instantly set upon by waiting pigeons. 'It's life we need, and life we have. I come here most lunchtimes to see it.'

He smiled at a mother walking past with three children – one on her hip, one in a buggy and one holding her hand.

'Look, can we just get on with things?'

'Patience, my dear.' Ian opened his flask and poured hot green tea into its curvy lid. 'What do you have for me?'

'A will.'

'Goodness. How exciting. Whose will is it?'

'Tom Morgan's.'

'Love's husband? How marvellous.' Ian took a lilac hand-kerchief from his pocket and wiped his hands. 'Do show me.'

Lili slid the paper from the envelope and handed it to him carefully.

'Where did you find this document?' Ian asked, scanning the tiny writing.

'My Uncle Jeff had it,' said Lili. 'His dad gave it to him.' She paused for a moment. 'He told me there's been talk of the letters for years. That they have something to do with a family secret. That's what Mum thought too.'

'It's sad for a family to have secrets.'

'What family doesn't?'

'Oh, my dear.' Ian frowned. 'Not all families are secretive.' He closed his eyes. 'I have a feeling. A very strong feeling. There *are* secrets in your family. Hidden things. It's all to do with the youngest member.' He opened his eyes again and tilted his chin dramatically upwards.

'I'm the youngest member,' said Lili.

'Are you?'

'Yes. My Aunt Karen's daughters are both older. Darren's older. I'm the youngest.'

'Well, well.' Ian gripped the paper and held it at arm's length. 'Very interesting fellow, this Tom. What do you know about him?'

'Just that he was married to Love.'

'Tell me about your uncle,' said Ian.

'There isn't much to tell. He's just a normal bloke. Well, except that he's a millionaire.'

'There's always more to people than meets the eye,' Ian announced. 'You need to learn what people are hiding, or you'll struggle to find what you're looking for.'

'The letters.'

'The letters, yes, but what you're *really* looking for.'

Lili was silent for a moment. 'Like I said before, some sort of goodbye from my mum. So I can stop being angry.'

'And what about yourself?' Ian asked. 'Is there something of yourself you might find in these letters?'

'I don't know.'

Ian studied the will again. 'Your uncle – he's had this document for some time?'

'As far as I'm aware.'

'He inherited it?'

'Yes.'

'And he was happy for you to have it?'

'Sort of.'

'So you must be good friends,' Ian decided.

'I suppose we are,' said Lili. 'I mean, I hadn't seen him in years, but we always got on. He really helped me out, actually. When I was younger.'

'How so?'

'He got me work when I was too young to work. He bought drink for me and cigarettes when I had no money. I know to normal people that doesn't sound good, but how I grew up I was pleased for any help I could get.'

'And you worked in, how can I put this, a gentlemen's establishment?'

'It was a godsend,' said Lili. 'I don't know what I would have done if Uncle Jeff hadn't got me a job at the Bricklayers.' She laughed. 'Whenever I tell anyone my uncle got me work at a topless place, their mouths always fall open. *What sort of uncle gets you a job as a stripper?* But I wasn't like other girls. Even at fifteen.'

'Were you happy to perform nude at that age?'

'It was no problem,' said Lili. 'I had a good body. I was too young to know what to do with it, but that wasn't Uncle Jeff's fault. And he wasn't a perv, before you ask. He's never once watched me perform or seen me with no clothes on.'

Ian held his hands up. 'No, that's not the feeling I get. May I ask – how long did you work in this establishment?'

'Years,' said Lili. 'I lost all my friends from school over it. They were jealous, I thought, but now I just think they found it scary. They were right. It could be scary. I hated it by the end.

'When I first started, we just danced on the stage and walked around topless, picking up money from the customers. But then they brought in private dances, and you had to be really one-on-one, like you were their girlfriends, and it just got horrible.

'But I'll tell you something – it taught me a lot about stripping. I wouldn't be where I am now if I hadn't worked there. The first night I was there I just got up on stage, took it all off and danced like I was in a night club.

'This older girl, Chaznay, she showed me how to use my eyes to draw people in. How to stroke parts of my body, use what I was wearing. How to sew my own costumes with special hooks that meant I could take them off and look sexy doing it.'

Ian put a hand on hers. 'My dear. I don't think Love will come to us today.'

'What? Really?'

'No.' Ian stared up at the blocks of flats surrounding the park. 'I can't feel her.'

Lili swallowed. 'Can't you keep trying?'

'No.' Ian looked sad. 'She won't come.'

'Is there anything you can do to make her come?'

'No. I can't feel a thing. This document – it's too formal. There isn't enough *life* in it.'

They sat in silence for a moment.

'Fine. So we're stuck again. I'll call my Aunt Karen.'

Lili slid her bulky Nokia from her bag, noticing she had a text message waiting. She pressed a button and cubic writing flowed over the screen.

She stared.

'Something wrong, my dear?'

'No, no nothing.' Lili stood up. 'Nothing's wrong.' But everything was wrong. 'Ian. Sorry. I've got to go.'

As Lili stood, she felt the text message burning her hand. She glanced at it again, in case she'd misread the sender. But she hadn't.

The text was from Viv Morgan.

Act II

The Death-defying Leap

31

Life's a Stage by Lili Allure

Lili Allure's lessons from the dearly departed

You've heard the phrase 'standing on the shoulders of giants', right? Well, it's doubly true in the burlesque business. Us neo-burlesques, as the more exciting among us are called, are simply adding a modern twist to a very old business.

The original burlesque performers – women like Lili St Cyr (my namesake) and Bettie Page – performed at a time when shaking your thing in your underwear was as daring as it got. Fully nude pictures were illegal and burlesque girls were often arrested mid-performance for indecency.

Nowadays, girls like me spend hours watching old showreels of burlesque legends to inspire our acts. We watch how they move, scribble pictures of the outfits they wore and borrow their music scores. Of course, we add our own spin, but none of us ever forget that if it wasn't for those ladies, burlesque wouldn't exist.

Lili raced from the park, nearly bumping into an obese man in an electric wheelchair. She apologised and hurried to Whitechapel Road, where she stopped by a Bangladeshi shoe shop and stared at the message.

The sender's name was unmistakable.

Viv Morgan.

'Who's doing this?' Lili whispered, feeling sick. She thought of her mum, cigarette in one hand, bottle of pink Lambrini in the other, laughing and laughing. 'Who's *doing* this?'

Lili had forgotten she had Viv's mobile phone number. Darren had given it to her last year, when it became clear he was going back to prison. He'd wanted Lili to stay in touch with Viv, make sure she was all right. No doubt Darren had given Viv her number, too.

It was a telling sign of their relationship that Lili had entered Viv's details as 'Viv Morgan' and not 'Mum'.

The phone felt hot in Lili's hand.

Taking a deep breath, she read the message.

I'm always watching. The letters are mine. You stopped being family a long time ago.

Lili read and reread the message, trying to make sense of it, trying to understand. She didn't believe in ghosts. It really didn't make sense.

As Lili read, the screen flashed and then went blank.

What?

The message had disappeared.

Lili began to shake. She pressed keys, searching, searching for the message, but it had vanished. The text was no longer on her phone.

It was here. I read it. A text message from Mum's phone.

Her fingers trembling in their gloves, she searched her phone for Viv's number and hit the dial button.

She listened as the number rang and rang. After a moment, she tore the phone from her ear and disconnected the call.

What did I expect? Mum's hardly going to pick up and say Hi, is she?

The street was lunchtime busy. All around were windows – dark, net-curtained eyes. Who was looking out from those windows?

Enough is enough, Lili thought. PC Fletcher had told her to phone any time. Well, now it was time.

32

'Hello? PC Fletcher? Yes. Maureen Fletcher, please. It's Lili Morgan.'

The phone hummed and Maureen Fletcher came on the line.

'Hello, love.' Maureen clearly had a mouthful of something. 'Is this about the bedroom?' Crunch, crunch.

'What? Oh. Mum's bedroom. No . . . it's not about that.' The phone jiggled against her perfectly set hair, and she pressed it against her ear to hold it still.

'Must have been quite a shock,' Maureen said. 'To see all that. It was for us too. I should have stayed with you.'

'No, really, it's something else . . . I got a text message.'

'Oh yes?' Maureen sounded intrigued.

'From Mum.'

Silence. Maureen swallowed and said: 'I think I must have misheard you, love – did you say, a text from your *mum*?'

'Yes.'

'You understand, don't you, love, your mum has passed away? The coroner has given permission for the burial to go ahead. Perhaps after the funeral—'

'Not actually *from* Mum,' said Lili. 'I mean, from Mum's mobile phone. Someone sent me a message from Mum's mobile phone.'

'From Vivienne Morgan's mobile phone?'

'Yes,' said Lili.

'And what did the message say?'

'Something about not being family any more, and someone watching me.'

'Can you read the message out to me, love?' Maureen, at least for the moment, seemed to have stopped chewing.

'That's the thing,' said Lili. 'It disappeared from my phone almost as soon as I read it.'

'Disappeared?'

'Exactly.'

'Love. You've had so much to cope with. All on your own.' Maureen's voice was soothing. 'We've got a great chappy here—'

'I wasn't *seeing* things. I got a message from Mum's phone. I'm not saying she sent it. Someone else has her phone and sent me a text message.'

'And why would someone do that?' Maureen resumed her crunching. 'I think you've had a nasty shock, but messages don't just vanish from mobile phones.'

'Don't they? Isn't there a way someone could make a text message vanish? Using satellites or something?'

'Nothing I've ever heard of,' said Maureen. 'And I've heard it all.'

'Do you know . . . was my mum's mobile given to anyone?' asked Lili. 'Do you have any record of what happened to it?'

Maureen sighed audibly. 'Hang on.' She came back with rustling papers. 'I'll check.'

'Was it passed to a family member, perhaps?'

More page turning. And crunching. 'No, there's no record of anyone taking anything from the flat. I'm looking at the crime scene log.'

'Can you find out who was guarding the flat? Ask if they let anyone in?'

'They would have made a note of anyone coming and going,' said Maureen. 'And there's nothing. Only the coroner, the doctor and police. You were the first non-official to have access.

'Look. Let's say someone was sending you messages from your mum's old phone. How could a message just disappear? People in grief see things, hear things. When you're not sleeping properly or eating right . . .'

Lili let Maureen chatter on about the things grief did to people. She felt stupid for thinking the police could help. When had they ever been on her side? All they'd ever caused her were problems.

'There's something else,' said Lili, deciding to play her trump card. 'My dressing room. Someone broke in the day after I visited Mum's flat. They wrote something on the mirror.'

'Why didn't you call us?'

'I wasn't sure . . . I wanted to handle it myself.'

'You said someone wrote on the mirror – what sort of thing?'

'It said, "Stay away from the letters". Something like that.'

'Letters. Like what your mum wrote on her wall?'

'Yes. But she didn't write "stay away". She wrote: "Lilian, find the letters".'

Maureen let out a long breath. 'Love. It must have been a nasty shock, seeing all that stuff your mum wrote. It put the wind up me too. This writing on the mirror, is it still there by any chance?'

'I rubbed it off.' Lili felt embarrassed, suddenly, to have bothered PC Fletcher. To have shown her vulnerability.

'There's someone I think you should get in touch with,' said Maureen. 'Jerome Sherlock. A bereavement counsellor.'

'Shouldn't he be a detective?' Lili couldn't help herself.

Maureen didn't laugh. 'He's NHS,' she continued, 'but if we put you forward, he can push you up the waiting list.'

'I'm fine. Really. Thanks.'

'Suit yourself. He's there if you need him. Well, I must get on.'

'Wait!' Lili gripped the phone. 'PC Fletcher, don't you think . . . I mean it's so strange, Mum not leaving a suicide note. I've been so angry at her, but . . . maybe something else is going on.'

'What's the implication there?'

'Maybe Mum didn't commit suicide.'

'That's for the coroner to decide. But – please don't take this the wrong way – I've heard a lot of things in this job, and when they found your mum . . . Well, let's just say it was pretty clear cut. Lots of people don't leave notes. Most, in fact. I think after the inquest you might see things a little more clearly.'

'And when will that be?'

'Four to six weeks.'

'Thanks for your time.' Lili hung up the phone. She put her head in her hands, aware people on the street were beginning to give her a wide berth.

It was all such a mess. She felt like a complete idiot, talking about disappearing text messages and writing on the mirror.

Perhaps PC Fletcher was right. Grief was making her see things. It was more reassuring than the alternative.

There might still be smudges on the mirror where the writing was. I should check. If there are marks there, the police might take me seriously.

At Kate Hamilton's, the house lights were up. The club by day looked unremarkable. Ticket stubs, crumbs, cocktail sticks and olive stones littered the auditorium floor. Nightly glamour and magic became a daytime job for the cleaners.

Charlie, the lighting technician, was on stage muttering to himself and making notes. He was a large, balding man who wore a T-shirt covered in holes and paint stains.

'Hi, Charlie.' Lili picked her way through the tables facing the stage.

Charlie looked up in surprise. 'You've come round the long way. I thought I heard you downstairs already.'

'No. I just arrived. The get-out van was in front of the stage door. You heard someone downstairs?'

'Probably just someone outside.'

'Right. How's Graham?'

'Fine. Only a fracture in the end. He's at home eating sausage rolls and watching *The Sopranos*.' Although Charlie was gay, he was a million miles from the theatre stereotype of a camp homosexual. He and his partner raced monster trucks in their spare time, and Charlie was a former darts champion.

'Good to hear he's getting better.'

'Oh, bollocks.' Charlie squinted at a blown bulb. 'That one's gone too now. Another trip to Ransoms.' He patted his pockets. 'You're not going anywhere, are you?'

'Only to my dressing room.'

'I'll lock the front doors when I leave, then. We're the only ones here.'

Ransoms was the nearest hardware store to the theatre. It sold everything, from fuses and bulbs for Charlie, to glue-gun cartridges and fishing wire for the dancers. The joke was, being a central London supplier, it charged a king's ransom for everything. Everyone complained about prices, but no one quite got around to stocking up out of town.

Lili looked at the dark, cavernous doorway behind the stage. It led all the way down to the concrete tunnels under the stage and the dressing room.

'Pete not in yet?'

'Nope.' Charlie clambered down from the stage. 'It'll just be you and the ghosts.'

'Ha ha.'

'I'll be back in twenty.' Charlie tucked a pencil behind his ear and bumped between the tables.

Alone in the bright auditorium, Lili stared at the dark doorway. Then she headed into the sloped, concrete passage that led underground.

33

Under the stage, stone tunnels looped into storage areas, staff toilets and Lili's dressing-room-cum-bedsit. The whole area was the unmade-up face of glossy, glamorous Kate Hamilton's. If the Supper Club was a champagne-sipping burlesque superstar, backstage was that same star first thing in the morning. No hair, no make-up and a thumping hangover.

Like all theatres, colour, polish and perfection were for the audience. Behind the curtain, smiles, perfect costumes and fine dining became fast-food wrappers, tatty bits and pieces fallen from costumes and the chain smoking and teeth chattering of nervous dancers.

Probably that's why I feel so at home here, Lili thought. *That's how I am – flashy on the surface, but a mess underneath.*

As Lili wound her way under the stage, she heard a noise. She stopped and listened. The faintest scraping sound, like the sole of a shoe running over concrete.

'Hello?' Lili called out. The dressing-room door was slightly ajar, and she held her breath.

'Who's there?' Her voice wavered.

There was a scuffling sound.

She pushed the door open.

'Oh!' Lili gasped, a hand to her chest.

There, standing by the full-length mirror, was Gretchen. She wore a corset and Lili's green-jewelled high heels. Lili had spent weeks gluing the little gems onto those shoes.

Gretchen had drawn wonky, black lines above her large, brown eyes and stuck on false eyelashes, one of which hung from the corner of her eye like a dead spider.

When Gretchen saw Lili, she wobbled a little and smiled. She looked happy.

'Don't I look beautiful?' she asked. 'I know my legs are a bit big, but . . .'

'You scared the life out of me,' said Lili. 'But I'm glad you're here. I was racking my brains, trying to work out how to get hold of you. I spoke to Uncle Jeff and – wait. How did you even get down here?'

Gretchen's face fell. 'Oh. The stage door was open so I just came in. There was no one around. I thought you'd be down here.'

'Gretchen . . . tell me honestly, did you come to the dressing room before? Did you write something on the mirror?'

'What?'

'Never mind.' Lili put her suspicions in a drawer, to be tidied later. Catching sight of herself in the dressing-table mirror, Lili sat down and began reapplying her ever-so-slightly-smudged eyeliner.

Once that was done, she looked at the full-length mirror for signs of writing. There were none – no fragments of black, no matter how closely she looked. She touched the mirror to be sure, but it was clear.

'I look nice though, don't I?' said Gretchen.

'Honestly?' said Lili. 'Yes. But I think you look nice without make-up too.'

'How can you say that?' said Gretchen, trying to walk and catching herself on some free-standing metal shelves. Glitter fell over her long, brown hair. 'You get to wear make-up all the time. Do you feel like *you're* nice without it?'

Lili looked at herself in the mirror. Without the fake eyelashes, perfectly drawn lips, skin illuminated by various cosmetics and thick swooshes of eyeliner, she was nothing – at least that's how she felt. Actually worse than nothing, because without the distraction of make-up and costume, everyone would see what a screw-up she really was.

'It's different if you're on stage all the time,' said Lili. 'I'm used to it now. When I don't wear make-up, I don't look like me. I look tired. Plain.'

That was an understatement. Every morning, when Lili saw her bare face and unstyled hair, she felt a shadow of herself. It was always a mad dash to put her face on before the cleaners arrived.

She lived in terror of a photographer getting a picture of her without make-up. That would be the end of her career, she was sure of it.

'It's fun to wear make-up,' said Gretchen. 'Isn't it? It's nice to look . . . you know. So people fancy you. Mum never lets me wear anything like this.'

'You seem pretty tough to me,' said Lili. 'Why don't you just tell your mum you're going to wear what you like?'

'Mum runs a dictatorship,' said Gretchen. 'If I step out of line, she's got ways of making my life miserable. She takes me to school like a baby, or won't let me watch *Pop Stars* so I'm the geek at school who doesn't know who got voted off this week, or just, all sorts of ways. I've learned not to cross her.'

'Sounds miserable.'

'It's no fun at all. But this is, isn't it? Wearing a costume and make-up.'

'There's a difference between having fun with make-up and *needing* to wear it,' said Lili, wondering when things had changed for her. When she was Gretchen's age, make-up had been fun. But now it was hard work, when 'just being you' wasn't enough.

'Mum won't buy me make-up or the clothes I want,' said Gretchen, patting the corset. 'She's always pulling my school skirt down. She won't even let me get a bra, even though I need one.'

Lili looked at Gretchen's bust, spilling over the top of the corset.

'Why not?' asked Lili.

'Because it scares her. Me growing up.'

'You really, really shouldn't be down here on your own, you know,' said Lili. 'Promise me you won't come here again without telling me.'

Gretchen wrinkled her nose. 'Fine. Do this, do that. That's all I ever hear.'

'Seriously, Gretchen. It's not safe. Someone vandalised this room the other day.'

'Okay, okay. But we're still looking for the letters, right?'

Lili glanced at Gretchen in the mirror. She saw herself years ago, full of hope, ambition and courage. How had she ended up stuck in the same theatre day in, day out? Performing the same old acts, then falling asleep drunk on the same lumpy couch? For two years.

Because there was no family there to catch me when I fell, Lili thought. 'You do know I'm not a good role model, don't you, Gretchen?'

'What?'

'Well . . . that's why you're hanging out with me, right? You don't get on with your mum, so you're looking for someone to fill the gap.'

'I don't know. Maybe.'

'Well. I'm not the best person for the job.'

'Why not? You do care about me, don't you? I mean, you lent me your coat and you didn't tell on me for skiving and you let me hang out with you.'

'Of course I care about you.' Lili put an arm around her shoulder. 'Who wouldn't? You're great.'

Gretchen threw herself against Lili's waist. 'You see? Mum never says things like that to me. I think you're a great role model. Even if you do live in a dressing room.'

'That's why I can't stop looking for these letters, even if I wanted to,' said Lili. 'I can't carry on living this way. Finding those letters is my way forward. I've been stuck here for too long. I'm sinking and if I don't get free soon, I'll drown.'

Gretchen looked at her blankly. 'So . . . does that mean we're still looking for the letters?'

'Yes. But you can't do things like coming here again on your own. Okay? Whatever you do, I'll have to be with you.'

'Why?'

'I told you. Because someone broke into my dressing room.'

'Fine.' Gretchen blew hair out of her eyes.

'I should tell you what I found out. I spoke to Uncle Jeff, and he told me about Love and Tom's son, James.'

'The workhouse baby?'

'Yes.'

'I *knew* he must have survived,' said Gretchen. 'I've been checking over everything. Dates and stuff. Love died just a few months after James was born. So if all her other children died before that, he must have been the one that lived on and had children of his own.'

'Yes, he did,' said Lili. 'He had a partner called Catherine and they were in and out of workhouses. Oh – and Uncle Jeff told me Love's maiden name. Avery. James and Catherine lived in Whitechapel. Are there many old records for Whitechapel?'

'Some.' Gretchen stepped down from the high heels and began pulling at corset strings.

'Where?'

'Most of them will be at the London Archives.'

'Will the archives be open now?' Lili checked her thin gold watch, a 1950s original.

'Just about,' said Gretchen.

'Then let's go.'

LOVE MORGAN b. 1831,
             d. 1865.

Nee
Avary

Love Morgan   M   Tom Morgan
1831 - 1865   1836 - 1874

James Morgan
1864 - 1889

Fred Morgan
1899 - 1972

Vivienne Morgan
b.1965

Jeff Morgan b.1958

34

Life's a Stage by Lili Allure

Lili's London: The London Archives

The London Metropolitan Archives sit on a quiet, serious street just off Farringdon Road. A red-brick building with tall sides and few windows, it looks a lot like a prison. A good look for a building that holds thousands of criminal records from centuries past.

The archive building was as warm as a hospital, and every bit as busy. Visitors crowded the tables and microfilm desks, and staff constantly ferried documents back and forth.

Lili and Gretchen worked among people of all ages, everyone sorting through pages and rolls of historic documents. Lili didn't pretend to understand the documents Gretchen studied, but she didn't need to – Gretchen knew exactly what she was doing.

'Found anything yet?' asked Lili.

'We need to speak *quietly*,' Gretchen whispered. 'This is like a library. We have to be respectful.'

Gretchen certainly knew her way around the archives. Within moments of their arrival, she'd flashed a well-used history card at the front desk and greeted the roaming, elderly historians like old friends.

She'd ordered an abundance of documents and now pored over maps of 1800s London, sanitation reports and Old Bailey court records.

'It's hard going,' Gretchen admitted. 'Morgan's a really common name.'

'Can I help at all?'

'No! I can do it.' Gretchen sighed, stretched and went off to get more documents.

Lili absentmindedly scanned the document Gretchen had left. There were lines and lines of handwritten names, all tiny and hard to read.

Gretchen returned with an armful of documents. 'More court records,' she announced, dumping them on the table. 'This is a nightmare. I've found four different spellings of Avery so far.'

'Can't we just check them all?'

Gretchen laughed. 'Do you know how long that would take?' She ran her finger down the page.

The minutes ticked by, and soon the tannoy announced the archives would be closing soon.

'Okay. Well we can forget the court records,' said Gretchen. 'There isn't time. But I just want to check one last thing before we go.'

Gretchen pulled a huge, black book towards them with *Child Welfare in the 1800s* stamped in dusty gold on its cover. She began turning pages. 'No. It's not here. Right, let's go.'

'What are you looking for?'

'A picture. I had a page reference but it's not there.' Gretchen sighed. 'Look, they're closing up. We'd better head off.'

'It doesn't look like the sort of book to have pictures,' Lili remarked.

'I know. I must have got it wrong.'

'Here.' Lili took the book and turned dusty pages. 'They haven't thrown us out yet. Let's just look through.'

Gretchen put black fingertips to her face. 'We don't have time now.'

Lili turned pages faster. Gretchen checked her watch.

'What about this one?' Lili showed Gretchen a pencil sketch of a boy in ragged trousers, standing by a market stall.

'No. Come on, Lili, I come here all the time. I don't want them to get annoyed with us—'

'I'm hurrying.' Lili flicked gossamer-thin pages. 'No, no, no
– wait. Here's a picture.'

'No, that's of an NSPCC inspector.'

'Okay.' Lili flipped faster. 'Okay, that's a workhouse. Wait. How
about this one?'

'Let me see.' Gretchen looked closer. Then she read the text
under the picture.

'Well?'

Gretchen took the book from Lili. 'I think . . . wait a minute.'

The picture was a black-and-white ink drawing of a tiny room
with wooden floorboards. There was a baby crawling on the floor,
a clothes line hanging across the room and a woman slumped
in a corner, her head in her hands.

'So?' Lili asked.

'You won't believe this,' said Gretchen. 'But I think this might
be the one.'

'The one what?'

'Well, it might, just might, be your great, great, great grandparents' house. The residence of James Morgan and Catherine
Long.'

LOVE MORGAN b. 1831, d. 1865.

Nee Avary — Love Morgan (1831 – 1865) — M — Tom Morgan (1836 – 1874)

James Morgan (1864 – 1889) m. Cooky Morgan (Catherine Long) b. 1863 – d.?

Fred Morgan (1899 – 1972)

Vivienne Morgan (b.1965)

Jeff Morgan (b.1958)

35

'What?' Lili stared at the picture, her eyes running along the rough ink lines and scratches. 'How can it be James Morgan's house? Love and Tom's son . . . I don't understand. Why would there be a sketch of this? Our family were just normal people. Just ordinary.'

'It was part of a report by the NSPCC,' said Gretchen, flicking through papers. 'They went around the slums checking children were being looked after properly. This is a drawing made during one of their checks. It was to show the authorities things needed to change. That children were being neglected.'

'It's amazing,' said Lili. 'So the woman in the drawing. Is that . . . Catherine Long? Cooky? One of my relatives?' She held the picture close to her face.

The woman in the sketch looked hard-faced and angry as she glared through her fingers at whoever was drawing her one-roomed house. She wore a grubby, torn white apron and boots with holes in them. Her pale hair was swept under a dark bonnet. She sat next to a weak-looking fire in a square fireplace.

'I suppose they thought James' and Catherine's house was particularly bad,' said Gretchen.

'It looks it,' said Lili. 'There's no furniture. Where did they sleep?'

'On the floor, probably,' said Gretchen. 'Not many slum people had furniture.' Her lips mouthed words as she scanned the text. 'Workhouse . . . bad air . . .' She pressed a chewed fingernail to the page. Then she looked at the picture again. 'Look there,' she told Lili. 'Tell me what you see.'

Lili looked. Above the limp fire, there was a mantelpiece with an object on it.

'Papers,' said Lili. 'Wrapped in something – maybe cotton rag. Could they be—'

'Love's yellow letters,' said Gretchen. 'The inspection notes what's in the property . . . wash bowl, wooden bucket, broom and – wait for it – letters on yellow paper wrapped in red cotton. Just like the ones found on Love's body when she died.

'There's a note about the letters. It says that even in the poorest houses, literacy can triumph, and the fact this family kept letters, pride of place on the mantelpiece, shows how much they valued reading and writing. It says they were very protective about the letters. When they went out, they carried the letters with them.'

'Wow.' Lili stared at the picture. 'This is amazing. So James and Catherine had the letters. They were passed down to James, just like the will instructed.'

'That's what it looks like,' said Gretchen.

'The London Archives is now closed . . .' shouted the tannoy.

'We should go,' said Gretchen. 'I'll see if I can come back tomorrow.'

'I wonder if James passed the letters down to his son,' Lili said. 'Like Tom's will told him to. If James followed his father's wishes, then he would have passed the letters down to his only surviving child, Michael.'

Gretchen took a camera from her bag and took pictures of the documents. 'Maybe we should have searched for Michael today, instead of James.' She packed the camera into her bag.

'Yes, maybe. But I should probably find out more about him first. Give you as many facts to work on as possible.'

Visitors made their way towards the exit, and Gretchen and Lili followed with them.

'My aunt might know about Michael – that's what Uncle Jeff thought.' Lili looked at Gretchen's rucksack, still stuffed with the unworn winter coat. 'Gretchen. Can I borrow your camera?'

They were out on the street now, the sky blue-dark above them.

Gretchen was reluctant. 'Why?'

'The pictures you took. I need to show them to someone.'

'But I need to study them. They'll be good for leads.'

'I'll give it back to you,' said Lili.

'When?'

'Tomorrow. First thing. Promise.'

'How about we meet at your mum's flat,' said Gretchen. 'I can sneak up there for a few minutes, no problem.'

'I suppose that makes sense,' said Lili. 'But don't go in there without me.'

'How can I? It's all locked up.'

Lili looked at the dark sky and knew that, once again, she was in danger of running late for her show. Three nights in a row. Taxis sped past.

'How are you getting home?' she asked Gretchen.

'Walking.'

Lili knew London was safe enough. She certainly didn't think girls from Whitechapel needed protection, but she still didn't like the idea of Gretchen walking back on her own.

'We'll take a taxi,' Lili said, 'and while I take you back, there's someone I need to call.'

36

Life's a Stage by Lili Allure

Lili Allure's thoughts on first impressions

You know the saying 'You never get a second chance to make a first impression'? It's doubly true on stage. The first glimpse your audience sees of you has to be mesmerising.

Aim high.

Imagine they might remember it for the rest of their lives. When it comes to curtain up, make the entrance of your life every time. Never let the audience down. You're only ever as good as your last show.

9 pm at Kate Hamilton's Supper Club and curtain-up time for Lili Allure.

At Lili's request, the velvet curtain rose slowly, tantalisingly, revealing the stage a little at a time.

Guests paused, mid-conversation, mid-drink, mid-forkful, to watch the swaying burgundy cloth rise and rise. This is what they were waiting for.

Ian Batty sat alone at a table near the stage, a complimentary ticket laid carefully by the flickering candle in front of him.

'I say,' he said, as the curtain revealed the bottom of a white sledge amid a fairyland of fake snow. 'How jolly wonderful.'

Kate Hamilton's, however, wasn't so delighted with Lili's choice of guest. Ian occupied an 'emergency' table usually reserved for high-rolling celebrities without bookings. So far, Ian had failed to order anything but iced water.

Carol-Ann did her house manager duties, hanging around Ian's table doing her best to up-sell.

'Would you care for a cocktail, Mr Batty?' she asked, tapping a velvet-covered notepad. 'We have a trained mixologist on staff. How about a Kate Hamilton? Champagne, brandy and sweet almond liqueur.'

'I'm afraid alcohol and myself don't get along,' said Ian. 'We were friends once, but it proved to be a false friendship and I'm glad to be rid of it.'

'And will you be dining with us this evening?'

'You're very sweet, but no.' Ian patted his stomach. 'I had an early supper of baked brie. I'm full as an egg.'

The pen in Carol-Ann's hand ground into the notepad, making an angry dimple, but her smile remained fixed.

'So you're friends with our Lili?' she asked, curious as to how or why Lili fitted in with this colourful, old teetotaller.

He was something of a character, she'd give him that. In fact, Ian was probably the most elaborately dressed of anyone in the audience. He had pinned the head of a sunflower to the lapel of his lilac suit, and wore an especially tall top hat.

'I'm helping her with a psychic consultation,' said Ian. 'And I must say the energies in this theatre . . . well! To be among an audience like this . . . it's a very good thing for spiritual vibrations.'

'Well – you take care of her. She needs some taking care of more than ever, right now.'

Carol-Ann left Ian to it. It was a shame he wasn't a big spender, but if having him as a guest kept Lili happy then so be it.

Bookings had tripled since Lili became the club's signature act, but Carol-Ann knew her popularity would wane. It always did when a star stayed in one place. She'd told Lili time and time again – performers need to tour and see new audiences. But as long as Lili was still selling tickets, Kate's was happy to have her.

On stage, the curtain continued to inch up.

More of the sledge appeared. Fake snowflakes fell from the

ceiling and pale blue lights spun and shone over glittering, bare trees.

But there was no Lili.

'Shitting hell,' Carol-Ann murmured, watching the bare sledge appear on stage, minus the great Lili Allure, who was usually draped over it, wrapped in bright, white fur. 'Where's Lili?'

Lili not on stage for curtain up – it just wasn't possible.

Carol-Ann turned to Charlie at the lighting desk, mouthing *Where is she?*

37

The music reached its 'ta da!' crescendo as the last inches of curtain rolled up, but there was still no Lili. The beautiful stage set, with its winding, winter trees and feather-covered sledge, looked sad, like a Christmas window display in January without Santa.

There was a painful silence as the music stopped. Then a clatter and muffled voices from backstage.

A long pause.

Lili Allure hip-rolled onto the stage holding armfuls of white fur, eyes large and full of sexual promise, chest out, rear-end doing figures of eight.

The music started again and Lili began her routine. She was flustered, although the audience would never have known it. The Four Seasons *Winter* began to play, and Lili held up her legs to lace on a pair of original 1940s ice skates, then began twirling on a circle of plastic ice.

Little by little, she removed her gloves, shook her hair loose and teased the audience by unlacing her corset bit by bit, being sure to keep her naked body covered until the right moment. She pretended to slip and slide on the ice, a look of exaggerated surprise on her face as her 'falls' became bumps and grinds.

Like every good burlesque performer, Lili's 'effortless' routine was a perfectly choreographed dance, and every drop, bounce and flash was perfectly timed. She worked hard to get back in sync with the music.

Once she was in rhythm, Lili made the striptease look easy. But it wasn't. The audience saw clothes unpeeled and thought: *If I didn't have cellulite, if I didn't hate this or that, if I hadn't had a child I could be a burlesque dancer.* But they couldn't. Not without an awful lot of practice.

Keeping her teeth flashing, Lili adjusted her lace pulls and corset drop to match new points of the music. She was infinitely adaptable. Anyone who'd worked their way up knew how to change an act when the wrong CD played or the set broke or a drunken audience member misbehaved.

Ta da!

Lili's big reveal was perfect as always, her glowing white skin sparkling under blue lights. Wearing nothing but blue pasties and a G-string, she fell onto the waiting sledge, threw her hair back and posed, posed, posed. The audience took great big breaths, drawing her into them.

Curtain down.

Lili hurried to the dressing room. She'd thought of nothing but meeting Ian since she'd arrived at the theatre, and every minute on stage had been agonising.

As she ran down the concrete hallway, someone grabbed her arm.

'Hey!' She shook her arm free and slapped a face before she saw who it was. 'Oh! Pete! Don't grab me like that.'

'Are you all right?' Pete pulled out a pocket mirror and checked the stinging red creeping over his cheek. He gave his eyebrows a quick groom. 'You weren't on stage . . .'

'You scared me.' Lili thought of the text message. 'What are you doing sneaking around the corridors? Oh, right. I was late. Yes. I know. I've got a lot of things on my mind.' She marched into the dressing room.

Bryony was there, making a hasty repair of a silver corset. 'Lils, are you okay?'

'I'm all right, Bry. Don't you worry about me.'

Pete followed. 'You're never late. And on stage – you weren't moving right. You were all jerky.'

Lili went to her dressing table. She'd left Gretchen's camera by the mirror, and wanted to take the pictures up to show Ian.

But the camera was gone.

'Where's my camera?'

Lili combed through the things on her dressing table.

'Where's my camera?' She was screaming now. The camera was nowhere. Not on the floor or the chair . . . 'It doesn't even belong to me. It's Gretchen's.'

'Give me a minute and I'll help you look,' said Bryony, knotting cotton thread and chewing the end free.

'It had some pictures on it.' Lili, naked except for a G-string and tasselled pasties, pushed make-up aside.

'What pictures?' Bryony asked.

'Just . . . stuff I was looking into about Mum.' Lili fell to her knees, crawling under her dressing table to search.

Bryony watched with concern. She'd been friends with Lili before Lili hit the big time, when she still bought her stockings from Tesco. She knew that under the expensive costumes and perfect make-up was a girl more fragile than most.

Her manager stealing her show and running off with her best friend – that had really knocked what little confidence Lili had. But now her mum had died in such a terrible way . . . Bryony worried that Lili might never recover from it.

Bryony knelt beside Lili. 'What did it look like? Lils?'

'I need that camera. It doesn't even belong to me.'

Pete knelt down too. 'That's all you're upset about?' He pulled at his tight jeans.

'Yes.'

'But why?'

'Someone's meeting me here tonight and I need that camera and it doesn't belong to me . . .'

'That old bloke in the top hat?'

'Yes.'

'Who is he?'

'A friend of my mum's.'

'Oh.' Pete smoothed his T-shirt. 'You're sure the camera was here?'

'Right here. I left it on the dressing table.' Lili put her head in her hands. 'So stupid. So, so stupid. I was running late, and . . . what was I thinking?'

Bryony put an arm around her shoulder. 'Don't worry. How can you think straight with everything you've got going on? I know I couldn't. It'll turn up.'

'It will,' said Pete. 'It's safe down here. Well, except for the break-in.'

'I'm such a screw-up.' Lili put her head in her hands. 'What am I going to tell Gretchen? She trusted me. Cameras don't just disappear. *Things* don't just *disappear*.' She chewed a bright red fingernail. 'I don't believe in ghosts.'

38

Heads turned as Lili climbed down from the stage, wearing a fitted midnight-blue dress and white fur stole. People stared as she sat beside the colourful, dapper gentleman in the top hat.

'Ian. I'm so sorry, I've done something really stupid.'

'Oh, my dear. Whatever is the matter?' Ian leaned onto the table, his creased face and rounded nose turning orange in the candlelight.

Lili sat beside him. 'The thing I had for you. I don't have it any more.' She paused. 'It was on a camera and someone took it. I can get it for you again. I'll go back to the archives tomorrow.'

'Goodness me. Very interesting.' Ian drummed his fingers together. 'Taken.'

There was an ominous pause, and Lili had a moment to imagine how someone could have crept into the dressing room and taken the camera. It wouldn't have been difficult.

While Lili performed, the performers waited in the wings for their final curtain-call number. The dressing room was empty and the stage door unlocked at that time. Anyone could have come in.

Lili looked around the audience. They all could have done it – even Ian.

'Well,' said Ian. 'Why don't you tell me about what you found.'

'It was a picture of my family from years ago, in their slum room. James Morgan – that's Love's son. And Catherine Long, his partner. From an NSPCC report.'

'Sounds interesting.'

Lili put her head in her hands. 'I was really . . . *looking forward*, I suppose, to you talking to Love again.'

'Still an unbeliever though?'

'Does it matter? We're trying to uncover what Mum told you, right? If this is the only way to do that, it's fine by me.'

Ian flexed his large, knotty hands. The joints looked like marbles. 'Doesn't matter in the slightest. The spirits don't care if you believe or not. I feel Love is already very close to us tonight.'

'Really? I thought . . . You said you needed things, documents and so on, to bring her nearer.'

'Usually, but not always,' said Ian. 'Tonight, in this fine theatre, the spirits are chattering away. They're so excited by the vibrations in this building. They're full of energy. They *want* to speak.'

'Will Love?' asked Lili, glancing around. The sounds of people talking and laughing hung over the club like a friendly mist.

Ian closed his eyes. 'Yes,' he announced, taking a gulp of water. 'Yes. She is here.' He leaned back in his chair and looked to the ceiling.

He closed his eyes.

'How the devil are you, madam? Oh. I do apologise.' Ian laughed. 'She's not on best terms with the devil these days. You'd like to take us to the time just after your son was born. Righty-o. You are working very hard. Well, I can imagine.'

He cupped his hand to his mouth and whispered to Lili: 'She's eaten some bad bread. It snapped one of her teeth, but she has matchboxes to glue together and must sit and do the work, or else no one will eat tonight.

'Little James sleeps in the corner, wrapped in one of her bonnets to keep him warm. He has been crying three days straight, but today she has given him . . . I'm sorry . . . the *quietness*.'

'The quietness?' Lili asked.

Ian scratched his head. 'I believe she means opium, or something in that family. She's given the baby a spoon of something so she can work. She is furious about the work she is doing. Some rich man makes a fortune while she toils for pennies, and she knows when she's done she'll be so sore that she'll want nothing but sleep.

'Tom tells her now she has a little one who lives, she can't sin any more as she did. She can't go about the streets asking men for business. But she tells me she'll be back on the streets by tomorrow night, God help her. She won't work and work all day for a bowl of salted gruel and fingers that can't light a candle.

'I like to walk the streets, she tells me, free as a bird. That's how I earn my money best. And who cares if what I do is a sin? The likes of me aren't long for this earth at any rate. I may as well use my time happily.

'She likes to talk as she works, and wants to tell me about . . . a love affair.'

'A love affair?' said Lili, leaning closer. 'Whose love affair?'

'My goodness.' Ian turned pale. 'Really? You can't mean . . . *him*, can you? Dear me, there's a thing. You want to tell me about an affair with . . .'

'Who?' Lili asked.

'Love,' Ian announced theatrically, 'wants to tell me about an affair with *William Peavy*.' He paused. 'What do you think of that?'

'William Peavy.' Lili stared at Ian. 'Did Mum tell you Love worked for him? An affair? Is that what Mum told you?'

'There's no need to be ashamed, Love, my dear,' Ian continued. 'Attitudes are quite different now. We don't see things the same way. Love isn't a bad thing, in this day and age, no matter how it is expressed.'

'You're saying,' Lili said, 'that Love is . . . she's telling you she had an affair with William Peavy? The author?'

'We must tread gently,' Ian whispered. 'Times were different back then. Love is a married lady. She may not want to speak about . . .' His head dropped. 'Well, I'm glad! No, my dear, I welcome it. Please. Do tell me.'

Lili leaned closer.

'William Peavy,' said Ian, 'isn't the gentleman people think he is, she says. He has secrets. He has a grand house where . . . no, I think I misheard you. Oh. Yes. Your father-in-law. George Morgan – that's Tom Morgan Senior – still works at William Peavy's house. Even after you and your husband were sacked.'

Lili's eyes widened. 'Where are you getting all this from? George Morgan – you say he was Tom's father?'

Ian continued. 'The love affair has been going on for many years, she tells me. It is a great secret, as William Peavy is a married man and, of course, very well-known, as he still is today. It will cause great scandal if this affair is revealed.

'She . . . oh, good Lord. Oh, I'm so sorry.' Ian was silent for a moment. He felt at his forehead. 'Love is telling me she is so tired today. The baby . . . oh, my dear. The baby screamed and screamed all night. He is very sickly. If a friend hadn't given him a spoonful of the *quietness* she doesn't know what she would have done.

'She has hundreds of matchboxes to glue before the end of the day, and her fingers are very sore.'

Lili watched Ian's brow furrow and unfurrow, his fingertips patting the tablecloth. Where was he getting this information from? Memories from his consultations with Viv, or his own research?

'Love tells me William has a great many perversions,' Ian continued. 'Unspeakable things. He takes part in abnormal sexual practices. He is a loving man, but she cannot forgive his abominable behaviour.

'Love's husband, Tom, is very angry about the love affair. Furious. It burns him up inside, she says. He beats her, because he is so angry about it. He must keep it a secret. He wants to keep it a secret but she . . . she wants the affair made public.'

'Why?' Lili asked.

'I . . . she's not telling me.' Ian put a hand to his cheek. 'May I suggest . . . is it money? No, my dear, I apologise. Love? My dear?' He opened his eyes. 'Oh dear. I've upset her.'

There was a long silence and then Ian said: 'She's gone.'

'Can you get her back?' Lili asked.

Ian shook his head. 'Not tonight.'

'We have to meet again soon,' said Lili. 'I'll arrange to meet Gretchen tomorrow and get more documents for you.' She remembered the missing camera. 'If she'll ever speak to me again.'

39

When Gretchen suggested Viv Morgan's flat as a meeting place, Lili hadn't been keen. It was a grey, stormy morning and rain made Viv's flat more depressing than ever.

There was a special coldness, Lili thought as she waited on Viv's couch, that hung around empty homes. Sad and unloving.

As Lili perched on the slumpy, bumpy burgundy sofa, the magazine picture of Viv looked down at her from the living-room wall. Viv's eyes were slate grey and bewitching, her face young and beautiful. The paper was bulging with damp.

Lili looked away.

Then she heard a noise.

A low laugh coming from somewhere nearby.

Lili kept perfectly still.

There was a bang. Viv's smiling face caught her eye.

The front door squeaked.

'Hello?'

'Who is it?' Lili shouted, her voice wobbling.

'It's only me.' Gretchen clattered into the hallway.

'Gretchen,' Lili said, relieved. 'Thank goodness. You look tired.'

'Who did you think it would be?' Gretchen asked. 'I was up until four in the morning doing research. Have you got my camera?' She went into the kitchen and opened one of the cupboards. 'God, didn't your mum *ever* go out and buy new food? This stuff is ancient.'

'Do you want me to make you something to eat?' Lili asked.

'No, I need something unopened to show Mum I've been to the shop.' Gretchen picked through various, half-opened jars of things – Nutella, pineapple jam, marshmallow-swirled peanut butter. All dried-up or mouldy or both.

'Here.' Lili opened her handbag and threw Gretchen an unopened packet of chewing gum.

'Thanks.' Gretchen caught the gum and took a seat next to Lili. She threw her rucksack to the floor and took out a handful of print-outs. 'Look at these.'

'What are they?'

'Court records,' said Gretchen. 'It took hours and hours. After the first three hundred records, I nearly gave up. But then I saw there were only three hundred more to go, and once I get into something, it's hard to stop. I went through twenty years of court records in the end.'

'Last night? How?'

'The Old Bailey records are online,' said Gretchen, rubbing her neck. 'I wish someone had told me before. I could have saved myself loads of trips to the archives. Still, it's nicer to look at paper than a computer screen. Look at my eyes.' She pulled down the skin under one eye, and Lili saw red veins.

'Gretchen, you're amazing.'

'Love turned up under two different names – Avery, spelt A.V.R.Y and Morgan. There were a few petty thefts and drinking offences that could have been, but these ones I've brought here are *definitely* her.'

'How do you know?'

'Because everything matches up. Names, dates and the other people in the records. You'll never guess what. She was only caught stealing from William Peavy while she worked for him. Listen to this.'

Gretchen flicked pages.

Love Avry, stealing 2 capes, 3 gowns, 1 scarf and other articles, value £151. 6s.; the goods of William Peavy, her master, in his dwelling house.

'She stole from William Peavy?' Lili asked.

'Yes,' Gretchen laughed. 'That's why she lost her job. She was found guilty and confined for six months. That meant she went to prison. To think, a relative of yours, stealing from someone so famous. You should be very proud.'

'Ha ha.'

Gretchen scanned the paper. 'Actually, she didn't lose her job for stealing. She lost her job for having improper relations with the footman, Tom Morgan. They were both sacked for it, and *then* Love stole a load of stuff before she left. Sort of like revenge.'

Lili eyed the paper. 'Tom and Love were both servants at William Peavy's house *before* they got married?'

'Yes,' said Gretchen. 'This is what the lady of the house, Mrs Gertrude Peavy, said about the theft.'

We are quite sure the theft occurred as a revenge of sorts, because Love Avry and her friend, Tom Morgan, were dismissed from our home.

Poor Tom is a shy, dear little lad and has been with us since the age of fifteen. We were very sorry to let him go, especially since his father, George, has been in our employment for some twenty years. Unfortunately, I had it on good authority that Tom and Love behaved improperly in our house.

I felt Love, who is some five years older than Tom, was the corrupting influence. She is a forceful woman, several years his senior, and is known to have a violent temper. However, the only course of action I could take was to dismiss both parties, for I couldn't sack one without the other for the same crime.

Love Avry was only in our employment for seven months, but was known among the other servants as being a 'bad sort', and I wasn't sorry to let her go. She was often in trouble for quarrelling and I had been told by a household member that Love liked to invite Tom Morgan and other household members to her room when she was in a state of undress.

She was also most indiscreet in the company of my husband, telling bawdy jokes and on one occasion showing him private parts of her body that only a doctor or female friend should see.

My husband is greatly embarrassed by women behaving improperly. He spoke to Love, privately about her bawdy behaviour on several occasions, but alas, there was no change in her.

The morning Love left the household I noticed items missing . . .

'George,' Lili murmered. 'So he wasn't making it up. Ian said Tom's father was called George.'

'Maybe he read this record too,' said Gretchen.

'Maybe. Or maybe Mum told him.'

'Listen to what Love said in court.' Gretchen rubbed an eye and yawned. 'She sounds like a real character.'

The lady of the house is drunk for most of the day and wouldn't know it if a mouse came and ate from her dinner plate. You may as well listen to a lunatic, for all the truth she tells you. Tom and I are planning to marry, and there is nothing improper about that.

Yes, I took the things she says I did. I will not say where they are now. Why should I not take something, when she has as good as sent us to the workhouse? For well she knows we won't find other servants' work now.

'This is great,' said Lili. 'It means we know roughly what years they worked for Peavy. Right.'

'There's more.' Gretchen turned pages. 'Tom Morgan, prosecuted for assault. The record mentions his wife, Love Morgan. He's accused of *Unlawfully assaulting John Robins, causing him actual bodily harm*. That's the charge. Now here's the evidence. Listen. A testimony from John Robins – the man Tom is accused of assaulting.'

40

I live at 31 Old Nichol Street, the house belonging to myself. In December, Tom Morgan was living in a downstairs room with his wife, Love Morgan. On the night of 11th December, between 9 and 12, I heard them quarrelling – I heard screaming and went to their door.

Mrs Morgan said, 'It is a sin, and I can't bear to carry the shame any longer. I will sell the letters and let all of England know. I will sell them and pay the rent at least.'

I said, 'If you do not pay rent, you shall not live here any longer.' They were behind in some rent money.

'Letters,' said Lili. 'They were fighting over letters. Do you think they could be *the* letters?'

Tom Morgan up with his fist and struck me in the face. He asked me what I'd heard, and I said I had not heard anything at all. Then he called me an old B— and struck me under the jaw.

'And there's another testimony,' said Gretchen. 'From their neighbour. I think the prosecution were trying to prove Tom was violent too. Listen. This is by a woman called Cathy Batty. She lived in the same building as Tom and Love:

I now live in Brick Lane – I did live at 31 Old Nichol Street when Tom and Love Morgan occupied the back room. I am a single woman and live by myself.

Gretchen held the paper away from her. 'Single woman. That probably means she was a prostitute. Lots of poor women back then were. Sex was the only thing they had to sell.'

'Carry on.'

Gretchen shook the paper and continued.

'Okay. This is still Cathy Batty.'

I did not see much of Tom and Love as they were in the habit of drinking. I have heard them quarrelling and him threaten her. Once or twice he said he would kill her.

Lili nodded. 'Do you think Tom killed Love?'

'Could have,' said Gretchen, her voice emotionless. 'Jack the Ripper had nothing on domestic violence back then. The most dangerous place for women was at home. There are plenty of court records here about men beating up women. And a couple about men who murdered their wives.'

'Keep going.'

'Right. Okay, so this is still Cathy, the neighbour, talking:

Once I went in and saw Love lying on the floor, with Tom standing over her with his fist clenched. It looked like he was kicking her. I asked him what he was doing and he said if I did not go out of the room, he would serve me the same. I went out. I remember Love showing me marks on her arms and face. They looked like knife marks.

She told me Tom said now he had disfigured her, she could not leave him. I have no idea where the marks on her face came from.

'Then there's a testimony from Love herself.'

Our landlord is ashamed to have been hit by a woman, for well he knows it was me who struck his jaw. Tom, for all his faults, is a gentle soul and would not hurt a fly.

Cathy doesn't know what she says. She wishes Tom married her instead of me and so tells lies because she wishes to see us parted. Tom may not be the husband I wished he was, but he is not a violent man.

Gretchen stopped reading. 'That's fairly typical of women back then. There are loads of accounts of women defending their husbands in court after they've been beaten up. Anyway. Tom was found not guilty. Here.' She handed Lili the pages.

'Gretchen, thanks so much. This is amazing. To stay up so late . . . why are you doing this?'

'Doing what?'

'Bending over backwards to help me like this?'

Gretchen shrugged. 'When I find out stuff for you, you're really happy with me. I feel really clever and good about myself. And I don't feel good about myself very often.'

'Gretchen, I need to tell you something.'

'Uh oh.'

'Look, I'm so sorry. Your camera . . .'

Gretchen's eyes went blank. 'You didn't.'

Lili reached out, but Gretchen stepped back.

'It was taken from the dressing room,' said Lili. 'I don't know who took it, but I'm going to find out. It may even turn up – perhaps it's just mislaid. I've got you a new one, just in case.' She reached into her bag and held out a brand new Fujifilm camera. She'd bought the most expensive one in the shop.

'I thought you liked me,' said Gretchen, her brown eyes suddenly vulnerable. 'How could you let that happen?'

'Of course I like you,' said Lili. And she really did. Gretchen could appear strangely emotionless at times, but Lili knew it was largely an act, and that Gretchen needed looking after.

'Then why didn't you take care of my camera?'

Lili thought for a moment. 'I was late . . . I was running on stage . . . I thought the dressing room was safe . . .'

Gretchen shook her head. 'You said there'd been a break-in a few days ago. You knew it wasn't safe.'

'I'm so sorry,' said Lili.

Gretchen hung her head. 'It doesn't matter. Nobody likes me, anyway. I don't know why I thought you did.'

'I do. I do like you.'

Gretchen sighed and suddenly looked much older. 'Let me think. So. It's okay. The people at the archives might scan the pages and email them to me – they know me, we're friends. I'd better write down what I remember.' She took a notepad from her rucksack and scribbled on it. 'Lucky I'm a genius.'

'I'm really sorry Gretchen. Here – take this.' She held out the new camera. 'I know it doesn't make up for things.'

Gretchen plonked herself next to Lili. 'Thanks. It looks like a good one.'

'The best I could get.' Lili liked the way Gretchen could go from upset to fine in seconds.

'I looked into stuff about William Peavy last night, too,' said Gretchen. She slung her rucksack around her shoulders and checked her watch. 'But I've just hit dead ends. There's just SO much stuff on him. Have you found out any more from your family?'

'Not exactly,' said Lili. 'But Ian said . . . he thought Love was having an affair with William Peavy.'

41

'Who cares what that old psychic guy said? That stuff you found out from your uncle – it was brilliant. I'm not looking into stuff based on the hunch of some old psychic guy.'

'But he was one of the last people to speak to Mum – and all this spirit world stuff is his way of remembering—'

'No.' Gretchen held up her hand. 'It could be a complete waste of time.'

'I'll go see my Aunt Karen,' said Lili. 'Find out what she knows about Michael Morgan. It'll be hard though – I haven't seen her in years.'

'Lots of things are hard,' said Gretchen, her voice flat. 'My real parents didn't love me enough to keep me. My foster mum doesn't like me very much. Do you hear me complain about it?' She looked at her leather lace-ups. 'Do you really think these letters will help you understand why Viv . . . you know, took all those pills?'

'I don't know,' said Lili. 'But I think they'll at least give me a goodbye, somehow. Maybe. And help me understand what was going through her head, those last days. I want to forgive her. To move on.'

'Your Aunt Karen is the one who's horrible about you, isn't she?'

'I don't remember telling you that.'

'You didn't. Viv did.'

'You two spoke about Aunt Karen?'

'We spoke about lots of things,' said Gretchen. 'Viv was really nice. Sometimes. When she wasn't ill.'

Lili assumed by ill, Gretchen meant hungover.

'What did Mum say about Aunt Karen?' Lili asked.

'She said Karen didn't talk to any of you for years. She used to bad mouth you and your brother, but she's changed – that's what your mum said. See?' She looked proud of herself. 'People say I don't listen, but I do.'

'Really?' said Lili. 'Mum said Aunt Karen had changed?'

'That's what she said.'

'Well, it doesn't matter whether she's changed or not. I'm going to do everything I can to find those letters. There's nothing to go back to, now. Since Mum died, it's like my life is under some great big spotlight.' Lili looked around the tatty flat. 'And what I see . . . it's not so different from how Mum was living, and I know how that story ends.'

'I'll look into this William Peavy thing,' said Gretchen. 'I can't do anything right now, though.' She patted her rucksack straps. 'Re-vi-sing. And writing more of my coursework.'

'Oh. Really?'

'Really. I'd better get back. Thanks for the chewing gum.'

'I'll see you soon.' The door slammed shut and Lili found herself alone. She looked at Viv's bright, twenty-something face on the wall, so self-assured and full of life. The magazine advert was from a simpler time when women were supposed to like beauty and housework above all things. Viv looked delighted as she vacuumed a carpet.

Lili thought: *Aunt Karen's eyes are just like Mum's.* And suddenly the idea of visiting Karen didn't seem okay after all. But what she'd said to Gretchen was true – there was no turning back. At least visiting Aunt Karen meant leaving the chaotic, sad flat with its strange noises.

Lili locked up her old home and headed south towards Aldgate East tube station.

42

Lili's London

London isn't really a city – it's a group of small villages all squashed together. There are rich villages, poor villages, arty villages, business villages . . . all sorts of people living side by side, fused together by an underground train network.

Loughton is a London village. Located near the end of the Central line, its little group of houses and shops are pretty enough. There are a few nice churches. There's a cricket club. There's a Café Rouge. The women wouldn't dream of leaving their homes without hair, nails and make-up done, and men drive around in new, highly polished Peugeots.

Loughton residents are lovingly referred to as 'East Londoners done good'. People who started life with nothing and built their own fortunes. Good people. Happy people. Family people.

Aunt Karen's home was a Loughton cliché. A five-bedroom mock-Tudor house with two garages and a shiny, red alarm system. It was the sort of home many Whitechapel and Mile End Londoners dreamed about moving to.

Lili pressed the doorbell and stood back from the porch, too apprehensive to stand near the front door. Gravel rearranged itself around her high heels as she rolled her lips together to spread her lipstick.

I will not let her get to me. I won't let her make me feel like nothing. I'm a success, I'm a somebody. People love me.

The door opened.

'I thought you'd be round sooner or later.' Karen stood on her doorstep, blue nails on the UPVC doorframe. She wore a silky blue dress that matched her nails, and pearls around her neck. Her short hair was feathered and highlighted. The perfect Loughton mother. She looked like she was about to appear on a detergent commercial.

'Nice to see you too,' Lili said.

'You've changed,' said Karen. It was an accusation. She took a pack of Marlboro Lights from a shelf beside the door and lit a cigarette.

There was no 'Good to see you' or 'What a nice surprise,' but Lili hadn't been expecting that. She dug her heels into the gravel path, waiting to see if Aunt Karen would invite her inside.

'It's about—'

'I heard,' said Karen. 'Ben told me about the funeral, but I'm not a hundred per cent sure I'm going to make it. We have a dozen meetings for Jessica's wedding that day. *Loughton Life* are doing a photo shoot, and naturally we need to finalise arrangements with them, run them through the schedule, make sure everything turns out perfectly . . .' She ticked things off on her fingernails.

Lili laughed in disbelief. 'You're her sister. How could you think of not coming to the funeral?'

Karen didn't smile. 'I suppose you'd better come in.'

Karen's kitchen, the heart of the home, was all cold surfaces like steel and marble. It had large, glass doors that opened onto a giant, green garden and outdoor swimming pool.

Lili sat on a hard stool by a marble counter and watched Karen shoo a Yorkshire terrier outside.

Karen didn't offer Lili a drink.

'I'm sorry we couldn't invite you to Jessica's wedding,' Karen said. 'But it was close friends and family only.'

'I didn't even know she was getting married.' Lili liked her cousins, Jessica and Rebecca, although she hadn't seen them since she was little. They had been nice little girls, back then. Scared of Aunt Karen of course, but what child wasn't?

Karen flew off the handle about things that made no sense to children. What eight-year old understood why rearranging ornaments on the mantelpiece or drawing a steamy smiley face on the bathroom window was cause for a telling off?

'You hadn't heard about the wedding?' Karen put her palms to her cheeks. 'Are we living on the same planet? Don't you read the newspapers?'

'Not often. Maybe *Bizarre* magazine sometimes, if I'm on the cover. Anyway, I don't care about Jess's wedding. I'm here to talk to you about—'

'Then you don't know who she's marrying?'

'I haven't a clue,' Lili admitted.

'She's engaged to Toby Samson.'

'Who?'

'To think, not so long ago, I was living in the East End, and now my daughter—'

'You're still in the East End,' Lili pointed out. 'Just a bit further out. Away from all the good food and interesting shops.'

'You know what I mean. Well. Yes. Anyway, I'm so very proud of her. Marrying into the *Samson* family.' Her voice became a delighted squeal. 'She's living in Kensington. Toby takes her shopping at Sloane Square. Harrods. Lord Samson is a *very* well known businessman. Anthony Samson. Famous.'

'I've never heard of him,' said Lili. 'And I've got more important things to think about. I need to ask you about—'

'Well – I suppose people mix in different circles.' Karen glanced at Lili. 'You haven't even asked about Rebecca. She lives nearby with her boyfriend. Doing ever so well. Two new cars this year, a Jaguar for him, a Kia for her. Both brand new. And they have their own cleaner.'

'I came to talk about Mum,' said Lili.

'Yes.' Karen had the decency to look down. 'She'd been unhappy for a long time.'

'Uncle Jeff said—'

'You spoke to Jeff?' Karen looked surprised and irritated. 'What does he know about it? He hardly saw her.'

'You didn't see her either,' Lili said. 'When I lived with her, you never did. Uncle Jeff came over, but never you.'

'I saw her the day she died,' said Karen. 'How old were *you* when you left? Fifteen? You know what a state she was in. You didn't hang around when she needed you – her own daughter.'

Ouch.

'Don't you think I feel bad about that?' Lili's voice was hard. 'It was her or me. I couldn't stay there, the way she was.'

'Darren stayed with her.'

'Darren's in prison now.'

Karen opened her neat little mouth, but no words came out. Eventually she said:

'So you'll be attending the funeral?'

'Of course I will.' Lili didn't let on how angry and numb she felt. How she hadn't cried. How scared, no, *terrified* she felt at the idea of seeing her grandma. And how finding some old letters had become crucial to grieving and letting go. 'Did it occur to you I'd rather not go either? But I never thought not going was an option.'

'I wasn't really involved with Viv's life,' Karen said. 'I'm not sure I should really get involved now. Considering the circles we're mixing in. The sort of people Viv knew.' Karen gave a little shake of her head. 'That boyfriend of hers, the market traders and the men from the pub. Not our sort of people.'

Karen picked a dog hair from her dress. 'Mum and Dad always used to joke Viv should have gone to a different family. She was always the black sheep. It was always me and Jeff. Then Viv.'

'You say you saw Mum the day she died.'

Karen nodded, blowing out smoke. 'Yes.'

43

'I've seen Viv a few times this year, actually,' said Karen. 'More than I wanted, in all honesty. She was very distressed, that last day.'

'About some old family letters,' Lili filled in.

Karen's eyes sharpened. 'That's right. Yes. I suppose she told you all about those letters.'

'No, but she wrote about them on her bedroom wall. She asked me to find them.'

Karen's plucked eyebrows shot up her forehead.

'Yes,' Lili continued. 'She was obsessed by them. And looking into the family tree. And then she killed herself. I want to find those letters, Karen. Do you know what they are? *Where* they are?'

'I have no idea what or where they are.' Karen tapped her cigarette butt. 'But I do know this. Those letters weren't hers or yours to find. She had no right to be looking for them. I told her that.'

'Why not?'

'They belong to the family.'

'Then she had a perfect right to look for them,' said Lili, 'just as much as me or any other Morgan. Mum was your family, whether you wanted her or not. And so am I.'

'What do you want with them?' Karen asked. 'What's the big deal? They're just old family letters.'

'Mum didn't leave me a goodbye note when she died,' said Lili. 'She just wrote something on the wall asking me to find the letters. And a load of other stuff, about a family secret. I want to know what was so bad she felt she couldn't go on living any more. Maybe even understand why she spent her whole life angry.'

'Vivienne was always angry,' said Karen. 'That was her way. There wasn't necessarily a reason – she was born that way.'

'People aren't born angry – Mum always said the family made her that way.'

'She never said anything like that to me.'

'How was she the day she died?'

'She really wasn't herself,' said Karen. 'She wasn't thinking clearly. A bit of a state, actually.'

'Did she talk about the letters?'

'Just that she was looking for them. She asked if she could use my bath, and got water all over the floor. Then she tried to make a cup of tea, forgot the teabag and made herself a mug of hot water and sugar.'

'Did she seem very unhappy?'

'Yes,' Karen said. 'Like I said, she was in a right state.' Her faux-posh accent had slipped a little. 'Questions, questions, wanting to know all about old relatives, who the letters had been passed to. I told her I didn't know. I've never been interested in family history.

'She'd had a fight with that boyfriend again, the one from the market. She was banging on—' Karen stopped to correct herself '– *talking* about getting back together with him and asking me over and over about the letters.'

'And what did you tell her?'

'Nothing.'

There was barking from outside as Karen's terrier threw itself at a cat.

'And you don't even have enough respect for Mum to come to the funeral.'

'Well, that's a very unfair way to put it,' said Karen.

'True though.'

'The timing . . . there's so much to do for the wedding. I really can't.'

'Will you come to the inquest then?' Lili said. 'Mum at least deserves that. A fair final hearing. Will you come and tell the court about how she was before she died? It might make a difference to the outcome—'

'No.' Karen's lips snapped closed. 'No, I certainly couldn't do that, Lilian.'

'Please—'

'I said no. It's bad enough they suspect suicide. I'm not going to help them prove it.'

'It's not about proving anything, it's about showing Mum respect—'

The phone rang and Karen answered, her voice resuming a clipped, formal tone – the lady of the manor. 'Yes. Darling, I'm with somebody. I'll call you straight back.'

'Don't you know anything about the letters?' said Lili. 'What did Mum ask you about?'

'Oh.' Karen threw her hands in the air. 'A few things. About our grandmother. Look, I've really got things I should be doing—'

'Then cancel them,' said Lili, resting her elbows on the breakfast bar, just like Karen told her not to when she was a kid.

'There isn't much to tell, and I'd appreciate—'

'Jeff said you might know about Michael Morgan,' said Lili. 'Your grand-uncle Fred's dad. Did Mum ask you about him?'

'No.' Karen shook her head. 'She didn't, and Jeff got that wrong. Grand-uncle Fred never talked to any of us about Great Grandad Michael. Michael was a violent man. A gangster. Grand-uncle Fred wanted to forget him. He went to America to forget him. And to be a comedian. Dolly came along for the ride, and ended up being the star of the show.'

'You don't know anything about him at all?'

'Only that he lived in Whitechapel,' said Karen. 'Really. I don't know any more than Viv or Jeff. Viv never asked me about Michael, I promise you.'

There was a bleeping sound and Lili jumped. She took her mobile phone from her bag.

A text message waited for her.

'Hang on, just . . .' Words fell away.

Stay away from Karen.
The letters are mine.
Stay away, stay away, stay away.

'What's wrong?' Karen asked.

'A message.' Lili sensed something outside the window, but when she looked there was nothing. Only bare trees swaying in the wind, a green lawn and the tarpaulin-covered swimming pool.

She stared at the text.

The house phone rang again and Karen answered it. 'Now? I'm a little busy . . . no, no, of course, if you must.' She hung up. 'Look, I really do have things—'

'Wait.' Lili held out her mobile phone. 'Read this.'

'Read what?' Karen looked at the phone.

'The message. And the sender.'

'There is no message.' Karen turned the phone to her.

The screen was blank.

'It was here.' Lili searched the phone. 'It was right here.' She turned the phone off and on. 'The message was here.' But it had gone.

'I really do have things I need to do.' Karen got to her feet. 'So if you don't mind.' She crossed her arms.

'Yes,' said Lili, barely hearing her own voice. 'Fine. I'm going.'

She left Karen's home in a daze, and wandered along the driveway deep in thought. It was good to be out of that cold, sterile house, but she was still on an empty street miles from home.

Against winter trees, the large houses felt hostile. Seeing the sky was strange after being so long in the city.

'Whoever's doing this, you're wasting your time,' she told the grey clouds. 'I won't give up. I'm going to find those letters and move on with my life. I won't end up like my Mum.'

Who knew I was with Aunt Karen? Only one person could have possibly known Lili was there at that exact moment.

Gretchen.

44

Bang, bang, bang!

Lili pounded on Gretchen's front door with her palm.

No answer.

She made a mallet of her hand and pounded some more.

The door rattled and Gretchen's mother, Carol, appeared. She had a tea towel wound around her hands and looked like a mouse peeping from its hole.

'Who are you?' said Carol, pushing her glasses up her nose. 'Oh. Yes. Viv's daughter.' She closed the door a fraction. 'The caretaker handles—'

'I need to speak to Gretchen,' said Lili.

'Gretchen's very busy. She was too sick for school today, but she still has her coursework to do. I don't think now is the time—'

'Yes,' said Lili. 'Now is the time. Let me speak to her please.'

'Oh . . .' Carol looked alarmed. 'Is there something I should know about? If there is, as her mother I really feel—'

'It's between me and Gretchen.' Lili could hardly tell Carol she wanted to ask Gretchen about threatening text messages. 'I've got some things for her history coursework.'

At the mention of coursework, Carol seemed to reconsider. Her face sagged.

'Well, just for a moment,' she said, stepping back to let Lili inside. She led her down the hall. 'Gretchen!'

Gretchen's bedroom door was open and Lili saw a pink-fairy duvet under a shelf of Enid Blyton books – all unread if the perfect spines were anything to go by. Sprawled on top of the crisp children's books were bashed-up teen novels about ghosts and vampires.

Gretchen sat at an old-fashioned school desk, its inkwell full of pastel-coloured biros. She appeared to be making notes, but from the open library book at her feet Lili guessed she'd been reading.

'Lili?' Gretchen turned around in mock surprise. Lili smiled – Gretchen must have heard her in the doorway. 'You're here with something for my history coursework, aren't you?' She spoke like an answer-machine recording and it was clear she was lying, but Carol didn't seem to notice.

'Mum. Can Lili stay and help me with my coursework?'

Carol's lips thinned. 'She said she had some *things* for your coursework. I didn't agree to anyone staying.'

'*Pleeease* Mum. I don't want to fail.'

The word 'fail' made Carol jump. 'I suppose if you need her for your work. Oh, Gretchen – this project. I never should have let you get involved with—' She caught herself. 'I'll bring you some tea.'

When Carol left the room, Lili shut the door.

'Listen, I need to talk to you. I've been getting text messages. You haven't been sending them, have you? As a joke or something?'

'How could I send you text messages?' said Gretchen. 'I don't know your number. I never have any credit, anyway.'

'Not from your phone,' said Lili. 'From my mum's phone.'

'From *Viv's* phone?' Gretchen looked at her like she was mad. 'Yes.'

'How could I do that?' There was a pause. 'Oh. I get it. You think I stole your mum's phone. Thanks a lot.'

'Whoever's sending me messages knew I was at Karen's house this morning,' said Lili. 'Only you knew that. Did you tell anyone else?'

'Who could I tell?' said Gretchen. 'Kids at school think I'm weird enough already. Mind you, at least they don't accuse me of stealing.'

Lili sighed. 'Honestly, I don't think you'd steal things, Gretchen, but nothing else makes sense.'

'Maybe you told someone and then forgot,' Gretchen suggested. 'I do things like that sometimes.'

'No. I didn't tell anyone. I spoke to you and went straight to Aunt Karen's.'

'Well – who could have your mum's phone?' Gretchen asked. 'Think of it that way.'

'I don't know. That flat's been locked up since her death.'

'Well I didn't take it,' said Gretchen.

'I spoke to the police,' said Lili. 'There's no record of the phone. They think I'm seeing things.'

'No offence, but maybe you are.'

The door opened and Carol appeared with a mug of mint tea and a carob bar. She placed them by Gretchen's elbow.

'Sorry – you didn't want anything, did you?' Carol asked Lili.

'Yes, I'll have a black coffee – filter if you have it,' said Lili, deciding that if Carol was rude enough to bring Gretchen a drink without offering her one, then she was rude enough to ask for whatever she fancied.

'Oh.' Carol looked flustered. 'Right. Okay.' She left the room.

Gretchen ducked down and pulled a laptop from under her bed. It was a sturdy, no-frills machine, built for work and study. 'I've found a few bits and pieces about William Peavy. Nothing earth-shattering. There's not so much I can do, stuck at home.'

'Well, anything is better than what I have right now. Aunt Karen didn't tell me a thing, and it seems like the rest of my family are ex-directory.'

Gretchen jabbed the enter button and said, 'Mum thinks I can't go online when she's not here, but all she did was hide the internet desktop logo.' She rolled her eyes. 'Anyway.' She turned her laptop to face Lili. 'Look.'

Lili leaned towards the screen. She saw a white document with swirly handwriting on it.

'It's a letter,' said Gretchen. 'Look. See who wrote it?'

A creak of footsteps came from the hall.

Gretchen snapped the laptop closed and stuffed it under the duvet. Lili was sure she practised that move many times a day.

The bedroom door opened.

'Coffee,' said Carol, looked from Gretchen to Lili and back again. 'I'd prefer this door left open if you don't mind.'

'She's fifteen years old,' said Lili. 'Shouldn't she be allowed to close her bedroom door if she wants to?'

'That's really none of your business,' said Carol, putting the coffee down. 'Open,' she told Gretchen, pushing the door wide as she left.

Gretchen waited a moment, then pulled her computer out again.

'William Peavy,' Lili read from the screen. 'This is a letter from William Peavy?'

'No,' said Gretchen. 'It's from one of his servants. Ann Hadley. She wrote about things that went on at William Peavy's house while she worked there. There are loads of these letters. Loads.'

Lili looked closer at the bunched-up writing. 'Gretchen – where did you get this?'

'The William Peavy Museum,' said Gretchen, swirling a finger on the mouse pad. 'They're scanning the letters and sending them over for me.' She pulled up more pages. 'It's information overload though, you know? Too much to look through, just like everything else. I haven't found anything useful yet. But still – it's good to have access to it all.'

'There must be a way to search for names in the letters,' said Lili.

Gretchen shook her head. 'They're all handwritten. Someone would have to write them all into a computer, and why would they? They're just servants' letters. The only reason they've been kept is because the servants worked for William Peavy. We can sort of search by date, but half of them are in the wrong order.'

'We know a date,' said Lili. 'The court records said the date Love and Tom were working for Peavy. Or at least, the date they were sacked.'

'I know, but the servant who wrote most of letters – Ann Hadley – she wrote LOADS of them. Like three a day for the entire time she worked for the Peavy family. She was a lady's maid for William Peavy's wife, and later on a housekeeper, so there were all these little boring details she wrote about, like the price of coal and how to get out stains.'

'The court document said Love only worked for the Peavys for seven months,' said Lili. 'So. Let's take the date of the court document and work back to around the time Love was hired. Surely the lady's maid would have written something about it, if she wrote letters every day. What else would she have to write about?'

'The price of carrots, the price of flour . . . you'd be surprised,' said Gretchen, clicking at pages. 'But okay. So. That would be . . . January.' She leaned towards the screen, squinting at the bunched-up handwriting. 'Stuff about Christmas deliveries and the price of meat. It's no good, Lili, half of these aren't even from January. They've been mis-filed. Even if she did write about her, it could be in a completely different month's worth of letters.'

'Let's just carry on looking through January.'

'Okay.' Gretchen yawned. 'Just this one month.' She began clicking open letters. 'Nothing, nothing. See? Just dreary stuff.'

'But lots of these were written in January, though. Keep going.'

'Twenty-ninth, thirtieth – she wrote three that day. But nothing. And then the thirty-first. Only one. To her sister.' Gretchen's hand froze over the mouse pad. 'Wait.'

'What? I can't read the writing.'

'You get used to it. There. Look. Right there. You're right – there's something about Love getting hired.'

LOVE MORGAN b. 1831,
d. 1865.

George
Morgan

Tom
Morgan
1836 – 1874

*Nee
Avary* — Love
Morgan — M
1831 – 1865

James Morgan — m. — Cooky Morgan
1864 – 1889   (Catherine Long)
b. 1863 – d.?

Fred Morgan
1899 – 1972

Karen   b. 1960
Morgan

Vivienne
Morgan
b. 1965

Jeff   b. 1958
Morgan

45

Lili leaned over Gretchen's shoulder.

The new maid is called Love Avary and is a lowed women who is always making a show of herselve. I can't pritend to like her. There are rumours she left her last job after some skandalls with the master, and the way she is here I can well beleive it.

I was pasing her bedroom this mornin when I saw the door wide open and her on her pot in just a shifft. Mr Peavy or any of the men could have seen her.

She is very bad for young Tom Morgan, hoose father, George Butler, is such a dear friend. With Tom so young and such a sweet lad, I fear Love will leed him down the rong path.

'Scroll down,' said Lili.

Gretchen did. 'Boring, boring. She just goes on about her day off. Walks in the country and stuff.'

'It's just like what Mrs Peavy said in the court records.' Lili moved a curl from her cheek. 'About Tom being sweet and Love being a bad influence.'

'It's still going to take a long time to find anything else, Lili. There are too many letters. Hundreds. We need more dates.'

'Ian Batty said Love was having an affair with William Peavy,' said Lili. 'Is that something we could look into?'

'The old psychic guy? Who cares what he said?'

'I do,' said Lili. 'He spoke to Mum the week before she died. She might have told him stuff, family history stuff, that he's sharing with me in his own special, slightly weird way. And don't you think, reading between the lines, maybe Peavy had an affair with Love when she worked for him? It's possible, don't you think?'

'Maybe,' Gretchen whispered, watching the hallway. 'Have you heard of *The Lady of the Lake*?'

'Sort of,' said Lili. 'It's one of William Peavy's books, isn't it?'

'It's not a book,' said Gretchen. 'It's a short poem from a collection of poems about Camelot. Together, they're all just a few pages. They were published after Peavy died – most people think he never really meant them to be seen by the public.'

'What are they about?'

'They're poems about Camelot and King Arthur,' said Gretchen. 'You know – Merlin, the Lady of the Lake, all of that. *The Lady of the Lake* is the most famous. When it was first published, people said Peavy must have written it about his wife.

'But then later, people read between the lines – Peavy was *such* a genius, always ten different meanings in everything he wrote – and now some scholars think that poem is *really* about the master of the house in love with a servant. So you never know. Maybe your old psychic guy is right. And maybe Viv did tell him something about Love that she never told me.'

'Actually, I think I remember reading that poem at school,' said Lili. 'Something about underwater, or something. Love underwater. Can we look at the poem on your computer?'

Gretchen screwed up her face. '*Really* quickly.' She typed into Google and opened a page titled: *The Works of William Peavy*.

'Here it is,' she said. *The Lady of the Lake*'.

> *Underwater, men are true,*
> *where we hide, me and you,*
> *Our feelings drowned within the lake,*
> *For no one would our marriage make.*
>
> *The lady holds the sword in hand,*
> *Excalibur for married land,*
> *Hidden, love will always be*
> *Underwater, you and me.*

'That line – *For no one would our marriage make*. What do you think that means?' asked Lili.

'Some people think he's saying something about how sad he is to be separate from his wife,' said Gretchen. 'He wrote the poem when she was living away from him. But other people think he's talking about an affair outside of marriage.' She snapped the laptop closed and sat on it. Carol walked past the door.

'You've got good reflexes,' said Lili, as Carol disappeared into the kitchen.

'I have to, living in this flat,' said Gretchen.

'I take it your mum doesn't know about your virtual boyfriend.'

'Shuush!' Gretchen waved her hands. 'Of course she doesn't. She'd kill me.'

'These servants' letters . . . how many more of them are there exactly?' Lili asked.

'Thousands. I'm going to carry on working through them, but honestly Lili, without dates it's going to be hard to find anything in a hurry. It could take weeks. How about I research today, then meet you at your theatre later. Seven o'clock. I'll tell Mum I've got a drama class.'

'I don't know, Gretchen. I don't want you falling out with your mum.'

Gretchen laughed. 'You can't fall out with someone you're not friends with.'

'Okay. Fine. I've got a dress rehearsal at six, but – yes, let's meet after that.' Lili sighed. 'And I still need to work out what happened to Mum's mobile phone.'

'What about asking Viv's boyfriend?' Gretchen asked. 'He might know. He was always round her flat. Well, last year anyway. And he knows all her friends and everything.'

'Yes, I need to thank him anyway. For everything he's done so far. And say sorry for not speaking to him before.'

'He works on Whitechapel market,' said Gretchen. 'I see him sometimes on the way to school. He's really nice. He sells sat navs.'

'Did he and Mum fight a lot?'

'All the time.' Gretchen drummed her fingers on the laptop shell. 'But it was always Viv who was doing the fighting. He was the one trying to calm everything down.'

'Sounds about right,' said Lili. 'That was Mum. Always angry.'

46

Life's a Stage by Lili Allure

Lili Allure's guide to SIY – sew it yourself

In my early days of striptease I taught myself to make my own costumes. To be truthful, I'm more of an off-the-peg girl than a Blue Peter enthusiast, but knowing your pins from your needles is an absolute must in the burlesque business. I've lost count of the number of times a beautiful couture outfit has fallen to bits just before a show. If I didn't know how to work a sewing machine, I'd have had nothing to strip off – imagine that!

I first made costumes because there were only a handful of shops in London selling striptease outfits and I was on a serious budget. There was no way I would spend half a night's wages on a strip of sequinned lycra when I could buy fabric for 50 pence a metre and sew sequins on myself. So my fellow strippers and I would scour Whitechapel market for showy fabrics, extra glittery sequins and strong thread to sew it all together.

Whitechapel is a Mecca for any striptease girl in search of showy material. Every fabric imaginable sits fading behind shop windows or under market tarpaulin. Sari fabric, fake fur, sparkly zebra print, curtain velvet and lycra in every shade and colour – it's all for sale, come rain or shine.

Even though I stripped at a spit-and-sawdust club in my early years, I was always more interested in old-school glamour than loud colours and 'look at me' fabrics. While the other girls tested the stretch on a roll of mirrored lycra, I'd be twirling around chiffons and fake furs, and ducking into secondhand shops for 1940s bargains.

Whitechapel High Street was shiny with rain as Lili went from stall to stall. She held a theatre programme over her curls as she passed tables of tracksuits, mobile-phone cases, alarm clocks and fruit in metal dishes.

Poking her head under green-and-white striped tarpaulin, she asked:

'All right? Do you know anyone selling sat navs? Ben? No. Okay.'

Market traders huddled by their wares, puffa jackets zipped right up to the neck, drinking tea from polystyrene. Heads shook and backs turned.

As rain sprayed onto her white cheeks, Lili noticed the warm-looking shops facing the market stalls. *I could try the shopkeepers.* At least she'd be dry that way. She saw a second-hand clothes shop: *Vintage Raz.*

Lili laughed out loud. 'I don't believe it. Who better to ask?'

She'd bought armfuls of secondhand clothes from Vintage Raz in the days before she went big time. Raz, the owner, was a hyperactive party girl who knew everyone in Whitechapel. If Raz didn't know Ben, no one would.

The shop window was just as Lili remembered, give or take a feather boa here and there, and the familiar bell jangled overhead as she came in out of the rain. Something else was familiar too – the ripple of excitement Lili felt when she saw rows of musty old clothes.

It was her favourite kind of treasure hunt, searching for rough diamonds in rails of rock.

Inside the shop, electronica played too loudly and Lili felt she was walking into a party. It was just like old times.

A girl appeared from behind a rail of fur coats. She wore daisy-covered plastic platform boots and a purple kaftan – both 1970s originals.

'Raz,' said Lili. 'Is that you?'

'Lili?' Raz had elaborate plaits woven in a crown around her head, and her shoulders danced to the music as she wove through rows of clothing. Her hair, which used to be treacle brown, was now dyed black – perhaps to cover creeping grey – and deep lines ran around her mouth. She was the same age as Lili, but looked much older. 'Hey! Look at you. How long's it been? Four years? Five?'

'Try ten,' said Lili. 'How have you been?'

'Good, good. You know.' Raz pulled a floor-length blonde coat from a hanger and fluffed out the sleeve fur. 'From an old lady in Chelsea. Just your sort of thing, am I right?'

'It's gorgeous,' said Lili. 'But I'm not looking for clothes. I'm looking for a guy called Ben. Someone told me he works on the market.'

'You mean, the guy your mum's seeing.'

'Yes,' said Lili, not surprised that Raz knew. *Was seeing*.

'Always drinking coffee,' said Raz. 'Trades as Behnam's, does sat navs.'

'I don't really know him,' said Lili. 'Only what Darren's told me. I haven't spoken to Mum in a long time.'

'Why are you looking for him?' Raz took a sip of Red Bull from a can on the counter. The bin underneath was full of empties.

'Oh – just . . . I've got to ask him a few things, that's all. Do you know where he works?'

'Yeah. He's about ten stalls along, near the Sainsbury's end. You'd better hurry – it's nearly six o'clock.'

The market was closing by the time Lili reached Ben's stall, and she almost passed the good-looking man stacking sat navs into cardboard boxes. Only the sign over the stall that said *Behnam's Ko-ordinates* stopped her walking past.

'Excuse me.'

The man shivered and turned around. He was tall, with a thick quiff of black hair, black eyes, white teeth and beautiful brown cheekbones. He wore a thin Adidas sports jacket.

'Can I help you, love?' He looked her up and down.

'Are you Ben?' Lili asked.

'Who's asking?' He had the typical Whitechapel accent. Bouncy, East London English, spoken with the soft edges of some other language. Like many Whitechapel residents, he'd probably grown up somewhere warm and exotic, and somehow ended up on England's damp pavements.

'Viv's daughter.'

Ben stared. 'Viv's daughter?'

Lili nodded.

Ben wiped rain from his nose and shook her hand warmly. 'Good to see you. I mean it. So good to see you. I know, I know . . . it was all too soon. Me calling you. I hope I didn't do anything wrong. I didn't mean to take over, but—'

'No. I'm glad you're sorting everything. Can we talk?'

'Sure.' Ben looked over Lili's head and signalled to a man at the next stall. 'Hassan will pack up for me. Come on. We'll have a cup of coffee.'

47

Café 2000 offered everything the new millennium Londoner could want. Internet access, coffee, sandwiches, secondhand mobile phones, laptops and watches. It had a window full of adverts and a shop of empty tables.

The owner, Sofi, was a bald man as wide as he was tall. He didn't look up from his magazine as Lili and Ben pushed through the glass door.

'I used to bring Viv here all the time,' said Ben, leading Lili to one of the few tables without an ageing computer on it. 'Good to see you, Sofi. Espresso and—' He pointed at Lili. 'Tea?'

'Yes please.'

'It's what Viv always used to have.' He pulled back a chair for her. 'The funeral directors told me you stopped by, so I guessed the police must have passed on my message.'

'Yes,' said Lili.

'I tried to choose things Viv would have liked,' said Ben. 'Colour. Songs. You never expect anything like this to happen . . . not so young.' He sighed. 'I was happy to do it, but it should have been family. I grew up in Iran, you know? Family, tradition . . . all very important. But Viv hardly saw her family.'

'Did you manage to invite any of them to the funeral?'

'Hardly any. Just Viv's brother and sister. And you and Darren. That's it. No one has any numbers for anyone – it's like you're all strangers. The hardest person to find has been Viv's mother. No one knows where she is.'

Lili found it hard, suddenly, to swallow her tea. 'So you haven't got in touch with Gran yet? That's a relief, actually. The thought of seeing her . . . I don't know. They look alike, her and Mum.

She'd probably end up getting the sharp end of how I feel about the way Mum died, and that wouldn't be fair.

'The police said they'd help me track her down. It'll be sad if she can't make it. Already, Viv's sister is trying to back out.'

'We're not like most families,' said Lili. 'And Mum could be difficult.'

'Viv and I were always rowing.' Ben squeezed his eyes together and tears appeared. 'About everything. I wanted to move in with her, make a proper relationship, but she said we fought too much. For her it was always tomorrow, tomorrow. I knew she wasn't happy. But I never thought she'd go and do something like this.'

'I need to ask you something,' said Lili. 'My mum's mobile phone – do you know what happened to it?'

'Viv's phone?' Ben took an espresso from Sofi. 'I don't know. It would be in her flat, wouldn't it? Unless the police took it. Why?'

'I don't think it's in her flat. Someone's taken it.'

'Taken it?' Ben sounded upset. 'Why would anyone do that? I bought her that phone. She loved it. Have you searched the flat?'

'No,' Lili murmured. 'Not properly.'

'I'll never forgive myself for Viv,' said Ben. More tears. 'I miss her so much. If I hadn't left her alone, if we hadn't been fighting . . .' He put his head on the counter and sobbed.

'Hey.' Lili patted his hand. 'It's okay. Don't feel bad. I left her too.'

Ben lifted his head and swiped tears away. 'She died all alone. All *alone*.'

'When did you last see her?' Lili asked.

Ben sniffed. 'November. At the White Hart. She'd had her hair done, but I didn't notice, so we rowed. Both so stubborn. Then we did our usual thing, lots of late-night phone calls. Shouting. Bad words. I called her—' His shoulders began to shake. 'A *mess*. Those were the last words I said to her. I'll feel guilty for as long as I live.'

Lili watched him cry, hating how easily emotion poured from

him. 'That's just like Mum.' Her voice frightened her, the way it trembled and boomed. 'It's not enough for her to feel bad, she has to share it around. Make everyone else feel like shit.

'And then, at the end of it all, she just checked out of life without a thought for anyone else. Ran away, just like she always did.' She poured more tea, her hand shaking with fury. 'She doesn't deserve your guilt. Or your pity. Everything that happened to her, she brought on herself.'

'I just wish she'd at least said goodbye.'

Lili felt a wave of tiredness. 'I know. That's exactly what I want. Mum wrote on her bedroom wall, asking me to find some old family letters, and maybe . . . I'm hoping that might be her way of saying goodbye to me. Did Mum tell you she was doing her family tree?'

'Family tree?'

'She was looking into the family history when she passed away. She wrote about it on her wall.'

'She never spoke to her family. Why would she be writing on the wall about them? What wall? What did she write?'

'In the bedroom. Stuff about finding some old family letters. It doesn't make all that much sense. I think she was in a bad place.'

'I know she wasn't happy.' Ben's lip trembled. 'I'm so sorry to be this way. I keep it together most days, but it comes out sometimes, you know?'

'I wish I did. I haven't even cried yet. I feel so awful knowing Mum was unhappy, but on the other hand I just think, Serves you right. Everything's so messed up inside. One minute I'm angry. The next I'm . . . I don't know. Empty. And hurting at the thought of her suffering. It's like I'm fighting with myself.'

'So these . . . what did you say, *family* letters?'

'I'll be honest, I'm desperate to find them. Some sort of goodbye from Mum would help. A lot.'

'You think that's what these letters are? Like a suicide note?'

'Who knows? Mum liked playing detective games, didn't she? I think there'll be something in them that'll be her explanation.

I have to think that. Otherwise I'm lost.' Lili had a vision of herself surrounded by wine and pill bottles, curled up on the dressing-room sofa. Her skin felt clammy.

'There hasn't been an inquest yet,' Ben said. 'Are you sure . . . I mean, she might not have killed herself. She didn't leave a note.'

'Maybe it was an accident, you mean? A cry for help? Yes, perhaps. But I'd rather believe she meant to do it. At least that way, she got what she wanted.'

Ben fixed his brown eyes on her. 'The police took lots of things from the flat. To check. You know. For a crime. But I don't think . . . you're her daughter. In my heart, in your heart, I guess we know what the truth is.'

'That she didn't want to live any more.' Lili felt her body go cold and heavy.

'You look so sad,' said Ben. 'How about we go for a walk? Fresh air.' He gestured to the busy main road outside.

'No, I should be getting back to my club.'

Ben looked at her meaningfully. 'See you Saturday, then. We have to look after each other, okay?'

'Okay.'

Lili watched Ben bounding down the road and felt sorry he'd got himself messed up with her mum. Viv could drag anyone down with her – God knows, she'd dragged Darren low enough. But then again, people made their own choices.

As Lili got up to leave, she felt for her mobile phone. There were no text messages. There were, however, five missed calls.

Oh shit, shit, shit. The dress rehearsal. She checked her watch. *If I hurry, I might catch the end.*

She threw money on the table.

'Something wrong, love?' Sofi asked as she hurried out.

'Oh nothing,' Lili answered. 'Just my career.'

48

Kate Hamilton's was dark and quiet when Lili arrived. It wasn't a good sign. If the rehearsal was still going on, the auditorium would be bright with stage lights.

Lili saw a single candle flickering by the stage and curls of silver smoke. She recognised the smell of Benson & Hedges cigarettes and realised Carol-Ann was sitting by the stage.

'Caz.' Lili walked over soft carpet. 'I know. I'm late for the rehersal. I should be dressed already.'

'Sweetheart, you *missed* the rehearsal,' Carol-Ann replied. 'I was worried about you.'

Lili sighed and took a seat. 'I'm so sorry. It's been a weird day.'

'What happened, Lils?'

'It's just all this stuff with my mum.'

'No one's going to think any less of you if you want to take some time off.' Carol-Ann scratched a patch of dry skin on her chin. 'I mean, you're owed a holiday by now. You must be getting pretty bored, doing the same old numbers night after night. People do get bored, staying at the same place. Look at me. I've been here donkeys years and I'm bored as anything.'

'Maybe you're right, Caz. But anyway, I'm meeting someone in the dressing room, and—'

'Don't take this the wrong way, Lils, but I'm worried for tonight's performance. You haven't been at your best on stage.'

'What?'

'Not there for curtain up. And your act a bit sort of forced. Stiff. Look, you know me. I'm your friend. I tell it like it is. When you're great I tell you. If you're shit I'll tell you too. But it's not only me saying it. We've had some audience feedback. Complaints they weren't getting what they paid for.'

'The audience said that?'

'On those little cards we give them.'

'I'll be perfect tonight.'

'Perfect, smerfect. There's no such thing, Lils. Even the best of us mess up sometimes. But I just think at the moment, you need a rest. It's not good for your image, getting bad reviews.'

Lili chewed her lip and tasted lipstick. 'Shit, shit, shit. I'm so sorry, Caz. I'll sort it out. I will. Don't stop me performing – it's the only thing keeping me sane right now. Anyway. Look I'm so sorry, but I have to go. I'm meeting—'

'Who?'

'Just . . . someone.'

'Come on, Lils. Look, you know I'd never tell you what to do. Lord knows, I've tried and failed. But have you seen the time? If you're saying the show tonight is going to be perfect, why aren't you rushing off to get ready? You look exhausted.'

Carol-Ann stubbed out her cigarette, her white fingers bending in the ashtray like ballerina legs. 'Pete is really worried about you. And so am I. And Bryony and the girls. We're all a family here, we look after each other.'

'I know. And I love you all right back.'

'You know Pete would do anything for you.' Carol-Ann gave her a wink. 'Don't you?'

'I suppose so.'

'You could do a lot worse. Right. I'm off to the wholesalers before they close. I'll leave you to it.' Carol-Ann disappeared out front, and Lili heard the splutter of her old Mini.

Bad reviews. Oh shit. Lili hurried towards the stage, but a rustling sound behind the bar stopped her.

'I thought she'd never leave.' Gretchen's head appeared by the premium spirit bottles.

'Gretchen! Will you stop scaring the life out of me.'

'Sorry,' said Gretchen. 'You do look well scared.'

'How long have you been hiding there?'

'Nearly an *hour*,' said Gretchen. She checked her watch. 'Actually, one whole hour. That Northern cow told me I couldn't wait, so I snuck behind the bar when she wasn't looking. It's freezing outside and I wanted to see the rehearsal – it was *brilliant*.'

'She's not a cow. She's one of my best friends—'

'Oh my God. I *so* want stockings and suspenders now. Where do you buy them from?'

Lili noticed a rucksack on Gretchen's back. 'Have you got something for me?'

'Yes.'

49

'What?' Lili asked. Suddenly, the show was forgotten. 'More servants' letters?'

Gretchen unzipped her bag. 'One. After like, five hours. I was looking and looking, and then I thought – hey. What about checking the letters written at the time Love was taken to court by the Peavys?'

'Good idea.'

'I know. I am brilliant. But actually, there was nothing about the court case in any of the letters. I was really disappointed, but maybe all that stuff is just too complicated for servants to write about.

'Anyway. I was about to give up, when I found another letter from Ann Hadley to her sister. She was a housekeeper by that time. It's amazing she found time to write – those women worked from six in the morning to midnight most days.

'Anyway. She wrote about Love and the Morgan family. I printed it out. Here, you can read it. Her handwriting's a bit better on her later letters.'

Lili leaned over her shoulder and read:

Mr Peavy is a kind man, but he does himselve no favowers when he visits white chapal and a certan Morgan family. For this kindnyss, there may be rumurs of skandall if he is not very carefull.

What a good man Mr Peavy is that he can't see a family go rong. He gives charety because the Morgans are in need, and does not care a bit that their need is of their own making. He is a true Christian.

For my part, I feel if Tom and Love are to go hungry they have only themselfs to blame. Mr Peavy does too great a kindnyss when he lets himselve be seen with the likes of Love Avary. Now she is Morgan, we are told, as she and Tom have wed. I am so very pleased Mrs Peavy gotten ryd of the pair of them. If it was down to Mr Peavy, he would have kept them both on, even with Love caught for stealing.

'Interesting,' said Lili. 'Don't you think? William Peavy visited Love at home. And Ian Batty thought they were having an affair.'

'Well, I don't know about that,' said Gretchen. 'I think he had a different motive for going to their home. In fact, I know he did.'

'How?'

She took a bunch of white pages and slapped them on the table. 'My virtual boyfriend sent me this book he found online. It came as a PDF so I downloaded it and printed the pages – it took me for-ev-er. But it's a great book. Lots of detail.'

Lili read the top page. '*William Peavy – The Arsenic Saviour*. Peavy wrote about arsenic, didn't he? In some of his novels?'

'Yes,' said Gretchen. 'But more than that. This book's all about how he campaigned to teach poor people about the dangers of arsenic. He was a hero, really. For years, lots of people didn't know, and traders would use it in food and things like that.

'Even when people began figuring out how deadly arsenic was, plenty of poor people still didn't know how dangerous it could be. Peavy campaigned to save lives. He helped get the law changed, so people at least had to sign a register before they could buy bags of arsenic. And they put an age limit on buying it too. Obviously under-age people still bought it, just like the corner shop near school lets me buy cigarettes, but at least there was a law—'

'You shouldn't smoke,' said Lili. 'But listen, Gretchen. Can you get to the point? What's this got to do with the letters?'

'Just *listen*,' Gretchen snapped. 'William Peavy went around poor neighbourhoods and tried to educate people about how easy it was to poison your family when you had a bag of arsenic around.

'He told them how to spot the symptoms of arsenic exposure – burning skin, hallucinations, confusion. And about all the different things made with arsenic that could be deadly in the wrong hands.'

'Such as?'

'Cleaning products. Use the wrong cleaner to scrub your walls or floors in a tiny lodging house, and you could kill your whole family. Peavy had a laboratory at home where he ran the tests, and he had bag-loads of confiscated arsenic from traders in his cellar. Out of harm's way. His lab found arsenic in beer. And wallpaper.

'For a while, arsenic was used to dye wallpaper green. Anyone who lived in a house with green wallpaper got sick. Really sick. Some people died. Did you ever read a book called *The Emerald Peril*?'

'No. Gretchen, what's the point of all this?'

'He wrote it in eighteen fifty-nine,' said Gretchen. 'His first book about arsenic. But he wrote loads more – stories about arsenic being mistaken for flour and all sorts. Poor people read his books – he was one of the first authors working-class people actually read. They say his books saved thousands of lives. Stopped a whole load of accidental deaths.'

'Okay, Gretchen, this is all fascinating—'

'Just *listen*. This book, *The Arsenic Saviour*, documents all the things Peavy did to save the poor from arsenic, and it mentions a visit he made to the Morgan family, who *had previously been in his employment*. And they had a son called James.'

'Let me see.' Lili took the book from Gretchen, opening it where a page had been dogeared, and some text highlighted.

When Peavy learned that two former servants of his, Mr and Mrs Morgan, had a sickly infant, he was greatly concerned and announced his intention to visit them immediately.

The Morgan infant, a baby of two months, was said to be covered in a livid red rash and 'screaming morning, noon and night'. Doctors tried and failed to treat the condition, and no amount of bathing eased the infant's discomfort. The child's mother had syphilis, and so it was assumed the baby had been born with the disease and was therefore a hopeless case.

On Peavy's arrival, Mrs Morgan refused the great man entry to her home, saying she would take no charity. However, Peavy insisted on seeing the infant and immediately concluded that arsenic was causing the distress. He asked to take the baby's clothes, bedding and other articles for chemical testing.

It was soon discovered that a lavender soap used to wash the baby contained arsenic. The mother admitted to stealing the soap after a doctor insisted her infant, already sickly with syphilis, should be washed regularly to treat his skin sores.

The soap was destroyed and gradually baby James recovered, although his ribcage and legs were malformed due to the syphilis infection. Without Mr Peavy's intervention it is likely yet another unfortunate child would have died.

Other households were warned about the soap and countless lives saved.

'Wow,' said Lili.

'I know. Just think – William Peavy saved the life of your great, great, great grandad.'

'Love didn't want to let Peavy in the house. That's odd, don't you think?'

'Maybe she didn't want the neighbours talking.'

Shrieking female voices came from the foyer.

'Oh shit.' Lili looked towards the ticket office and saw a group of women wearing peacock feathers, short skirts and wedding veils – a hen party, if ever there was one. 'The audience are arriving and I'm not even dressed.' She looked at Gretchen. 'Can I take those papers?'

'No way. I don't trust you to look after *anything* any more. Do you have a photocopier here?'

'Yes, but – Gretchen I'm running really late.'

'You either want them or you don't.'

'Fine.' Lili checked her watch again. 'Great. I'll make a copy. The show will just have to wait.'

50

Life's a Stage by Lili Allure

Lili Allure's guide to burlesque etiquette

Burlesque girls are usually all good friends. We treat each other well because there are enough people who treat us badly. Here's my guide to etiquette when working with other performers:

- *Never apply silicone spray on stage, no matter how bad the dressing-room facilities are. It makes a slippery film on the floor that is lethal for ladies in high heels.*
- *Always share everything backstage. Champagne, pastie glue, sewing kit and disaster stories.*
- *If you're the star of the show, remember you're no more important than anyone else. The lighting guy, your backing dancers, the cleaner . . . they're all just as crucial as you, even though your name tops the bill. Be a diva and your career won't last long; be humble and you'll be loved.*
- *Turn up to all rehearsals, no matter how tired/busy/hungover you are, and even if you personally have done the routine a million times. It shows respect for the people you're working with and that's vital if you want to last in this business.*

In the dressing room, Bryony and the girls gave cordial 'hellos', but Lili sensed their concern. If the big star couldn't turn up to rehearsal, what did that say about the show?

'Look, girls—'

Orchestra music played above them and the dancers took last glances in the mirror, then hurried past Lili up to the stage.

'Break a leg,' Lili called after them, but no one answered.

Lili stripped naked, hanging her dress, stockings and suspenders on her clothes rail. She knew she should be focusing on the show, running through routines in her mind, but Gretchen's news, as usual, meant her thoughts were elsewhere.

The great William Peavy saved the life of one of my relatives. Weird. And maybe he had an affair with Love. Even weirder. Are the yellow letters something to do with William Peavy?

G-string.

Lili unclipped the string underwear, sewn with ice-blue Swarovski crystals, from a hanger. She pulled the jewel-covered thong between her buttocks.

Some performers sewed rhinestones to the waistband of their G-strings, but that simply wasn't dazzling enough for Lili.

She wanted the fire of Swarovski crystals, and the blaze that came from attaching them to every centimetre of her underwear. Whenever she bent, turned or stepped, the audience saw glistening crystals.

Her pursuit of glamour came at a price. The crystals felt like little rocks against her skin, and pinched and pulled as she moved.

Love and Tom's son nearly died of arsenic poisoning. And then Love did die of arsenic poisoning. And William Peavy wrote about people dying of arsenic poisoning, and tested things for arsenic . . .

Pasties.

Lili took a Godiva chocolate box labelled 'Snow Queen' from a metal shelf and slid off the lid. Two snowflake-shaped pasties winked and sparkled inside the box from a bed of blue tissue paper.

Sewn with clear and ice-blue crystals, the pasties were intricately cut like the most delicate of lace. But they weren't delicate. As she picked them out the box, Lili felt the hard nodules of dried glue on the rough buckram backing.

She squeezed a coating of adhesive over glue lumps and stuck the pasties in place, high up and centred for the most flattering bust.

Who would be trying to frighten me about the letters? Lili thought. *Someone related to William Peavy? Or someone in my own family?* Then a malevolent voice said: *But only you saw those text messages and the writing on the mirror. Who's to say you're not seeing things?*

Corset.

Blue silk and silver laces. Lili needed help to tighten the corset to 19 inches at the waist, but there was no one around. Today she'd have to let it all hang out at 21 inches. She stepped into the corset, tightened it and waited. After a few moments she tightened it some more.

I need to find who has Mum's mobile phone. Ben thought it could still be at the flat.

Gown.

A blue gown of net and chiffon, sewn with silver snowflakes, hung on the rail, and Lili slid it from its hanger and pulled it up over soft, curved hips. Fastening it with two snowflake pins at the shoulders, she pouted at the mirror and applied another coat of lipstick.

I will find those letters. No matter what. And these disappearing text messages. If I find whoever's sending them, I might find out where the letters are. Or at least why Mum was looking for them.

Shoes.

Lili's heels were more than just high – they were Monument. With a slight platform at the front, the shoes stopped just shy of throwing her forward onto her face and every inch of them was covered in blue crystals.

Okay. I'll search Mum's flat for her mobile phone. No stone unturned. Tonight. After the show is finished.

Crown.

This was the agonising part. Lili had a crown specially made by her milliner, and it weighed the best part of four pounds. Wearing it hurt and, as soon as she put it on, all she could think about was taking it off. But that was show business.

The audience didn't have a clue, behind Lili's Vaseline smile, that she was in pain a great deal of the time.

The orchestra died down and Lili knew it was nearly her cue. *Showtime*.

51

It was gone midnight by the time Lili arrived at Viv's flat. The tower block was silent and dark. Lili's footsteps went *smack, smack, smack*, as she climbed the dark steps. The sound echoed around the black windows and grey concrete walls.

Viv's front door looked beaten and sorry for itself. It swung open with a long whine.

Lili fumbled for the light switch, but two short clicks told her the electricity had gone. Maybe the electricity company had cut off the flat, or maybe the meter had run out of credit.

She hovered on the threshold, smelling the familiarity of her mother's hallway – the sweetness of alcohol mixed with food, vanilla perfume, damp and cigarettes. It smelt like her mum, she realised, and felt a lump in her throat.

A memory came: Viv pulling Lili and Darren into her tobacco-y bosom and gripping them so tightly, as if she was scared they'd get away.

The dark flat beckoned.

Behind her, the front door creaked shut, thinning out the light from the stairwell. Then it clicked into its latch, throwing the flat into moonlit shadows.

Lili tried the kitchen light, just in case, but it didn't work. Nor did the lounge light or the light in Viv's bedroom. In the kitchen, she felt the greasy outline of the electricity meter, but she didn't have any pound coins.

Viv had candles in the house somewhere, Lili was sure of it. They'd be in the kitchen cupboard, under the leaking sink. Blue mould had already been growing there when Lili left; she wondered at the state of the cupboard eighteen years later.

Flicking her lighter, Lili followed the shaky flame to the sink in the kitchen. She felt edgy.

'*HISSSS*. Ha.'

Lili jumped and the lighter burned her little finger.

What was that?

The noise had been just behind her shoulder. She took a deep breath and turned. Shadows swarmed over each other and became looming monsters. Lili nearly screamed, but then everything was still and Lili knew the monsters were just a trick of the light.

But that noise . . . it had come from somewhere in the flat, Lili was sure of it.

There was a rustling, like fabric rubbing together.

Lili bit her lip.

'If someone's there,' she called out, 'you shouldn't be. This is my mum's flat.'

Silence.

She waited a moment, but the silence remained. Still, the air felt alive.

Lili threw open the cupboard under the sink, the flame a blue-and-yellow jelly in her shaking hand.

There was an almighty clatter and Lili gasped and bit her tongue as objects tumbled out.

Okay, okay. Calm down.

All manner of things were now on the kitchen floor – packets of soap, body spray, stacks of shoe polish in every colour imaginable, a single sock with a hole in it . . .

Lili reached into the cupboard and felt around one-handed, touching something slimy, then something sharp, then something that rustled.

She pulled out a box of plastic-wrapped fire lighters.

For the barbecue Mum was planning in her balcony-less, garden-less, high-rise flat.

She rummaged further and found a teddy bear in a box.

For the grandchildren neither I nor Darren had given her.

And then . . . candles. Five bundles of them in different sizes and fragrances. She lit one of the fatter ones and the cheap scent of fake vanilla wafted into the kitchen. Viv loved vanilla. She used to say it smelled like chocolate.

As Lili stood up to the level of the kitchen counter, something caught her eye.

All along the counter were smashed shards of crockery – a bumpy layer of chocolate-brown saucers, plates and cups all beaten to pieces.

Lili blinked at split saucers, broken plates and stray cup handles. She put a hand to her mouth.

I wanted to do that. I wanted to smash up all mum's crockery when I first saw the flat. Did I . . . ?

Stepping back, she bumped into the cooker and let out a shriek. The cooker was hot. Not warm. Hot.

Okay, okay, okay.

Lili left the kitchen, white wax dripping on her hand.

Get out of here, get out of here, a voice screamed.

There was another shuffling sound, and this time it was right beside her. Lili looked at the grease-stained hallway wall.

'Whoever is here, you'd better leave,' Lili shouted. 'Now.'

Silence.

'Get out,' she said, looking into the lounge. She threw open her mother's bedroom door. No one.

There was only one room left to try. Lili's old bedroom.

The door was shut tight, and the bulky stainless steel bolt on the outside had been slid into place.

Lili ran it open.

She put a hand against the nicotine-stained gloss paint and the candle flickered. She paused, noticing the grubby marks of old ET stickers by the handle. Seeing her bedroom again . . . she'd be opening more than just a door.

Someone could be hiding in there.

The anger resurfaced. Pushing hard, Lili felt resistance. Her mind raced with images of monsters and dead bodies, but she shook them away and put her shoulder against the chipboard.

Managing to scrape open half a metre of space, she saw boxes. No intruder. No monster. No dead body.

Lili let out a breath she didn't know she'd been holding.

The bedroom was a wall of shadowy cardboard and plastic. Boxes and tubs towered over her from the top bunk.

It had been cramped when Lili and her brother lived here, but that was nothing to how it was now. Viv's hoarding really had got out of control.

Under the towers of cardboard and plastic, Lili could see the shape of the room she and Darren grew up in. The bunk beds, the thin window and a few games and clothes from long ago poking out from under the bed.

In a strange way, it was a relief that boxes concealed most of the floor. They hid a life Lili didn't want to remember.

I always thought I'd come a long way since I lived here, thought Lili. There had been no room to breathe back then. She and Darren used to hang clothes from the top bunk because there was no room for a wardrobe, and games and shoes had covered the half metre of floor.

Yet now Lili slept among piles of things, drinking every night and sleeping all day. *Just like Mum.*

Under one of the bunk beds she saw the corner of a shoebox, covered in little diamanté stickers. 'Oh my God, Mum. You kept it.' The words sounded weird in the silence. She pulled the box from under the bed.

Dust had worked its way between the shiny stickers, which she'd bought from the 50p stall at Petticoat Lane market. She slid off the lid, and couldn't help smiling at the pages of folded magazine articles, fabric clippings and photographs inside. It was her memory box, from a younger Lili she'd thought long gone.

Look at all this stuff. These old photos – I look so young! I never realised my skin was so good. And my figure . . . and Jimmy and Carly, I'd forgotten about them. And Simon.

She unfolded magazine pages of dresses she'd loved but couldn't afford. Now she could afford them all, she didn't love them that much.

A very old showbill caught her eye.

Sensational Dynamite Dolly performs the Dance of the Seven Veils.

Lili laughed, turning over a black and white photograph of a beautiful, glaring woman with thin eyebrows and dark lips, wearing a fur stole.

'My great grandma Dolly,' she said. 'My role model. The burlesque performer.'

52

Life's a Stage, by Lili Allure

Lili Allure's history of burlesque

Now, please don't look at me like that. History doesn't have to be boring. Anyway, I won't talk about it for long. I just want to point out that burlesque is nothing new.

My great-grandmother, Dolly Morgan, was a burlesque performer back in the 1930s – and burlesque wasn't all that new then either.

'Dynamite' Dolly, as she was known, lived at a time when women set their hair every day, married at eighteen and baked pies for their husbands. Burlesque was rather daring – and big business. Most men were lucky to see their wives naked, let alone get a prolonged gawp at a beautiful stranger in the nearly nude.

Dynamite Dolly performed in 1930s America, when glamorous ladies stripped to a live orchestra, and 'waist-cincher' corsets were all the rage. Burlesque theatres were packed night after night, and big-name striptease artists like Dolly were at the top of the bill.

In the US, burlesque (sort of) began when lovely ladies were employed to strut around the stage during comedy-show set changes to keep the audience from getting bored. Some bright spark soon worked out that these ladies were often more popular than the shows. So they started giving women centre stage, and gradually the comedy acts slid down the show bill.

When burlesque first came along – nearly 100 years ago now – it wasn't the fancy-schmancy posh night out it is today. There were no three-course meals. People paid a few bucks for a night of comedy, a tub of popcorn and a lady taking her clothes off. Who could ask for more?

'You met Dynamite Dolly once, didn't you, Mum?' Lili addressed the shoebox. 'But you said she wasn't keen on meeting her grandkids. And she was always on the road. Even when you were living in the States, you didn't see her much.'

Lili tapped the photograph. 'And she didn't marry, I remember that. This guy,' she pulled out a picture of Dolly on stage, with a man waiting in the wings, 'he was the stagehand she had kids with. Tony. But she didn't want to settle down. So the children took her name – Morgan – and she sent them off to England to live with her parents. I guess those parents must have been Michael Morgan and his wife.'

She took the showbill, careful not to tear the powdery old paper.

For One Week Only, read the showbill, *on Her Sell-out American Tour*.

The bill was for the Empire Burlesk Theatre in Newark, and in the picture Dolly looked old and a little on the saggy side. She sat on a brown trunk, one leg kicked in the air, holding a veil over her mouth.

'One-trunk Dolly,' said Lili, smiling at the paper. 'She used to travel everywhere with it, didn't she? They called her one-trunk Dolly, because she only ever needed one piece of luggage. Of course, she made sure it was a good piece of Louis Vuitton, if I remember right.'

Lili's phone rang from her bag and the showbill jumped in her hand. She slid her Nokia from the silk lining, expecting to see Pete's number and mentally cursing him for calling at such a stupid time.

But it wasn't Pete.

The low green glow of the phone lit Lili's gloved hand, and her whole arm started to shake.

Viv Morgan was calling her.

Lili slowly brought the phone to her ear and pressed the answer button.

'*Stay away*,' whispered a voice. There was a hiss and a pop. Then the line went dead.

Lili backed out of the room, hitting the 'recent calls' button and seeing Viv Morgan's number, clear as could be.

Someone needs to see this.

She stumbled over lumps of clothing and boxes, and knocked stray bottles as she manoeuvred along the hallway. The candle fluttered from her bedroom.

Who? Who can I show?

The tower block was sleeping. She could knock on a door, any door, and ask whoever answered to read the message, but knowing the neighbourhood she doubted anyone would answer the door past midnight. Most windows and doors had bars on them – her mum's flat was one of the few which hadn't 'modernised' with wrought-iron grilles.

Gretchen was in the flat below, but there was no way Lili would get her in trouble by knocking so late. However, Gretchen's bedroom was right below Lili's old bedroom. The windows were on the same stretch of concrete.

Keeping her eyes on the phone and pressing buttons so the screen stayed glowing, Lili stumbled back to her old room.

The narrow floor space, where Lili used to iron her school shirts, was stacked with plastic crates of odds and ends. For a moment Lili thought she couldn't reach the window. Then she leaned forward and just managed to grab the catch and push.

Cold air rushed in and the candle wavered and nearly blew out.

Lili checked her mobile phone again. The message was still there.

Taking a plastic rabbit from a crate, Lili dropped the toy down so it struck the window below.

There was a clunk, then silence, then a gentle *creak, creak*, and Lili held her breath. She looked down and saw Gretchen's head poking out of the window.

'*Gretchen,*' she hissed. '*Up here.*'

'Who is it?' The sleepy teenager turned her head upwards. She smiled as she saw Lili. 'I knew you'd come! How did you know?'

'Know what?'

'Hold on,' said Gretchen. 'I'll come up.'

'No,' whispered Lili, feeling goosebumps on her arms. 'I'll come out and meet you. See you on the stairwell.'

Cold as it was outside, Lili felt nothing but relief to leave the flat. She'd been a fool to come at night. *What am I trying to prove? I'll search tomorrow. In daylight. And I'll phone the police and tell them someone's been in the flat.*

She closed the door firmly behind her.

'What's with the midnight visit?' Gretchen's face peered around the concrete steps.

'I was looking for something.' Lili held out her phone. 'Tell me I'm not going mad. You can see I got a call from Mum's phone, right?'

'What? Where?'

Lili looked at her phone. There were calls from Pete, Annette, a few of the dancers . . . but nothing from Viv Morgan. The call record simply wasn't there. A chill ran from her shoulders to her toes.

'Wait – is this about those text messages you thought *I* was sending you?' said Gretchen. She wore candy-striped pyjamas and a dressing gown that said 'Cute' on the lapel. There were pink rabbit slippers on her feet.

'Sort of.' Lili sat on the step and put her head in her hands.

Gretchen sat beside her. 'So – you didn't come to ask me what I'd found out?'

Lili sighed. 'No.'

'There's something I need to tell you, then. William Peavy wrote letters to someone who lived in Whitechapel. One of them had a poem in it, about Camelot. Written on yellow paper.'

'What?' asked Lili.

'His private letters were always written on yellow paper. I found that out today. And one of his servants used to deliver them. When you said about the psychic guy saying Love and Peavy had an affair, it got me thinking. So I started looking for stuff about how he might have cheated on his wife.

'It's hard finding anything bad about Peavy at all. Everyone makes him out to be a saint. All the bookshops and libraries were like, Peavy was a happily married man, he never had an affair, you won't find a book saying anything of the sort. And there was nothing online either.

'But on the way home, I stopped in this old secondhand book shop, and there was a nineteen seventies out-of-print book called *The Secret Life of William Peavy*. It really tears into his private life, saying his wife was miserable and he had an unhappy marriage.

'And it talks about sending Ann Hadley, his housekeeper, to Whitechapel to deliver letters.'

'Really? What – he couldn't trust the post?'

'Not if he was sending something *really* private. But get this. Ann Hadley read the letters, and wrote to her sister saying she'd never reveal the contents to anyone. But she said there was a poem in one of them about King Arthur. And the letters were on YELLOW PAPER.'

'He was sending secret letters to someone in Whitechapel on yellow paper?' said Lili. 'With poems in them. Do you think these could be the letters we're looking for?'

There was the eerie squeak of a door being opened below them, and Gretchen jumped.

'Gret-chen! Gret-chen!' It was Carol. She sounded on the verge of hysteria.

'Oh shit.' Gretchen got to her feet. 'It's Mum.'

'GRET-CHEN!' Carol was really wailing now, and Lili saw the flash of a torch beam below.

Gretchen went to the stairs.

'Tell me quickly,' Lili hissed. 'Please.'

'Yes. I think so.' Gretchen looked over the staircase. 'These yellow letters. The ones Viv was looking for. I think they're love letters from Peavy to Love Morgan. I think they prove, once and for all, that his Camelot poems were really written to a servant and not his wife. Which means they're worth a lot of money.'

There was a clip-clop below as Carol climbed the stairs.

'I really better go,' said Gretchen. She vanished into torch beam and shadow.

53

Viv's front door looked no cheerier in the morning light, especially
as rain tumbled from a grey sky. Lili felt for the front-door key
and beside her PC Maureen Fletcher paused to get her breath
back.

'Six floors and . . . lift out of order,' Maureen panted.

'The oven wasn't just warm,' Lili said, inserting the key, 'it was
hot.'

'I heard you the first time.' Maureen was making no secret of
the fact she'd rather be elsewhere. 'Well, let's take a look.'

They opened the door, letting slicing winds race along the
hallway.

'The cups and plates were in the sink when you let me in last
time,' said Lili, leading Maureen into the kitchen. 'But someone's
smashed them up on the counter—'

They both looked at the kitchen counter. It was empty, except
for a few of Viv's usual stray items: a packet of tights, two dirty
mugs and a broken fake-gold watch.

'This counter?' said Maureen.

'But it wasn't . . . last night . . . everything was all smashed
up . . .'

Maureen looked at her kindly. 'You know, sometimes death—'

'The cups and plates were *there*,' Lili murmured. 'In pieces.
I'm sure . . .'

'I can still refer you to a counsellor—'

'I'm all right.' Lili decided not to mention last night's disappearing phone call.

'Well.' Maureen patted her on the shoulder. 'I should be getting back. What are your plans – don't stay here long, will you? On your own.'

'I will for a little bit,' Lili admitted. 'I need to search for Mum's mobile.'

'Ah yes . . . the disappearing text messages. My money's on that phone turning up in this lot somewhere.'

'I could ring it,' said Lili. 'I mean, while we're in the flat. Then you'd see it's not here. I'm not making this up – someone's taken it.'

Lili took out her phone and dialled the number.

They both listened, and heard the faintest sound of Viv's favourite song – *Staying Alive* by the Bee Gees.

'Do you hear that?' said Maureen. 'A phone ringing. Nearby.' She took Lili's phone and walked from room to room. 'Very faint, though. Sounds like it's coming from *outside* the flat, if anywhere. Probably buried under something.'

Abruptly, the faint ringing stopped. 'It's gone to answer machine now.'

'Right.' Lili looked at the boxes, the nicotine-stained walls – anywhere but into Maureen's eyes. 'So it's here somewhere.'

'Keep ringing. I'm sure you'll track it down.' Maureen passed the phone back to her, and Lili was grateful she didn't say 'I told you so'.

'You know, love, the inquest will be coming up in a month or so. Often, people are, how can I put it, *restless* before it's all done and dusted. How are you feeling right now?'

'Oh. You know. Like someone's taken out my heart and replaced it with razors. Wanting to kill someone half the time, and the other half just wanting the pain to go away.'

'Time heals all wounds. Well, I best be going.'

As Maureen left, Lili looked at the cupboard and shuddered. The flat felt even more unfriendly as the front door banged shut, and Lili realised she was afraid. Not of the flat or ghosts, but herself.

Lili pulled boxes aside, peered between them, opened and closed drawers and felt down the sides of the sofa. No phone.

I'll ring it again, Lili thought, pulling out her mobile and dialling.

Viv's old number rang immediately, and once again there was tingly music, so faint as to be other-wordly. It seemed to be coming from the floor, if anywhere. Lili strained to listen.

Ring, ring. Ring, ring. Click.

'Buon giorno.'

Viv's voice.

Lili's heart pounded. She smelt stale wine.

'There are plenty of frogs out there, but not many princes,' Viv said, her voice slurred and tired. 'So if you're a prince, leave a message.'

There was a beep. The answer machine. Of course.

Hearing Viv's voice after so many years was a shock. A frightened, sick feeling churned inside and Lili thought she felt tears. But she didn't cry. She couldn't. Not while she was so angry with Viv.

She carried on searching, periodically ringing the phone and listening. At first, the ringing seemed to be coming from under her, but then the sound grew fainter and moved towards the front of the building. Then it cut out altogether and went straight to answer machine. Lili supposed she'd used up the battery.

Several hours later, covered in dust and a sticky something or other, Lili surveyed the mounds of boxes. She'd searched barely a quarter of them. The whole flat would take days, weeks.

'I won't stop looking for the letters,' she told the empty flat. 'I'll do whatever it takes. There's no way back now. I won't end up like you, Mum.'

54

Life's a Stage by **Lili Allure**

Lili's London: Spitalfields Market

Old Spitalfields Market sits between Brick Lane and Liverpool Street, dividing the sleek, glass windows of Liverpool Street's high-rise offices from the rough and tumble flats of Whitechapel.

Years ago, before London ate up the countryside and became one great, smoking city, Spitalfields used to be Spittal Fields – green fields on the outskirts of the city. Now those fields are long gone, and the outskirts have shifted miles east, burying Spitalfields in a maze of buildings.

Serious on one side, fun on the other, Old Spitalfields Market is a bridge between work and play. The market itself lives in a clear-roofed warehouse, with a fancy brick arch on the east side. Londoners of every income and persuasion crowd the stalls come Sunday morning. They have done for hundreds of years.

Ian Batty sat on a wooden picnic bench by a Mexican food stand, a half-eaten chilli taco by his elbow. He clasped the hands of a dishevelled, grey-haired lady who sat opposite. The woman gazed at him, tears in her eyes.

Lili had arranged to meet Ian at Spitalfields Market at noon, but clearly he was in the middle of an appointment with someone else.

She waited by a homemade, organic soap stall, watching impatiently. It was tempting to march over and demand Ian speak to her, but the dishevelled lady looked so needy, so enraptured by Ian, that she held back.

After a few moments, the woman's face softened and a huge smile made apples of her cheeks.

'*Thank you*,' Lili heard her say. '*And God bless.*'

When the lady walked away, Lili cut through the crowds.

'You're running late,' she told Ian.

'My dear, I'm so sorry,' he said, brushing taco shell from his purple and green paisley shirt. 'You *are* right. I despise lateness. My consultation did indeed overrun, but the lady I was seeing arrived a little late herself and . . . well, I can't cut a consultation short when a client needs my help and love.'

'I've got something for you,' said Lili, pushing forward the papers she'd copied from Gretchen.

'Ah! Some new information for the spirits to digest. Tiny writing, though.' Ian took the pages and balanced a pair of red-framed glasses on his nose. 'Yes . . . yes. *Most* interesting. And so very sad. So many children died in those days. Thank heavens baby James survived, or you wouldn't be here today. And all thanks to William Peavy, well, well, well.'

'Do you think Love will speak to us again?' Lili asked.

'She may,' said Ian. 'But my dear – do you understand why I've arranged to meet you here this morning?'

'There's lots of life around?' Lili guessed. 'Like the park – plenty of people going back and forth? The spirits like being around the living.'

Ian shook his head.

'I don't know then,' said Lili. 'Why?'

'Well. We're rather near your mother's flat, aren't we? And I feel *certain* that your mother wants to come through today. I felt it as soon as you called. That's why I arranged to meet here. Near her old home. Viv has things she needs to say to you.'

'I'm here to talk to Love,' said Lili.

'But your mother—'

'No,' Lili interrupted. 'That's not how I want to do things.'

'Very well.' Ian flexed his fingers. 'In that case, let's talk about you for a moment.'

'Ian—'

'We have to warm up the spirits one way or another.'

'But I brought you—'

'My dear.' Ian held up a hand. 'I don't tell you how to do *your* job. Now. Your house manager, *Carolyn* I believe her name was. We had a little chat when I came to your theatre, and she divulged something most interesting.'

'What?'

'She said before you arrived at Kate Hamilton's, you were touring all over the world, but then a friend let you down and you haven't toured since.'

Lili frowned. 'Carol-Ann has a big mouth.'

'She cares about you. Tell me about this friend.'

'Friend?' Lili laughed. 'That so-called friend stole my whole act. My career, really. Carol-Ann's right – I stopped touring after it happened. It's funny. Since Mum's suicide . . . it's like the curtain's come up and I see myself. I've been hiding away, feeling angry. I don't want to do that any more. It's time to let go.'

'Stole your act?'

'There's this rule in burlesque shows – whoever owns the props owns the act. I spent years designing all my acts, putting shows together, building props. But my manager paid for everything, so technically, he owned the props and my show.

'Then he and my backing dancer, Janey, got together, and one day the two of them and all the props vanished. I got an answer machine message saying the show legally belonged to my manager – who was now my ex-manager – and Janey was performing in my place. That was that. No more show for me. I got a solicitor, but there was nothing he could do. Years of hard work down the drain.'

'Very insightful.' Ian adjusted his hat. 'Shall we go for a walk? We're very near the streets where Love used to live. Her spirit will be easier to contact if we're walking her neighbourhood. The spirit world needs many bridges.'

As Lili and Ian walked up Shoreditch High Street, Ian spread his arms and turned full circle.

'Can you feel the history of this street?' he asked, ignoring the odd looks he was getting from passersby. 'It used to hold a marketplace years ago, back in Love's day. This street was what separated the Nichol slum from the City itself.'

'The Nichol slum where Love lived?'

'Yes,' said Ian. 'We'll be there soon. Of course the slum isn't there any more. No, no. It's all nice houses . . . some ex-council, some private, but everyone doing very nicely, thank you very much.

'That public house over there.' Ian pointed to the Ten Bells pub, next to the huge white steeple of Christ Church Spitalfields. 'It was frequented by slum dwellers and prostitutes. You know all about Jack the Ripper, I take it? Some of his victims drank in that pub.'

They walked further north, past Shoreditch station, and Ian led Lili down a series of leafy roads.

'Ah! Here. This is Old Nichol Street,' he announced, stopping in the middle of the road. 'The centre of the old slum. This is where Love and your family used to live.'

The street looked innocent enough, with tarmac pavements, modernised Victorian brick buildings and some new builds of glass and steel. The bare branches of trees hung over the quiet road. It looked like a lovely place to live.

'Some of the slum buildings remain,' said Ian, patting a wall. 'These very bricks have seen entire families living in one room, plaster coming from the walls, damp all year round. Starvation. Disease. These were black, winding streets back then. Nothing like today.

'Hungry slum children would run out from the Nichol like little mice, steal food from the market place, then tear back to their bare lodgings. Few traders would follow them into the Nichol maze.'

Ian closed his eyes. 'Are you there, my dear?' He smiled. 'Yes! Love is here. Love, my dear . . . you sound out of breath. Oh goodness. She's running. Why are you running?'

55

Ian started breathing faster. 'She is running from a policeman. She has her baby in a bundle of rags at her chest.' He wrapped his arms around his middle. 'But her skirts are too heavy to run fast. She is tripping as she runs over the cobbles. What's in there, my dear? Oh, I see! Two sausage rolls and a bar of soap. She has stolen food and soap and put them in the cloth with the baby.

'A policeman is shouting after her, running too. People on the streets see Love – one of their own – and step aside. Someone trips the policeman and he stumbles, but keeps running. It's dusk. He carries a bull light and wears a heavy cape, but he is fit enough and well fed and gains by the minute.

'Every one of us here is starving, Love shouts. A day at a time. My baby is sick, his sores need washing. And we need food. My neighbour died last week, starved to death. I saw her body, all skin and bone. She died alone and hungry, like all of us will.

'Love is slowing now. She can't hear the policeman behind her and thinks maybe he gave up the chase rather than venture too far into the Nichol. She leans against a wall and gets her breath back.

'If he catches me he'll tell me *the church gives charity*, she tells me. Charity! Judgement, more like. Those women with their husbands and houses and servants. They don't give to the likes of me. They know I'm beyond saving. I go along regular to see what charity I can get, but they give nothing to me, only gruel to children who'll go to their Sunday school.

'Love hears footsteps and heavy breathing. The policeman still gives chase. She pulls herself from the wall and carries on running.

'He is gaining now, and Love is labouring under the weight of her baby and heavy clothes. He is only feet away, but she keeps running. If he catches her, she is done for this time. She is sorry to have sunk so low as common street theft, but needs must.

'She only wishes she would not get caught, because her baby will die if she goes to prison. After so many stillborns and her daughter dying not two years ago, that would be worse than death.

'The policeman grabs her arm, but she is strong. She pulls away. And then . . . a door opens. She runs through it. A gate is opened too. Then another door. People turn from the policeman and close doors and gates in his path. A bucket of muck is thrown at his feet.

'You are one of us now Love, say the looks of those on the street. We don't have much, but we look after each other.

'Love passes through a doorway, straight through a house and through an open gate.

'Thief! shouts the policeman. Stop her or I'll arrest the whole lot of you!

'But the Nichol know the policeman can't arrest them all. Smiles are shared as Love slowly but surely loses her pursuer in the warren of passages that open for her, but close against the man who doesn't belong.

'God will judge you, the policeman shouts after her.

'There's no God in the Nichol, Love shouts back. You only need walk these streets to see that.

'When she knows he's given up the chase, Love falls, exhausted, into the Victory pub. Tall Sal is behind the bar.

'Sal, let me rest here a while, she says. I've sunk so low I see no way out of the Nichol. James is my only reason for living, but he won't survive the winter on a few thieved sausage rolls. Lord help me. If I didn't have James, I'd throw myself in the Thames. William Peavy, God have mercy on his soul, has given me this child, so I suppose truly he is my saviour.'

Ian opened his eyes and stared at a brick archway filled with glass. He let out a sigh and his shoulders slumped. 'She will tell me no more.'

'You think James was William Peavy's child?' Lili asked. 'Ian . . . please. Try and remember. Did Mum tell you that?'

Ian pressed his lips together. 'Perhaps, but I don't really recall. My memory. I share what the spirits share with me. I can't speculate as to their exact meaning. It matters little where information comes from – only whether it's useful to us.'

'But do you think . . . perhaps if Love had an affair with William Peavy . . . Gretchen found a letter from one of his servants. It said William Peavy visited the Morgans at home. After they left his employment. And one of his servants delivered yellow letters to someone in Whitechapel.'

'It wouldn't be the first time the master of the house had improper relations with a servant,' said Ian.

A car accelerated towards them and Lili and Ian headed for the pavement.

'If they had an affair,' said Lili, 'and Love was pregnant with his child and the yellow letters prove it, that really is a big deal. That would make us direct descendants of William Peavy.'

'Indeed.'

'His estate must be worth thousands. His books still sell.' Lili watched a young, hungover couple gaze queasily at a curry stall. 'The spirits won't say for sure if Love had a child by William Peavy?'

'I can never say anything for sure,' said Ian. 'The lines between here and the spirit world are crackly at the best of times.'

Lili gave him a long, hard stare. 'I need facts. Answers.'

'Lili, my dear,' said Ian. '*I* only want to help you. You do understand that, don't you?'

'But I don't know if you are helping me,' said Lili. 'That's the trouble. Gretchen's been getting servants' letters from the William Peavy Museum. They deal in facts, there. Reality. Maybe they can help me.'

She turned and walked away, west towards the centre of London. The museum was in Holborn, if she remembered correctly. Records of the past held just a few roads away from Covent Garden and Kate Hamilton's – her present and future.

56

Life's a Stage by Lili Allure

Lili Allure's guide to tassel twirling

It's what burlesque girls are famous for – the tassel twirl. If I had a pound for every time I've been asked how to twirl tassels, I'd be drinking champagne every night instead of cava.

Every burlesque performer worth her salt has a pair of tasselled pasties and can spin them in any direction she fancies, whether she's upright or even hanging upside down. I'm no exception.

For my Snow Queen show, I wanted to tassel twirl while spinning in my hoop. Not easy! It took months of practice to make that particular twirl look effortless, but I always put the hours in for my audience. After all, when you come to my show you deserve the very best, don't you think?

I can twirl with the best of them. However, a basic tassel twirl isn't as tricky as it looks. There are dozens of different ways to bump your breasts and set your tassels in motion, but here's a simple one for beginners.

Put your arms above your head and bounce on the balls of your feet. After a few bounces, your tassels will be twirling. Simple!

It didn't take Lili long to find Bethnal Green Road. Buses charged past the pound shops and tatty newsagents. She couldn't see any taxis around, but there was a bus stop ahead.

As she got closer, she froze.

On the side of the bus stop was a full-sized poster advertising Lili's show, *The Snow Queen Striptease*. There was nothing strange about that in itself – Lili posed in adverts all over London, corseted, pouting, legs stretched in the air. But this particular advert wasn't like the others.

It had been vandalised.

Lili looked closer.

On the scratched laminate covering the poster, someone had drawn a noose around Lili's neck, and a black tongue hanging from her mouth.

Down the side of the poster was written:

Lilian, I'm watching you.

Not Lili – the name she'd been known by, on and off the stage since she was a teenager. Lilian. The name her mum had given her. The name only her family knew her by.

No one calls me Lilian any more.

Lili felt sick. 'Who did this?' she heard herself say, and people on the street turned to stare.

The vandalism was so violent. So bloody. As if someone hated her.

I'm watching you.

Her footsteps were uncertain as she headed down Bethnal Green Road. The street and the people on it felt hostile. Malevolence buzzed from the pavement. She ducked down Brick Lane, thinking she was leaving the horrible, violent scribbles behind.

The vandalism, however, had only just begun.

Posters for her show, pasted near the Old Truman Brewery, were slashed, scribbled and ruined. Every one.

On the brick walls, Lili's face hung in tatters. Knives, nooses and chainsaws were drawn at strategic places, threatening to strangle and saw off limbs.

And those words again, scrawled on her snow-white cheekbones . . .

Lilian, I'm watching you.

The venom pouring from the walls nearly knocked her over.

Lili walked faster. She didn't want to be here any more, alone in East London. She wanted to scurry back to her theatre and never come out again.

Watery grey night was stealing the afternoon sky by the time Lili reached Kate Hamilton's. She wondered if summer would ever come – the short winter days seemed to have gone on for ever.

Men were carting lighting equipment back and forth at the stage-door entrance, so she went through the auditorium and found Pete on a stepladder adjusting the lights.

'Hey,' she said, hurrying onto the stage. 'I need to rehearse. Will you do the lights?'

As Lili spun inside a silver hoop, the spotlight created two perfect silver moons of her suspender-clad behind. When she dipped forward, the light focused on the tasselled pasties stuck to her breasts. They glittered and glowed under the white beam. She twirled the pasties left, then right, then left again in time to the music.

Maybe sometimes it's okay to hide away. I'm stuck. I feel angry. So what? No one can hurt me that way. I'll just do what I always do – perform until the pain goes away.

Finally, the spotlight reached her face and she swung back and forth, hair flowing, face tipped back, pouting and smiling at an imaginary audience.

'Don't take this the wrong way, but you look sort of . . . like you're holding back,' said Pete, as the hoop gently lowered Lili to the floor.

Lili tiptoed across the stage in bare feet. 'Holding back?' She thought of Carol-Ann and the audience cards.

'A little. So.' Pete lounged against a side curtain, a mug of tea at his feet. 'Are you going to talk to me?'

'Since when did we talk?' Lili picked up scattered clothing from around the stage. During the live show, Bryony scooped up dropped items, but during her solo rehearsal she had to keep a tight check on everything herself.

'Sometimes we do. When you're *really* drunk.'

'What should we talk about?' Lili picked up a stocking and scanned the stage for its partner. Even seemingly mundane items, like stockings, were expensive when you were Lili Allure and ordered the finest, hand-seamed hosiery from Paris. Everything had to be carefully accounted for, both during rehearsals and the shows themselves.

'Your mum.'

'Right.' Lili retrieved a glove. Audience members were the worst for taking stray gloves, especially in intimate venues like Kate's. Backing dancers earned their fees many times over by rescuing a hand-decorated lace, silk or velvet glove from drunken, grabby paws.

'I think you probably need to talk to someone,' said Pete, as Lili counted her costume pieces. 'Your act is suffering. It's hard to see someone so talented only do half of what she's capable of.'

'Someone defaced my posters,' Lili blurted out. She looked up, hoping Pete wouldn't think she was going mad. 'It wouldn't usually get to me, but . . . I don't know. There's a lot of things going on, and I feel like someone wants to stop me finding something really important.'

'What posters?' said Pete.

'In East London. Near my mum's.'

There was a pause.

'What a shitty thing to happen,' said Pete. 'Look, it was probably kids, but I'll get—'

'It wasn't kids,' said Lili. 'They wrote Lilian on the posters. Only family calls me that.'

'Should I call the police?' Pete asked, taking out a soft pack of Marlboro Reds and offering her one. The theatre was non-smoking, but when the audience weren't in, the chainsmoking cast and crew took no notice of the ban.

Lili slid a cigarette from the pack. 'The police already think I'm crazy. They'll have better things to do.' She accepted a light, inhaled and blew a thin line of smoke towards the ceiling.

'Is this something to do with the dressing room?' Pete asked.

'Maybe,' said Lili. 'But it's all right. I won't let those posters scare me. What's the time?'

'Four-thirty.'

Lili dropped her cigarette into Pete's tea mug, where it hissed and steamed. 'I'm going to get changed. There was somewhere I meant to go earlier. Thank God there's no show tonight. I think there's still time.'

Life's a Stage by Lili Allure

Lili's London: The William Peavy Museum

William Peavy's London townhouse on Bedford Square is still standing, more than a hundred years after the great man's death. The beautiful five-floor Georgian property, with towering chimney stacks and striped stone archways around the door, has been turned into a museum and research centre to celebrate Peavy's life and works.

As a property, it is worth millions, but as a piece of history it is priceless.

In the heart of bustling London and within walking distance of the theatres, Peavy's townhouse allowed him the metropolitan life he loved. He wrote many of his masterpieces sitting in a second-floor room at Bedford Square and watching 'all of London life pass by'.

Peavy's wife preferred the country and remained at Peavy's Hertfordshire estate, while William worked in London. The months of separation gave rise to the Camelot poems, which were published after his death, and are thought to speak of the anguish he felt at being apart from his wife and family.

On his death, Peavy donated the Bedford Square townhouse to the city of London. It is now a famous museum, maintained by Camden Council and open to visitors all year round. Original items relating to Peavy, such as clothing, furniture and original documents, are available for public view, and the museum is popular with researchers from all over the world.

★　★　★

A light snow fell as Lili stepped out of the cab at Bedford Square, dusting bare tree branches and clinging to black railings around the William Peavy museum.

Even though it was just gone five o'clock, night had fallen and soft yellow lights glowed behind the chequered museum windows.

Lili brushed snow from her coat and walked up stone steps, worn into curves by years of footfall. A gold plaque next to a huge black door read:

Here lived William Peavy, champion of the poor, saviour of the poisoned.

A sign on the door itself, next to the intricately carved silver doorknob, read:

The door and doorknob are originals. They have been restored and are now lovingly cared for. Please treat them gently.

Lili thought, *Love's and Tom's hands probably touched this door.* It was a strange thought. Maybe generations from now, her great, great, great-grandchildren would touch the doors of Kate Hamilton's and think of her.

She was about to push the door open when it swung inwards and an elderly woman with badly dyed, grey-brown hair appeared. She wore a bright green coat with yellow buttons and matching green-framed glasses.

'That's lucky,' said Lili. 'I thought maybe the museum was closed.'

The woman looked her up and down. 'Goodness, what are you wearing dear? Why would you bother with such an uncomfortable outfit in the age of elastic?' She pulled the door shut. 'The museum *is* closed. You'll have to come back tomorrow.'

'Please,' said Lili. 'You've been helping a friend of mine – Gretchen. And I wondered—'

'Gretchen! Oh, she's a lovely little thing, isn't she?' The woman took out a bunch of keys. 'So interested in history, and at such a young age. Yes, you tell her – I'm scanning letters for her as quickly as I can.' She inserted a key into a dead bolt and turned. 'As quickly as I can.'

'I wondered,' said Lili. 'Could I have a look at the letters you're scanning for Gretchen?'

'There won't be time for that – not tonight.' The woman shook keys at her. 'We're all volunteers here. We don't get paid overtime.'

Lili thought of the posters. 'It's *really* important. I won't take long.'

'You won't,' the woman agreed, 'because I'm closing up.'

'But you don't understand,' said Lili.

'I think it's you who's not understanding,' said the woman, folding her arms. 'I'm going home for my supper. We open tomorrow morning. Nine o'clock. If it's that important, you'll be here first thing.'

The woman marched off, leaving Lili trembling with frustration. She banged a gloved fist on the solid, wooden door until blood came through the fabric.

Lili thought of the rough-and-tumble dressing room; the smell of paint and spilt port. She couldn't go back there, not tonight.

The twirling snow made Bedford Square quieter. Lili turned to the chessboard windows. They had sliding latches.

With acrobatic ease, she placed a narrow heel on the railing and used the door knocker to pull herself up to window level. Taking an ivory shoe horn from her bag, she slid it to open the window catch.

There's something to be said for original features, she thought. *They're much easier to break into.*

Lili wrenched open the window and felt the panes rattle. Then she slid her body through the tiny gap and found herself in a dark room of tables and books.

She was about to close the window when she saw someone. A big, bulky someone, watching from the pavement. She darted behind a curtain, and when she looked again the figure was gone.

Probably just a homeless person.

Lili closed the window and felt her way around the tables. She didn't dare turn the lights on, but the snow gave the room enough of a silvery glow to see by. There were filing cabinets all around. She opened one up, tensing at the noise the drawer made.

Lili began rifling through files.

Pages and pages of photocopies were stuffed into foolscap files. *This was a stupid idea*, she thought, pulling out a folder marked 'A'. *I can hardly see and, like Gretchen said, without dates to guide me, I'm hardly likely to find anything in a bunch of paperwork. But at least I'm doing* something.

She went to the desk and began examining the papers. For a moment, she thought she saw a shadow at the window again, but when she glanced at the dark snow outside there was no one there. The documents quickly regained her attention.

58

Squinting in the grey light, Lili read dark handwriting on white paper.

These are photocopies of letters written by William Peavy's servants, she realised. *Probably the same ones the museum staff are copying for Gretchen.*

She sat down to read, knowing she was probably wasting her time, but glad to be doing something, anything to move her forwards.

Soon, Lili's head was filled with the punishing schedule of Peavy's servants' lives. Their work was gruelling. Up at dawn lighting fires in the freezing cold, then scrubbing the house from top to bottom, baking bread, pies and puddings, washing clothes by hand . . . the jobs were endless.

They cooked, washed, mended, polished and dusted from 6am until 11pm, six days a week – sometimes seven. However, the servants had nothing but praise for Peavy, who was clearly a better employer than most. Lili couldn't find a bad word said against him. The only half-juicy letter she came across was an argument between the housekeeper and the footman about Peavy storing boots on a marble floor.

Lili's eyes burned as the sky outside turned muddy, then milky, then bright white. By the time daylight came, she hadn't even finished reading one filing cabinet drawer, let alone found anything useful.

Sun lit up the snow, floating over the railings and lamp posts, and Lili realised staff would be arriving soon. She let herself out of the front door, then sat on the cold step. Pulling her knees to her chest, she waited. It didn't take long before everything went numb.

* * *

'Oh. You made it here then.'

'What?' Lili's aching body felt joined to the stone step.

I fell asleep.

One side of her cashmere coat was white where snow had built layers. She looked up to see the woman from yesterday standing over her.

'I'll need to let myself in,' the woman said, climbing the steps.

Lili stood and felt heavy, frozen water clinging to her left-hand side. Judging by the thickness of snow around the square, it had snowed all night. It was so bright. She blinked and rubbed tired eyes, sore with yesterday's make-up.

Bedford Square looked like a Christmas card: railings, rooftops, chimneys and trees were dusted with a layer of shining snow. It was beautiful. The square was born again.

The woman pushed past her up the steps. There was a click of locks as she opened the museum. The door swung inwards, then closed again.

For a moment, Lili was too tired and stunned to realise what had just happened. Then she turned and hammered on wood. 'Hey! Let me in!'

After five minutes of banging, the door swung open. The woman poked her head out and took a breath of freezing air. She wore a Victorian lady's outfit which Lili presumed to be some sort of uniform. A plastic badge on her blouse said: 'Betty – here to bring history alive.'

'I told you it was important.'

'I suppose you'd better come in then.' Betty held the door open. 'Out of the cold.'

She led Lili into a marble-floored entrance hall. A sweeping staircase flowed down into the hallway, and met a beautiful stone fireplace at the bottom. Lili thought: *Maybe Love and Tom warmed themselves here when they worked for Peavy.*

It was good to get inside again, and Lili knocked snow from her shoes against an old boot scrubber.

'Don't touch that,' Betty scolded. 'It's an original – William

Peavy himself used it. We haven't quite opened up yet, so if you could wait here and try and stay out of trouble . . .'

'Your sign says nine,' said Lili, gliding past her towards a door marked Research Room. 'This is where you keep all the records, right?'

'We don't like people going in there without a member of staff,' said Betty, catching up with her. 'So if you could just wait until—'

'No,' said Lili, lightly. 'It's important. I have to look.'

Betty sighed. 'Right. I suppose you're here bright and breezy. Shows willing.' She went to the research room and opened the door. 'What was it you were after? The servants' letters, like Gretchen wanted?'

'Yes.'

'Well then, we'll see what we can do for you,' said Betty, waving her arm. 'Come on then – we've got cabinets of letters just through here.'

In daylight, the research room, with its rows of gunmetal-grey filing cabinets, appeared stark and cold, but the temperature was warm.

'This room is used by academics mainly,' Betty explained. 'It's nothing like it would have been in Peavy's day – the rest of the museum gives a much better idea of—'

'It's fine,' said Lili. 'That's all I'm here for right now. Research.'

'You can't touch the letters themselves,' said Betty. 'They're stored in the basement in controlled conditions. Up here we keep the copies. They're arranged by sender and date. Here.' She pulled out a drawer. 'Andrews, Atkinson . . . then filed in date order. I've got to open everything up – I'll leave you to it.'

'I don't suppose there's any other way of searching?' Lili asked. 'By keyword or—'

Betty shook her head. 'The council's been talking about that for years, but the funding never quite makes it here. Keyword this, keyword that, online catalogue this, online catalogue that.

'Silly idea, anyway. It would mean hand-typing everything into the computer, and then what? Who'd come and visit if they could find it all online? No, no, they'll never get around to it – not in my lifetime.'

59

'How are you getting along?' Betty asked, appearing in the doorway with a William Peavy Museum mug of tea.

Lili nodded at her, tired. 'Nothing so far.' She'd barely made a dent in the second drawer, and the swirly writing and odd words were hurting her eyes. Servants, it seemed, generally couldn't write all that well, and used 'sound-a-like' words a lot of the time. Him instead of hymn. Goayst instead of ghost. That, coupled with the unusual turns of phrase, made reading slow going.

'It takes time,' said Betty. 'Academics can spend weeks looking through, and for people who don't know what they're doing . . . well, it can take months. Everyone's in such a hurry these days, but some things you can't rush.'

'Will you help me?' Lili asked. 'I can't do this on my own. I don't know how.'

'I'm afraid I've got a museum to run,' said Betty.

Lili thought for a moment. 'Gretchen. Do you happen to have an email address for her?'

'I'm sure I do somewhere,' said Betty. 'You seem very determined. Let me go and look for you.'

A moment later, Betty reappeared. 'Yes – Chris had it. Here it is. I suppose you'll be wanting to email her on our computer?'

'I'd love that.' Lili found she was blushing. 'Thanks so much.'

Gretchen,

Help please. Researching WP servants' letters at museum, taking for ever, think I must be doing it wrong. How did you find things out so quickly?

Love,

Lili

The old computer rocked as Lili typed. She guessed that Gretchen, being more computer savvy than her mum, had ways of making sure her emails weren't checked. The virtual world was probably the only place Gretchen was free.

Lili thought of her own childhood. It wasn't perfect, and she still felt angry when she thought of her mother, sleeping all day, too drunk to walk, generally being unfit to care for children. There had been plenty of stress and worry, but at least she was allowed to be whoever she wanted.

It was only after she clicked 'send' that Lili realised she hadn't eaten a thing since yesterday lunch time.

The screen flashed and an email from Gretchen appeared.

Lili!
    How cool is the WP museum? I love it. My second favourite museum in London. Sit tight and keep reading what you can. Mum grounded me, so I'm stuck at home, but I'll see what I can do. Check your emails in an hour. BTW – I found something out about Michael.
    G xx

Michael?
Lili fired back another email:

What about Michael?

She waited five minutes, but getting no reply she returned to the research table. Soon, she was engrossed, but every other letter she went back to the computer to check if Gretchen had replied. She hadn't.

Twenty letters later, she heard a voice in the hallway, high and light like a teenager.
Is that . . . Gretchen?
She chased the thought away. Gretchen was grounded.

Then she heard another, older voice. 'I think we'll learn a lot today.'

Carol.

Leaning back in her chair, Lili tipped her head so she could see into the hallway. She was rewarded with Gretchen's round face, smiling.

Behind Gretchen stood Carol, glasses splashed with melting snow. Her head was bent over a leaflet about the museum.

They both wore thermal anoraks, but Gretchen had pulled her hood down and snow was caught in her dark brown hair.

'Okay, Mum,' Gretchen said, winking at Lili and putting a finger to her lips. 'I'll be in the research room, just for an hour or so. How about you look round the house and then we explore the top floors together?'

Lili leaned away from the door just as Carol turned around.

'There's no computer in there, is there?' she heard Carol ask. 'You're not jumping on the internet again as soon as my back's turned?'

'Mum! Let it go. That was one time.'

'Do you have everything you need for your coursework?'

'Yes.'

'Okay, fine.' Carol sighed. 'It's a shame. I thought we could have a day together. I've spent too much time on my own this week.'

There was the creak of stairs and then Gretchen came clattering into the research room, throwing her rucksack on the table.

'Gretchen!' Lili stood up and gave her a relieved hug. 'It's so good to see you. I've been at it for hours. I haven't found anything useful. What did you find out about Michael?'

'Something *really* interesting.'

LOVE MORGAN   b. 1831, d. 1865.

George Morgan

Tom Morgan
1836 – 1874

Nee Avary

Love Morgan
1831 – 1865

M

James Morgan
1864 – 1889

m.

Cooky Morgan
(Catherine Long)
b. 1863 – d ?

1877 – 1912 Michael Morgan

Fred Morgan
1899 – 1972

1900 – 1970
'Dynamite' Dolly Morgan

Karen Morgan   b. 1960

Vivienne Morgan   b.1965

Jeff Morgan   b.1958

60

'I couldn't find Michael's birth certificate,' said Gretchen. 'I looked and looked, but Michael is such a common name, and there were so many different spellings of things back then.

'I found five Michael Morgans in Whitechapel, but none matching anything else to do with your family. Lots of births weren't even registered back then, so most likely he slipped through the net and never had a birth certificate.

'I got a bit down about that, to be honest. I hit a real brick wall. There were no death certificates either, that I could match up for certain. But the website I was looking on offered me army and ship passenger records, and I thought, what the hey, I'll take a look.'

'Was Michael in the army?'

'I couldn't find anything that said he was,' said Gretchen. 'At least not for sure. But get this. There's a record of a Michael Morgan stowing away on a ship to New York. His address is registered in Whitechapel, in the Nichol, just north of my tower block. I thought, probably it's not him. There were lots of Michael Morgans in Whitechapel. But I'll take a look.'

'And?'

'This particular Michael Morgan was caught stowing away on a ship to New York. He was discovered and sent back to England.'

'He was a stowaway?'

Gretchen nodded. 'He was probably trying to start a new life away from poverty. Lots of people did that back then.'

'Did he ever make it to New York?' Lili asked. 'My great-grandma, Dynamite Dolly, moved there with her brother. And Grandma and Grandad lived out there for a while too.'

'No, this guy never made it,' said Gretchen. 'At least, not off the boat. He was caught and sent back. After that, it looks like he stayed in East London, on Old Nichol Street.'

'So . . . how do you know it's the Michael Morgan we're looking for?'

'That's the interesting part,' said Gretchen. 'Yellow letters were listed as part of Michael Morgan's possessions when he stowed away. The ship records detailed everything he had on him, and that included a bundle of yellow letters wrapped in red rags.'

'Yellow letters . . .'

'Bit of a coincidence, don't you think?'

'Too much of one.'

'They must have been important to him,' said Gretchen, 'if he chose to take them to America. He wouldn't have had luggage if he stowed away. So whatever he did bring would have been of either actual or sentimental value.'

'So, let's say Michael inherited the yellow letters from his father,' said Lili. 'Would he have passed them down to someone else?'

'That's if they were *the* letters,' said Gretchen. 'They could have been something totally different.'

'Unlikely, though, isn't it? Yellow letters wrapped in rags. Michael Morgan. It all matches up. But what did Michael do with them?'

Gretchen picked up the pile of servants' letters Lili had been searching. 'How's the Peavy research going?'

'Slowly.'

'No wonder.' Gretchen flicked through pages. 'You've just pulled out all the letters in the A file and started reading through.'

'So show me a better way.'

Gretchen gathered up the pile on Lili's desk and pushed them to one side. 'You're not even searching letters from the servants who worked *here*, in his *London* house.'

She went to the filing cabinets and whisked open a drawer, her fingers whizzing over files. 'And you need to read letters from

the *important* servants first. Like the housekeeper or the butler.
Plan your trip too, if you're coming somewhere like this. I bet
you just turned up here this morning and started reading, didn't
you? No packed lunch? No flask of coffee? No notepad? No
idea what you're looking at?'

Lili laughed. 'You've got me there.'

Gretchen opened her rucksack and took out a brown Thermos,
two cheese sandwiches and a packet of custard creams.

'Here,' Gretchen said, pouring a lid of plasticy coffee and
passing Lili a sandwich. 'I bet you're hungry.'

Three cups of coffee later, Lili had learned more from Gretchen's
selection of letters than she had all morning from her own.

'Peavy was obviously much happier in his London house than
his country estate,' Lili said, as she read yet another account of 'Mr
Peavy's black days' when he was due to visit the countryside.

Gretchen nodded. 'He was hardly ever in the country. Look
at these letters from the eighteen seventies. There are only about
four of them mentioning Hertfordshire. You see why I said we
should read letters from his London servants first, don't you?
His country servants hardly knew him at all.'

'All his servants seemed to like him, though,' said Lili. 'No one
says anything bad. His housekeeper keeps saying how sad it is
that Mr Peavy doesn't have children.

'Listen to this: *For such a kind man not to be a father is a very
great sadness.*'

She put the paper down and stared at falling snow. 'If Ian is
right, we'd be William Peavy's only direct relatives.'

'What?'

'Nothing,' said Lili. 'Just thinking. Anyway. It's a bit unusual,
isn't it? For someone to marry and not have children? In those
days, anyway.'

'Maybe his wife wouldn't have sex with him,' said Gretchen,
seeming to feel Carol's presence at the word 'sex' and checking
over her shoulder. 'Or maybe they just couldn't have children.
Perhaps one of them was infertile.'

They kept reading.

'This is hopeless,' said Gretchen. 'Even searching only the London letters, it could still take months.'

'But at least we're doing something,' said Lili. 'You said before about dates. Why don't we search some more key dates?'

'Like what? We don't have any.'

'Yes we do. What about when Love died?'

'But she didn't work for William Peavy then,' said Gretchen. 'She was sacked ages before that newspaper article about the poisoning.'

'Let's check,' said Lili. 'You never know.'

'Lili.' Gretchen held a letter close to her face.

'What? Have you found something?'

'Maybe. This letter here. It was written by Peavy's London housekeeper on the thirteenth February, eighteen sixty-five.'

'The day before Love died,' said Lili. They both leaned over the letter.

My Dearest Sister,

I do not know how to thank you for your kindniss in doing the dresses for me. How I would have finished them the Lord only knows, because I have ardly had any time this week.

The coal delivery was late three weeks runnin and so the mornin fires are low and the house cold all day today. This mornin John Footman left the back door open and a runway dog got into the parlour and destoid a mornin of cooking.

That set the lunch back an ower, so Mr Peavy can't have been best pleased, though was too good to say so.

When lunch was cleared, Love Avary turned up at the dor wanting to see the master. She looked very sickly with many marks to show the sin of how she is living since she left the house.

Jane Maid tried to send her on her way, but Mr Peavy asked her in for tea and teld me to bake scones, so another job to do and for someone I'd soner not do it for.

Jane Maid says Love was blakmalling the master, talking of

*sellin stories to the neeyouspaper. I did not hear anythin
of that sort and Jane does talk so, but as I passed the door
I eard Mr Peavy say: Love is love and I am not ashaymed.*

*I am very sure the master has nothing to be ashaymed of,
but Love has plenty.*

*Love left within the ower, but was treated with more kindniss
than needed. George Butler, who is Love's father-in-low now (as
Love and Tom Morgan are married) showed her into the
drawing room and Master William served her tea as if she were
a lady guest. So there are still some in this house who think of
her fondly, but I never will.*

*When Love left, Jane and I cyrtsyed to her as if she were a
lady of high standing. How we laughed.*

With fondest love to all,

Affect. Sister,

Elizabeth Reeves

Gretchen and Lili looked at each other.

'What does it mean?' Lili asked.

'I don't know,' said Gretchen. 'Sounds like Love was trying to
blackmail William Peavy.'

'Yes,' Lili agreed. She thought for a moment. 'Peavy had stocks
of arsenic in his cellar. He tested things for arsenic, didn't he?
At his home. So there was arsenic around. When Love visited,
he could have given her something with arsenic in.'

'Could have happened,' said Gretchen. 'Arsenic is flavourless
. . . colourless. The perfect poison. She didn't even need to
drink it or anything. If they had sex or something, he could
have rubbed it somewhere.'

'Really?'

Gretchen nodded. 'Arsenic is deadly. All you need is a tiny bit
to contact porous skin. But . . . I don't know. Everything in history
says Peavy was a really nice man. He spent his life looking after
poor people and doing charitable things.'

They flicked through more letters, but after a few minutes
Gretchen slapped down pages and put her hands on her hips.

'Look, there's not much point reading past the date Love died.'

'I've got a visitor's pass to see Darren tomorrow,' said Lili. 'Maybe he'll have some things to tell me.'

'Your *brother*?' Gretchen complained. 'What's *he* going to know? You need to talk to *old* people. Don't you have grandparents?'

'My grandad's dead.'

'Grandma?'

Lili bit her lip. 'Yes. I have a gran.'

'So why not speak to her?'

'It's hard to explain. Even if I knew where she was . . . the thought of seeing her again . . . I don't know if I could be civil to her. I might just end up shouting and swearing at her for making Mum the way she was. She's hard to track down, anyway.' Lili rubbed her eyes. 'She might be at the funeral.'

'That's *days* away, isn't it?'

'Just two days. Anyway. I can see Darren before that. He's worth talking to, I promise. He knows things I don't. He lived with my mum longer, and he lived with Grandad's sister for a while.'

'Fine. Better than nothing. Why do you need a visitor pass to see him?'

'He's in prison.'

A shadow fell over the doorway.

Lili turned to see Carol, glasses steamed up, lips pressed together in a tight, white line. She had a teary expression, like she'd eaten a hot chilli.

'Gretchen.'

There was an awkward silence.

'Mum, guess who I happened to bump into—'

'Don't.' Carol put a hand to her lined forehead. 'The trust is gone now. It's gone. To think you'd be so deceitful. To tell lies . . . We're going home right now, and you'll go straight to your room and—'

'Carol,' Lili interrupted. 'It's true. Gretchen was just—'

'Stay away from my daughter.' Carol's voice was low as she

grabbed Gretchen by the arm. 'I mean it. I won't have her associating with people like you.' She cut herself off abruptly with a zip of her anorak.

'Email me after you visit your brother,' Gretchen whispered, as Carol dragged her out the room.

61

As the number 71 bus bounced past the tabby-cat-coloured walls of Wandsworth Prison, Lili pressed her face to window. The big red bus dragged itself over tarmac, and she willed it to go faster.

The first time Lili had visited Darren, she'd arrived at the prison gates in a taxi. That had been a bad idea. The collection of convicts' mothers, girlfriends and wives, many with small children hanging from them, had given her a wide berth.

Prison staff had made sure she was last in line, and that they took their time processing her visitor order. She'd better not think she was getting any special treatment. Prison was the great leveller, but toffs were levelled just that bit more than everyone else.

Now Lili did what most visitors did – she arrived by bus.

She felt the familiar sickness at the thought of Darren inside those dirty walls. She'd cried on her way home the first time she'd visited him, but that was many years ago.

The bus passed searchlights on tall poles, towering above the prison turrets, barbed wire and acres of tarmac.

A rare glimmer of winter sunshine shone as the 71 pulled up beside the PACT visitors' centre, a small, homely building just outside the prison walls.

Next to the huge turrets of the prison, the PACT centre looked positively cosy – a farmer's cottage beside a nuclear power station. Lili had whiled away many an hour inside, drinking weak tea and waiting, waiting, waiting.

As Lili stepped off the bus, an emaciated woman with long, straggly blue-black hair caught up with her. She wore the market version of a designer puffa jacket, frayed jeans and knee-high pink boots with pointed toes.

'Hey Li.' The woman, whose name was Joanie, walked beside her. 'Didn't see you on the bus.'

'I was upstairs.' Lili walked quickly, not wanting to be slowed down by a conversation. But Joanie kept up.

They walked inside the visitors' centre and headed towards the desk where their visitor orders were checked and approved.

Joanie pulled her folded VO from a Gucci handbag – a genuine one, by the look of the lining. 'Billy's getting moved. Cat C.' She smiled a little-girl smile, completely out of place in her wrinkled, cigarette-raddled face. Joanie was thirty-five but looked fifty. 'How have you been?'

'My mum passed away,' said Lili, hoping Joanie would understand that she wasn't up for talking. Lili couldn't quite say 'died' yet, but 'passed away' felt okay.

'I'm so sorry.' Joanie put a bony arm around her shoulder. 'And for Dazza too – to be stuck in here when something like that happens. What a shame. Will they let him out for the funeral?'

'I don't know yet.'

They checked their bags into the lego-brick wall of red lockers. To Lili's relief, the guard led her through immediately to be searched.

'No waiting today,' said Joanie with a whistle.

Lili had purposely dressed in a plastic-boned corset so she wouldn't set off the metal detector. Still, something set it off anyway, and the guards seemed positively languid as they searched her.

'Can we get a bit of a move on?' Lili asked.

The prison guard smiled at her colleague and shook her head. 'Your brother going somewhere, is he?'

The guards led her along an open-air painted-on pavement and then into a prison building.

This was always the worst bit as far as Lili was concerned. The prison was vast, and the thought of her brother lost in this maze of concrete and metal was so lonely, she could hardly bear it.

They passed green and white walls, and Lili thought of the

workhouse where Love had given birth to James. *The walls so blank, my shadow I thank for falling there.* Then they reached the blue door to the visitors' hall.

Lili saw Darren immediately, his long, skinny limbs folded around a laminated bench. His mousy blond hair stuck up in tufts, and his thick brown eyebrows were pulled close together. Across his nose were long bruises – swollen black stripes tinged with red blood.

LOVE MORGAN b. 1831,
            d. 1865.

George
Morgan

Nee
Avary

Love   M   Tom
Morgan   Morgan
1831 - 1865   1836 - 1874

James Morgan   m.   Cooky Morgan
1864 - 1889   (Catherine Long)
                      b. 1863 - d.?

1877
- 1912
Michael
Morgan

                    1900
                    - 1970
Fred Morgan   'Dynamite'
1899 - 1972   Dolly Morgan

          Francine
          Morgan 1933
                  - 2000

          b. 1960
Karen   Vivienne   Jeff   b.1958
Morgan   Morgan   Morgan
                   b.1965

Darren
Morgan

62

Darren wore a prison-issue fluorescent orange tabard and was tapping Nike Air trainers. All around him sat other prisoners, looking eagerly towards the door. Darren's big blue eyes watched the door too, forlorn and slightly glazed.

'Lils.' Darren smiled when he saw her, and Lili thought the smile must hurt. The bruises leapt around his face and resettled. He stood slowly on unsteady feet and gave her an awkward hug. Lili noticed one of his hands was bound with bandages.

'Daz—'

'It's worse than it looks,' said Darren, sitting on the screwed-down metal bench. His words were slow and his voice hoarse. Now she was close, Lili could tell he was on heroin. It was easy enough to get hold of in prison. His movements were slow and soft, like he was moving underwater. The smile probably hadn't hurt him after all.

It doesn't matter, she thought, sidestepping the usual disappointment. *You know he won't get clean in here. He needs an escape more than ever.*

'Are the guards looking?' Darren asked.

Lili turned to the blue counter at the far end of the room, where two guards stood watching them.

'Yes,' she said.

'Just like always,' Darren gave a half smile. 'They fancy you. Or me.'

As a heroin user, Darren was always watched extra closely in case visitors brought him drugs. But the guards were out of luck. Lili never brought anything. She fuelled Darren's drug habit by sending him cheques – something she'd long ago made her peace with.

'Two of them.' Darren glanced at a bald prisoner sitting across the room. 'Toothpaste tube full of gravel. Me and my mouth.'

'You should know by now,' said Lili.

'Good news,' Darren said. 'I got compassionate leave. For the funeral tomorrow.'

Lili took a seat opposite. 'I'm so sorry, Daz. I meant to phone the prison. I forgot. I should have – but it's okay, right? You got leave? How did you know about the funeral?'

'Ben got in touch. He told me he was doing the funeral. What that bloke has put up with, I'd have thought he'd want to run in the opposite direction. But he said he was happy to do it.'

'I know,' said Lili.

'I gave him such a hard time when he and Mum first got together. Him being so much younger, I thought – user. But he couldn't be a user if he tried. He's looked after Mum, he really has. More than the rest of us.'

'You looked after her, Daz. When you could.'

Darren put his head in his hands. 'Our family. We can't even manage our own funerals.' He looked up. 'They told me about the inquest – they've given me leave for that too.'

'The inquest.' Lili had forgotten about that, perhaps purposely. 'I want Aunt Karen to come, but she says she won't.'

'Do you care?'

'Yes,' said Lili. 'She says she might not make the funeral. The least she can do is show up for the inquest. Out of respect, you know. I mean, I'm angry with Mum – I've got a right to be. But she hasn't. How did you find out about . . . you know. What happened.'

'A guard came to my quilting class.' Darren looked at the table, and Lili noticed one of his canine teeth was newly chipped. 'I didn't crack. Not until I was back in my cell. They didn't tell me much – just that she died at home and it looked like suicide. Have they told you anything else?'

Lili shook her head. 'The inquest won't be for weeks. But they seem pretty sure it was suicide. She wrote all this stuff on the wall. *I will die today.*'

Darren's eyes grew wet. 'I knew she'd do it one day. It's good to finally cry for her. I wanted to every day she was alive.' Tears poured down Darren's face, and Lili watched him enviously. Even in the 'can't feel, don't care' land of heroin, Darren had emotions.

'I haven't cried,' Lili admitted. 'Even when I went to her flat I didn't cry. I wanted to but I'm too angry with her. She doesn't deserve my tears. She left us. After everything she did, she went and left us.'

'You just have your own way of dealing with things. You'll cry. And when you do, you won't be able to stop.'

'Daz, Mum was looking for some old family letters before she died. From years ago. They were something to do with one of our relatives, Love Morgan. Did she ever talk to you about any letters? Or write to you about them?'

'No.'

'When you lived with Mum or Great-Aunt Francine, did they ever tell you stories about our family? Especially about the older relatives – people who lived before we were born?'

'Like old war stories, you mean?'

'I suppose.'

'Why?'

'Mum wrote on her bedroom wall, *Lilian, find the letters*. She meant these old family letters she was looking for. Like one of her detective games, you know? I think it's her way of saying goodbye. So I want to find them. And the more I know about our family, the easier it'll be.'

'She wrote on the bedroom wall?'

'Yes. Loads of stuff. About the letters and family.'

'What about me? Did she write about me?'

'No, Daz, but I think these letters – they're her way, you know? She asked me to find them because she knows you're in prison. So she wanted me to understand what was going through her head before she died. So we can move on. Get over it. Because I'm stuck, Daz, I'm completely stuck. I'm so angry.'

'You really think she wanted you to know what was in her head before she died? And finding some old letters will tell you that?'

'I don't know. It sounds stupid when I say it out loud, but yes. I think these letters are her way of saying goodbye.'

'Sounds a bit like wishful thinking, Lils.'

'Maybe. But there's something else too,' said Lili. 'Some weird things have been happening, and part of me thinks – you know, it's so odd for Mum not to leave a note. Even after me not seeing her so long. She would at least have written to you. So maybe, I don't know. Maybe there's more to all this than suicide.'

'Like what?'

'Like, Mum was looking for these old family letters, and maybe someone didn't want her finding them. So . . . they stopped her.'

63

'Really, Lils?' said Darren. 'You know how Mum was. This wasn't her first attempt. She wrote stuff about wanting to die on the wall. The police found pills. I know it hurts that she didn't say goodbye, but—'

'Wouldn't it be better if it wasn't suicide? Better than her leaving us, after all she put us through, without even writing a note?'

'I can understand you feeling that way,' said Darren. 'But Lils, didn't you always feel like she'd do something like this one day?'

'God, she was such a terrible mum. If she hasn't even said goodbye to us, someway, somehow, I don't know how I'll stand it. I'll crack up. If I'm not cracking up already.'

'She did the best with what she had, Lils. She didn't have it in her to do better. Don't you feel relieved? She's at peace now.'

'I just feel angry.'

'You've always been angry. Just like Mum was. She wasn't perfect, Lils, but that's just how she was. You have to let it go.'

'I can't. And Darren, I'm so scared. Because if I don't let it go, if I carry on feeling this way, I'm going to turn out just like her. Angry. Stuck. Did she ever tell you why she was so angry at our family?'

'No. Never.'

'Did she ever tell you any family stories? Maybe about someone called Love Morgan?'

'Mum never said much to me about the family,' Darren said. 'But Great Aunty Francine used to tell me stories.'

'I was jealous when you lived with her,' Lili admitted. 'I always wondered what it was like in that nice flat. I thought you got a good deal.'

'It was all right,' said Darren. 'She was like a cross between Gran and Mum. I was lucky she took me in – none of the rest of them would have done. It was the life of riley, really, living with her. Pocket money, packed lunch, the lot. But nothing lasts for ever.'

'I still feel bad about that,' said Lili. 'I should have looked into it. Filled in the right forms—'

'It's that social worker who should feel bad,' said Darren. 'Never there when you need her, and then she fucks it all up when everything's going okay. Still, Aunty Francine's gone now, and I'm grown up. So what does it matter.'

'Tell me about Francine,' said Lili. 'What sort of stories did she tell you?'

'Lots,' said Darren. 'They're a right load of villains, you know, our lot. Don't listen to what Gran says.'

'I haven't spoken to Gran yet.' Lili looked at the table. 'She may not even know about Mum. But I guess if Ben got hold of her, she'll be at the funeral tomorrow. Ben's been trying to bring the family together, without realising some families prefer to be apart.'

'You haven't tried to get in touch with Gran yourself?'

'No. I tried, but I haven't tracked her down yet. Anyway, I'm not ready. Not yet.'

'If she turns up at the funeral, you'll have to see her.'

'I know. And maybe that's a good thing. She might know about these letters. Or have some old family stories. Anyway. Who did Francine tell you about?'

'Uncle Fred,' said Darren. 'You know. Mum's great-uncle. Dolly's brother. He was a right character. A stand-up comedian in the old burlesque shows – sounds like a real laugh. Wish I'd met him.'

'What about someone called Michael Morgan – he would have been her grandad.'

'Oh yeah, her grandad. She told me all about him. She and Grandad Albert lived with him for years while Dolly was touring America. He was a real hard man. Lord of the Nichol slum. He lent money, broke legs … proper East End gangster.'

'Did he have a wife?'

'He wasn't married,' said Darren. 'Not properly. Aunty Francine said he lived with a woman called Margaret Collins. They were common-law husband and wife. They lived together, but no wedding ceremony.'

'So tell me about her.'

'She was a big, rough, tough woman who didn't take any nonsense, that's what Francine said. They were all terrified of her, all the grandchildren. She'd had fights with half the men in the Nichol and most of them had come off the worst for it.'

'What did she do for a living?'

'Aunty Francine said she was a fence. Everyone knew she was the one you came to if you needed something. Lots of people owed her favours, but Aunty Francine said you never wanted to owe a favour to Margaret Collins. You'd end up owing her for the rest of your life.'

'Do you know anything concrete about Michael Morgan?' Lili asked. 'Dates, places he worked … anything like that?'

'He wasn't in respectable employment, Lils, he was a gangster. They don't keep pay stubs.'

'Please Darren. You've got to remember.'

'I don't know dates or anything like that,' said Darren. 'But him and Margaret worked as a team. He'd go around threatening anyone who didn't pay up. Professional finger snapper, that's what Aunty Francine called him.

'She said between Michael and Margaret, the Morgan family ran the Nichol slum. She was pretty proud about that. They were Lord and Lady Morgan, she said. Their neighbours all slept on the floor and had shitty fires and no furniture, but Lord and Lady Morgan burned as much coal as they needed and had chairs, beds … the lot.'

'Sounds like paradise,' said Lili.

'Back then it was,' said Darren. 'Most people in the Nichol were slowly starving to death. They ate paint, chalk, all sorts. If you lived in the slum, blimey, *this* place would be paradise. Michael and Margaret were East End royalty. Money to lend and food on the table. That was as good as life got.

'Aunty Francine said she had no end of trouble being related to them, though. As soon as anyone found out she was a Morgan, they gave her a wide berth. Scared of having their legs broken. No one wanted to get on the wrong side of Michael Morgan.'

'What about letters?' Lili asked. 'Did Francine mention anything about letters?'

'No,' said Darren. 'Sorry, Lils. I wish I could help you. Why am I always stuck in this shit hole when people need me? When Mum—' He banged his hands on the table.

The guard appeared at Darren's shoulder. 'Any more of that and your visitor will be leaving.'

'All right, all right.'

'None of your lip.' The guard pulled Darren to his feet.

'Hold up,' Darren croaked, shaking the arm away. That was a mistake. The guard smashed his face against the table, forcing his cheek onto the cold laminate. Other guards came running to help pin him down.

'You can kiss goodbye to that compassionate leave, Darren Morgan.'

'Any excuse,' came Darren's muffled response.

Lili pulled at the guard's hands and was rewarded with a backwards slap that sent her a few feet across the room. 'Leave him alone,' she said, as a guard grabbed her arms and led her away.

'Your brother has just relinquished his right to compassionate leave,' said a voice as she was taken from the room. 'Next time you see him, ask him how he gets his drugs in. Tell him we don't like piss takers in here.'

64

Life's a Stage by Lili Allure

How to deal with striptease prejudice

There are all kinds of people in the world – some think striptease is sexy and fun, others think strip clubs and burlesque girls are cheap and worthless.

At Kate's, I'm in something of a bubble. The only people I see are paying ticketholders, which means they all love burlesque and treat me with the greatest respect. But out in the real world, people can be much less kind.

When I worked at a strip club in the East End of London, I met all sorts of people – some good, some bad. The bad spoke to me and the other girls as if we were nothing. They thought just because they had the money to pay for a dance, they could behave without care or consideration. To them, the world was divided into worthwhile people and those who didn't count.

Those people taught me a thing or two about power and how not to abuse it. No matter how well known I become or how much money I make, I always treat everyone with respect.

Lili retrieved her handbag from the locker, then threw the door furiously shut with a metallic clang that echoed through the visitor centre. While Darren was in here he was nothing, and they could treat him as they liked. Prisoners' self-esteem was ground to powder, and society wondered why criminals reoffended.

'Coming or going?' asked a white-haired Caribbean lady, holding a shopping bag stuffed with multipacks of crisps.

'Going,' said Lili, looking past the lady to a table of tired, sad women sharing Jaffa Cakes and holding wriggling children. They looked like life had defeated them.

Waves of heat rose from the electric heater as Lili sat, sipping a black coffee in the theatre office. She tapped on a little metal-bar keyboard that looked thin enough to snap in two, crossing and uncrossing her legs to stop the heat scorching her stockings. Web pages flowed over a huge Mac screen.

Darren did tell me something new, she thought, as she typed in 'Margaret Collins' and clicked the search key. *I didn't know Margaret's name before.*

She'd signed up to a family tree service called ancestry.co.uk and had already patched together different threads of the family, working forwards from Love and Tom in order to find out when Margaret might have been born.

Outside the 'boom boom' of sound checks sent a hum through the floor, but Lili was used to loud noise. At night, the dressing-room window let through central London's nightclub music, shouting, screeching and the sounds of throwing up in the gutter.

There you are.

Margaret Collins, born in Bethnal Green, 1880. According to the website, the record matched another she'd found for Dorothy 'Dolly' Morgan – Dynamite Dolly. Margaret was her mother. She clicked through and found details of Margaret's birth certificate:

Name: Margaret Morgan

Date of registration: Jul – Aug – Sept 1880

Registration district: Bethnal Green

Now she knew the year Margaret was born and the approximate month. If she wanted, she could order her birth certificate and find the exact date of her birth and her father's occupation.

The sound check finished and Lili waved as the crew left. Auditorium lights dimmed, then turned dark.

'Thought this was your day off,' Charlie called through the office door.

'It is,' said Lili. 'Just a few things I'm looking up. I'll be done soon.'

'Have a good night.'

She heard the theatre doors closing and the click of the locks.

Letting out a long sigh, she leaned back and blinked at the screen. There were so many records to search through, but so few details to work with. Poor people weren't well recorded. They lived and died quietly, while wealthy people filled the history books.

There was a rattling sound, like someone pushing at the theatre doors, and Lili looked away from the screen.

'We're closed,' she called, hoping her voice carried far enough. 'No show tonight.' People often tried the theatre doors late at night, not realising it was all closed up. She blamed Pete for insisting the theatre posters outside were lit 24 hours a day.

Losing patience with the ancestry website, Lili decided the Old Bailey records were worth a try, now she had a new name to search with.

Rattle, rattle.

'We're closed,' Lili called again, feeling uneasy. People usually left once they realised the doors were closed.

She chose a date range between 1880 and 1913 – the latest date the records went up to – typed in Margaret Collins and watched two records appear.

LOVE MORGAN b. 1831, d. 1865.

George Morgan

Love Morgan (Nee Avary) 1831 – 1865 **M** Tom Morgan 1836 – 1874

James Morgan 1864 – 1889 **m.** Cooky Morgan (Catherine Long) b. 1863 – d.?

Margaret Collins 1880 – ? Michael Morgan 1877 – 1912

Fred Morgan 1899 – 1972 'Dynamite' Dolly Morgan 1900 – 1970

Francine Morgan 1933 – 2000

Karen Morgan b. 1960 Vivienne Morgan b. 1965 Jeff Morgan b. 1958

Darren Morgan

65

Lili leaned closer to the computer screen.

Margaret Collins, Breaking Peace, Other, 23rd August 1904

Margaret Collins, Breaking Peace, Wounding, 13th January 1913

She clicked the first record and found it was an arrest for 'habitual drunkenness'. A medical practitioner living in the area had been called as a witness, and said:

The prisoner is known to me. She is, in my judgement, suffering from chronic alcoholism. She told me herself she was so drunk she fell in the Thames and had to be pulled out by two men. I would describe her as a habitual drunkard.

Lili scanned down the page, and saw something that made her smile.

The next witness testimony was by Michael Morgan, cited as the prisoner's common-law husband.

Michael's testimony simply said:

Sometimes Maggie is the worse for drink, but she is not as bad as she was last year.

Lili clicked through to the next record, and found a lump in her throat.

341. Margaret Collins (33), Unlawfully attempting to commit suicide

Suicide. What an ugly, awful word. She felt her fingers scratching the desk and her teeth clench. 'The coward's way out,' she told the screen, but she was beginning to understand the appeal of escaping anger and emptiness. Life could be so painful. A few pills and it could all be over.

She looked back at the witness testimonies. There was one from Martin Jenkins, a railway constable.

On the 22nd December I was on duty at Aldersgate Station. I saw the prisoner and her daughter, Dolly Morgan, from the booking office. Both were known to me. They were quarrelling near the centre platform. The prisoner was trying to unbutton her jacket whilst her daughter was trying to button it back up again.

The prisoner said: I am better off under a train. I've no husband and no home. Give me the letters or I'll do for myself.

Lili blinked and reread the last sentence. *Letters.*

There was a rattle at the door again, but Lili couldn't tear herself away from the screen.

I heard Dolly Morgan reply: With me they are in safe hands. He knows you'd sell them for drink.

The prisoner said: What else do I have to live for?

Then Dolly Morgan said: He'll be back again in a day or two, and he'll do for you if the letters aren't kept safe. They're mine now, not yours.

On the approach of the train, the prisoner took off her jacket and ran to the edge of the platform, where I grabbed her and prevented her throwing herself in front of the engine.

She said: My husband has left me. I was promised some valuable letters, but they were given to my daughter. I have nothing to live for and my daughter won't do right by me.

The Prisoner: I was not attempting suicide, the train was not coming into the station. I was standing on the platform waiting for a train to come. The arresting constable has a spite against me.

*   *   *

Lili leaned closer to the computer. Margaret was sentenced to twelve months' hard labour. *Good. Serves you right for trying to abandon your family.* She decided to print out the pages to show Ian, in the hope they might jog his memory.

'I've no husband, no home. Give me the letters or I'll do for myself.'

Lili started up the noisy printer, which made the desk wobble violently as it shot out pages. When it finished and fell quiet, Lili heard a sawing sound coming from the auditorium.

She went rigid.

'Hello?' Lili tucked the pages into her handbag and came out of the office. 'Charlie?' The auditorium was dark. She wove around shadows of tables and clicked the light switch.

Frozen outlines of women appeared on stage and she yelped in fright. Then she remembered – the girls had been rehearsing their mannequin act that morning.

Five clothes-shop mannequins were lined up for the girls to play real-life dolls around, their dance moves jerky, their expressions blank. It wasn't an easy act to perform and new girls frequently ended up in tears after rehearsals.

One of the dummies looked strange.

'Gretchen?' Lili called, but there was no reply. The theatre was completely silent. She was alone.

Lili noticed pink plaster sawdust on the stage and metal filings, and a round object at one of the dolls' feet.

What's going on?

Lili realised the round object was the dummy's head.

The mannequin had been decapitated.

She looked closer and saw the dummy's face had been scribbled over by an angry hand.

The body had been marked too.

Crosses were placed over the breasts and crotch of the dummy, like a plastic surgeon's marks, and there was writing scrawled in odd places across the ribs and stomach.

FAMILY   FAMILY   FAMILY

                                                    FAMILY

Lili's legs buckled and she found herself grabbing the doll, falling into it. She felt the rough cuts of metal at the sawn neck.

There was a snapping sound.

In darkness, the ragged neck tore Lili's fingers. The dismembered head screamed from the shadows.

Lili turned and ran.

66

Life's a Stage, by Lili Allure

Lili's song lyrics
The Great Pretender by The Platters, sung by Freddie Mercury

Please be in. Please, please, please.

Lili hammered on Pete's apartment door. She was familiar with his communal hallway, having been there many times for drunken 'what the hell' sex, but hadn't noticed the pretty art deco flourishes, or the bright green palm trees.

Pete opened the door wearing tight underpants, trying to affect casual surprise. 'Lils, what are you doing here?'

'You were nearest to the theatre,' Lili gasped.

'Do you want to come in for a drink?'

'No . . . not a drink. But can I come in? Please?' Lili knew what Pete meant by drink. Probably he'd seen her through the peephole and stripped in preparation. 'I'm not here for what you think I'm here for.'

'You're not?' Sex was a fair assumption on Pete's part. Lili had slept with him too many times to call him a 'one-night stand', and going to him in her time of need was, in truth, entering dangerous territory. But there was no one else to turn to.

'Something's happened.'

Lili knew she must look frantic, and Pete noticed her expression and stopped flexing his biceps.

'What's wrong? Is it about Janey?'

Lili put a hand against her lips and realised it was the first time in years she hadn't worn her gloves in public. 'Why would it be about Janey? That was years ago.'

'Look, come in.' Pete led her into his living room, a space just big enough for a sofa, TV and a corner of kitchen units. He shared the flat with an artist who made sparkly splatter paintings and the living area was covered with canvases and glitter. 'Janey just got a new show. In Vegas. I thought you might have heard.'

'I couldn't care less.'

'It should be you out there,' said Pete. 'That's the career *you* should be having. She stole your show. All your props and routines—'

'You're right . . . bloom to perish, isn't that what they say? But who cares? I think I'm going crazy.'

'Here – sit down.' Throwing a tumble of tabloid pages from the sofa, Pete took a whisky bottle from the top of the fridge and poured a generous measure into a Baywatch mug.

'Thanks,' said Lili, taking the drink. The flat smelt like a pond, but it was warm and friendly and a long way from sawn-up mannequins in dark theatres. It felt safe.

Pete disappeared into his bedroom-of-the-exploding-laundry-basket and returned fully clothed and holding a tracksuit.

'Here. You can wear this.'

Lili looked at him. 'I'm not wearing your old tracksuit.'

'But you've got all that tight stuff on. How can you relax?'

Lili perched on the sofa in her rigid corset and thought: *Don't you know by now why I wear all this stuff all the time? If I relax, I'll fall apart.*

'Pete – I don't want to stay at the theatre tonight.'

'Why not?'

'Someone was in there while I was in the office. One of the stage props was vandalised. I was right there.' The words caught and Lili couldn't finish the sentence.

'Someone broke in again? Call the police. I'll be back.'

'No! It might be me. It might be my imagination. Mum's funeral is tomorrow and I think, maybe, I don't know.' She gave a hysterical laugh. 'I'm going mad or something! The police already think I'm seeing things . . . Can we go down there tomorrow? Just the two of us?'

Pete sighed. 'If that's what you want. Come on. You can sleep in my room. I've always hated you staying in that dressing room anyway. You want me to come to the funeral with you tomorrow?' He held his hands up. 'Not like that. Just as friends.'

'No. It's all right. Where will you sleep?'

'On the sofa. Unless you want the company – but you probably haven't had enough to drink yet.'

Lili stared into the mug, swilling orange whisky around its sides. She put it on the floor. 'Share the bed with me. I don't want to be on my own.'

The next morning, Lili woke with a sore throat but no hangover. Pete was sleeping next to her, snoring with his mouth open. She climbed out of bed as quietly as she could, dressed and creaked open the door.

In the cold light of day, the mannequins seemed like a murky dream. Not real. Last night, she'd felt plaster dust on her fingertips, but this morning her hands were clean and she was less sure than ever of what had actually happened.

She checked her watch. Ten o'clock. The funeral was at eleven. There was time to show Ian the print-outs before the ceremony.

Later, she and Pete could check the theatre, but waiting for Pete to wake up was just too much to deal with. She knew he'd insist on coming to the funeral, and she wanted to go alone.

Pete rolled over and Lili leaned down and kissed his forehead, then jumped back in case he woke up. She grabbed Pete's black blazer from the sofa on her way out – her last-minute funeral outfit.

Let's get this over with.

Act III

The Grand Finale

67

Life's a Stage by Lili Allure

Lili's London: St Botolph's Church

St Botolph's Church stands on the outskirts of Whitechapel between Aldgate and Liverpool Street – a beautiful reminder of historic London.

The giant cone-shaped spire has seen many buildings come and go across the city, and will live to see many more. Around it, green fields have changed to concrete roads, its foundations have felt the clip-clop of horses become the rumble of motor cars, its spire has watched bomber planes turn into easyJet air buses.

Within its walls, hundreds of marriages, deaths and births have been marked.

Clinging to a generous patch of grass and trees by Aldgate station, the church is a sanctuary circled by cars, a spiritual haven among glossy storefronts. It has seen hundreds of years of London, and will most likely outlive you and me to see hundreds more.

By the time Lili reached St Botolph's, a yellow sun was creeping into a cold blue sky. The clock on the church spire showed 10.30am, and a young vicar with floppy blond hair threw open the church doors and smiled at the sunshine.

Lili had no desire to smile back. She was cold and tired, and clung to a paper cup of cappuccino as she stood by the church railings.

'Hello, my dear.' Ian Batty approached the church gates, looking especially lively and flamboyant. He wore a checked shirt of yellow and blue, and a red jacket with two medals on the lapel.

On his head was a tweed flat cap, as if he were about to go grouse shooting.

'Ian. Thanks for meeting me.'

'Not a problem. How are you feeling today?'

'I don't know. A bit scared about the possibility of seeing Gran.' She reached into her bag. 'Here are the records.'

'Lovely,' said Ian. 'But please don't forget, I'm also here to pay my respects to your mother.'

'I hardly dare ask,' said Lili. 'But if you're here for the funeral too, why aren't you wearing traditional black?'

'Vivienne liked bright colours, did she not?'

Lili nodded, and felt something that could have been a lump in her throat. 'You're right. Mum did like bright colours.'

'So I'm wearing something that celebrates *her* life, and if it doesn't please the other people, I don't give a damn. Shall we go inside? It's a little breezy out here.'

Lili smoothed her crumpled blouse, realising that today she didn't care about being well presented.

She knew people in grief forgot to take care of themselves. Maybe that's why she hadn't gone back to the theatre for a change of clothes, or fixed her make-up. But she didn't feel like she was grieving. She still felt angry.

'Can you feel the energy of this church? It's seen so many things.' said Ian, as they walked up the path towards the brown-and-cream building. 'Did you make use of it when your lived here with your mother?'

'No,' said Lili. 'Mum talked about visiting and getting forgiven, but we knew she'd never get around to it. Drinking was her religion – she was always hungover on Sunday mornings.'

'People search for themselves in different ways,' said Ian.

'We were never a religious family. Anyway. Ian – the print-outs . . .'

'You don't need to be religious to make use of these buildings,' said Ian. 'They're for everyone. It's spectacular, don't you think, that something built by the hands of man can outlive all of us. And a sign, don't you think, of eternal life?'

'I suppose so,' said Lili, struck by how light and uplifting the decor was.

The walls were finished in white plaster and a second tier, running around the church, was lined with white balustrades. The altar was covered in a patchwork quilt like Joseph's coat of many colours, and behind it sat a pale-gold painting of a tree.

'Aren't you going to read the print-outs?' said Lili. 'We don't have long before—'

'The church narrowly escaped bombing, you know,' said Ian. 'World War Two. A bomb struck the roof, but didn't explode. And later, in the sixties, there was a fire and much of the building was burned.'

'It was destroyed?' said Lili, looking at the angel plasterwork and stained glass windows. 'But it's so beautiful now.'

'Some things are better when they're destroyed and remade.'

'Right. Anyway. Take a look at the records.' They walked across the marble floor and chose a pew. Above them, the huge gold organ pipes organ shone. 'They're not about Love, they're about my great-grandma, and my great, great-grandma. But I thought, maybe . . . I don't know. They might help you somehow.'

Ian nodded at the documents. 'Not up to your usual standards,' he remarked, scanning the papers. 'These are unlikely to build a bridge to Love. However, perhaps if you wanted to make contact with your mother . . .'

Lili shook her head. 'Nice try.'

Ian flipped through the pages. 'There is nothing else?'

'I've found out lots of things, but I don't have any paperwork.'

'What sort of things?'

'I went to the William Peavy Museum and read some of the servants' letters.'

'Really?' said Ian. 'Do tell. Sounds intriguing.'

'It is. Love visited William Peavy's home the day before she died. The servant thought she was trying to blackmail him. That she wanted to sell stories to the newspapers.'

'Fascinating. What sort of stories?'

'I don't know,' said Lili. 'But I feel I'm getting closer to understanding who could have killed Love. She was poisoned by arsenic – something William Peavy used to test in his basement. And the servant thought Love might be blackmailing him. It's a big coincidence, don't you think?'

'Coincidences are what we detectives treasure,' said Ian. 'They point to synchronicity. And synchronicity gives us motive and probability.'

'And perhaps if they had an affair,' said Lili, 'James Morgan was William Peavy's son. Maybe he wanted that covered up.'

'Perhaps.'

'So you think Peavy could have killed Love?'

'Never discount a coincidence,' said Ian. 'The man had the means and potentially a motive.'

'But William Peavy was known as the saviour of the poor,' said Lili. 'He really cared about people. And all his books . . . they were about being good. Not acting selfishly. He was a good person. People loved him. They still do.'

'*Facta non verba*,' said Ian, pointing to a Latin inscription on the stained glass window. 'Deeds not words. Never mind his books – what were Peavy's actions?'

'He lived apart from his wife most of the time,' said Lili. 'I suppose that's not necessarily the action of a nice man.'

'Interesting,' said Ian. 'Although not conclusive. Marriages were different back then. Often they were more like business arrangements. Love worked as a servant for William Peavy, isn't that right?'

'Yes,' said Lili.

'Tell me, do you know how Love procured a job at such a prestigious address?'

'No idea,' said Lili. 'Her father-in-law, George, worked as William Peavy's butler. So I suppose that's how her husband, Tom, ended up working there. But I don't know about Love. Maybe she was just a very good servant.'

Ian nodded. 'That information is certainly something that's missing from the puzzle. Perhaps, as you say, she was simply a sought-after servant. But maybe there was something else – an attraction between Love and William Peavy that earned her the job.' He closed his eyes and was silent for a long moment.

'Ian.'

'Hush, my dear. I'm listening.'

68

Lili waited. The young vicar strolled down the aisle and tapped her on the shoulder.

'I'm sorry to interrupt your worship,' he whispered, 'but I have to tell you there's a funeral here in about twenty minutes.'

'Yes,' said Lili.

Ian didn't seem to have heard. 'I know. I'm . . . it's a relative of mine. I'm here for the funeral. We both are.'

'I see. My apologies.' The vicar glanced over their clothes, then walked away.

Ian's eyes snapped open. 'She's here,' he said, gripping the pew. Blue veins showed around his knuckles. 'We have her. Love. Welcome, my dear. Yes, you remember this old place, don't you? It used to be known as the prostitutes' church back in your day, did it not? Ladies of every description parading around, offering their services.'

Ian laughed. 'Yes. Women like yourself weren't allowed to loiter on street corners, so they'd walk *around* the church and the police couldn't arrest them. It's still here, all these years later. Yes, of course, you never liked the folk who came here. They weren't your sort of people. Well, I hope you'll forgive our meeting here today.'

Ian's face fell.

'Oh, my dear. You're quite sure?' Ian gave the briefest of nods. 'Well, if you're certain.' He turned to Lili. 'She'd like to remember how she was poisoned.' He closed his eyes again. 'She's . . . *banging* on something. Oh yes, of course. A door. She's banging on a door and ringing the door bell. Over and over again.

'She's been ringing for a long time. It is a very good house indeed, a large house for a wealthy gentleman. Why, is it indeed? William Peavy's house. And what are you doing there, my dear?

'Oh! No time for that. A servant has answered the door. Love is shouting I want to see the master.

'The servant is shaking her head. Mrs Morgan, the master will not . . .

'Show her in, a man says. The butler, Love's father-in-law. He is still kind to her, even if no one else in the house is.

'Love is being shown along the hallway. What a fine hallway! You're here to . . . oh, my goodness me. To threaten William Peavy.' Ian shook his head. 'It's not very becoming to threaten, but I hear what you're saying. Morals are for those with money. She is being shown into a room – a very fine room, with a large fire and many books.

'Mr Peavy is standing by the fire. He asks for tea to be brought for his guest. Love has dusted this room many times, and it makes her laugh now that she is a guest. Really, there's no reason to cry, my dear.'

Ian patted his cheeks.

'Yes, of course. You lost the most precious thing of all that afternoon. Well, life is an unusual gift. People often only see its value when it's slipping away from them.'

Lili thought of Viv, and how she couldn't throw anything away, yet discarded her own life as though it were nothing.

Ian frowned. 'It's the tea, she is saying. When I drank it I should have known. There was dirt or plaster in it. I felt the grit on my teeth. I thought the maid was playing tricks, but it wasn't the maid.

'She is looking now, at the man who took her life. It is . . . No. Surely not.' Ian blinked, confused. 'What would he be doing in that house?'

'Who?' said Lili.

Behind them, the vicar paced in the doorway.

'Who?' said Ian. 'It's . . . it's her husband. I see her husband. Tom.'

'Tom?'

'Yes.' Ian laced his fingers together. 'I need to see more. Love, please show me more.'

'Excuse me.' The vicar bobbed at Lili's shoulder. 'Are you a close relative? These front pews are reserved for close relatives.'

'Oh,' said Lili. 'I'd prefer to sit at the back anyway. Out of the way.'

The vicar frowned.

'We need to move,' Lili whispered to Ian, leading him to his feet. Ian looked bewildered, but obliged, letting Lili guide him to the back row near the open doors, where cars and vans inched past.

Lili turned and stared at the traffic. 'People hardly ever talk about death, do they?' Emptiness overwhelmed her, and she wanted to be away from the church. 'But it's the one thing we can all be certain of.'

Ian blinked as he followed her gaze to the sunshine. 'Indeed. The end of this great adventure we call life. My dear, I can still feel Love.'

Lili wanted a cigarette, then changed her mind. What good could it possibly do? The blankness she was feeling couldn't be lifted by smoking, drinking, or even performing – it was on another level. 'Well. Let's hear what else she has to say.'

Ian closed his eyes. 'Yes, Love, my dear. Apologies. Some disruption. We have to make way for the living, of course. You understand. It would have been a rudeness not to.'

Lili saw a black cab pull up in front of the church and two tanned, middle-aged women climbed out. Viv's friends from her modelling days, Paula and Suzie.

She gripped the pew, wondering if Gran would show up.

'Please, Love,' said Ian. 'Show me more. Show me everything you can see. That man . . . the man who poisoned you. He looks like your husband, but how could he be there, in Peavy's house? The lines are confused, my dear. I don't wish to upset you.'

Paula and Suzie walked past Lili without noticing her, and took seats a few rows ahead.

Three more women arrived, all with slack, mournful faces. Viv's friends from the pub – they didn't recognise Lili. She wasn't surprised. She looked very different from in the days when they'd known her.

Two were dressed in black, but one, a sturdy woman with a lumpy, salt-and-pepper bob, wore a bright red dress. In her hand, she held a black-and-gold trimmed photo of a young, suntanned Viv.

'Oh, she's laughing now,' said Ian. 'What's so funny? Love? Tell me.' Ian put a hand on Lili's shoulder. 'She won't tell me any more. She's getting fainter.' He shook his head. 'She's gone.'

But Lili wasn't listening. The church was filling with people who looked dimly familiar. More friends from Viv's pub, the man from the corner shop, two women with Ben's eyes and nose, whom she presumed to be his relatives.

She scanned every arrival for Gran and felt a mixture of relief and disappointment every time it wasn't her.

Uncle Jeff arrived.

'Hello, love,' he whispered.

'Where's Aunt Karen?' Lili whispered back. 'And Grandma? Did she get the invitation?'

Jeff looked uncomfortable. 'Karen got hers. I don't think she can make it. It was all a bit much for her. You know. How Viv went and everything. I don't know about Mum. No one's sure where she's living.'

'Is she still in her caravan?'

'Last I heard love, yes.'

'Are they coming to the inquest?' Lili asked.

'If we can get Mum's address by then, I'm sure she'll come along. Not sure about Karen. Darren didn't get day release then?' He eyed the empty front pews.

'No.'

'Are you coming to sit at the front?'

'I can't.' Lili's lips were tight. 'I can't sit at the front and play the loving daughter. I just can't.'

'Well . . . I think I'd like to.' Jeff went to the front pew.

Lili turned to see a sleek black hearse pull up by the church gates. Behind it was a black limousine and Lili saw Ben in its leather interior.

In the back of the hearse was a coffin.

It was exactly what Ben had asked for – a blue lid with bright yellow daffodils painted around the sides. A wreath of red roses sat on top. Black-suited men lifted it effortlessly to their shoulders. Ben took a front corner, tears rolling down his cheeks.

Lili watched the coffin and felt nothing but anger and emptiness.

If I don't get free of these feelings, I may as well be dead. Feeling this way is no kind of life.

The box was placed on a stone table at the front of St Botolph's, the church Viv had never been brave enough to attend in her lifetime. Save for Jeff, the front pews were still empty.

Lili didn't remember much about the ceremony, except that it started raining. Ben read a poem, the vicar read from the bible. There may have been some singing – she wasn't sure.

69

Behind the church, Lili hid in a tiny grassy graveyard and sucked on a cigarette that tasted of nothing. She felt blood beating at her temples.

'Finding a little peace and quiet for yourself?' Ian picked his way over the spiky grass. 'Everyone's leaving now. Don't you want to say goodbye?'

'I don't want to talk to anyone. The only thing that can help me right now is finding those letters. Look, Ian. What you were saying before, it doesn't make sense. If Love's husband poisoned her, how did he get into William Peavy's house?'

'I only convey what the spirits tell me.'

Lili watched the empty black funeral limousine drive past. 'Love's husband . . . maybe he had reason to poison her. Husbands and wives – there's a lot of emotion there. But in William Peavy's house?'

'Sometimes the spirits—'

'I'm sorry, Ian, but you must be wrong. Whatever you're basing your information on – even if it's something Mum told you – it can't be right.'

Ian nodded. 'It is a strange conundrum. Poisoning in itself is a cold-hearted way to kill. It's not a passionate crime.'

'I don't have time for guesswork right now. There are real things going on.' She took out her mobile and dialled Pete's number.

'Pete. Are you at the theatre yet?'

'You left,' Pete said.

'I know.' Lili remembered the mannequin and felt uneasy.

'You were right,' Pete said. 'One of the mannequins has been vandalised. The head's been sawn off.'

Lili swallowed. 'Did you read the writing on the body?'

There was a pause. 'What writing?'

'The writing,' she whispered. 'There was writing on the doll. On the body. And scribbles on the face.'

'Hang on.' There was a clumping sound, then a crackle as Pete picked up the phone. 'There's no writing, Lils. But the doll's head has been sawn off. I've called the police – they're here now. They say there's no sign of a break-in.' An even longer pause. 'They say it must have been done by someone with access. Maybe an employee.'

It took a moment for Lili to understand what Pete was getting at.

'No, no, no.' She shook her head at the phone. 'It wasn't me. The stage door could have been open – I always leave it open when I'm upstairs. I was in the office. It couldn't have been . . .'

'Where are you?' Pete asked.

'I'm out. Near my mum's house.'

'Tell me where. I'll come meet you.'

'No,' said Lili. 'No, it's okay. I'll come to the theatre.'

'I could come pick you up and we can talk about the writing—'

'NO! It's okay. I must have just . . . it's okay. It was late at night, I must have been seeing things. Silly. Anyway, I'd better go. There are things I need to do—'

'Lils, you haven't forgotten about this afternoon, have you?'

'What?'

'The afternoon tea show?'

'No, I hadn't forgotten exactly. It's just really important I find these letters Mum was looking for, and—'

'Lili, the big boss is here.' He lowered his voice. 'You're under contract. If you miss the show today, she's going to take legal action.'

'I don't respond well to threats.'

'Don't be an idiot, Lili. If you're thinking of having any kind of career revival, you don't want to begin it with a court case.'

Lili closed her eyes. 'Fine. I'll be there.'

In the theatre dressing room, Pete made two teas and added a generous splash of vodka to each mug.

'So tell me about the funeral,' Pete said. 'I tried to find out where it was. I wanted to come.'

'It was fine.' Lili waved her hand. 'A relief actually.'

'To get it over and done with?'

'No. Because my gran wasn't there.'

'You look tired. Exhausted.'

'I haven't done my make-up properly.'

'No. It's not that. Maybe you should talk to Carol-Ann. Ask if she can sign you off for a few days.'

Lili laughed and took a sip of steaming tea. 'She's already offered me time off. But you know me, the show must go on. Anyway, performing is probably the only thing holding me together right now.'

'Well, go straight to bed after that.'

'I can't. There are things I need to do. Research. Stuff to do with my mum.'

'Tonight?'

'Of course tonight. I'd do it right now if I didn't have a show to do.' She noticed a fetish flyer stuck to the mirror and put her head in her hands. 'Oh shit.'

'What?'

'Caz booked me to appear at the fetish club tonight, didn't she? Midnight. Right? She booked it ages ago, when I was, you know, *sane*, and doing three shows a day seemed perfectly normal.'

'Oh yeah. Well you could try and cancel—'

'No.' Tea and vodka splashed from Lili's mug onto the black painted floor. 'Like you said, I'm contracted. There's no getting out of it. Anyway, you can't turn down a show, not in this business. Not if I ever want to tour again.'

She looked into her tea and thought of the nooses drawn around her white neck and the doll's head rolling around the floor.

70

Life's a Stage by Lili Allure

The burlesque motto – never turn down a show

We're busy bees, us burlesque bunnies, and we have to be to make a living. Never turn down a show, that's the burlesque motto. You don't know when you'll be asked again. Reputations are everything in this business, and you want to be known as the girl who never says no.

Of course, that being said it's absolutely vital you take care of yourself between shows and relax when you can. Otherwise you'll run yourself ragged.

Lili slumped against the window of a cab and watched the night sky and the lights of Vauxhall tube station bob past. It was midnight but, despite an exhausting day of two live shows, she somehow had to muster the energy to entertain hundreds of people.

She was on her way to perform at a fetish night called Club Pedestal at an enormous venue overlooking the Thames. The booking had been made weeks ago, when performing had been the way Lili distracted herself from the life she was living. Now all she could think about was how soon she could get on the internet, and what Gretchen might have found out.

Lili's mind had been stretching and flexing all day.

Did I really see the word family *on that doll? Or was it all in my head?*

She looked at Pete, who'd insisted on coming along. He'd been stealing concerned glances at her the whole journey.

'I'm not feeling one hundred per cent,' Lili admitted.

'It was your mother's funeral today, no wonder you're feeling weird.'

Lili felt Pete skirting around the sawn-up doll issue. It hadn't been mentioned explicitly since that afternoon. Lili didn't know whether Pete secretly believed Lili had flipped and done it herself – but he hadn't had the locks changed at the theatre.

'It's not just *feeling* weird. Strange things have been happening since Mum died, but . . .' She looked at her lap. 'Death sometimes makes people see things, doesn't it?'

'Maybe,' said Pete. 'But I'll tell you something real. You were terrified last night.'

'I know. I'm not crazy about doing such a public performance tonight, to tell you the truth.' Lili caught sight of Pete's outfit. He wore black jeans and a T-shirt with *Nobody knows I'm a lesbian* written on it – the closest he could get to a fetish outfit. 'And I'm not sure they'll let you in wearing jeans.'

'Then I'll wait outside and make sure you get home safe.'

'Right.'

'What sorts of people come to this sort of thing?'

'Women, mainly,' said Lili. 'Just like a big girls' night out, but with lots of high heels and men wearing leather straps and aprons. Everyone's free to express themselves. But anyone can come in – it's not like at Kate's. No one's names are recorded.' She looked at him. 'Thanks so much for letting me stay last night.'

'You're staying tonight as well.'

Lili didn't say anything, but she was relieved. She didn't want to sleep alone in the dark theatre.

The taxi pulled up outside the club.

'Here we are.'

The house mistress, dressed in a buckled-up corset and red plastic gloves, greeted Lili at the door.

'Welcome. We're so very pleased to have you as our performer. One of our slaves will show you to the stage area.' She looked at Pete's jeans. 'I'm sorry, but your friend isn't dressed appropriately.' She tapped sharp, red fingernails together. 'Absolutely no jeans. If he has a change of clothes, we can lend him a dog collar.'

'Pete's my security,' said Lili. 'A few of my posters have been slashed, and there was an incident at the theatre.' She glanced at Pete. 'So . . .' She let the sentence slide away.

'I'm afraid unless he has a change of clothes we can't let him in.' The house mistress took out a dog collar and ran the chain through her fingers.

'I don't,' said Pete. 'I'll wait outside.'

A male house slave in an apron appeared from the shadows and knelt at Lili's feet, presenting her with a red rose.

'Pete—'

'It's fine.' He went to the doorway and lounged against it.

The slave took Lili's equipment bag and led her into the dark depths of the club. Techno grew louder with every step, reminding Lili she had a bad headache.

Anyone can come in here. Not like at Kate's.

Few people paid attention to Lili as she strutted towards the stage in a plastic corset and bright yellow thigh-high boots. She was perfectly ordinary, if not a little plain, in a club of spiked seven-inch-high heels, candyfloss-coloured wigs, buckles, leather, whips and severe red and black make-up.

She passed the trampling cage, where bare-backed men lay waiting for high-heeled women to walk over them. At the end of the night, she usually obliged male guests by walking over them in especially sharp heels, but tonight she planned to go straight back to Pete's and sleep.

Someone tapped Lili on the shoulder and she jumped.

'Where may I put your bag?' It was the house slave.

'I'll take it. Thanks.' She headed towards the stage, feeling a murmur pass through the crowd as people realised who she was. Heads turned, and for once she wished people wouldn't look. She felt so exposed.

What's wrong with me? I'm a performer. I love people looking.

There was a whip-crack and she flinched.

Calm down.

She dropped her CD at the DJ booth, climbed on stage and began unloading her equipment – wrought-iron fire fingers with meth-soaked bandages at the ends.

As Lili knelt to light the bandages, giving the crowd a good look at her electric-blue plastic suspender belt, she felt her red patent handbag vibrate. She grabbed her phone, thinking it would be Pete checking up on her.

'Hello?' She held the phone against her chin as she arranged the iron fingers.

'Lils.' It was Darren.

Lili dropped the metal sticks and everyone turned to stare. 'How are you calling me?' The only prisoner phones were in the wing outside the cells, and could only be used at designated times – which definitely did not include the early hours of the morning.

'I nicked my cell mate's mobile,' Darren croaked.

'How did he get a mobile in prison?'

'You don't want to know. Listen. I've got to be quick – he's asleep. Did you ever meet Grandad's brother, Ron?'

'No,' said Lili, walking to the side of the stage, covering her ear. 'But I remember Grandma talking about him.'

'Really nice bloke. Lives in Stepney Green, or he did. You know you wanted stories from relatives and all that? Well he's pretty old and he might know bits and pieces about the family. I don't know if he's still alive but—'

'Do you know his address?'

'No,' Darren whispered, 'But I remember his telephone number. Aunty Francine rang his wife, Rose, every Saturday, and she had a song for the number. 5818722.'

'That's too short for a London number,' said Lili, hearing a shout from the crowd and huddling further into the corner. She repeated the number in her head: *5818722.*

'I know, but they added sevens didn't they? Zero two, zero seven. Hold on MATE. MATE!' There was a clatter and the line went dead.

Lili squeezed her eyes shut, trying to fend off the image of Darren in yet another fight.

'Lili.'

It was the house mistress, looking at her with concern.

'Do you need help setting up?' She tapped her watch. 'We're running over—'

'No, no!' Lili looked at her unlit bandages. 'Sorry – no, it's fine.' She signalled for the DJ to start her music, but nothing happened. Lili's face and hands began to tingle. It was too hot.

'Oh shit,' Lili said, watching the DJ's panicked expression as he pressed buttons, ejected and reinserted the CD. 'The CD's not working.'

She looked at her fire sticks and saw her hands were red and sweating in her fingerless PVC gloves. The poles slipped around in her fingers. Everyone was staring.

I'm watching you, Lilian.

The slashed posters and the doll's head whirred around and around.

What's wrong with you? Your music's crashed plenty of times. You have to improvise.

Orange-red light pounded at Lili's eyeballs. She tried to move, but her body was stiff and wouldn't fold into any of her usual poses. Then the firesticks fell to the floor, and she grappled to pick them up, but her movements were clumsy.

What's happening to me? Why can't I perform?

She tried again to pose, the firesticks slipping around, her legs turning at graceless angles.

Everyone was staring at her, and she felt their confusion and disappointment.

I need to get out of here.

On six-inch heels, dressed in red-and-yellow plastic, Lili pulled herself to her feet and stumbled out of the club.

By the time she reached the exit, she fell against a wall, tasted cold air and felt her chest heaving and falling.

'Lils.' Pete appeared from the shadows. 'What happened?'

'I couldn't do it.'

'You know, Lils, sometimes when people have a trauma . . .'

'I'm dealing with things in my own way. Mum was looking for

something. When I find it, I can let everything go. I'll be even better than before, you'll see.'

'Let's get a taxi.'

'My stuff,' Lili heard herself stammer. 'It's down there. The show. I've got to go back.'

'No, we're leaving,' said Pete, and he led Lili to a waiting taxi.

71

Lili woke the next morning staring at scarves pinned to a cobwebby ceiling. She saw a black duvet and realised she was in Pete's bed. Again. He wasn't beside her, but she could hear him snoring from the living room.

Well, this is a first.

She'd never slept at Pete's flat and woken up with her underwear still on.

Sliding out of bed, she noticed plastic clothes folded on the floor and held her head.

Last night. Oh shit.

She crept into the living room and saw Pete lying on the sofa, one arm and leg grazing the carpet. The room was warm with Pete's body, and the loose, sash window, which let in flurries of winter air, glittered with condensation.

Lili saw her equipment bag next to the sofa and a folded skirt and blouse next to it, with shoes on top. Her shoes. Her skirt and blouse too.

'Pete.' She shook him awake. 'How did you . . . My bag? And the clothes?'

'What? Oh.' Pete sat up. 'A mate of mine picked up the bag for you. Don't worry about last night – they totally understand.'

Lili sat on the arm of the sofa. 'They'll never hire me again. And the big boss will go mad. Trust me. Reputations in this business—'

'Lils.' Pete put a sleep-hot hand on her knee. 'They get it. Your mum. Look, a friend of mine counsels soldiers who've been to Afghanistan, and—'

'I don't need a counsellor.' Lili picked up the clothes. 'I need to find Mum's letters.' She returned to the bedroom and dialled the number Darren had given her, pushing the door closed as the phone began to ring.

The throaty, bits-and-pieces voice of an elderly East London woman answered.

'Oh – hello,' said Lili. 'Are you Rose?'

'Speaking.' The woman sounded delighted. 'Daisy? Is that you?'

'No, it's Lili. Albert's grand-daughter.'

'Oh.' A pause. '*Lilian*, did you say? Darren's sister?'

'I was Lilian. But I'm Lili now.'

'Oh. Right. Right. Yes, of course. No, I remember now. Lily. Yes. Viv's daughter. I always said to Albert, Viv should bring you over. Darren, I saw quite a bit, but you were still with Viv. But I always told him. Where are you now love? Still in London?'

'Yes, in the West End,' said Lili.

'My two are in Australia,' Rose said. 'They come back from time to time, but I hardly ever . . . well. How's Darren? I haven't seen him in years. He was a little monkey.'

'Oh. He's good. You know. I'm doing some family research, and I wondered – might I come see you and Ron? Ask a bit about the family?'

'Of course you can,' said Rose. 'Yes, yes of course. When would you be thinking of coming?'

'I was hoping today,' said Lili. 'Now, if possible.'

'Oh, well I'm not sure if I can manage this morning. I'm visiting Ron you see, I go every morning so, well—'

'Oh. Is Ron not at home with you?'

'No,' said Rose. 'He's in hospital.'

'Can I come visit him with you?'

'Well, yes, come along. Why not? The more the merrier. He'll like the company. I have to warn you, he's not saying much of anything at all. He's resting quite a bit. He had a heart attack you see, and . . . well. We can meet at the hospital – the Royal on Whitechapel High Street, do you know it?'

'I can—'

'Take the tube to Whitechapel. Or if you prefer the bus, there are plenty. You'll see the hospital easy enough. Ask someone to show you to the critical care unit. We can meet in the relatives' room outside.'

'See you there.'

LOVE MORGAN b. 1831, d. 1865.

George Morgan

Nee Avary

Love Morgan 1831 - 1865

M

Tom Morgan 1836 - 1874

James Morgan 1864 - 1889

m. Cooky Morgan (Catherine Long) b. 1863 - d.?

Margaret Collins 1880 - ?

1877 - 1912 Michael Morgan

Fred Morgan 1899 - 1972

1900 - 1970 'Dynamite' Dolly Morgan

Ron Morgan b.1937

Francine Morgan 1933 - 2000

1935 - 1995 Albert Morgan

Karen Morgan b. 1960

Vivienne Morgan b.1965

Jeff Morgan b.1958

Darren Morgan

72

The sign on the coffee machine said: *Free hot drinks for visitors. Please donate what you can afford. Suggested donation: 20p per drink.*

Lili dropped three pounds in an empty plastic cup by the machine, then pressed for a black coffee. A spray of coffee granules clattered into a beige cup, followed by steaming water.

Lili was glad the relatives' room was empty. No sobbing, emotional visitors reminding her what an unfeeling monster she was.

She read a poster on the wall about keeping germs out of the critical care unit.

'Lily?' An overweight woman in a flowery dress appeared at the door. She had flat, grey hair in a pixie cut, a red, sweaty face and a nervous expression. A cotton-and-plastic Fanta shopping bag with two battered biscuit tins inside swung from her fingers.

'Rose?' Lili asked.

Rose gave a shy smile. 'I wasn't sure if you'd come. I made some profiteroles and a pork pie. I don't know, sometimes people don't eat meat so I thought I'd better do a couple of things.'

'Thanks so much.'

'You're ever so nicely dressed,' said Rose, reaching out to stroke Lili's skirt. 'Lovely material. A bugger to sew, though. Are you ready to go through?' She put the shopping bag under a plastic chair.

'Yes,' said Lili, sensing her nervousness. 'I'll follow your lead. I'm so glad you and Ron were able to see me today.'

They went through double doors and Lili, noticing a hand sanitizer, sprayed her hands.

'I always forget,' Rose admitted, taking a spray herself. She pressed a buzzer and a nurse led them through.

'No change from yesterday,' the nurse told Rose.

She showed them to a bed, where a pale old man lay sleeping. He had large ears and deep lines in the thick skin of his forehead. Bright white hair, short and straight like a GI's, stuck up around his head.

'Hello, Ron,' Rose said, snatching his limp hand and stroking it with vigour. 'Love, it's Rose. I've brought a friend.'

'Can he hear you?' Lili asked, noticing the crumple of Ron's eyelids and long, stray hairs shooting from his eyebrows. It was intrusive, she realised, staring at someone while they were so helpless. She looked away.

'They say he can't,' said Rose. 'They say his oxygen supply was cut off for too long. Even if he comes round, he won't be able to understand much. He might not even recognise me. But I don't pay any attention to all that. I still talk to him. I'm like a radio. It must be so boring for him in here. So I tell him about what's been on the news, that sort of thing.'

Ron's chest moved in slight, jerky breaths.

'He's not suffering,' Rose continued. 'That's what they say. Just in limbo. Not here, not there, not anywhere. He looks cold, don't you think? When he first came in here, I thought he was cold. But they kept telling me, no. He's not cold. He's just pale. Something to do with lying down all day.'

'I'm sure he's comfortable.'

'You must think I'm heartless, being so matter of fact. I was in floods of tears when they first brought him in. Funny how you get used to things. At first I was so sad for him. I thought, it's the worst place to be. Not one thing or the other. But I've got used to it, and I'm just glad he's still with me.'

Rose shook Ron's hand. 'This is Lilian, Ron. Albert's granddaughter. You never met her, but she's come to say hello.' She turned to Lili. 'Tell him about yourself, if you like.'

'Hello, Ron,' said Lili. 'My name's Lili. I'm Viv's daughter. I'm a showgirl in the West End.'

'A showgirl. Listen to that, Ron. She's come to visit. I've made you a pork pie today, and a few profiteroles.' Rose turned to Lili. 'Don't think I've cracked – I can't bring the food in here. Germs, they say. He can't eat it anyway. So I just talk him through it, then share it out in the waiting room after I've seen him.'

'Right.' Lili watched Ron's sagging face. It was blueish-white, but soft, and she could feel heat coming from his cheeks. There was still life there.

'They say it's only a matter of weeks, but they said that three months ago,' said Rose. 'And he's still with me. Aren't you, love? You're still here. Doctors see death all the time, they're bound to think the worst. At the moment he's just stuck. But he can't stay like this for ever. There has to be a change soon.'

'I wanted to ask you. I hope this isn't inappropriate or the wrong moment or—'

'No, no. Don't you worry. Ask away. Anything you like.'

'Well, I'm doing some family research and I wanted to know . . . I wanted to find out as far back as I can. Do you know much about the Morgan family? The ones who lived before I was born?'

'Not much,' said Rose. 'Ron doesn't know much about my side of the family either. What about your nan? Ron's sister, Ginny? Have you spoken to her?'

Lili shook her head. 'Not yet. I'm not sure where she's living right now.'

'She'll be over the moon to talk to you.'

'I'm not so sure about that. I haven't seen her for a while. I'm sort of, I don't know . . . not quite ready to see her yet.'

'Why's that?'

'I'm not sure exactly. When I think about seeing her, I don't feel good.'

'Well, if you want to know about your family history, Ginny's the best one to ask. She's an interesting woman. Got up to all sorts when she was in the States.'

'Interesting? Are you thinking of the same person? This is my gran who lives in a caravan, who won't travel abroad. Who goes to church every Sunday and stopped talking to Mum after she did underwear modelling.'

Rose burst out laughing. 'Well that's the pot calling the kettle black!'

'But Gran is so . . .'

'She is now,' said Rose. 'Who wouldn't be, after that dreadful thing?'

'What dreadful thing?'

'The dreadful thing. In America.' She looked at Ron. 'Horrible. Horrible experience for her. They left America, of course.'

'What happened to her?'

'Oh . . . you ask her yourself, she'll tell you.'

Neither women spoke for a moment, and Lili absorbed the stillness of the intensive care ward. She saw a teenage girl, maybe twelve or thirteen, by the bedside of a young woman – a sister, perhaps. The woman was unconscious, and the girl watched her stoically, not crying, just being with her, waiting for her to wake up.

They were all frozen, Lili realised. Stuck in one place, waiting for life or death to claim them. They didn't have a choice. Change would come when it wanted to.

She realised nothing – no threats to body or sanity – could be any worse than being trapped in one place, slowly wasting away.

'Did Gran or Grandad Albert ever mention some family letters?' Lili asked. 'Old ones – from Victorian times?'

'Letters? The ones Albert kept in his trunk, you mean? Yellow ones. Well, I say Albert's trunk. It was Dolly's originally.'

Lili stared at her. 'Dynamite Dolly's trunk? The trunk she travelled around with? There were yellow letters inside it?'

'Oh Dynamite Dolly,' said Rose. 'I haven't heard that name in a long time. Yes, the letters were inside her old trunk. She was always Dorothy to me. I only met her once – she was quite something. Ever so lady-like. Glamorous. She put the wind up me, I can tell you. She never saw my girls. Not once.'

'So tell me about the letters and the trunk.'

'Your Grandad Albert loved that trunk,' said Rose. 'Dolly's brother inherited it, and passed it on to Albert when he died. My girls were always playing with it. They found this sliding bit at the bottom with these old yellow letters inside. Albert went ballistic. Don't you touch those, this and that.'

'The letters – what did they look like?'

'Oh, just old letters, you know. Dear so and so. Address at the top. Old paper, yellow, and writing from an ink pen with lots of spots everywhere. We used to dip pens in inkwells, you know, before fountain pens and biros came along. Messy business.'

'How many letters were there?'

'A handful. Three at most, I'd say.'

'Did you notice who wrote them? Or who they were addressed to?'

Rose scratched her red cheek. 'I didn't. Or if I did, it was so long ago I can't remember.'

'Do you know what happened to them?'

'Albert put them back in the trunk, away from sticky little fingers. But I've no idea what happened to the trunk after he died. Perhaps your gran still has it.'

'Right.'

'Go see your gran,' said Rose. 'She'll know more than anyone.'

'The thing is, no one knows where she's living,' said Lili. 'I thought she'd come to Mum's funeral, but she didn't.'

'She's at a static caravan site in Epping,' said Rose. 'On the west side of the town. There's only one. She came to see Ron a few weeks back, told us all about it. The manager is letting her stay there for free over the winter. He's even thrown in the electric.'

'Epping? That's on the Central line.'

'That's right. Easy.'

'Oh, I wouldn't say it'll be easy.'

As Lili left, the hospital security guard hurried across the tarmac. Lili made to step aside until she realised he was heading for her.

'Excuse me – are you Lili?'

'Yes,' said Lili, surprised.

'She was dead right about you being easy to recognise. I've got a message for you.'

'A message for me? From who?'

'Someone called Gretchen.'

'What?'

'Gretchen. She rang a while ago. Described you down to a tee. Lucky I caught you. She was frantic, the receptionist said. Really upset, poor thing. Desperate to track you down.'

'How did she know I was here?' said Lili.

'No idea.' The security guard gave her a piece of paper.

Lili, I know who's sending you text messages, and they know I know. Meet me at the theatre at noon, love Gretchen.

Lili noticed the time scribbled at the top of the paper, showing the phone message had been taken an hour ago. It was already gone noon.

She reread the message.

They know I know.

73

Life's a Stage by Lili Allure

Lili Allure's guide to playing with fire

Now girls, you should never play with fire – unless you're on stage, that is. Not all venues can accommodate a fire show, but if you have access to a large, well-ventilated stage with a safety curtain and fire extinguishers on standby, oh – please make use of it.

It's one of my biggest regrets that Kate Hamilton's isn't suitable for fire shows. Too small, too old, wooden floors, yada yada yada. But I do so miss playing with fire! Before Kate's, fire was the centrepiece of my performance. Fire is passion, heat and danger. What else could a burlesque girl ask for?

There are all sorts of whirling, twirling fire toys you can bring into a performance – double-ended devil sticks, x-shaped chaos sticks, fire fans – the list is endless. Buy, experiment and find your toys of choice.

I have flaming pastie tassels – yes, you heard right. I set each tassel on fire and twirl with all my might. Just like my inspiration, Satan's Angel (burlesque legend and flaming-tassel twirler extraordinaire), years of practice means I don't have a single fire scar.

My favourite flame toys are the oh-so-simple fire fingers. You can buy as many as you please (of course, I buy a full set of ten, but that's just me), and create real magic on stage – elegant and dreamlike if you dance, or whoosh, bang boom if you swallow fire and spit it out. It's up to you.

The roads were clear between Whitechapel and Central London, but as Lili's cab turned into Long Acre, it hit a traffic jam the whole street long.

'Come on, come on,' said the taxi driver. 'What's going on? The congestion charge was supposed to have got rid of all this.'

Lili noticed a crowd on the pavement up ahead. There was a red and white cordon blocking the way to the theatre and police were waving traffic away.

'I'll walk from here.' Lili jumped out of the cab. She wove in and out of the crowds.

'Fire,' she heard someone say. 'Theatre,' said someone else.

Lili walked faster, smelling burning wood and noticing black smoke hanging over shop roofs.

Turning a corner she saw two fire engines banked up on the pavement.

She looked up.

The wedding-cake turrets of Kate Hamilton's were black and scorched, and smoke slid from second-floor windows. There were popping sounds, and the smell of burning chemicals crept inside her nostrils.

Gretchen.

She lifted the tape cordon, but a fire fighter, wearing a white tabard with *Incident Commander* on it, blocked her path.

'You can't go through this way.'

'Please.' Lili fought to keep her voice steady. 'I was meeting someone here. There might be a girl inside.'

The fire fighter lifted the cordon. 'Under you come. Someone inside, you say?'

Lili ducked under the tape. 'I don't know. People aren't supposed to know this, but the stage door is almost always unlocked. Gretchen knows you can get in that way.'

'This Gretchen. Does she have access to the building?'

'She shouldn't. But she's got inside before.'

'Can I have a physical description?'

'She's fifteen,' said Lili. 'Medium build, tall – about five-foot six, brown hair. Very pretty.'

'Do you know much about the layout of the building?'

'Please,' said Lili. 'You've got to send someone in. Please. She could be—' Glass shattered and Lili winced. She tried to move towards the building, but the fire fighter stood in her way.

'We'll be able to search the building much more quickly if we know the layout.'

'Right.' Lili tried to weave a path through her messy mind. 'There are tunnels downstairs where the dressing room is. An office upstairs. The auditorium and bar. Ticket office. There's a bar upstairs too.'

'Do you have keys?'

Lili nodded, pulling a large bunch of silver and gold keys from her bag, holding out the one for the main doors.

The fire fighter took it and shouted to four others, who put on breathing equipment, took the keys and disappeared inside the building.

'Is there any way to contact this girl?' the commander asked. 'Perhaps rule out the possibility that she's inside?'

'Oh. Right. Of course.' Lili coughed on smoke that tasted of rubber. 'I don't have a number for her. She has a mobile but it'll only take calls from her mum.'

'Can we contact her mum?'

'Yes,' said Lili. 'I know her address. I'll go there but . . . Please, I can't leave now. Not when she might be inside. I have to be here.'

Time crawled along.

Lili watched flames curl around roof timbers and knew she should feel sad about the theatre. Even violated. It was her home, after all. But as little green flames burned chemical-covered wood, she couldn't care less about the building. The theatre could go to hell. Only Gretchen mattered, and for Gretchen her knees faltered every time a gust of wind fed the fire.

When fire fighters trooped from the charred innards of the theatre, it felt like hours had passed. Their movements were solemn and for a heart-stopping, acid-throated moment, Lili thought the worst.

Oh my god. She was inside. They found her.

But then one of the fire fighters lifted his mask and shook his head.

'We didn't find anyone, but there's a lot of damage. A *lot* of damage. It began in more than one location.' He looked meaningfully at the boss. 'It's going to take a long time to get under control.' Behind him, other fire fighters sprayed great loops of water over the roof.

'You're sure there's no one in there?' Lili asked.

'We can never one hundred per cent rule it out until the fire's under control and we've done a complete search,' said the commander. 'The best thing you can do now is get in touch with her mum and see if you can track her down.'

Lili nodded, watching flames poke through the roof tiles, accompanied by great clouds of pigeon-coloured smoke. She thought about the quickest way to get to Gretchen's house.

Head up to Charing Cross Road – no, the traffic might be blocked there too. Walk south?

'Do you know when the fire started?' Lili asked.

'It's been burning for at least an hour. It should have triggered the alarms. It wasn't until it spread outside the building that someone called in.'

Lili checked her watch, feeling beyond uneasy as she realised it was gone one o'clock. *Gretchen wasn't inside. She wasn't.*

A stocky fireman approached the commander. 'Evidence of a break-in round the back,' he said, and the commander nodded.

'I'll tell the police. They'll want to make it a crime scene.'

'A break-in?' Lili's eyes watered as a piece of hot ash landed on her eyeball. The commander seemed oblivious to the burning grey petals that were settling all over them. 'Oh no. Gretchen. She could have broken in and still be trapped in there.'

'You think this young girl might be responsible for the fire?'

'No, no. That's not what I meant. Just that she might be in there.'

'It's unlikely, if the lads didn't find her first time around.' He nodded at a police car outside the cordon.

A police officer approached. 'John?'

'Can you take this young lady to – where does the girl's mother live?'

'Whitechapel.'

74

Life's a Stage by Lili Allure

The only one of William Peavy's poems I remember . . .

> *The filthy air of Whitechapel,*
> *Is something to be seen,*
> *For ne'er did I see a fog,*
> *Of red and black and green.*
> *Come noon the air is thick and foul,*
> *And dangerous to breathe,*
> *As all of London's soot and smog,*
> *Blows eastwards on the breeze.*

From *The Pretty and the Poor* by William Peavy

Lili thought the worst day of her life had been and gone. She was wrong. As she rode in the police car towards Carol's flat, trying to figure out how to tell her Gretchen might have ventured into a burning theatre – *her* burning theatre – she wanted to open the car door and throw herself into the oncoming traffic.

Life was awful. Full of despair and ugliness. Smoke from the theatre had followed her, cloaking her in black air, suffocating and dimming everything.

The world had fallen into tiny, dreamy little details.

Sirens.

Traffic clearing.

Falling against the side of the car as they took a sharp corner.

Building.

Building.

Tower block.

Lili thought she could still see smoke overhead, but it was just rain clouds.

A locked communal entrance.

'It's okay,' Lili heard herself say. 'My mum used to live here. I have a key.'

Concrete.

Chewing gum stuck to the floor.

Stairs.

A freezing black rail under her bare fingers.

Door. Orange wood.

Black bars and glass reinforced with glass wire.

Geraniums in a pot.

A doorbell too clean and bright white for the building, like teeth in a tanned face.

Lili put a shaking finger to the button and felt smooth, cold plastic under her naked fingertip. Smoke clung to her skin and clothes and she knew her face was dirty.

Turning she saw the police officers and supposed they must have followed her up the stairs, but didn't remember hearing them.

The front door opened and Lili saw Carol, wiry hair combed close to her head, sharp, frantic eyes behind her glasses.

'Yes?' Carol didn't look at Lili, but at the police officers standing behind. 'What's happening?'

'Is Gretchen here?' Lili asked.

Carol pulled thin arms around her chest, her head bobbing between the police officers and Lili. 'I thought I told you to stay away from my daughter.'

'Is she here, Carol?'

'No. She's gone to drama group. Has something happened?'

'There's been a fire.'

'Oh!' Carol's hand shot to her mouth. 'Is Gretchen okay?'

'It was at my theatre,' said Lili, not knowing how to answer the question. She felt as if cold water had been thrown over her. The fragile hope that Gretchen would be home, messing around on Facebook in her bedroom, evaporated. 'In Covent Garden.'

'Oh.' Carol's hand lowered and she let out a breath. 'I was worried. I thought something had happened to Gretchen.'

Lili heard the shuffle of feet behind her and felt an ache in her stomach.

'Carol, we don't think Gretchen was inside the theatre, but there's a chance—'

Carol blinked. 'I don't understand. Gretchen's nowhere near Covent Garden. Her drama group is in Bethnal Green.'

'She sent me a message,' said Lili, 'arranging to meet me at my theatre at noon today, but when I got there . . .' *The theatre was in flames.*

'A message?' Carol's arms wove tighter around her ribcage. 'What sort of message?'

'A telephone message.'

'No, she couldn't have. She doesn't have any phone credit. Anyway, she's been at drama group all morning. It must have been someone else.'

'Maybe she found a way to put credit on her phone.'

Carol sucked in her cheeks. 'For your information, her mobile phone is right here – she dropped it in the washing-up bowl last night. It's broken.'

Carol disappeared down the hallway and returned with a pink mobile phone. Its screen looked like a lava lamp, with grey blobs moving around inside it. 'She couldn't have called anyone.'

'What about a pay phone?'

'She's at drama group,' Carol repeated, but Lili could sense her floundering. 'She didn't have any money. I cut off her pocket money after the museum incident. What did the message say exactly?'

'It said Gretchen wanted to meet me,' said Lili. 'I was given the message by a hospital security guard this morning.'

'So you didn't speak to her?'

'No.'

'Wait there.' Carol disappeared into the house. Five minutes later, she came back in tears.

'She's not at her drama group. They say she called in sick. Oh Gretchen. Gretchen.'

Lili looked at the police officers, both of whom stared at the floor.

'Come with me,' said Lili, reaching out to her. 'Come to the theatre. Bring your mobile phone. We'll find her, Carol. I promise we will.'

75

By the time the police car pulled up at the theatre, fire had ravaged Kate Hamilton's completely. Charred roof joists were exposed to the sky like bent, burned knuckles. The building looked naked, and Lili shivered as winter winds curled around the blackened wood.

A police cordon had been stretched all around the theatre, and a policeman with a clipboard was logging people in and out of what was now a crime scene.

The fire commander recognised Lili and approached the cordon. 'There was no one inside. You can breathe easy.'

Carol, standing beside Lili with a crumpled tissue at her nose, sagged inside her quilted jacket. 'Oh, thank God.'

Lili couldn't speak. Her throat was too tight.

'Are you the young lady's mother?' the commander asked Carol.

Carol nodded into her tissue. 'You're sure, you're absolutely certain, she wasn't inside?'

The commander put a hand on her shoulder. 'There's a lot of damage, but nothing has been found to suggest anyone was in there.'

Still, Lili couldn't bring herself to feel relieved. Brisk winds turned black smoke thin and grey above the theatre, but guilt still clung to Lili.

Carol nodded, grasping at the good news. She lifted her glasses to wipe away tears. 'But I need to know where she is. She's missing. Please.'

'Give some details to this gentleman,' said the commander, pointing at one of the officers who'd been at Carol's flat, and now loitered behind the cordon. 'See if he can help you locate the young lady. I'm sure there's no cause for alarm.'

Lili turned to the officer, noticing him in detail for the first time. He was young – perhaps twenty years old – and kept fiddling with the zip of his fluorescent yellow jacket.

'Please.' Carol stuffed her tissue from her coat pocket. 'My daughter. My child. She's supposed to be at drama group, but she's not there.'

The police officer checked his watch and said gently: 'As the fire commander said, I'm sure there's no cause for alarm. Sounds like she's done a bunk from her drama class and she'll turn up when it's supposed to finish. Phone her friends, check her usual haunts. No cause for panic just yet.'

Carol looked at Lili, confused. 'Usual haunts?'

'Is there anywhere she likes to hang out?' Lili asked.

'I don't know.' Carol pushed glasses up her nose. 'She doesn't hang out. She goes to school, does her homework, goes to hobby groups.' She began to sob again. 'She's been grounded this week.' Carol turned to the police officer. 'How could this happen?'

'Maybe her school friends know something,' said the police officer.

'She doesn't have friends at school.'

'Everyone has a few friends. Don't they?'

Carol shook her head. 'She doesn't get on with children at the local school. If it wasn't for . . . circumstances . . . she'd be in private education.'

'But she doesn't always go to school,' said Lili. 'And she said she was thinking about running away. She's not all that happy at home.'

'What?' Carol looked devastated.

'She skived off a few days ago,' Lili admitted. 'Look – I hate telling tales, but I was with her. I thought she was better off with me than roaming the streets on her own.'

A bad choice of words.

'Roaming the streets. Oh good God. Look, is this something to do with Viv? Some sort of revenge or something?'

'What?'

'Oh – never mind.'

'She'll be all right,' said Lili. 'She's somewhere near. I'm sure. She might even be at home by now.' The words felt hollow and dipped in guilt.

'Yes.' The police officer agreed. 'Why not head back and wait. I'll take a few details, just to be on the safe side. What's your daughter's full name?'

'Gretchen Carmichael,' said Carol.

'Do you have a photo of her?'

'Right, yes. Of course. A photo. I'm sorry. I'm in a state.' She looked in her handbag. 'I have her passport here.' She rifled past chequebooks, then stared at the officer in amazement. 'It's gone. Her passport's gone.'

'Maybe it's just been misplaced,' said the officer. 'In the stress of the moment—'

'No, it's gone,' Carol shouted. 'Gone. Oh good God.' She stared into her bag. 'Oh no, no, no.' She glared at Lili. 'Did she tell you she was taking her passport?'

'No,' said Lili. 'She never said anything about her passport. Maybe it's just been misplaced, like the police officer said.'

'Right. Yes, maybe. Perhaps it's at home.'

'What was Gretchen wearing, Mrs Carmichael?' asked the police officer.

Carol rubbed her forehead. 'A brown jumper I think. And her quilted coat. Navy blue, from Laura Ashley. Like this one.' She tugged at her own coat sleeve. 'Blue jeans – I don't like her wearing jeans, but you know what children are like. Black lace-up shoes. What else? Pink gloves.'

'Where did you last see her?'

'At home.'

'And what time was that?'

'About ten o'clock this morning.'

'And who was she with?'

'No one. She asked me for bus fare for her drama group – it's a mile or so away near the animal sanctuary in Mile End – and then off she went. I should have driven her.'

'And her drama group haven't seen her?'

'They said she called in sick. But I don't know how she could have called them.'

'It sounds to me if she called in sick – don't take this the wrong way – that she's done a bunk and is off having fun somewhere. No cause for alarm. Do you have any numbers for friends? Names and addresses? What about a boyfriend?'

'She's too young for a boyfriend.' Carol turned to Lili. 'Do you know of anyone? Friends from school?'

'I don't,' said Lili, adding carefully, 'Carol, she does have a boyfriend. A few, by the sounds of it. Online.'

'What on earth does that mean?'

'She calls them her virtual boyfriends. She's friends with a student on Facebook. He's been helping her with research.' Lili bit her lip. 'I told her he seemed a bit old, but I thought it wasn't any of my business.'

Carol retrieved her tissue and blew her nose. 'Well, who is he?'

'I don't know. Just someone she met on Facebook. I don't think she ever met him in person. There's no reason to think that's who she's with. She's probably at home right now.'

The police officer put a hand on Carol's shoulder. 'I think the best thing to do is go home. Most likely, she'll come back of her own accord. She might even be there already.'

'Yes.' Carol sniffed and dabbed her nose. 'Yes, you're right. Of course. That's where she'll be. She'll be at home already, and we'll get all this mess sorted out. She's in a lot of trouble. I'll be having serious words with her.' The idea of telling Gretchen off seemed to cheer Carol up.

'Have there been any rows recently?' the police officer asked.

'Rows?' Carol replied.

'Between you and your daughter. Anything she was upset about?'

'No, nothing. She's a good girl. Well behaved.'

'Carol.' Lili saw ash floating onto Carol's hair and shoulders. 'She may not have spoken to you about this, but Gretchen felt a little . . . suffocated. She wasn't as happy as perhaps you think she was.'

'Check your daughter's bedroom,' said the police officer. 'See if any of her clothes are missing, or personal items.'

Carol shook her head and pushed the tissue closer to her nose. 'She wouldn't run away.'

'It's worth checking, that's all I'm saying,' said the police officer, before adding kindly, 'Look, she's probably home already.' He knocked on the car door. 'Bill? Whitechapel area – what's the nearest? Brick Lane?'

After a nod from the officer in the car, he turned back to Carol. 'Call one zero one, or drop by the Brick Lane police station if she's not home when you get there.'

'I should go home,' said Carol stiffly, turning away from the police officer.

'I'll come with you,' said Lili. For a moment she thought Carol would refuse, but the exhausted woman merely nodded.

'Yes, I'd like that,' she said. Despite their differences, they had something very important in common. All they wanted was for Gretchen to be safe.

76

As soon as Carol opened her front door, Lili felt the emptiness inside the flat and knew Gretchen wasn't there. Carol darted from room to room, but Lili didn't need to. She went straight to Gretchen's bedroom and stared out of the window.

Wherever you are, please come back.

The bedroom, with its sickly pink bedspread, curtains and carpet, looked like a catalogue advert for a little girl's furnishing range. But Gretchen wasn't a little girl. She was fifteen, missing and capable of getting into trouble.

'I'm so sorry Carol,' Lili said, as Carol came in and searched drawers. 'Truly. If it wasn't for me . . .'

'I'm aware of that,' said Carol, pushing aside folded, ironed jeans and white socks with frills at the top. 'Very aware. But being angry with you won't help.'

Carol went to the wardrobe and pushed clothes around. 'I'm certain her jeans . . . No, she has more clothes than this.' Carol ran frantic fingers over school shirts and skirts. 'She had more than . . . and her bag.' She fell to her knees and threw aside a pink rucksack with a teddy bear on the front. 'Her overnight bag . . . things are missing.'

'Are you sure?'

'Of course I'm sure!' Carol reached up to fling clothes back and forth. 'She's taken vests, jumpers, jeans.' She went to the drawer. 'And underwear.' Sitting on the bed, she put her head in her hands. 'She's okay, she's okay, she's okay.' It was a mantra Carol had been murmuring all the way back to the flat.

'She is,' Lili agreed, although fear and guilt chased each other around her body. Missing clothes and an overnight bag weren't good news.

This is what feelings do to you, she thought, wondering when it was exactly that she'd started caring about Gretchen. *They scare you to death.*

'I'm phoning the police,' said Carol.

From the hallway, Lili heard her on the phone.

'. . . *daughter . . . yes, missing for several hours . . . only fifteen . . .*'

Lili looked around the neat room, noting the perfectly made bed, not a crease or crumple in sight. The open wardrobe showed hangers of straight clothes arranged by item order. Jeans, jumpers, blouses. It looked like a lawyer's wardrobe.

Under the bed, Lili caught sight of Gretchen's laptop. By the time Carol came back into the room, Lili had the computer open and was on the internet

'There won't be anything on there,' said Carol. 'I've fixed it so she can't go on the internet.'

'She does,' said Lili.

Carol shook her head. 'She wouldn't.'

'What did the police say?' Lili asked.

'The police? Oh, they're useless. Useless. I don't know. They're sending someone over, but they say the circumstances aren't worrying because she phoned up her drama class. They think she'll turn up after her class is supposed to finish.

'They don't seem concerned that her clothes are missing. When I told them about the theatre fire, they asked me if she carried a lighter around. Can you believe it?'

Lili clicked through screens and opened up Facebook. It automatically logged into Gretchen's account.

'What are you looking at?' Carol asked. 'Are you on the internet? How did you get on the internet?'

'I went through the menu,' said Lili, adding pointedly, 'like Gretchen does. This is her Facebook page.'

A profile picture of Gretchen, in a black swimming costume with the straps pulled down and tied at the back, all warm-brown skin, rounded shoulders and pink lips, smiled at them.

'How did she get that picture?' asked Carol, leaning towards the screen.

'I guess she took it on her phone.'

'I had no idea Gretchen had a photo like that. No idea.' Carol's face had gone pale. 'And I told her she wasn't allowed a Facebook page.' She said the words brashly, but Lili could tell by the way she chewed her lip she was frightened. Her little girl was slipping from her control.

'It's just a social site,' said Lili. 'Harmless, really.'

'What would she want to mess around with a social site for?' Carol took a breath as she watched Lili scan down Gretchen's wall. 'Who *are* all those friends? They can't all be from her school.'

Lili scanned down further.

'I can't stand this.' Carol paced back and forth. 'These people have been contacting my daughter without permission. I'm calling the police again. They have to do *something*. We can't just wait around here doing nothing.'

She marched out the room and Lili heard her shouting down the phone.

Lili opened the profile of a student called Jack Dredger who'd been sending Gretchen messages titled 'Morgan Family Tree'. A green dot showed he was online and available to chat.

She scrolled through Facebook messages, reading embarrassingly personal chat between Gretchen and Jack.

Great smile beautiful girl, but what's under the smile looks better.

Maybe I'll take more pictures for you and show you even more.

Carol's voice floated from the hallway.

'. . . *online . . . my daughter . . . perverts . . .*'

Lili tapped out a message:

Hi. Gretchen has gone AWOL, is she meeting you today?

Within a few seconds, Jack replied.

Who's that?

Lili wrote back: **Her friend. Don't worry.**

Jack wrote back. **No, we don't meet in real life ☺ She's a great girl, hope she's okay. Jack xxx**

Lili noticed Gretchen had a 'favourite friends' box, and hovered the mouse arrow over it. The box contained two people – Jack

Dredger and someone called Harrison Blakely. There was no profile picture for Harrison, only a photo of a giraffe.

Another virtual boyfriend? Lili wondered, and opened up Harrison's profile. Harrison had only one friend. Gretchen. *That's very odd.* There was no green dot to show he was online, but she tapped out a message anyway.

Hi. This is Gretchen's friend, Lili. Gretchen's gone missing. Need to find her. Is she with you?

Harrison replied almost immediately:

I've taken her. I warned you to leave the letters alone.

Oh my God.

Then the message disappeared.

Lili ran into the hallway, seeing shadows of cubic lettering behind her eyes.

'Carol. May I speak to the police?' Without waiting for an answer, she snatched the phone. 'Hello? Yes.' Lili prayed she was going mad, prayed that the shock of her mum's suicide was making her hallucinate. But if the message was real . . .

'Gretchen might have been kidnapped,' she blurted out, seeing Carol's panicked face and feeling awful. 'Please send someone straightaway.'

'What's going on?' Carol shrieked, hanging up the phone. 'Kidnapped? What are you saying? My Gretchen. Oh no. Please no.'

Lili watched Carol crumple against the Habitat wallpaper and felt wretched. *What if I'm seeing things?*

'Carol – I could be totally wrong. I've been . . . I don't know. Since Mum died. I don't know. Maybe I've been seeing things.'

'Seeing things?'

'There was a message. On Facebook. But—'

'Let me see.' Carol marched into the bedroom.

'Carol – wait.' Lili followed. 'It's not there any more.'

Carol snatched up the laptop. 'Who sent the message? Which one of these people was it?'

'Him,' said Lili, sliding the mouse arrow to Harrison Blakely's name. 'But look, the message is gone. Whoever sent it must have deleted it straightaway. Or maybe I imagined it.'

Carol's hand moved slowly to her mouth. '*He* sent a message,' she whispered. 'This person? Harrison Blakely?'

'Yes. At least, I think he did. Like I said, maybe I'm – I mean he doesn't even look like a real person.'

'It is a real person,' said Carol. 'I know him. I know who it is.'

'What?'

'Harrison Blakely. That's the name Gretchen's father uses when he emails me. He uses it so if Gretchen ever reads my emails she doesn't know who he is.'

'Carol, I don't understand.'

'Harrison Blakely,' said Carol. 'Is Gretchen's biological father.'

77

Life's a Stage by Lili Allure

Lili Allure's Guide to Making Your Clothes Disappear

I suppose a burlesque act is a bit like magic – a girl comes on stage and then, Poof! her clothes disappear. Just like many magic acts, you know what's coming, but that's okay. The excitement comes from seeing how my clothes disappear. I work hard to be original, exciting and, above all, elegant every time.

Not all corsets are made equal, and sod's law says that the most beautiful, hand-stitched, silk covered designer corsets are the most difficult to take off. Mr Jean Paul Gaultier, hang your head. Such beautiful corsets, but so difficult to remove.

The trick, of course, as with everything on stage, is to rehearse. With some outfits it's taken me weeks to perfect an elegant removal and I even have razor blades hidden behind stage props so I can cut myself free if necessary.

I've never had to slash a costume yet, but never say never!

The police announced themselves with a firm knock on the front door.

Lili watched Carol greet the two female officers, one blonde, one dark-haired, with apologies.

'Sorry, I don't have any real coffee. Sorry the lounge is a mess. Sorry for all this.'

'I'm Officer Hawkins,' said the blonde officer, who was tall, thin and gym-toned. Her orange tan and freckles didn't suit her heavy black uniform. She made herself at home on the sofa. 'And this is Officer Greeves.'

'We understand your daughter is absent from the home. Is that correct?'

'Yes,' said Carol, clearly relieved by the clinical language. 'Absent.'

'Please,' said Lili. 'It's important you know this. Gretchen and I were searching for some letters together and—'

'And you are?'

'A friend,' Lili replied.

'And you're the girl's foster mother?' Officer Hawkins asked Carol, taking a black book from her uniform.

Carol nodded.

'Right. And her birth parents. Where are they?'

'Her biological father lives in the area,' said Carol. 'I'll find his address. Hang on.' She returned with a paisley-covered address book. 'Cambridge Heath Road. There's a number for him. And I have his email too.'

'He lives nearby?' said Lili. 'Gretchen thinks he lives abroad.'

'And her mother?' Officer Hawkins interrupted.

'Her birth mother passed away,' said Carol. 'Gretchen thinks both her birth parents live in France. It seemed easier not to tell her the truth. What she doesn't know can't hurt her.' She glanced at Lili, her face tight. 'And I'd rather she wasn't told otherwise.'

Lili flinched. 'Gretchen talked about running away to meet her parents. If she thinks they're living in France—'

Hawkins made a note. 'We'll look into it. What's her relationship with her birth father like?'

'She's never met him,' said Carol. 'But it looks like he's been using the internet to spy on her. Pretending to be someone else. On Facebook.'

'But the two of you are in touch? Yourself and Gretchen's biological father?'

'Yes. Off and on. More so recently, since my husband left. He's started giving a lot of opinions about how Gretchen should be brought up.'

Hawkins's kindly expression turned serious. 'And you think there's a chance her father may have abducted her?'

'I don't know. I'd never have thought so, but with this Facebook thing. Who'd have thought he'd spy on her like that? And this young lady thought she saw a message. But we're not so certain about that.'

Carol glanced at the carved, wooden body of an elephant wrapped around a clock. 'It's gone four.' She began to sob quietly into her hand. 'What do we pay our taxes for? There should be people out looking for her.'

'Mrs Carmichael, we need to take things one step at a time. We'll be contacting the father and potentially conducting a search, but I need details from you first.'

'Don't you want to know about the message on Facebook?' said Lili.

Hawkins gave Lili a lovely smile. 'I'll talk with you in just one minute – I just need to take some details from Mrs Carmichael. Okay?'

'But—'

'Listen, I know you're concerned. But let's speak to Gretchen's carer first. There's method to our madness. Mrs Carmichael. Would you tell us about this Facebook message?'

'I didn't see it. This young lady thought she did. But she's not certain.'

'Right. May I see the message?'

'It's not there any more,' said Lili.

'I don't follow you,' said Hawkins.

'The message was there, and then it disappeared,' said Lili, feeling hot behind her ears. She knew her face was going red. 'I suppose whoever sent it must have deleted it.'

'When did you receive the message?'

'Less than an hour ago.'

'And you're sure you're not getting confused? Misreading some other message?' Hawkins gave her an I've-done-plenty-of-silly-things-myself look. 'When emotions run high, it's easy to get in a muddle.'

'No. At least, I don't think so, but honestly I don't know.' She sighed. 'Maybe yes – I've got it all wrong.'

'Let's work with what we know for certain,' said Hawkins. 'Some of Gretchen's possessions are missing, is that right?'

'Clothes,' said Carol. 'And an overnight bag.'

'Right. So we could be dealing with a runaway situation. You're sure her things are missing? Not just mislaid?' Her cheeks dimpled. 'Easy enough, with a teenager in the house, not to know where everything is.'

'I'm certain,' said Carol tightly.

'Okay dokey. Well. Let's do an open door search, and if it's not too much trouble, Mrs Carmichael, perhaps you could show us to any computers Gretchen's been using.'

'Of course,' said Carol.

'Does she have a mobile phone?'

'Yes – it's been water damaged.' Carol retrieved Gretchen's mobile from the dresser. 'She left it here.' She burst into tears.

The police began moving through the flat, opening doors and looking behind them. Lili watched them stoop to look under Gretchen's bed.

After a few moments, they returned to the lounge.

'Well, that's done,' said Hawkins. 'Looks silly I know, searching for someone in a flat this size. But it's a procedure we have to follow. Now. Let's talk about computers and mobile phones.' She put a hand over Carol's. 'We also may take fingerprints and DNA samples.'

'Yes,' Carol whispered. 'Yes, do whatever you need to do.'

'Based on what I've heard,' said Officer Hawkins, 'I don't classify this as a high-risk situation. We're not going to throw everything at it just yet. It seems most likely to me that Gretchen is out with some mates and will turn up in the next few hours.

'Worse case scenario, a day or two. The fact she's packed a bag tells me she's left willingly. And if she's never met her father, odds are she's not with him. All the same, given her age, we're taking the situation seriously.'

'Yes.' Carol looked relieved.

'Do you have any photos of Gretchen?'

'Of course.' Carol took a brown album from a drawer. 'Here. This is a recent one.' She showed them a picture of Gretchen, frowning in her school uniform, the sun glowing on her brown hair.

'Thank you. May I ask about Gretchen's religious background?'

'Agnostic,' said Carol. 'Like me. But her family background – her father is Muslim. He wasn't fussed before, but recently he's been suggesting Gretchen attend religious study groups . . . things like that.'

'I see.' Hawkins tapped her fingers on her leg. 'Well.' She glanced at her colleague. 'That's certainly worth looking into. We'll be getting in touch with her father ASAP.'

'But she's never met him—'

'All the same,' Hawkins insisted. 'It does happen. Fathers abducting their daughters. Do you have her passport?'

'It's been mislaid,' Carol admitted.

'Find it as soon as you can.'

'Yes, I will, officer.'

'Wait,' said Lili. 'There's something else I need to tell you. Gretchen left me a message . . . before she disappeared. Asking me to meet her—'

Hawkins held a hand up and turned to Carol. 'Sexual orientation? Boyfriends? Girlfriends?'

Carol fidgeted. 'I wasn't aware of this until today, but apparently she has something called a virtual boyfriend.'

'A fella online, you mean?'

'Yes. But I'm not the sort of mother . . . all of this went on behind my back. I had no idea—'

'What's his name?'

'Jack something. She talks to him on Facebook. And that's where her father has befriended her too.'

'We'll look into that,' said Hawkins. 'Let's take her laptop and chances are she'll be home in twenty minutes saying, Goodness me Mum, who's been messing up my room.' She put the laptop under her arm. 'So we'll head off now, and you call us if she comes back of her own accord.'

'Wait.' Lili stood up. 'Please. The message—'

'I've made a note of it,' Hawkins assured her. 'But without seeing the thing it's difficult to get a gauge on . . .'

'No, I mean the other message Gretchen left. She arranged to meet me at my theatre earlier.'

'I'll make a note of that too.'

'So what will you be doing now?' Carol asked.

'Contacting her birth father and circulating her description. We'll also be checking her laptop, seeing if we can find any details about where she might be staying. And looking into what you suspect is her father's alias on Facebook. It's not against the law to use a different name to chat online, but when there are minors involved it's worth looking into.'

'What if she's not staying anywhere? What if she's been taken?'

Hawkins's eyes crinkled. 'A bag and clothes are missing and she left the home willingly. Doesn't sound like an abduction to me. Maybe she's meeting up with this virtual boyfriend, Jack. If she's not back this evening, we'll bring out the big guns.'

'And what about the theatre?' said Lili. 'Maybe we should look around there. She was supposed to be meeting me.'

'Which theatre?'

'Kate Hamilton's.'

Hawkins looked at her colleague. 'There was a fire there this morning. Big one. Most of the roof has gone.'

'Yes,' said Lili. 'Gretchen asked me to meet her there at twelve, but I was late and the whole theatre was on fire by the time I arrived.'

'Just throwing a theory out there,' said Hawkins. 'But perhaps Gretchen was messing around at the theatre, started a little fire, got scared and ran. Not on purpose,' she added quickly, trying to smooth over the outrage on Carol's face. 'No. Perhaps an accidental fire, but when it caught she didn't want to get in trouble so she grabbed a few things and now she's at a friend's house lying low.'

'Maybe,' said Carol. 'I went out for an hour or so this afternoon. She could have come back. I don't know. I really don't know.'

'Please,' said Lili. 'Will you send people out looking for her? The text message—'

'Let me know straightaway if you get another one,' said Hawkins. 'But for now, let's just follow the standard procedure and if I know my onions she'll be home in the next few hours.'

'What should we do?' Lili asked.

'Contact any friends of hers, visit places she might be, have a search around the streets – but the most useful thing you can do is make sure there's someone here to meet her when she comes back.'

When the police left, the living room felt empty and unnaturally quiet.

'You can wait here if you like,' said Carol awkwardly.

Lili stared out the window over East London.

'No,' she said. 'There's someone I need to talk to.'

'Who?'

'My gran.'

78

Life's a Stage by Lili Allure

Lili's London: the end of the (Central) line

At the end of the Central line, as far east as you can go, lies the town of Epping. A quaint town of two-storey cottages, small pubs, green trees and little churches, Epping is everything London is not. Quiet and rural, not a tower block in sight, and surrounded by trees.

It is built around one large, long road that cuts through its centre, and years ago, when horse-drawn mail coaches took news from London to the East of England, horses would charge along Epping High Street, or rest in one of the many inns by the roadside.

Beside Epping is Epping Forest, a popular woodland for nature lovers and campers. There are several campsites around the Epping Forest, and their grassy fields, wooden lodges and static caravans are popular in summer.

In winter, the campsites are all but deserted.

Lili stood at the edge of the campsite, under the straggly branches of bare horse chestnut trees. A road of blond and brown static caravans lay ahead under a navy sky. They were all dark, except one. Her gran's caravan.

She trod a path of concrete set with hard pieces of gravel and saw a sliver of silver moon overhead. It was getting late. The temperature was freezing, but she barely noticed.

For years Lili had tucked her family away, out of sight – her mother especially – and she'd thought it was all under control.

But it had never really been under control. Bad feelings had been eating her up since she'd left home.

Seeing the caravan across the wind-ruffled site, Lili felt as though glass was trapped under her skin. It was guilt, she realised – not anger – that was causing the pain. It poked and prodded. There was no more putting it off. Seeing Gran meant cutting herself open and fishing everything out.

The lit-up caravan had a curved front window, lace curtains and half a wooden wagon wheel nailed into the roof fascia. Its corrugated sides were yellow with age and splattered with brown stains.

Before Lili knew it, she was standing by the metal pull-down steps, looking at the insulating strips hanging out around the hinges of the front door.

Lili went to knock, but a desperate scrabbling behind the door made her step back. She caught her ankle on a wrought-iron furniture set and felt pain in every bit of her body.

Three sharp barks told her there was a dog inside.

She glanced at the lace curtains, looking for the Salvation Army sticker that used to be in the window, but saw only soot-coloured dust clinging to lacy white flowers.

'Who is it?' a voice yelled.

Lili tried to speak, but her throat was cold and her mouth dry.

'Well?' the voice demanded.

'It's Lilian,' Lili finally managed to say.

'What?'

The door was wrenched open and the insulating tape flapped free in the wind.

A Staffordshire terrier shot out of the caravan, barking and chasing around the garden furniture. Then it bounced and twirled over the pale, mud-patched grass of the empty campsite.

'Ruffles! Come,' the voice shouted from inside the caravan.

The dog slunk back and its claws clicked on the metal steps.

'*Who* is it?' A tired, angry woman appeared in the doorway, framed by dim orange light. Her hair was big and grey-blonde, hanging in bleached knots around broad shoulders, and her handsome nose and large blue eyes gave her the look of an enquiring bird of prey.

Ginny Morgan.

She'd put on weight, especially around the middle, and wore a bright red jumper, black trousers that fastened at the waist and flat, sensible shoes.

She looks so much like Mum.

Ginny reached for a pair of glasses – big ones with clear plastic frames – and fitted them over her ears. Then she looked down at Lili.

'Oh Lordy. Lilian?' Ginny patted her chest and gave a throaty cough. Cigarettes had turned her voice low and gravelly, and she'd lost the edge of American accent she'd had when Lili knew her.

Lili tried to push an actress's smile onto her face, but managed only to look nervous. *She sounds like Mum, too.*

'My little Lilian,' said Ginny.

Lili started to cry.

The wind whipped across the open field, stinging her bare hands, messing up her perfectly set hair, and she cried and cried. What was left of her make-up ran down her neck.

Darren had been right. Once she started crying, it was hard to stop.

'I wish you'd come before,' Ginny said, not taking her eyes off Lili. 'I didn't know how to reach you.'

The sobbing took hold of Lili's body, and tears fell onto her freezing hands. 'It's all my fault,' she said. 'Everything is my fault.'

'You'd better come in.'

Lili tried to nod, but her neck was stiff.

'I know, I know . . . I'm an old witch for not making the funeral,' Ginny said. 'But I was in no state that day. No state at all. And that man – that boyfriend of hers. I never liked him taking charge of everything. He's not family.'

Lili ran her tongue over dry teeth.

'The terrible, terrible waste of it.' Ginny looked at the field over Lili's shoulder. 'Well? Are you coming in, or not?'

79

Inside, the caravan smelt of baked potatoes and furniture polish. Lili took a seat on the dinette and rested her elbows on the table. She remembered spilling Alphabetti spaghetti on the pebble-patterned plastic oh-so-many years ago.

A gas fire blazed near Grandma's U-shaped sofa, and the warmth made Lili's hands throb.

Ginny filled a cordless kettle and smacked it into its plastic casing. 'I didn't know if you'd come. We haven't seen each other in God only knows how long.'

Lili nodded, her moist eyes running over the framed photos of Grandad Albert that decorated every wall surface.

'The police came the day after it happened,' Ginny croaked. 'I'd just come back from walking Ruffles. They didn't even take their hats off. Manners have certainly changed.'

She unclipped an overhead cupboard and took out two cups and saucers.

'Ruffles got a good walk that day. I walked round and round for hours, but you can't walk away heartache. You caught me on a good day – I'm dressed. I've been a mess, just imagining things, awful things. Why? Why my daughter? The Lord already took my husband.'

Lili's throat was too swollen to reply. She watched Ginny make tea – two cups exactly the same, more milk than water and three sugars. Then Lili swallowed and said:

'It's my fault. It's all my fault.'

'What's your fault?'

'Mum. The way she died. I thought I was angry with her. But the truth is, it's really me I'm angry with. It's all my fault. If I hadn't left her . . . it's all my fault.' Tears dropped on the plastic table.

'Lilian, goodness me, not at all. Not at all. Lilian, Viv isn't your fault.'

'Yes she is. I shouldn't have left her.'

Ginny sighed and rattled the cups and saucers onto the table. 'No one wanted to leave her. I'm her mother – do you think I wanted to leave her alone, the way she was? But you shouldn't feel guilty, Lilian. You're the child. She should have been looking after you.'

'I should have been there for her. I could have helped her.'

'She's a grown woman who made her own choices,' said Ginny. 'No one could have helped Viv but Viv. Oh, I could kill her, I could. If she walked through that door right now, I'd strangle her.'

'I thought I was angry with her too,' said Lili. 'But it was a lie. Deep down, it's myself I can't forgive. For letting her down. I'm so ashamed.'

'I know.' Ginny gave two sharp coughs. 'I know what shame is. Suicide isn't like other mourning. It's not clean. You end up blaming yourself – that's the way of it. But there was nothing you could have done. Viv has set us apart from everyone, dying this way.' She laughed. 'I guess that serves me right, for setting her apart.'

'I've been a horrible daughter—' Lili's voice was bruised and weak, and Grandma easily cut her off.

'The hell you have. Lilian, it's not your fault. You should have come before. You've been carrying all this around with you since she died?'

'Longer than that.' Lili wiped wet hair from her face.

'Well, that's very foolish. What made you decide to come here now?'

Lili reached for a tea and took a juddering sip. 'There's a girl, a friend of mine—'

Ginny squeezed herself into the dinette. 'If you're going to tell me you're gay, you've picked the perfect time. I couldn't care less. To hell with those Christians – they haven't said a word to me since Viv passed. But my girl's gone to heaven, sin or no sin.'

Lili shook her head. 'No – not that. Me and this girl, Gretchen – she's only fifteen – we were searching for some family letters, and then she vanished. I got a threatening message saying someone had taken her.'

'You got a threatening message? Well, what the hell are you doing here? Go tell the police.'

'I did, but they think I'm seeing things or something. They might be right. But if they're not, I need to find some letters Mum was looking for. Quickly. Because they might have something to do with Gretchen going missing.'

'Letters Viv was looking for?'

'Yes.' Lili sat up taller. 'Mum was looking for them before she died. She wrote about them on the wall in her flat and she asked me to find them. I thought they'd be her way of saying goodbye, somehow. That if I found them, I'd understand why she killed herself. Maybe even why she never came looking for me when I ran away. It would help me grieve for her. But now Gretchen's gone missing, I couldn't care less about me. All I want is for Gretchen to be safe.'

'This girl's fifteen? Like you were when you ran away.'

'Yes.'

'So you're looking out for her, just like Viv should have been looking out for you.'

'I'd never thought of it that way.'

'Christ.' Ginny took a lace-edged hanky from her trouser pocket. 'Here come the waterworks.' She dabbed at tears. 'Viv was all alone in that place – all that junk everywhere. I knew when I seen the state of it she was in trouble. But she wouldn't talk. She hated to talk. She thought I didn't know about the booze, but it was plain as the nose on your face.'

'Did she talk to you about the letters?'

'Sure.' Ginny nodded. 'Years ago. When Albert passed, Karen and Jeff got some bits and pieces, but Viv didn't get anything.

She thought Jeff or Karen might have inherited these old family letters Albert used to talk about.'

'Yes – those letters. Do you know where they are?'

'I don't.' Ginny put her large hands around her cup of tea. 'They were from Albert's side of the family. Maybe Ron has them. How are you feeling, honey? You look a little . . . I don't know. Softer than when you arrived.'

'I don't know,' said Lili. 'I don't know what I feel right now. I'm just . . .' She let more tears come. 'I have to find those letters. If anything's happened to Gretchen—'

'You spoken to the rest of the family yet?'

'Darren and Jeff. And Karen. I saw Rose Tanning. She said you weren't so straitlaced when you lived in America. She said something happened to you out there.'

'Oh, that was years ago. Years and years ago. Not worth remembering. I really don't want to talk about it.'

'Mum always thought you didn't love her as much as Jeff and Karen.'

'If she could see me now, she'd know how wrong she was. I'd give anything in the world to have her back.' Ginny put her head on the table. Her shoulders shook as she sobbed.

'Did Jeff or Karen inherit any letters?' Lili blew her nose.

'Not letters.' Ginny looked up. 'Jeff got an old will. And Karen got some things from when Albert and I were on the road.'

'What sort of things?'

'Costumes. Jewellery. A trunk. All sorts of things. They're all still in her loft. Ask her if you want to look through it.'

'A trunk?'

'Yes,' said Ginny, raising herself from the table and dabbing her eyes. 'An old steamer. It's got all the old clothes and everything else in it.'

Lili stiffened. 'Was it the one that belonged to Albert's mother – Dynamite Dolly?'

Ginny lifted her head. 'How in the world did you know that?'

'Research.'

'Good for you.' Ginny rubbed her eyes and took a sip of tea. 'You're right – it was Dolly's old trunk.'

'Did Grandad Albert leave Mum anything at all when he died?' Lili asked, feeling a wave of pity for her poor, second-best mother.

'No.' Ginny let out a long sigh. 'Lili – haven't you worked out the truth by now?'

80

'What truth?' Lili asked.

'You never wondered why Viv was so left out of everything?' Ginny replied. 'Why Albert never left her a thing in his will? Why she was always so angry at her family?'

'I've wondered all my life,' said Lili. 'It was like the family had something against her – not Jeff so much, but Karen and you and Grandad. She drank to get away from herself, because she never felt anyone liked her.'

Ginny started crying again. 'Christ, did I screw up. *We* screwed up, both of us. I'll pay for it the rest of my life.'

'So why did you leave her out?'

'When I had that trouble in America. When those men grabbed me and took me away in their car . . . I ended up pregnant. With Vivienne. Every time I looked at Vivienne, growing up, I saw those men's faces. Albert did too. We didn't mean to treat her different, but she *acted* different from the other children. It was like she was doing it on purpose.

'I'll pay for letting her down for the rest of my life. I can live with that. But don't you feel guilty – you did nothing but look after her.'

'But I left.' Lili's hands began to shake around her teacup.

'You got on with your life,' said Ginny. 'If you'd have stayed, you'd have wound up like Darren. She was happy you left.'

'She was?'

'Yes.'

'She told you that?'

'She told me that. She loved you – she didn't want you around her and her problems. She was proud of how well you were doing. It broke her heart Darren ended up where he did, but he was a car crash waiting to happen. We all knew it. Someone that young shouldn't have to take the weight of the world on their shoulders. He never stood a chance.

'But you got out. Viv had a good reason to feel bad about her life. She let her kids down. But you've a chance to get away from all that. Lilian – you've nothing to feel guilty about.'

Lili nodded. For a magical few seconds the guilt and pain and sickness lifted. 'I went to see Karen. She told me she didn't know anything about the letters, but if she has Dolly's old trunk . . . I should go back.' Lili got up. 'She might even know where Gretchen is.'

'I wouldn't go to see Karen now,' said Ginny. 'It's Jessica's wedding tomorrow – she's up to her eyeballs.'

'I couldn't care less.' Lili went to the door. 'What matters is finding Gretchen.'

Aunt Karen's drive was rammed with shiny, new cars when Lili arrived. Folded marquees and boxes of white flowers lay in the front garden. The house itself was dark – no soft lighting or even TV glow.

Lili banged on the front door, already knowing no one was home.

'Hey!' she shouted at the house. 'Aunt Karen. Hey!'

No one answered.

She threaded her way through the cars, went around to the neighbours' identical mock-Tudor mansion and rang the doorbell.

A smiling streaked-blonde woman with a Botox-frozen face opened the door. 'Can I help you?'

'Karen – next door. Do you know where she is?'

The neighbour craned her neck to look over the dividing hedge. 'You're not a photographer, are you?'

'A photographer without a camera?'

'Fair point.' The woman gave her a dimply smile. 'They've been *swarming* round here since, you know, the big story.'

'What big story?'

'You know. In all the tabloids. A few hookers have come out the woodwork, a checkout girl, a lap dancer and an ex girlfriend. All of them with naked pictures, text messages . . . all sorts.

'Jess's fiancé has been cheating left, right and centre *days* before the wedding. If he can't keep it in his pants now, it doesn't say much for him as a husband, does it? If it were me, I'd send him packing, but Jessie still wants to go ahead. She feels lucky to have bagged him.'

'That's sad.' Lili meant it. 'So do you know where Karen is?'

'She'll be out at Jessie's pre-wedding dinner. I wasn't invited to that – family only. Who are you?'

'Family. Pre-wedding dinner? What's that?'

'Oh, a meal before the wedding.' The neighbour rolled her eyes. 'As if she doesn't have enough to organise with this wedding of the year she's trying to pull off. Good luck to her, but the *stress*. Oh my word, I wouldn't take all that on.'

'Where is it?'

'In town. They hired out Italiano's on High Road – turned the whole thing white to match the wedding.'

'Thanks,' said Lili.

'You'll need an invitation,' the woman called after her.

81

Loughton High Road – a place of contrasts. Concrete and willow trees; boutique hair salons and betting shops; chain restaurants and cosy cottages.

The air was cool and clear, and Lili breathed it in as she approached Italiano's. Opposite the restaurant, yellowy branches of winter willows dangled – a hint that green things still lived, even if most were hidden. Perhaps spring wasn't so far away.

Karen sat behind restaurant glass, her posture upright, tapping something into her mobile phone. She looked fraught, tense and miserable. Beside her sat Jessica, looking equally fraught, tired and miserable. Like mother, like daughter.

On Karen's other side sat Uncle Phil, reading a newspaper, and Lili's cousin Rebecca. The rest of the long table was filled with, Lili presumed, the relatives of Jessica's fiancé.

Just like the neighbour said, the restaurant had been turned white – white tables, chairs, staff uniforms and plastic chandeliers. It looked too clean next to the scuffed grey concrete steps at the door.

Lili tapped on the glass.

Karen jumped, grabbed her gold Fendi handbag and hurried out to the street.

'What are you doing here?' Karen whispered. 'We kept things very private. The newspapers . . . how did you know?'

'Your neighbour told me.'

'I'm sorry, Lilian, but we simply don't have room for you. I've spent all day getting the seating plan right—'

'Karen – please.' Lili held up her hand. 'I couldn't care less about your meal. Look, I need to talk to you.'

'Not about the letters.' Karen's red lipstick stretched across her face in a thin, sad line.

'You guessed right.'

'I told you. I don't know—'

'Yes you do,' Lili interrupted. 'We're going back to your place. And when we get there, you're going to show me where those letters are.'

Gravel hissed as Karen's black four-by-four rolled onto her driveway. She brought the car to a stop, but stayed buckled up, staring straight ahead at the guest cars in front.

'Listen.' Karen turned to Lili, her leather seat squeaking. 'These letters. It's best they're left alone. Especially tonight – it's a big day tomorrow. As if we don't have enough scandal to deal with already.'

'Why should they be left alone?'

Karen drummed pink nails on the steering wheel, then unclipped her seatbelt.

'We'll talk in the house.'

In the hallway, boxes of white flowers were piled up.

'Phil has totally messed up,' said Karen, walking straight through to the lounge. 'He had the flowers and all the garden pieces sent here. Complete idiot. As if I don't have enough to do tomorrow, without organising getting this lot sent on.'

Lili followed her into the lounge, noticing an almost life-sized framed photo of Jessica with, Lili presumed, her fiancé. They were posing in sunglasses, and neither of their smiles looked genuine.

'Sit down,' said Karen.

Lili perched on an arm of a beige leather sofa. 'Tell me what you know about the letters. What you *really* know.'

'How did you know they were here?'

Lili smiled. 'You just told me.'

Karen wrinkled her nose. 'Viv thought they were here too.'

'She did?'

Karen nodded. 'She was desperate for them.'

'But why? *Why?* What did she want with them? And why does she want me to find them?'

'Money.' Karen reached for a packet of cigarettes on a polished table beside her and lit one. 'She wasn't in a good way. That boyfriend of hers – he was bad news. He stayed with her as long as she paid for everything. If she had money, they were fine. But if she ran out of cash, she saw the other side to him.'

'Ben? He's the only decent one amongst us. He arranged the funeral—'

Karen cut her off with a shake of her head. Smoke wafted left and right. 'No. He's a loser. Never had any money, never will. She could have done so much better. But Viv loved him.'

'I wasn't around when the two of them—'

'I know,' said Karen. 'When she met Ben, everything changed. If you thought she was bad before . . .' She shook her head. 'That's what love does to you. She was always buying him clothes, taking him out. He never had money to take care of her. And the less money she had, the more she hoarded. She had to keep hold of everything.

'It's the same old story. Young, good-looking guy and an older woman who thanks God she got so lucky. She came here crying more than once. But then she always went back to him the next day.'

'But Ben's a good guy,' said Lili. 'Decent. More decent than the rest of us, probably.'

'He's a loser. Viv knew she should leave him, but she couldn't. He was like an addiction. She got money and spent it on him. That's why she wanted the letters. She knew without cash, it would all be over. And she thought the letters were worth a bit.'

'Are they?'

'That's what I've been told.'

'And that's why Mum wanted them? For the money.'

Karen nodded. 'She was long past her prime – she wasn't earning anything herself. She knew she couldn't hang on to Ben much longer without a big lump sum. She was desperate – she said she couldn't live without him. She was like a junkie. I guess that's why she asked you to find the letters. Guilt money. She wanted you to have something of an inheritance.'

'How come the letters are worth money?' Lili asked.

'Something to do with William Peavy – the writer.'

Lili let out a long breath.

'I never could read the handwriting,' said Karen, 'but Grandad Albert told me they had to be kept safe – they'd bring scandal on the family. Something to do with an affair.'

'Why didn't you tell Mum you had them?'

'I knew she'd sell them and whatever the scandal is would be out in the open. And at a time like this, with Jessica's wedding—'

'A girl's gone missing—'

'Jessica's getting *married*,' Karen insisted. 'Tomorrow. If the press gets hold of any scandal, anything at all, it could ruin everything.' She flicked the cigarette daintily into a glass ashtray.

'By the sounds of things, the press already have a hold of plenty.'

'Those *slags*.' Karen was positively venomous. '*Days* before the wedding. They couldn't have waited. They've tainted her wedding day, that's what they've done.'

'Maybe those girls wanted to save Jessica making a big mistake.'

'Mistake! He's the son of a lord. You wouldn't understand. You've never been close to what we're close to.'

'No, you're right,' said Lili. 'I've never been close to being unhappily married.'

'Unhappy! I hardly think—'

'Have you looked at your daughter lately?' Lili shook her head. 'She's miserable. Who's this wedding for – you or her?'

Karen blew out a cool line of smoke. 'All *I* care about is Jessica's wedding and—'

'I need to look in the loft.'

'What?' Karen stumbled a little as she sat on the leather sofa. 'How did you know . . . who told you?'

'So I'm right,' said Lili. 'The letters – they're in Grandad Albert's trunk – in your loft.'

'You can't have them,' Karen insisted. 'Those letters, they're not to be made public.'

'If you're so scared about them being discovered, why haven't you thrown them away?' Lili asked.

'They're valuable,' Karen stammered. 'I'm not going to destroy something worth thousands . . . it's just the timing. Not *now*. Not with the wedding. The letters belong to me. Not you, not Viv. *Me*. Grandad Albert gave them to me. They're mine, okay?'

'Karen – do you know what's happened to Gretchen?'

'Who?'

'Gretchen. My friend. She was helping me search for the letters. She's gone missing.'

'I have no idea what you're talking about,' said Karen, pulling a lump of mascara from her eyelash.

Lili stood up. 'Karen, WHERE ARE THE LETTERS? This isn't a game. Someone's gone missing. A teenager. I've been getting threats. Have you been sending me text messages?'

Lili looked into Karen's frantic blue eyes and saw insecurity and confusion.

'Someone's been sending me threatening messages,' Lili continued. 'Telling me not to look for the letters. Telling me . . .' She felt tears coming. 'Telling me they've taken Gretchen.'

'Are you sure you're feeling all right? I don't know anyone called Gretchen, I haven't been sending texts to anyone about the letters.'

'I need to see those letters.' Lili went to the wide staircase, soft carpet springing against the soles of her feet.

'Wait.' Karen ran after her. 'Please – they can't be made public. Not now. *Please*.'

82

The landing was lined with marquee parts and crates of champagne. A stepladder and cans of paint rested by a bedroom door.

Lili saw the loft hatch immediately. She pushed a marquee pole up to click it open, and the hatch fell down with a bang. Taking the stepladder, she wobbled it under the hatch and climbed the steps.

'Wait.' Karen grasped the bottom of the ladder and shook, but Lili was already through the loft hatch, her fingers feeling dusty wood. She grasped a dangling light cord and pulled.

For a moment, there was darkness and bulky person-shaped shadows. Then white light flashed around the loft, showing a rail of clothes in dry-cleaning bags and a tower of identical plastic crates.

'Lilian,' Karen called from below. There was a creak as Karen climbed the ladder. 'Wait.'

A pile of frames and a black trunk sat by a water tank in one corner, under raw wood beams darkened by dust.

'Lilian, please.' Karen's head came through the loft hatch.

Lili ignored her and went to the trunk. It was perfectly rectangular and covered in old black leather, rumpled in places. Wooden strips were nailed along the flat top, and on the corroded handles Lili saw the all-important words.

Louise Vuitton.

A Louis Vuitton steamer from the 1900s. This trunk – it must be worth thousands.

She snapped open the three catches, feeling the dents of old nails along the top ridge, and lifted the lid.

'Stop.' A hand banged the lid down, catching one of Lili's fingers.

'Ouch!' She turned to see Karen leaning over her.

'You'd better get out of the way.' Lili opened the trunk, seeing cream lining stained with spots of rust where the nails had bled through. The trunk was filled with folded, tweedy suits, net dresses and costume jewellery.

'I'm not leaving without those letters,' Lili shouted. 'Don't you understand? How can you be so selfish? Gretchen could be hurt.' She threw aside old, musty clothing, and tore at the beautiful antique lining until shreds of cream silk hung away from the wood.

No letters.

'Where are they? Tell me or I'll tear this trunk apart.'

'No!' Karen's made-up face became three circles of surprise. 'Don't ruin the trunk. It's valuable. Here. I'll show you.' Kneeling down, Karen unbuckled a brown leather strap from around the bottom of the steamer. Behind it was an orangey-brown wooden beam, its varnish better preserved than the other strips.

Karen tugged at the beam and it rolled out from the trunk, revealing a special built-in drawer.

There was nothing inside.

Karen stared at the blank drawer with her mouth open.

'They're gone,' she said, after a moment.

'What?' Lili knelt beside her and reached into the drawer. It was empty.

'They were there,' said Karen. 'They've been there for years. They haven't been touched – not for years. Did you take them?'

'How could I have taken them?' Lili asked. She tossed aside old dresses and suits, praying to see pages between the musty fabric. But there was nothing.

'You were the only one who knew,' said Karen. 'The only one.' She put her hands on her hips. 'You said you did some research. That's how you knew they were in the trunk.'

'Yes,' said Lili.

'Who else could have done that research?'

'Anyone,' said Lili. 'Anyone who'd done a family tree and knew who was who.'

Karen pushed her lips together. 'Viv.'

'What?'

'She came here on the day she . . . Well, anyway. I knew something wasn't right. She asked to use my bath. It was all very peculiar. She was upstairs for over an hour. She must have got into *my* loft while I was downstairs and taken *my* property.'

'But Gretchen said they'd only just started doing research. She was sure Mum hadn't found them.'

'Do you know that for certain?' Karen countered.

'I don't,' Lili admitted. 'I searched the flat a little, but it was such a mess. There were so many things to look through.' She stared at the trunk and thought of Viv's hands touching it. Her heart ached. 'If she took the letters the day she came here, they must have been one of the last things she saw before she died.'

Karen shrugged. 'Maybe they were.'

Lili bit her lip. The ugly writing on Viv's wall raced around her mind, but not like before. It wasn't just a sinister logic problem now. It hurt to think of Viv so obsessed. So unhappy.

'Oh God.' Karen put her head in her hands. 'Those letters could be just lying around, waiting for some journalist to find them.'

'They could be,' Lili realised. 'Yes, they could be.' She wanted to laugh. 'They could have been in the flat all along.' She went to the loft hatch.

'Wait.' Karen held out pink fingernails. 'Let me go down first.' She took little clippy steps down the ladder. 'Wait until I'm down before you come,' she called. 'It's not safe to have two on the ladder.'

Lili should have suspected. Aunt Karen was rarely thoughtful, unless there was something in it for her. But memories of Viv meant she wasn't thinking clearly.

It only took a second for Karen to move the ladder away and jab the loft hatch shut.

'Karen!' Lili shouted. 'What are you doing? Karen – Gretchen could be hurt. Please Karen, please.'

She banged and banged on the loft hatch, then tried to lift the metal catch with her fingers. It was impossible. The heavy weight of the hatch pulled the metal hook tight into its fastening, and all Lili succeeded in doing was carving three bloody gouges into her fingertips.

'I'm sorry, Lilian,' Karen called through the wood. 'I need to phone our solicitor. Find out how we can keep everything confidential. I can't risk you leaving and finding the letters just yet. I'm sorry.'

'Karen! Karen!' Lili banged and banged, feeling a wave of terror at the thought of Gretchen, alone without anyone to look after her. 'This isn't a game!' The screech cut into Lili's throat. 'All for your stupid wedding. Let me out. I have to find her. Karen! Karen!'

But Karen had gone.

Lili's handbag and phone were downstairs. No one knew where she was and no one believed that Gretchen's disappearance was anything more serious than a teenager runaway. Every moment that passed Gretchen could be in more trouble.

With a pop, the fluorescent tube blew and the light cut out. Darkness.

Lili banged the loft hatch until her knuckles were raw.

Nobody came.

83

When Lili stopped banging, she heard ringing in her ears, then silence. The loft was perfectly still and quiet. And dark.

It was, Lili realised, the ideal situation for an overactive imagination to invent noises. And yet she could hear nothing. Nothing at all. It wasn't like Viv's flat with all the banging, creaking and sinister laughter.

Enough of this.

Lili felt her way around.

Where's that trunk?

Her fingertips met warm air as she groped forward, but finally her shin hit a hard, bulky object. It was the trunk, balanced across two wooden beams.

She got her fingers underneath and heaved it on to its side. It was empty now, but still heavy, and she felt heat in her wrists as she struggled with its weight. She hoisted the trunk onto a single beam, then heaved and dropped it onto the fibreglass packed between the two ceiling joists.

There was a splintering sound and a cracking. Yellow light shone in little needles from the room below.

She pulled aside the fibreglass, feeling its sticky sharpness, then stamped on the cracked floor.

A huge hole appeared, and she saw Uncle Phil's study below, his computer now dusted with white powder, his keyboard buried under chunks of ceiling plaster.

Hearing someone coming up the stairs, Lili sat with her legs dangling through the hole, then dropped down.

A warm, dull pain grabbed hold of her ankle as she hit the floor.

Karen appeared in the doorway, looking horrified.

'What have you *done?* Phil's room – we've got *company*.'

Lili hopped past her and down the stairs, grabbed her bag from the lounge and limped out of the house.

It was only on the street she realised she'd left behind her coat with her wallet in the pocket. There were only a few pounds of stray change in her handbag.

Her ankle was in agony. She considered limping back to the house, but doubted Karen would let her in. Anyway, time was precious.

'Taxi!' Lili waved at a passing mini cab.

The driver stopped and wound down his window.

'I've got no money,' Lili began, but before she could finish, the taxi sped away.

'Thanks a lot.' She hobbled on towards the tube station.

The freezing cold platform at Aldgate East had never looked so friendly, as Lili rolled in on the train. Covered in plaster dust and shivering in thin, chiffon sleeves, she went gratefully through the sliding train doors and limped along the platform. Her ankle felt like it was caught in a bear trap.

On the street, Viv's tower block, her old home, watched her struggle towards it.

At the wire-mesh security door, she rang Carol's bell on the intercom.

'Hello?' Carol's voice was frantic enough for Lili to know Gretchen hadn't come home.

'It's just me,' said Lili.

'Oh. Have you found her?'

'Not yet, but I'm getting closer I think. I need to search Mum's flat.'

'I'll buzz you in.'

84

By the time Lili made it up six flights of stairs, she realised the only way she was going down again was on a stretcher. Her ankle was so tender, every knock against the hard ground sent shocks of pain through her body.

At Viv's door, she leaned against brickwork and let the aching ebb and flow of blood subside. When the pain had settled to a pinprick aching sensation, Lili noticed Viv's front door was ajar.

Did I just open that?

She blinked and saw black spots.

Pain made everything fuzzy. She looked down and saw the door key in her hand.

I must have done.

The door made a 'poof' sound as she pushed it open.

Inside the flat felt warmer than before, like someone was home. Lili crept into the hall and listened carefully.

Silence.

She heard the rush of a bus passing outside, but the flat itself was quiet.

'Hello?' she called out.

Nothing.

She tried the light switch and, to her surprise, dull light lit the hallway. But then it shut off almost immediately, with a click that meant the electric meter, not the bulb, was at fault.

She groped her way into the kitchen and dropped a pound coin into the metal slot.

The hall light glowed as the electric dial began to swim around.

Did someone put coins in the electric meter before? Is that why the light worked for a few seconds?

Her old bedroom door was closed, and the lounge door was half open.

'Is anyone here?'

Silence.

She pushed aside uneasiness and thought of the letters. And Viv.

If Mum found the letters, where would she have put them?

Lili went into her mum's bedroom, seeing the biro scrawls cut into the wall like black scars.

I need to find them. Quickly.

Under the bed was a rubbish dump of old Christmas decorations, broken light bulbs, spent batteries and laddered tights. She was about to pull things out to search, but then changed her mind.

No. I know my mum. She wouldn't have hidden the letters under the bed.

To everyone else, the flat looked like heaps of broken things, but Viv only kept objects she felt were valuable. She had systems – systems people couldn't see unless they knew her really well.

I'd forgotten.

Where others saw chaos, Lili began to remember the way her mother organised things.

So where would she keep letters?

Lili sat on the bed and stared at the wall.

There were the piles of red credit card statements Viv used to keep in boxes above the kitchen cupboards. But no – the letters would have been more important to her than that. Karen said they were valuable.

Where did she keep valuable things?

She used to hide anything valuable, Lili remembered.

Fifty pound notes, holiday tickets, food vouchers – Viv would hide them in odd places around the flat. Sometimes, she'd give Lili and Darren some cryptic clue to work out where they were, and they'd play detectives until Viv fell asleep on the sofa and Lili and Darren took themselves off to bed.

It was fun. Really. You were fun, Mum.

Lili's mind raced around the house, like she and Darren had done as children. She thought of the kitchen drawers, the toilet cistern, inside the mattress, but none of those 'secret' places seemed to fit.

Then Lili remembered. *Our birth certificates. You hid them under the carpet by your bedside table. Would the letters be with them?*

Lili got to her knees and lifted the familiar frayed section of carpet and crumbly rubber underlay. A brown envelope lay on the concrete floor. Inside were birth certificates for Viv and Darren.

Darren never took his birth certificate, Lili realised. *He was always tied to this place, even as an adult. He never left Mum, not like I did. Except when he went to prison . . .*

There was a noise, like breathing or a murmur. Goosebumps ran over Lili's arms, but she didn't feel frightened. Just confused.

Mum, what's going on?

Lili stared glassy eyed at the writing on the wall, tears tickling her cheeks.

Then she noticed something. A nervous laugh fell from her grief-heavy chest.

I don't believe it.

She hadn't been seeing clearly before. In her anger and fear and frozenness, she'd blocked out everything. She hadn't seen what Viv had clearly meant her to see.

Mum. You were trying to talk to me all along.

Line by line, Lili scanned the writing on the wall.

Mine, mine, mine . . . FIND THEM . . .
. . . murdered by family . . . LOVE'S YELLOW LETTERS
I've looked BEHIND ME . . .

Her feelings were different now. The first time she'd read Viv's furious scrawl she'd felt coldness, anger, detachment. Now, as tears washed her face, she felt sorrow, loss and love.

Viv's writing was talking to her.

The underlined words . . . they're a detective game. They're Mum's final clue – her last cryptic puzzle to tell me and Darren where the letters are.

<u>**FIND THEM**</u>
<u>**LOVE'S YELLOW LETTERS**</u>
<u>**BEHIND ME**</u>

85

Lili chewed a fingernail.

Behind me . . .

She wandered around the bed, then into the lounge.

What would Mum mean by 'behind me'? Does she mean her past? Are they hidden somewhere to do with her past?

Viv's face, forever young and beautiful in the magazine advertisement on the wall, watched her walk around. Lili gazed back.

'I miss you, Mum,' she said. 'I'm sorry I left, but Gran was right. It was one of us or both of us.'

A breeze blew through the hall, gentle and benign. The magazine page fluttered.

And then Lili saw it. Just like that – pop! Something bulky, hidden behind the magazine advert. The page wasn't bulging with damp. There was something behind it.

No . . . I've passed this picture so often in the last few days, and I never noticed . . . Behind me . . .

She went to thin paper, unpeeling stiff old Blu-tack that snapped between her fingers.

There was a brown envelope behind the faded page. Lili took it and turned it over. On the envelope, written in calm, flowing biro, were the words:

For my children.

Lili fell to her knees, holding the brown paper to her chest. 'Mum.'

She cried as she tore open the envelope. Four old letters on faded yellow paper were inside, their folded creases crumbling. And something else – a white-lined biro-covered page of modern paper, torn at the top. It was covered in Viv's writing.

Lili sniffed and wiped her eyes. 'You left a note. I never really believed you'd leave us without saying goodbye. And you didn't.'

She put the white paper to one side, feeling Viv in the tear and smudged biro. Then she took one of the yellow papers and carefully unfolded it. The page was small and narrow, with loose ink writing flowing on the front and back.

At the top in stocky, embossed black letters were the words **WILLIAM PEAVY**, followed by a printed Bedford Square address and the date: 31st June 1864.

The handwriting underneath was artistic and hard to read. Lili held the page close to her face.

Dearest Tom,

Lili held the page away again. *Dearest Tom?*

> *Never did I know love, until you.*
> *Ever have I known life, since you.*
> *You are Arthur,*
> *To be Merlin,*
> *Betwixt the pair, Excalibur shown*
> *But parted, it remains in stone.*

Lili looked at the picture of Viv.

'It's a love poem,' she said. 'Like the famous ones printed after Peavy's death about King Arthur and Camelot. But it's not written to Peavy's wife or even Love. It's written to a man. Tom.'

She turned the page over and continued to read.

> *My love, my life, I miss you. Since you left my house I have not known myself. To have you as my tall footman was a blessing, to have you as my love a miracle.*

'To have you as a footman?' She stared at the page. 'He's talking about Love's husband. Tom Morgan.' She laughed. 'William Peavy was in love with Tom Morgan. They weren't letters *belonging* to Love. They were *love* letters. Love letters to Tom Morgan.'

She read on.

> *To live without you is agony, but I must set you free. The longer our friendship goes on, the more likely it is you will be discovered as my lover. I cannot have that for you, my dearest, not when you have so many good years ahead of you. I am an old man, but you will live on many years without me. I am determined those years will not see you as an outcast.*
>
> *It is no life when you are not near, but I will gladly lay down mine so you can have yours.*
>
> *However, on this parting note I must say you must not feel ashamed. What does London know about what we feel? It is the very purest, truest of love.*
>
> *Yours,*
> *William (Merlin)*

Lili put down the letter and looked at her mother's face, its smile bent in half as it curled away from the wall.

'William Peavy wasn't in love with Love at all,' Lili said. 'He was in love with her husband, Tom. And they had an affair.'

Silence.

'The Peavy Camelot poems,' said Lili. 'The famous ones that everybody loves. They're not about Peavy and his wife, or even Peavy having an affair with a female servant. They're about two *men* in love, an older man and a younger man. Merlin and King Arthur. Tom and William.'

Lili unfolded another letter.

> *Dearest Tom,*
>
> *I am so very proud of your courage, but I am firm in my thinking and no note nor word, no matter how gentle or persuasive, will change my decision. My darling, our friendship must end. You mustn't think I have the slightest care for my*

professional standing. I do not. It is for you, and only you, that I make this decision and one day, when I am long cold in the ground, and you are free to live your life as an ordinary man, you will thank me for it.

On the subject of your son, I beg you to reconsider. The poisonous air of the Nichol could yet prove fatal to one so sickly. He needs rest, away from factory smog and the bad air of the disfigured and diseased. It is no shame to take charity, no matter what your wife may say about it, and there at least I can help you, for no one would see anything amiss in an old rich man helping a poor family.

Even though we must be parted, I will love you for every moment of every day for as long as I shall live. When two people love each other, the world is beautiful. It is a very great sadness we could not share this beauty, as men and women do. Why did God see fit to have us scurry around, hiding, always fearing our love will be discovered?

Yours,
Merlin.

'No one knew William Peavy was in love with a male servant.' Lili thought about *The Lady of the Lake* poem. *No one would our marriage make . . .* 'Because he was in love with a man. And back then, that sort of thing wasn't acceptable.'

She took another yellow letter and unfolded it.

Dearest Tom,

I am eternally glad that even as an old man (and a lonely old man at that) I can be of use to you. It is unlikely I will still be alive to see your son grow into a man himself, but you have my word that I will pay James's medical bills for as long as I live.

As always, I enclose a small sum for doctor's bills and proper nourishment.

In response to your last letter, I believe your father may have had suspicions with regards to our friendship, but since you left

my house I feel these have firmly been laid to rest. As you say,
George is not a man who keeps his opinions to himself, and I
am quite sure he would have voiced his thoughts if he sincerely
believed anything untoward was going on.

With love,
William

Lili picked up the last letter from the floor. It was less yellow
than the rest, she realised, and coloured more by age than dye.
There was no 'William Peavy' stamp on the top, and the
handwriting was different – less flowing, lumpier and more carefully written.

For James,
I cannot leave this earth without you knowing you would
not be alive had it not been for my friendship with William
Peavy, the most loving, most kindest, most caring man I ever
met.

As a child you were very ill, and because of the caring
friendship William Peavy and I shared, William heard of your
sickness and called at our home.

He saved your life that day but his kindness did not end
there. He gave money for your doctor bills as you fort to get well
again. The illness you were born with needed a great deal of
care, and William saw to it that we were never without the hand
of a doctor.

Had it not been for him, you would never have lived.

Without him and his kindness, you would have ended up the
same place as Charlotte, James (1) and Jane and never grown to
be a man.

All this was done most secretly, as Mr Peavy and I had a
friendship of a pryvate kind. Mr Peavy himself always said that
ours was the very best of friendships and that one day people
would understand.

It is my hope that my and William's love will not dye with
me or him. I do not want it to be lost in time, but for people to

*know what a very great love we had, and what very great good
came of it.*

*I ask that you mind his letters to me, and that they are
passed down to your child'en and their child'en so each can
know.*

*Never forget that was it not for the love of William Peavy, you
or your child'en would never have been.*

Your loving father,
Tom.

Lili stared at all four loose pages.

'So these really are love letters,' said Lili. 'Because they make
sure a great love wasn't lost in time, and they share a story of
how lucky our family are to have survived.'

Her hand found the white, torn page.

'And if it wasn't for you, Mum, I wouldn't be here either. You
weren't perfect. But I understand now why you didn't come
looking for me. You thought you were doing the best thing. You
were setting me free. Like William did for Tom.'

She watched Viv's faded face and let a tear slide down her
cheek. 'I'm scared to read your letter.'

Her fingers found the white page.

'Terrified, actually.'

A breeze fluttered the magazine advert.

Lili picked up the white paper and looked at Viv's bubbly
writing, so different from the angry scrawl on the wall.

86

The Eyes Have It

Think of the screen goddesses of old. Marilyn Monroe, Elizabeth Taylor, Lauren Bacall … Now think of their eyes. Any kind of performance happens in the eyes first and the body second, whether you're on the silver screen or taking your clothes off in a pub with peanuts on the floor.

The eyes tell everything about a performance. Light, dark, sex, sorrow … it's all there in those bewitching little circles. That's why every screen icon you can think of exaggerates her eyes with lashings of eyeliner and yards of fake lashes. Think of Marilyn's famous eyelashes, Amy's long swoops of eyeliner and Elizabeth's thick kohl.

The eyes hold emotion, and it can't be faked. Whatever you want your audience to feel, you have to feel too.

My angels, Viv's letter began.

Lili felt more tears on her cheeks. She'd forgotten Viv used to call them that. Sadness crashed over her, a cold, suffocating wave, but it didn't drown her or wash her away like she'd been scared it would.

Please forgive me, but I can't stand the pain any more.

I have never felt so alone, so worthless. I have made such a terrible mess of my life, and there is no reason for me to be here any longer. I can give you nothing but my pain and misery, and for that reason I am better off gone.

Bump, bump.

The noise sounded like someone tripping over in the next room.

Lili looked around.

'Who's there?' she shouted.

Through the white paper in her fingers, Lili felt Viv, and suddenly she was certain the flat wasn't haunted. Those noises were human, just like the person who was sending the text messages.

'I know someone's here.' She waited for a reply, but there was none.

The letter pulled her back, and she looked down at the soft handwriting.

I have found Love's yellow letters (enclosed) and they are not what I thought. There was always talk that our family were related to William Peavy. I wanted that to be true. I wanted to be someone special. I wanted a family back again, even one that died a long time ago. But I am nothing, just like always. The black sheep.

The letters are for you all now – they are worth a lot, and at least I can give you something in death, even though I never could in life.

Darren, every time you go to prison you break my heart in two. You were wrong about Ben. I don't think he's ever really loved me. I hope you never have the pain of loving someone who doesn't love you back. It's no kind of life.

Lilian, I miss you more than you will ever know, but I knew you'd make something of yourself without me holding you back. Every day I have the pain of missing you, but I hope you have found everything you need in life and forgive me for not wanting to get in your way.

Gretchen, you are a clever girl and you have a wonderful mother. Be grateful for her, even if at times you don't get along.

To live without love is no life at all. I have only myself to blame, the way I lived means no one sticks around me and I've got what I deserve. I have nothing. I am nothing.

You mustn't blame yourselves. Thanks for the good times,
Mum.

Lili patted under her eyes with her fingertips, and discovered her
whole face was wet.

She looked at Viv's photo.

'Thank you,' she whispered. 'For saying goodbye. And for
helping me understand why you didn't come looking for me.
Who else is looking for the letters, Mum? The text messages –
has Karen got something to do with them?'

There was another thump.

'Seriously, who's there?' Lili got to her feet. A *bump, bump,*
bump, came from her old bedroom.

She went to the hall and tried the bedroom door. It held tight.
Lili saw the chunky slide lock on the outside had been pulled
across.

Did I do that? Did I lock it when I was here before?

She was certain she hadn't. Slowly, she slid the lock open and
pushed the door. There was a soft thud as wood hit cardboard
boxes.

Then a sound came from inside the room, low and steady.
Breathing.

Keeping her body perfectly still, Lili leaned her head around
the door.

'Oh, my God.'

There on the bed was Gretchen.

Gretchen was asleep, her eyelids sticky, her forehead ruffled into
a frown.

'Gretchen.' Lili went to her and shook her shoulder. 'You're
here. You're all right. Was it you all along? Were you sending
the text messages? Was it some kind of joke, Gretchen?' She
shook her shoulder again. It was then she realised something
was wrong.

Gretchen's eyelids flickered, and two narrow slits of white
eyeball appeared. Then Gretchen's pupils slid down, groggy and

out of focus. Gretchen stared at Lili, but didn't see her. Her eyelids closed.

'Gretchen.' Lili shook her harder. 'Wake up. What's wrong? Have you been drinking?' She lifted Gretchen's left eyelid and a pupil rolled around.

'Won't let me go,' Gretchen muttered.

'What?' Lili shook her roughly.

'Dad's here.'

'You must be having a bad dream.' Lili squeezed her hand, trying to wake Gretchen up.

'In the roof,' Gretchen murmured.

'The roof?' Lili felt cold. 'Who's in the roof?'

'Dad.'

'Your dad's in the roof? What are you talking about? I found Mum's note. I found the letters. They're not anything bad – Mum just wanted to be related to someone famous.'

'It was my dad,' Gretchen whispered, then closed her eyes. 'It was him all along. He's here.'

Lili heard a soft bang, and turned to see something swinging midair in the hallway. A pair of legs, hanging from the ceiling.

She threw an arm over Gretchen as she watched the legs, in trainers and a tracksuit, lower from a hatch in the ceiling and become a long torso, then a hooded head.

There was a soft pat on the hallway carpet as the man dropped down.

Lili saw a shadow lengthening over the boxes in the bedroom.

'Who are you?' Lili called out, gripping Gretchen tighter.

Lili reached into a box and grabbed something hard and plastic. 'This is my mum's house.' She looked down to see she was holding a plastic toy worm with a smiling face.

'You need to leave,' she said, looking closer at the man. There was something familiar about him – his height and the way he moved. She looked at the square, black maintenance hatch in the hallway ceiling.

The man reached up to snap the hatch into place, and his sleeve fell back to reveal a dark, hairy arm.

It was then Lili realised it was Ben.

87

Lili lowered the worm. 'What are you doing here?'

'It's my home,' Ben said.

'It's not your home. It's Mum's home.'

'I've practically lived here for years.' Ben's nostrils flared. 'I earned it.'

Lili stared at him. 'This isn't your home. You shouldn't be here.'

Ben shrugged. 'I wasn't planning on staying here after today anyway.'

Lili swallowed. 'You've been staying here?'

Ben pulled the hood back and Lili saw a hardness to his face she hadn't noticed before.

'Viv owes me. The state of her . . . the things I put up with.'

'You've been hiding in the roof?' Lili shook her head in disbelief. 'Whenever I've come into the flat, you've been up there.'

Ben pulled a key out of his pocket. 'She cut this for me. I can come and go when I like.'

Lili looked at the maintenance hatch in the hallway ceiling. 'You've been listening to us.'

Gretchen gave a murmur and Lili patted her hand. 'What's Gretchen doing here?'

'I'm her dad.'

'What?' Lili shook Gretchen, thinking Ben had gone crazy. 'Gretchen, wake up. We've got to leave.'

'She's not going anywhere,' said Ben. 'We're flying to Tehran in three hours.' He looked around. 'Viv promised me we'd get out of this dump but it was all lies. For years she said she'd sort the money. Now I've done it myself.'

'What money?' said Lili, feeling her lips turn white with anger.

'Look.' Ben spread his arms out. 'Viv was supposed to be good for money. You know? The whole time we were together, it was tomorrow, tomorrow. Tomorrow she'd get money for us – she had a bet on something, it would pay out. She had a pension coming, tens of thousands, but then it wasn't there.

'I don't understand.'

'Why else would I have been with an old boot like her? We never said it out loud, but it was an arrangement, you know? She got my body, I got her money. Except the money never came. I think the stupid old cow really thought I was in love with her.'

'How are you Gretchen's dad?'

'Gretchen is me and Viv's daughter.'

'You and *Mum*? What are you talking about?'

'Me and Viv had a baby for Carol and Daniel downstairs. They couldn't have kids, there were waiting lists, they wanted a baby, they couldn't wait. So me and Viv had a baby for them, they paid our rent for a bit and that was that. They fostered her. Private fostering. It's all legal.'

'You're . . . this is insane.' Lili looked at Gretchen, whose eyes were struggling to open. She saw Ben's dark skin, and for the first time something else. Viv's long nose and full cheeks on Gretchen's young face. And her own curvy lower lip and pointed chin.

'I would have known.' Lili turned back to Ben. 'Someone would have told me. Darren—'

'It wasn't anyone's business,' Ben snapped. 'It was me and Viv, our life. Darren was in prison. We didn't tell no one.'

'This doesn't make sense.' Lili chewed her lip. 'Gretchen's my sister?'

'We're all family.'

'Is it you who's looking for the letters?' Lili asked.

'Those letters were supposed to be it – the big pay-off. A cash sum so we could buy somewhere in Tehran. Finally, Viv was going to come good after all those years I wasted with her. Viv told me she found them, and then she went and killed herself without telling me where they were. I've been searching this dump for days.'

'But you said you didn't know anything about the letters . . . you said you hadn't seen Mum since November.'

'We were always making up and breaking up,' said Ben. 'I knew about the letters. It was her way to try and win me back. As soon as she found them, I promised I'd go back to her.'

'Those letters belong to family.'

'So what am I? I've lived with her longer than you have and I'm your sister's father. I *am* family. She hasn't *seen* you in years. What do you deserve? Nothing.'

'Look, you're right. I don't deserve anything, but I don't care about anything except Gretchen—'

'Viv promised me,' Ben interrupted. 'She knew how she was. I could do a lot better, everyone said so. But what does it matter now? I've found my own way.'

'What do you mean?'

'I've made a marriage arrangement in Iran. Gretchen and a friend's son. Viv never respected my faith – she didn't believe in parents helping their children to marry. But look how she turned out. Alone. No man respecting her. I've found a good family for Gretchen. They'll take care of me and her. They'll pay me. It's all arranged.'

He gestured to Viv's clutter. 'Years I've lived with this. She promised me day in, day out – Ben, I'll get money. I have money coming. We'll get our home in Tehran. I'll get you home again.'

'No she's – wait. Did you send me text messages? If you were in the roof – did you have Mum's phone the whole time? That's why it rang in the flat, isn't it? It was in the roof with you.'

Ben scratched his cheek.

'You did, didn't you?' Lili's voice wavered. 'But how did you—'

'There's an app I used. It removes your messages from someone else's phone. And I took out the record of the phone call too. I thought if I freaked you out, made you think some ghost was after you, you'd leave and not come back.'

'Did you come to the theatre?'

Ben looked shifty. 'I told you not to look for the letters. They're my letters.'

'The doll – you wrote on the doll, didn't you? And then – what? You came and rubbed it off again. And I suppose you wrote on the posters.'

'They're *my* letters, right?' said Ben. 'Viv promised them to me. I earned them. But I guess it doesn't matter now – I've found my own way out.' He glanced at Gretchen.

'What if I told you I've found the letters?' Lili asked. 'Would you take them and leave Gretchen here?'

'I've got an arrangement for Gretchen and I can't back out.'

Lili held him with her eyes. 'Gretchen's all groggy – how are you even going to get her on the plane? Don't be stupid. Leave us here. Take the letters and go.'

Lili took a step back, teetering over a pile of boxes.

'I've rung the airport,' Ben said. 'I told them Gretchen's scared of flying. Taken lots of medication, so she's drowsy. They'll have a wheelchair for her. It's all okay, they know about it, we're good to go.'

Lili took her mobile phone from her bag, but before she could lift it to her ear, Ben grabbed it from her hand. In one swift movement he smashed it on the white metal bed frame.

'I've got the letters,' Lili said. 'They're in the other room. They were behind her picture. Take them. Leave Gretchen here and take the letters.'

'I'll take both.' Ben grabbed her arm, and Lili fell onto her ankle and shouted in pain.

'No! Leave Gretchen.'

Ben's grip tightened. He pulled Lili from the room, and she fell over lumpy carpet, her ankle twisting and burning.

'Get off me,' Lili shouted, trying to swing at him. But her wounded ankle threw her off balance.

Ben pulled her into the lounge.

Lili tried to wrench her arm free. 'Hey – no!' She saw the hand coming towards her too late. Ben's palm hit her face hard and she fell to the floor. Black and yellow exploded around her eyes. The sting made her dizzy.

There were long marks on the carpet. Indentations, and Lili knew they were where Viv had been found, kneeling over. She put her palm against them.

I won't let him take her.

She saw a cricket bat dangling by track-suited legs. Then she heard a crack and felt aching at the back of her head. Her whole face felt like it was on fire – blood rushed into her eyeballs.

Viv's face flashed red and black, and Lili felt her hands pulled tight behind her back. There were ripping sounds. She tried to bite at a hand as her mouth was forced open and crumpled newspaper stuffed inside.

Something slapped against her teeth, and she felt thick, sticky tape on her cheeks. Then Lili felt herself being dragged along hot nylon carpet, her bare palms burning.

She saw the letters, white and yellow petals on cigarette-burned weave, jolt past as she was tugged towards the window.

Her legs were hoisted up and her ankles tied to a window catch.

She tried to shout, but the sounds were paper muffled and sticky tape dull.

From the hall, she heard heavy footsteps and Ben talking to someone . . . *Okay mate, yes, ten minutes* . . .

A slippery, sliding sound told her Ben was moving something from the flat. Bags? Suitcases? Gretchen? She held her breath and listened for breathing. She could still hear Gretchen, she was certain – her breathing groggy and irregular.

Then the lounge door slammed shut.

88

The nausea came moments later.

Lili felt burning around her tonsils and fought to swallow the bitter, throat-scouring liquid that filled her mouth, softening the sharp corners of newspaper.

She couldn't see Viv's pictures any more, only the dark London sky through the water-marked window. Blood was rushing to her upper body, and she twisted and turned to get her feet free.

They were held firm.

With a gasp, she tried to sit up, grasping at the garden twine that looped around her ankles. It took all her muscle control, and if she hadn't spent years spinning upside-down in a hoop she'd never have held herself in place for long enough, but she managed to reach the rope.

Her nails picked at a knot for a few seconds before, exhausted, she fell down again.

She choked on the liquid in her mouth and panicked, unable to breathe.

Calm down.

She pulled herself up again and continued to pick. The twine frayed and loosened under her fingers.

Nearly there.

The string slid free, and Lili's legs fell to the ground. She lay for a moment, thinking of Gretchen.

How did I never notice Gretchen looks so much like Mum?

She began to crawl like a worm along the floor, her ankles and hands bound. The letters were gone. She didn't care.

Ben was nowhere to be seen, but Lili could hear gentle breathing from the bedroom.

At the front door she pulled herself upright, but she couldn't get to the catch, not with her hands tied.

If I can just get outside and . . . and what? Shout? You can't shout. Throw yourself down the stairs and hope someone finds you before Ben does?

She closed her eyes and tried not to despair.

There was a noise from the other side of the door and Lili's eyes flew open.

Oh my God. He's back.

A shoe slid on concrete and Lili's whole body tensed. There was a cough – an older person's cough. It didn't sound like Ben.

Then there was a sharp knock on the door. 'Hello in there?'

The voice was unmistakable. It was Ian Batty.

'Mmmph!' Lili made as much noise as she could, but it wasn't loud enough, she knew.

Twisting her body, she threw herself against the door. When her shoulder only produced a dull, thumping sound, she gritted her teeth and banging her bruised head against the wood.

Darkness and gold spots came again, and the pain . . . the pain . . . For a moment, Lili thought she would pass out. Then she realised something much more frightening. She was going to be sick again.

A rush of liquid over-filled her mouth, swilling around the crumples of the newspaper, spilling out her nose and cutting off her airways.

She coughed and choked, her lungs inhaling splashes of liquid, her eyes wide and watering.

It didn't matter that Ian was outside the door – it was too late. He didn't have keys, he couldn't get in and rip off the gag. She was going to suffocate, metres from where her Mum had died, and Gretchen would be taken away.

Panic overwhelmed her.

Please God, I don't want to die. She thought of Viv, murdering herself. She felt the pain of it all – of Viv's loss, and the way she died – and she understood why Viv had wanted to escape a life that could be unbearable. She understood what Viv had sacrificed too – a relationship with her own daughters, both her and Gretchen, so they had a chance in life.

She thought of baby James Morgan, screaming and red-raw after being washed with arsenic, his bones malformed with syphilis. And his sister and brothers all dead because their parents were poor and diseased. She realised how unlikely it was for James to survive. Were it not for the love between William Peavy and Tom Morgan, he wouldn't have made it.

If James hadn't survived, Lili would never have been born. Nor would Gretchen.

I want to live.

The world began to go soft as grey clouds of unconsciousness came.

There was a thump, thump at the door.

Then a voice . . . *two, three.*

With a bump, the door burst open. The wobbly Yale lock fell easily from its screws and splinters of wood caught Lili's cheek.

As she squirmed and choked, she felt tape ripped from her face.

A cold hand pulled the newspaper from her mouth and she tasted metal. Then she was turned on her back and thumped hard with a flat palm.

Her breaths became fuller. Longer. Her lungs were still flecked with gritty bile, and there was burning pain as she took great gulps of air, but she could breathe. It was heavenly.

Tape was cut from her hands and feet and Lili gulped at a glass of water that was placed under her nose. She looked up and saw Ian, his hands on cream linen hips. He was wearing a safari suit with a crocodile print shirt.

'Thank goodness I came.'

'How did you know I was here?'

'Call it intuition,' said Ian. 'I had a feeling something was amiss. I conveyed my fears to the police, but of course they were unwilling to take action.' He knelt by Lili's side. 'They suspect I'm a crank.'

'Gretchen,' Lili spluttered. 'Has he taken Gretchen?'

'Who?' Ian looked bewildered.

Lili stood on shaky legs, and careered into a wall as she trod on her swollen ankle. She hobbled into the bedroom.

'Oh, thank God.'

Gretchen was still there, sleeping on the bed.

'Do you have a mobile phone?' Lili called to Ian. 'Mine's broken. We need to call the police. And we need to get Gretchen out of here before he comes back.'

'I don't believe in mobile telephones,' said Ian. 'They interfere with the brainwaves. You'll need me to help you, my dear, you can hardly walk.'

'Gretchen.' Lili went to her shoulder. 'We need to carry you out before—'

Lili turned and saw Ben in the doorway. He stared at the wood splinters in disbelief.

'Hey—' Lili shouted, but it was too late.

Ben bundled Ian into the kitchen and forced the door closed, fastening the bolt on the outside.

Ian pounded at the wood, his voice muffled, but the heavy-duty lock held firm. Viv may have fitted the locks on the wrong sides of the doors, but she'd done a good job of screwing them in place.

'No.' Lili stood in front of Gretchen.

Ben reached for duct tape that sat on a box in the hallway.

Lili tried to shut the bedroom door, but Ben was too quick for her. He jabbed a trainer in the way. She fought with him, and if she hadn't been injured she would have won. But her ankle felt like it was dipped in lava. She was losing ground every second.

'Someone help us!' she shouted.

'No one cares about their neighbours in this place,' said Ben, his foot inching over the threshold. 'You know how many days Viv was here before they found her?'

'Don't do this.' Lili forced her shoulder against the door. 'For Mum's sake. For her memory. You've got the letters. Just leave.'

'Her memory!' Ben scoffed. 'She gave me nothing. She owes me Gretchen.'

'No. You won't take her.' Lili shoved as hard as she could. The force shook the whole door frame and threw Ben's stocky body away.

Then there was a creaking sound from the roof.

Lili looked up at the hall ceiling through the widening slit in the door. For a moment she thought someone else was moving about in the roof. But the noise was different. Not banging, like footsteps, but a gentle creak like a ship's mast in the wind.

There was a click and a whine.

The maintenance hatch rushed away from its fitting. The painted white wood swung down and smacked Ben hard in the face, knocking him to the ground.

The hatch swung back and forth, and for a second Lili thought she heard Viv laughing.

Lili looked down at Ben, his palms pressed into the carpet, a dazed boxer knocked down, struggling to get up and fight.

She knelt beside him, took the duct tape that had fallen to the carpet and bound his hands and legs.

Pushing boxes aside, Lili let Ian out of the kitchen.

'What a disagreeable man,' said Ian, dusting down his jacket. 'Well my dear, I suppose it's best to advise the police about the situation.'

'Yes,' said Lili. She saw the yellow letters scrunched in Ben's tracksuit pocket, and pulled them free. 'And Gretchen's mother. She's downstairs.'

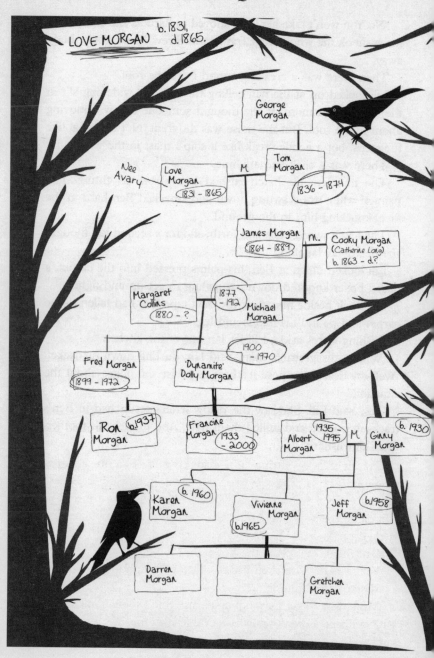

LOVE MORGAN   b. 1831,
                d. 1865.

George
Morgan

Tom
Morgan
1836 - 1874

Nee
Avary   Love
        Morgan   M
        1831 - 1865

James Morgan   m.   Cooky Morgan
1864 - 1889   (Catherine Long)
                      b. 1863 - d.?

Margaret
Collins   1877   Michael
1880 - ?   - 1912   Morgan

Fred Morgan   1900   'Dynamite'
1899 - 1972   - 1970   Dolly Morgan

Ron   Francine   1935 -   Ginny
Morgan b.1937 Morgan   1995 M Morgan b. 1930
              1933   Albert
              - 2000   Morgan

Karen b. 1960   Vivienne   Jeff b.1958
Morgan   Morgan   Morgan
                  b.1965

Darren   Gretchen
Morgan   Morgan

89

Life's a Stage **by Lili Allure**

Lili's London: Whitechapel Hospital

The Royal London Hospital stands opposite the scruffy market stalls of Whitechapel High Street, a building of beautiful archways, flat windows and flurries of stone steps.

Built in the 1700s to treat the poor and needy of Whitechapel, the hospital was originally surrounded by green fields. Patients arrived by horse and cart, pulled along dirt paths.

Nowadays, miles of grey roads are knitted around the hospital, and there is a helipad on site for air ambulances. Life is more precious than ever.

The raw, thorny stems of white roses cut into Lili's palm as she walked towards the hospital bed, her heels echoing around the hospital ward.

Gretchen was sitting up, watching a TV on a long, Anglepoise arm. She was wearing headphones. There was a tray table over her lap with a box of Malteasers on it and as Lili came towards her, Gretchen took a round chocolate and sucked on it.

'Gretchen.' Lili rested the flowers on the table.

'You're here!' Gretchen pulled out the headphones.

'Where's your mum?'

'Mum went to get me a hot chocolate. She's spoiling me rotten – it's brilliant. I didn't know if they'd let you in, since you're not family—'

'Gretchen—'

'There's nothing *wrong* with me.' Gretchen glared at one of the nurses as she hurried past. 'Why won't they let me go home?'

'They just have to check you over,' said Lili. 'They're doing some tests, just to make sure the drugs didn't do you any damage.'

Gretchen tutted. 'It was just, like *prescription* something he gave me. And I'm *fine*.'

Lili sat on a seat by the bed. 'How are you feeling?'

'Good. Except the internet on this thing is so *slow*.' Gretchen nodded at the TV. 'I'm having to watch daytime stuff instead of checking my emails.'

'Do you remember much of what happened?'

Gretchen shook her head. 'Not much at all. Ben met me on the way to my drama group. He was waiting at the bus stop. He said he was my real dad, and showed me my passport. He must have taken it from Mum's handbag. I was *freaked out*. I mean, he's been seeing Viv for years. Mum never said a word about him being my *dad*. No one did.

'He was like, let's go and have a talk. Phone your drama group. Tell them you're sick. Here's my phone. I've been trying to be in your life more since Daniel left, but Carol and I thought it best not to tell you who I was, but now we've decided it's the right time.

'He went on and on about faith and purity, and read me this passage about young women being spoiled if they didn't marry young. And he said my real mum wasn't pure and she never got married, and that had ruined her and I didn't want to turn out the same.

'I said, So who's my mum then? Is it Viv? Because Viv and Ben sort of lived together before . . . you know. And Viv always liked me, and not many adults do. But he said we'll talk about it some other time. I thought maybe Carol and Ben must have had an affair, or did surrogacy or something.

'Anyway. Ben said he wanted to take me out for coffee, and like an idiot I said okay. We went to this horrible café on Whitechapel High Street – it didn't do iced anything or syrups or whipped cream. Only, like really strong coffee that tasted like mud.

'He was talking to me about, how would I like a trip to Iran, and I was saying, no I wouldn't really. And he got really cross. Then he said he'd been watching me. That I was hanging out with you, and you weren't a nice person. And he said he knew I was helping you look for Viv's letters, and that they were *his* letters that Viv meant for him to have them, and he was looking for them too and we shouldn't look for them any more.

'And then I saw you, across the street, going into the hospital.

'Ben went to talk to his friend at the coffee counter – something about flights to Iran that evening. I was scared then, because he was saying about two tickets, and I thought him and Mum might force me to go.

'I didn't have your number, but he left his phone on the table, so I took it, got the hospital number and left you a message with reception. Then I started feeling weird. *Really* sleepy, like being massively stoned. Too stoned. He must have put something in my coffee. The hospital say it was di-azzy something.'

'Diazepam.'

'Right. And then after that I don't remember much. He said we'd go back and rest at Viv's place. I thought, at least he's not taking me to the airport. I think he locked me in when we got to Viv's.

'Who took the clothes from your bedroom?'

'He must have done,' Gretchen said. 'I had my front door key the whole time. I think Ben must have gone down and packed my things when Mum was out.'

'Gretchen, about your mum . . . your real mum.'

'What about her?' Gretchen's eyes widened.

'It was Viv. Your mum was my mum. So we're sisters.'

'Wow.' Gretchen stared at her. As usual, emotions didn't seem to register. 'I've always wanted a big sister. Will you lend me clothes?'

Carol appeared across the ward by the nurse's station. She held a paper Costa cup and pushed her glasses up as she approached the bed.

'Did you tell her?' Carol asked.

'Yes,' said Lili.

Carol sighed. 'We knew we were taking advantage.' She didn't meet Lili's eye. 'Of Viv, I mean. We both knew, Daniel and I, deep down. We had money, and Viv was desperate. She and Ben, they had an odd relationship. We knew that. I always suspected Ben wasn't quite right, but he had such a charm about him. He always made things sound like Viv was to blame. But of course I knew Viv had a drink problem. I knew she was vulnerable.

'You have to understand. We tried everything. We weren't allowed to adopt – not with Daniel's medical problems. When Ben suggested Viv have a child for us, it seemed like our dreams were coming true.

'But then Daniel left and Ben began to interfere. It was always there, unspoken. *I could take her back.* When Viv passed away, he began to interfere more and more. Dropping by for visits. I was so frightened he'd tell the authorities and have her taken away.'

Carol perched on the bed and put Gretchen's hot chocolate on the table.

'I blame myself for all of this. I'll listen more from now on, Gretchen. If you could have confided in me, none of this would have happened.' She wiped her nose. 'I failed.'

'It's fine. Mum, it's fine.'

'I was so frightened,' Carol's voice rose in panic. 'You hear so many stories about social services, the decisions they make . . . I never thought he'd interfere to this extreme.'

'Did Viv?' Lili asked. 'Did Mum ever interfere?'

'Never.' Carol shook her head. 'Quite the opposite. She'd avoid us when Gretchen was younger. She thought Gretchen should just have Daniel and me. That she would spoil things. I always felt extremely guilty about that, but it suited us so I kept quiet.'

Carol glanced at Lili. 'It was only recently . . . I don't know how it happened exactly, but the two of them became friends. I didn't know what to say about it. It was very uncomfortable, but Gretchen instigated it and I felt I couldn't say no. I owed Viv that.

'It scared the life out of me – I've never been certain of the legal situation after Daniel left. When Viv passed away, I wasn't sure if I'd done the right thing by keeping everything a secret from Gretchen. I was very sorry . . . I liked Viv.'

'So did I,' said Lili.

'Tell me about the theatre,' said Gretchen. 'I saw pictures in the paper of it all burned down. Are they going to rebuild it?'

'I'm sure they will.' Lili shrugged. 'But I'm not going to work there any more.'

'What?' Gretchen pulled herself higher on the bed. 'But it's your home.'

'No,' said Lili. 'It was never meant to be. It was just a resting place.'

'So where will you stay?' Carol asked.

'With the theatre manager, Pete. I'm going to work on new routines and doing big shows again. I'm going to have a proper career and a proper place where you can come and visit.' She turned to Carol. 'And stay over if you'll let her.'

'I think that would be nice.'

'I'm so glad you're okay, Gretchen.' Lili patted her hand. 'I have to go now, but I'll be back.'

'Where are you going?' Gretchen asked.

'There's a wedding I need to gatecrash.'

'Wait.' Gretchen stared at her, and big tears swam around her pupils. 'We've lost our mum. Haven't we? We've lost our mum.'

'I know.' Lili put her arms around Gretchen and cried too. 'I know we have.'

90

Jessica Morgan's winter wedding was white – and then some.

The Essex Hotel and Golf Club had been sprayed with synthetic snow and decorated with giant swathes of white silk. Inside the wedding venue, a long white carpet replaced the traditional red aisle, and explosions of white roses were pinned, stuffed and hung into every nook and cranny.

Guests, the registrar and hotel staff wore white from head to toe. They sat on chairs covered with white fabric and tied with white bows, and read from white wedding programmes.

Lili entered the ceremony room wearing a red dress of crushed silk. Amid the white suits and dresses she looked like spilled red wine.

'Aunt Karen,' she called over the white fascinators and top hats.

Karen, who had been bossing the registrar around, saw Lili and went as white as the fabric chair coverings. Lili smiled. Karen always did like to coordinate.

'Lilian.' Karen pushed aside chairs. 'Let's talk outside.' She gave curious guests sycophantic smiles.

'No. Here will be fine.' Lili reached in her handbag and pulled out a see-through make-up bag with the yellow letters inside. 'Do you know what these are?'

Karen tried to snatch them, but Lili pulled the letters away.

'Give me those,' Karen hissed.

'If you want them, you'll have to do something for me.'

'Look, I'm sorry about yesterday.' Karen twisted a heel against the floor. 'I was panicking. The wedding's sent me a little bit crazy.' She circled a finger at her temple. 'I shouldn't have . . .

you know. Done that.' She glanced left and right. 'I don't know what I was *thinking*. Phil gave me a good telling off when he got home.'

Karen pulled Lili to the side of the room, and whispered: 'There's a mighty great hole in our ceiling, and Phil's computer is ruined. So if you want revenge, you've already had it. I'm glad this *Gretchen* girl is okay.'

'You listened to my messages then?' Lili shook her arm free. 'Why didn't you phone me back?'

'Problem, Karen?' A woman, wearing an enormous showboat hat festooned with white netting, gave Karen a pointy canine grin.

'No Lady Ashcroft, just a little housekeeping. This girl doesn't have an invitation.'

'You don't need an invite to object to a wedding,' said Lili.

Lady Ashcroft's eyebrows shot into her hat.

'You wouldn't!' Karen hissed, and heads turned. Karen glanced left and right, patting her hair under her white fascinator. Her voice lowered to a whisper. '*You wouldn't.*'

'I would.' Lili waved the letters. 'I'd say there were family secrets the groom should know about before he marries into—'

'Don't you dare.'

'Come to the inquest.'

Karen's hand froze on her blonde hair. 'I never said I wouldn't come.'

'Oh, come off it.'

'Okay, fine.' Karen rubbed her tanned forehead. 'I just didn't want to rake over everything. Have you ever been to an inquest?'

'Have you?'

'No, but Phil's sister Mary's son had an unfortunate passing and apparently the inquest was worse than anything else. It's been painful enough. I want to put a lid on everything. Close the door.'

'Sweep it under the carpet. I don't think it works that way.'

Karen's taut face sagged. 'We all have our own ways of dealing with things.'

'So you'll come?'

'Promise me you won't do a *thing* to interfere with today.'

'If you'll come to the inquest, then I promise.'

Karen's lip quivered. 'Fine. I've never felt comfortable about missing the funeral – you do understand, don't you? I just didn't want to *deal* with all that all over again.'

A Whiter Shade of Pale began to play and Karen flapped her white fingernails. 'I should be in position. Excuse me . . . excuse me . . .' Her face was a whiter shade of distraught as she pushed to the front of the venue and took her place near the registrar.

The music grew louder, and everyone turned to see Jessica holding Uncle Phil's arm, wearing an ill-fitting copy of Kate Middleton's wedding dress. Her walk was strangely lolloping and it looked like Phil was tugging her along.

As Jessica walked haltingly past, Lili caught the look on her face – fear.

Jessica was patting at her throat, and her eyes were puffy. *I have to do this for my mother,* Jessica's face said, and for a moment, Lili pictured what things would have been like if she'd stayed to look after Viv. She would have been free of guilt, but slowly dying inside, never free to live her own life.

91

Life's a Stage by Lili Allure

Lili Allure's tips for dealing with a mother's inquest

Wear comfortable clothes. Have your family around you. And let the coroner take centre stage – you can't always be the star of the show.

Lili fiddled with the coroner's court microphone. It looked like a giant, bent spider's leg. She wore a loose, floral dress and a single pin in her hair. No corset, no make-up, no gloves.

Opposite was a witness box, where a policewoman stood giving evidence about Viv's death.

The policewoman's hand crushed the cardboard box of tissues perched by her own microphone. 'When we broke the door down, we searched each room of the property and found the deceased in the lounge, in a kneeling position. Her skin was purple, and there were pill bottles by her side.'

'And you tried to resuscitate Miss Morgan?' the coroner asked. He was a pleasant man who was clearly doing his best to put everyone at ease.

'Yes.' The policewoman nodded. 'But I'm afraid to say . . .' She glanced at the family benches where Lili sat with Darren, Gretchen, Karen, Jeff and Ginny. 'By the way her skin looked . . . it was very clear to us she'd already passed away.'

At the back of the court sat Ian Batty and a *Metro* reporter. Ian wore a fitted black suit with waistcoat and a black silk top hat. He was clearly itching to say something, and had been since court was in session.

'Thank you,' said the coroner. 'If you could just stay where you are for a second. Does anyone have any questions for this witness?'

Ian got to his feet. 'Mr Coroner—'

The coroner folded his arms. 'For the last time, you have not been invited to participate in this session. You are allowed in court as a viewer of the proceedings and nothing more.'

'But I was her counsellor—'

'You are not a registered medical professional, and nor were you present at her death. So kindly sit down or I'll have you removed.'

Ian sat, holding out his hands out to the reporter as if to say, *How can you deal with such people?*

Nobody had any questions, so the policewoman was ushered back to her bench while the coroner summed up.

The medical jargon washed over Lili until she heard the words, Death by suicide.

Suicide. The final judgment.

Lili squeezed Gretchen's hand.

Outside the court, trees sprouted green leaves and pink buds. The air was becoming milder and swifts darted around the pale blue sky.

Pete was waiting, leaning against the railings.

'How did it go?'

Lili managed a smile. 'Like I wanted it to.'

'Good.'

Lili felt a hand on her shoulder and quickly dabbed her eyes. She turned to see Ian.

'How are you feeling?' Ian asked.

'Pleased,' Lili replied. 'Very pleased. All the immediate family were there. It's what she deserved.'

'But you still have questions?'

'I'll always have questions. Thanks for coming along. It means a lot to have you here. I know you spent time with Mum, and I know you had things you wanted to say.'

'They fear what they don't understand.' Ian waved his hand. 'My dear, I hope I'm not intruding on your grief, but I feel Love very keenly today. I feel she would like to speak to you.'

'You know I don't really believe in all that stuff, don't you Ian?' Lili said. 'I mean, don't get me wrong, I'm tremendously grateful you found me in the flat. But there were things you said that didn't make sense. That Tom was in William Peavy's house—'

'I don't believe I ever said for *certain* it was Tom,' Ian insisted. 'I said a man who looked like Tom, in William Peavy's house.'

'But you never said anything about Tom and William Peavy having an affair. You thought Love had a baby by William Peavy. No offence, but I guess that's what Mum must have told you.'

'I don't recall ever saying anything was certain,' said Ian. 'And if you remember I said there were secrets to do with the youngest member of your family. And now I believe, it's been revealed that young Gretchen is your sister.'

'If you guess often enough you're bound to get something right,' said Lili.

'Right, wrong, that's not what connecting with the spirit world is all about.' Ian adjusted his top hat. 'It's not like that man in there, passing his judgments, putting life and death into order. No – death will always be a confusing business. Shall we go for a walk? Love is still seeking a connection.'

'Okay.' Lili turned to her family. They'd arranged to have a lunch together after the hearing, but there was plenty of time. 'I'll see you in a minute or two,' she called out, walking with Ian towards Poplar station and the glass high-rises of Canary Wharf.

'I sense Love very strongly around this area of London,' said Ian. 'Perhaps because there's so much life here these days. The skyscrapers and the money. So much energy. She would very much like a connection with us.'

'Well . . . maybe,' said Lili. 'For old times' sake.' A train rumbled overhead. 'Let's hear her.'

Ian placed his fingertips together. 'She is asking . . . do you have any questions for her?'

'Questions? Good guess, Sherlock. You know I have questions.'

'Then ask them.'

'Okay.' Lili stuffed her hands into wool pockets. 'I'd like to know who poisoned her. If she can tell us.'

Ian's forehead twitched. 'Yes. Yes, she'd very much like to tell us about that. Let me ask her. Love . . . Oh, good to see you. How are you today? Very well. Yes, it's been a good day, hasn't it? You'd like to take us back to William Peavy's house . . . where we were before.

'Well, certainly, my dear. Yes, I remember. The servant let you in and you were taken to the reception room. Yes, a lovely room, I quite agree.

'You're telling Mr Peavy you have his letters, and you'll tell the newspapers all about him. Yes. I remember. Goodness. So your murderer *is* in this house? Just as you told me before. Right at this moment? The tea. Of course. Well, that makes sense. The poison was put in the tea, so we must look to who served it to you.'

Ian raised a hand. 'I have him! Your father-in-law served you the tea. The butler, George Morgan. *He* was your murderer, am I right? Yes! Of course. He heard you blackmailing his employer, and learned of the letters sent to his son, and knew he had to act quickly.

'A relationship between two men – well! It could ruin his boy's life. Mr Morgan senior knew the newspapers would snap up such a story, and was damned if he was going to let his own sweet-natured boy be a social outcast for ever.'

Ian sighed and waved a hand. 'Yes, yes of course. It was a pleasure. Of course you may go, my dear. Your murderer has been named. A thousand farewells, and I will see you again in the next life.' He smiled and blew a kiss at the air. 'She is gone.'

'So in other words, the butler did it,' said Lili.

'That appears to be the case.'

'I guess we'll never know for certain what happened. But that's as good a guess as any.'

'Too true,' said Ian. 'As I've said many times, the lines between ourselves and the spirit world aren't particularly clear. Where history is concerned, we have to use our deduction too, if we are to find the truth. Now.' He clapped his hands together. 'There is someone else waiting.'

'Who?' A spring breeze stroked Lili's face.

'Why, your mother of course. Vivienne.'

Lili didn't say anything.

'Do you wish to make a connection with her?'

'Perhaps,' said Lili. 'Not because I believe all this stuff, Ian. But, you know, imagining her and what she might say – it might be good for me.'

'Yes, quite.' Ian closed his eyes. 'Ah! Yes. I have her. Vivienne? Vivienne, is that you? Of course. It's been something of a strange day, hasn't it? It's not often you hear people decide how you died. Not everyone has that privilege. She says she feels lucky to be so important. And there's something she wants to say to you.'

'What?'

'She says she's sorry she wasn't a better mother. She says she failed at everything she tried – her career, relationships, mother-hood. She saw Gretchen growing up with a good family down-stairs, and the older Gretchen got the more she realised she'd failed you. The pain grew and grew.

'She says she never blamed you for anything. Only herself. She says she thought of you every day. She wishes she could have said goodbye, but she knows if you saw her those last days, how unhappy she was, it would have caused you a lot of pain. Oh. And one last thing. She wants you to know how much she loves you.'

A light rain began to fall, gently soaking Lili's loose hair and summer dress. She looked up to the sky and wiped away tears. 'I forgive both of us.'

Through the misty rain, Lili saw Gretchen coming towards them.

'What you doing?' Gretchen asked.

'Just talking,' Lili replied. 'We're finished now. Shall we all go to lunch?'

'Yes. I'm starving.'

The three of them walked back towards Pete and the family.

'When does your new tour start?' Gretchen asked, patting rain into her hair.

'Next month.'

'What's it called?'

'The Big Reveal.'

Curtain Down

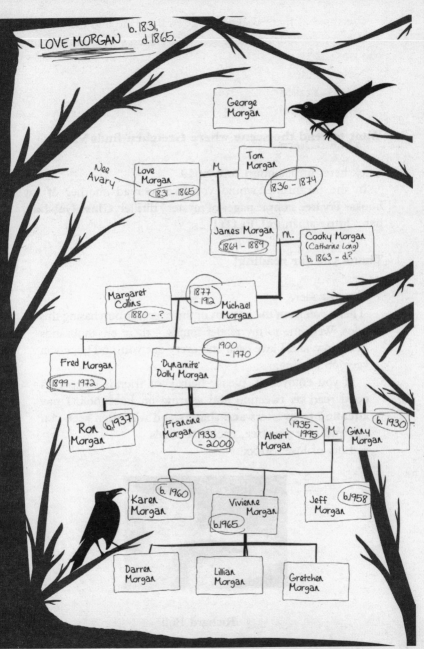

LOVE MORGAN b. 1831, d. 1865.

George Morgan

Tom Morgan 1836 – 1874

Nee Avary Love Morgan 1831 – 1865 M

James Morgan 1864 – 1889 m. Cooky Morgan (Catherine Long) b. 1863 – d.?

Margaret Collins 1880 – ? 1877 – 1912 Michael Morgan

Fred Morgan 1899 – 1972 'Dynamite' Dolly Morgan 1900 – 1970

Ron Morgan b. 1937 Francine Morgan 1933 – 2000 Albert Morgan 1935 – 1995 M Ginny Morgan b. 1930

Karen Morgan b. 1960 Vivienne Morgan b. 1965 Jeff Morgan b. 1958

Darren Morgan Lillian Morgan Gretchen Morgan

Want to read the scene where Gretchen finds Viv?

Click here: http://eepurl.com/znj49

In the meantime, would you like to read another of my books? Try free sample pages of mystery thriller, **Glass Geishas**, here: http://amzn.to/UFLOYJ

Thank you for reading!

Dear Reader,

Thank you from the bottom of my heart for purchasing this book. Welcome to my reader family – there are thousands of us now, and I love each and every one you, and hope you keep on reading.

If you enjoyed it, please help your friends discover a good read by tweeting and sharing on Facebook. I pay attention to tweeters and sharers and will often seek you out and give you free, exclusive reads.

Lots of love, Su xx

© Richard Boll